MEET THE AUTHOR

TEASERS,
TRAILERS & MORE...

BLUEBIRD DAY

A Novel

MEGAN TADY

ZIBBY BOOKS
NEW YORK

Library of Congress Control Number: 2024931687
Paperback ISBN: 978-1-958506-86-8
Hardcover ISBN: 978-1-958506-87-5
eBook ISBN: 978-1-958506-88-2

Book design by Neuwirth & Associates

Cover design by Vi-An Nguyen

www.zibbymedia.com

Printed in the United States of America
10 9 8 7 6 5 4 3 2 1

For Alex, the actual Sexiest Man Alive when he sings
(and when he doesn't)

We're legends. We always have been.

—Kipling "Kipper" Potts, 1972 Olympic gold medalist

1

Wylie

WYLIE'S SWEATING BUCKETS ON HER SPIN BIKE, suffering through a vicious ride over the Tuscan hills without leaving her bedroom. She's convinced: *this* is the most physically tested she's ever been.

Forgetting your sweat towel will do that to you.

Forgetting it on the bed just out of reach increases the torture.

Wylie's no whiner. As a former ski racer, she knows bodily misery. Ski racing is signing up to be constantly cold. The ice baths she submerges in these days are nothing compared to barreling down a mountain at ninety miles an hour, wind howling, temps hovering at nine degrees, wearing a skintight Spyder suit (there's no fur lining in those babies), fingers so frozen they could snap like brittle twigs. Lips cracked and bleeding at the hint of a smile. Cheeks simultaneously wind- *and* sunburned. Throw in period cramps, just for giggles.

But this? It's worse, somehow. She dips her cheek to her shoulder, but she's only in her faded blue sports bra, so there's no shirt to absorb the sweat. Moisture meets moisture. She emits a fierce growl into her bedroom.

The towel is so close, she could almost lean out of her bike seat and pinch it with her fingertips. Or swiftly dismount to grab it. But if she does that, she'll lose her lead, disappointing her boyfriend, Dan. He's tracking her stats like a hawk as they count down to the fitness competition in Berlin next Saturday. It's the Big Daddy of BodyFittest contests and comes with enough prize money to improve their lives: paying down Wylie's student loans, helping Dan set up his business as a fitness trainer.

"Now for the long climb," says the CycleTron instructor, Claudine Potts, her tush hovering over her seat. "Dig deep. We're in the thick of it now. Four minutes. You've got this."

At forty-eight, Claudine Potts is also a former skier, widely considered one of the best downhill racers ever, with five Olympic gold medals to her name. CycleTron has splashed images of her superfit bod and weather-whipped face across billboards with a message that reads like a dare: *Train with a GOAT.*

Greatest of all time.

But that's not why Wylie rides with Claudine three mornings a week.

On the bike, Wylie, signed in as ArtsyFartsy26, taps into another level of endurance, her legs firing, her hips acting as great, powerful pistons. Back when she was still skiing, she separated herself from the pack with a grittiness to ski fast through the last ten seconds of a two-minute downhill race, when fatigue smashed at her like a wall.

It's this grit she calls on now.

Wylie might have snatched Claudine's GOAT title, was headed that way. By ten years old she was skiing double black diamonds. But at the age of seventeen, when she was competing at the Junior Olympics—an important precursor to making the U.S. Ski Team—she abruptly quit the sport to go to college.

More specifically, art school.

By tossing away her talent and years of training, a rift opened between Wylie and her mom, one that's only deepened in the last few years. Wylie's tried to win her over by becoming an Important Artist, but garnering art-world acclaim—or simply finishing a painting—has proved harder than she thought. Her art supplies are covered in a thin layer of dust on the other side of the bedroom.

Sometimes she wonders if the parent who'd understand her is the one she's never met: her dad. The only tidbit she knows about him is that he was a "ski bum." Her mom refused to share any other detail.

"Release the tension in your shoulders," Claudine barks from the screen, giving her own a microshake to demonstrate.

Some riders choose Claudine because she's old-school, straightforward and direct. No flowery language, no rainbows-and-unicorns nonsense about accepting yourself as you are, no pumping music playlists or choreography. She's for the riders who long for that high school coach who'd get in your face while you were weeping, demanding thirty more. Burpees. Laps. Sit-ups. Push-ups. Whatever.

This no-BS rigor isn't why Wylie rides with Claudine, but she automatically follows the directions: looser grip, relaxed shoulders. Growing up, Wylie was constantly coached, every minute of her life calibrated to wring out the best results. Doing what she's told feels more natural than making her own choices. It's why she and Dan were such a good fit when they met at a BodyFittest studio three years ago. He provides the structure she craves; she executes.

Another rider, SheSpins4Lyfe, overtakes her, and admiration sprouts in Wylie's chest. *Get it, girl.* That level of fitness is truly impressive.

Then she remembers that the goal is to dominate—and being the best here translates to being the best elsewhere—so she reclaims her lead like she's shimmying through a concert crowd on her way to the bathroom. *Sorry. Excuse me. I'll just pass on the left.*

She's not aggressive, not really. She was graced with elite-athlete genes, but she's never cared to win for winning's sake. She wins to keep people happy with her. That dogged work ethic? It comes from knowing that losing means she's loved just a little bit less by the people in her life, a measuring tape retracted a few inches every time she fails.

And by "people," she means her mom. Wylie's a twenty-six-year-old grown woman who can't stop fantasizing about winning in Berlin and telling her mom: *I did it. First place, the best.*

She lifts her gaze from the touch screen to her bedroom window. The sky is a pot of boiling, darkened clouds, the tiny snowflakes a trail of steam. She takes a sharp intake of breath. Funny how a form of precipitation triggers so many memories—and not of building snowmen and drinking hot cocoa and enjoying a surprise day off from school.

In her world, snow meant going fast. Faster than a car on a highway.

And faster than she's going now. "C'mon," she shouts, regathering her focus, pumping herself up.

"Three minutes left," Claudine announces, her hazel eyes blazing. "Crank that resistance. Climb. Push it!"

Wylie activates inner beast mode. Gone is her sweatiness, her achiness—even the nagging loneliness disappears. The end of her braid whips across her neck.

Some riders choose Claudine Potts because, just as her rating suggests—8.75 on the difficulty meter—she leads the most grueling rides. A puke-in-the-wastebasket, gasping-for-breath, I-thought-I-was-in-shape, fifty-five-minute bender. But oh, the endorphin high.

And some show up for the community. The PottHeads, they call themselves, plug it into their social media bios: "Lawyer. Mom of 2. Devoted PottHead." If you know, you know. It's rumored that Matthew McConaughey, Meghan Markle, and Michelle Obama are PottHeads.

But these reasons aren't why Wylie rides with Claudine.

A flurry of goat emojis float up the screen, and Wylie rolls her eyes. Half these people have probably never watched an alpine ski race in their lives.

She imitates Claudine's posture, suspended just above her seat so her sit bones graze it with every revolution. Higher, higher, higher, her bike climbs to some imagined destination in the sky.

If she can hold this, she'll finish with her best time yet.

"Stay with me, people. Don't think, just do," Claudine says.

And with those four words—*don't think, just do*—Wylie's no longer in her North Adams apartment on a late-February morning.

She's fourteen years old at Burke Mountain Academy on race day, the weather as cutting as a snide comment, spitting ice crystals. She cracks her neck from side to side, pounds her gloved fists into her palms. "Ski mean," says her coach before giving her a little shove to the start gate, where Wylie, bent at her hips, feet trapped in ski boots, peers down at the run, at the small crowd below, and feels the ground beneath her slide away as if she'd been standing on hourglass sand. Her balance recedes; her head gets woozy with vertigo. Her legs shake uncontrollably. Heart detonating.

I'm going to die. It's her last thought before plunging downward at a pace dubbed breakneck for a reason.

Claudine's voice grows louder, snapping Wylie back to the present moment in her bedroom. "You want to quit? Go ahead, be a quitter."

Without noticing, Wylie has risen to almost standing on the bike pedals, and suddenly her right hand, slick with sweat, slips from its grip. She slams forward, nearly banging her face on the touch screen, her forehead inches from Claudine's, her right ribs smacking the hard edge of the handlebars. Had she been on pavement, her bike would've skidded out from under her, other riders swerving around her.

Her rank deflates like a punctured tire. Her sigh sounds like one. She taps Mute and slows her pace to stopping. There's no point in continuing.

One second, she's close to glory; the next, she's donezo. If this was a ski race, she'd get marked DNF: Did Not Finish.

So freaking typical.

It won't happen next week in Berlin with Dan by her side. It *can't.* She cannot handle another DNF next to her name. She couldn't live with herself.

Wylie unclips her shoes and reunites with the towel, holding it against her face as she steadies her breath, her chest heaving. Then she swipes her neck, followed by each arm, shoulder to fingers. On the screen, Claudine silently guides her PottHeads through a cooldown.

Wylie tenderly touches her right side. But it's her heart that's aching the most.

From beyond the bedroom, there's a sound of keys clanking into a wooden bowl atop the entryway table, shoes being kicked off, a duffel bag being hung on the peg rail, socked feet over hardwood.

Dan's home.

The doorknob opens before she has the chance to darken the screen.

"Hi, babe, good ride?" Dan was bullied as a chubby, overly mothered Italian kid, but he's since turned beefcake, his arm muscles rippling underneath his tight-on-purpose shirt. He's not shy about showing off his waxed chest and broodingly handsome face on Instagram: dark black hair, eyebrows as straight as diving boards, full lips. Wylie's still disbelieving that someone like him wanted her.

He's holding two green smoothies from the pricey juice bar down the street. Whenever Wylie pipes up about reining in their spending, he insists that winning in Berlin is about to make them 50K richer. Maybe she'll say it again now to distract him from the screen, her stats, Claudine—but he's stepped closer just as Claudine is signing off, another wave of goat emojis soaring toward the heavens.

"Wylie, you've got to stop torturing yourself," he says, groaning. Setting the smoothies on the dresser—a tag sale find, more shabby than chic—he gently pulls her to sit on the edge of the bed. "You know that, right? It's not healthy." She nods, pressing the place on her collarbone that calms her, tilting her head to rest on his shoulder.

He's right. But she cannot stop.

Her own reason for choosing Claudine: it's a way to see someone who can't see her. Because Claudine Potts isn't just a GOAT. She's Wylie's former ski coach.

And the mom she hasn't spoken to in two years.

2

Claudine

IN THE SHOWER, CLAUDINE SOAPS UP, SHAMPOOS and conditions her hair, rinses, shaves her underarms, and steps out. Dripping, she pauses the stopwatch on her phone.

One minute, eight seconds. Beat yesterday's time. It's silly, but a win is a win.

This is how a former Olympian gets her kicks, performing everyday tasks in under two minutes—the average time of a downhill ski race. You can take the competitor out of the game, but you can't take the competitive drive out of the athlete. And because Claudine was forced to retire—*Thanks a million, catastrophic knee injury*—she sometimes feels like she has unfinished business, more to prove. In the absence of any real tests of speed, she invents these daily challenges like she has a sibling nudging her in the ribs, saying, "I'll time you."

Today, though, Claudine needs to rush because the sportswriter Barry Haberman will be here at any moment to plead his case to ghostwrite her memoir. He's annoying, but he's a good guy; she's known him for years. She'll let him down easy. For the third time.

She resets the stopwatch and then rifles through her clothes, prioritizing warmth over style, still thawing out from racing all these years later. She and her husband, Gib, really should have moved to Maui and not this foggy, chilly seaside town in Oregon, but the bay views from their house make up for the weather—at least, when the fog isn't socking them in. She pulls on fleece-lined leggings and a sweaterdress that she still considers new even though she bought it five years ago. A brush of her graying bobbed hair, moisturizer on her face— no makeup—a gargle of mouthwash, and an annoying search for holeless socks ticks her just over the two-minute mark.

Claudine presses Stop. Dammit.

That interval of time is in her bones. One second slower than a competitor could make or break a career. It made hers. She was astoundingly, consistently fast.

Down the hall she strides, a hitch in her step from her aching left knee. When she rounds the corner to the kitchen to see Gib dicing red peppers into tiny uniform squares with a large kitchen knife, she halts and puts a hand to the wall. He looks up at her mid-dice, cracking a lazy, sexy half smile.

"Good morning, my love." How she adores his British accent.

"Should you be doing that?" she asks, trying to strip her voice of bossy apprehension.

"My tremors are good this morning." He holds out his hand. "Steady as she goes." Her face must betray her because he sets down the knife, moving around the kitchen island to pull her into an embrace. "I really am fine, promise."

"I'm sorry. I just worry," she says, slightly muffled by the soft gray flannel of his shirt.

"We've had enough of that lately." He releases her to slide across the kitchen floor in his socks, one arm out, showstopper style. "Look at me. I've still got it."

At sixty-three (fifteen years older than Claudine), Gib's as energetic as the day she met him, but she can spot the subtle changes, the stilted movements. Reaching for a coffee mug, Claudine tries to follow his lead, putting on a carefree air, all the while training one eye on his hands as he resumes the dicing. Finally, to her relief, he moves on to whisking the eggs for his signature frittata.

How long will he be able to cook? she wonders, not for the first time. She can't whip up culinary wonders like he does; she'll never share his glee over the *New York Times* food app. Poor Gib didn't marry a foodie. "You're a fuelie," he once joked. As in, she eats for fuel, not delight. She cooks this way too and has no clue how to "plate it."

Well, she'll just have to learn.

"Barry on his way?" Gib asks. In his warm-and-welcoming fashion, Gib insisted they serve Barry brunch, especially since he's coming all the way from Big Sky, Montana.

Whereas Claudine had been hoping to shake Barry in under two minutes. In a polite way.

"You mean Big Bear?" she asks, arching an eyebrow. Barry, the editor of *SKI Magazine* for twenty years, held on to his Dartmouth-ski-days nickname. Now he writes memoirs of retired skiers from his sprawling Montana ranch. "He texted me an hour ago. Should be here anytime."

"Wait," Gib says. "He goes by Big Bear, and he lives in Big Sky?"

"And he's a big guy with a big appetite. Just wait." She leans against the counter, sipping her coffee. "He probably thinks I'll have a harder time saying no—*again*—in person." As though puppy-dog eyes from Barry could convince Claudine to unearth secrets of her life for a memoir, including the one that she's kept buried all these years. A secret she's shared only with Gib, who miraculously stayed by her side despite knowing what she'd done.

Claudine turns her gaze to the window, to the choppy water below. "What do you think Wylie's doing right now?" It's a question she's asked Gib—and herself—countless times. Every time, it hurts deeply that she doesn't know the answer.

Gib looks at the clock on the microwave. "One in the afternoon her time. I bet she's hanging a Matisse."

The doorbell rings.

"Here we go," Claudine says. Another woman might smooth her shirt, run a hand over her hair. Claudine cracks her neck from side to side.

She opens the front door to find Barry Haberman in the flesh. "Claudine Potts," he booms. He's a girthy, jowly man—girthier and jowlier than she remembers—and he labors just climbing the threshold.

"Barry." She steps back, avoiding a hug. "Glad to see you, but I hope you haven't come all this way expecting a different answer." *He looks like President Taft*, she thinks, pleased with herself for remembering her U.S. history.

Barry appears not to have heard her. "I always prefer to meet with my authors in person." His cheeks are a mottled red.

She twitches a finger at him. "*Ah ah ah*. But I'm not one of your authors."

12

"*Yet*," he says. Then he sniffs the air. "Something smells good!"

"My husband's famous frittata. Follow me. I have us set up at the table."

She leads them into the dining room, indicating a chair for Barry facing the ocean. On the table, Gib's placed a plate of sliced cantaloupe and a small bowl of tangerines. How'd she get so lucky with him? Nobody's ever taken care of her like this.

Barry sits, folding his hands on his belly, peering around the room. "Didn't frame your golds?" he asks.

"What?"

"Where are your medals? Any racing pictures? Didn't see them hanging in the hallway either. It's like you didn't compete at all."

She lets out a stilted laugh, nodding to a sideboard populated with framed photos—Gib and Claudine's wedding day; Gib and his adult daughter, Phoebe, down on the beach; young Wylie. "There's a few photos over there." But he's right, there are no race photos, no medals. Claudine rarely has visitors; it's Gib who keeps a large social circle, hosts his poker nights. She sticks to herself, so it's strange to have someone in the house viewing her—and her things, her decorative choices—with her history in mind.

Truthfully, she didn't want to frame all her achievements, surrounding herself with proof that her best days are behind her. Her face on a Wheaties cereal box. Photos of her Letterman appearance. A *Sports Illustrated* cover.

She stores all that memorabilia in tubs in the garage, along with old equipment, weathered ski boots, items she could ship to a museum, like Kipper's gold medal in the Olympic downhill in '72, and her grandfather's Purple Heart from serving in the Tenth Mountain Division as a soldier on skis. She's even kept the news articles about her career-ending injury at the Salt Lake Olympics in 2002, when she'd been strapped to an orange stretcher and airlifted to the hospital, ten-year-old Wylie and Kipper watching from below.

"Huh," Barry says, as if he's not buying it. Then he slaps the arms of the chair. "So how is CycleTron?" He says the spin company's name in a sarcastic tone.

"Living the dream."

"You hate it. I mean, you must."

Claudine acts scandalized. "I'd never say that."

She says that all the time to Gib.

Two years ago, the CycleTron gig was a godsend, a new focus in her long struggle to transition to post-Olympic life. It pays well, for one thing, although she's not hard up for cash like she used to be, thanks to Gib's career as a music exec with Sony. CycleTron was a place to put her energy on days when all she wanted to do was stare at her phone, willing Wylie to call her back.

Quickly, though, the CycleTron shine wore off. It started to feel—well, a little depressing that her record-setting career, all her sacrifices and hardships and injuries and success, led to riding over pretend terrain, talking at people she can't see.

Now the job revs her engine about as much as a trip to the DMV does.

"You know what could get you off that hamster wheel?" Barry asks.

"Why do I have a feeling it starts with *b* and ends with 'ook deal'?"

Barry points a stubby finger at her. "You've always been funny. Your memoir could be funny."

"You're the only person who's ever described me as funny. And CycleTron's fine. I'm getting people moving. Keeping them healthy. I'm good with that."

Not really. She's withering on that bike, but it's hard to come up with a better plan. A plan that gives her more purpose, fills her with more passion the way ski racing once had. The way coaching Wylie once had. All of that is gone now. She couldn't even watch the Winter Olympics a few weeks ago, asked Gib to turn it off.

Gib sweeps in, a dish towel slung over his shoulder. "You must be Big Bear."

"That's what people tell me," Barry says, lighting up at the mention of his nickname.

"Barry, this is my husband, Gib. Gib, Barry."

The two shake hands as Gib sings the chorus to "Stayin' Alive." Claudine tilts her head, confused, and Gib kisses the top of it. "Barry Gibb was the lead singer of the Bee Gees," he explains.

"I'm more of a Tom Jones fan myself," Barry says. He gestures to the window. "What a view you have here."

"Coffee, Barry?" Gib asks. "Orange juice?"

Claudine cringes. "Oh, sorry, I should've asked." She doesn't want Gib to feel like the waiter. She's just terrible at this whole being-with-people thing, while Gib loves playing host.

"You know—I'll have both," Barry says. "You only live twice."

"Back in a tick," Gib says. "Brunch will be ready shortly."

"Want some help?" Claudine's half hoping for the excuse to ditch her guest for a brief reprieve.

"Hardly!" he calls.

Claudine misses Gib's levity the second he disappears into the kitchen, leaving her alone with Barry, who peels a tangerine in three fast strips and pops segments of it into his mouth like mints. "Don't you think Kipper would want you to immortalize the story of the Potts dynasty?" he asks, chewing.

Kipper. She shifts her eyes toward the garage. He's out there too, languishing for the last eight years. Well, his ashes anyway. It was a stroke that took down the lion, her firebrand of a father. She should finally, properly, ceremonially spread Kipper's ashes somewhere.

But a memoir she does not owe her father, and she resents Barry for playing that card, for possibly needling her a little with the word "dynasty." More than anything, Kipper would be disappointed by what she'd done to the dynasty, driven her daughter from the sport. "My answer is still the same as the last time we spoke: I'm not writing a memoir, Barry. I'm sorry. It's just not something that interests me."

Barry smooths a hand over his droopy cheek, his earning prospects draining away, and Claudine is nudged toward compassion. As far as reporters go, Barry hasn't been the worst.

From the time she joined the U.S. Ski Team at the age of eighteen, the media dubbed Claudine the Stone-Cold Killer for her stony demeanor in the start house before races, the way she appeared to stare blankly over the tops of snowy mountain caps while other racers were huddling with their ski techs or psyching themselves up in more animated ways. Barry never once called her that, not in print or in person.

She softens her tone. "Look, Barry. I appreciate that you came all the way here, I really do. If anyone has the skill to ghostwrite my book, it's you. If I ever change my mind, you'll be the first to know. Promise."

She'll never change her mind. But this feels like the only kind way to shake him.

Gib's back, setting down a mug of coffee and a glass of orange juice in front of Barry, his left hand shaking the tiniest bit.

"I'll take over," she says, moving to stand up. "You sit."

"And let you burn my masterpiece?" he scoffs.

"It's just—"

Barry smacks his lips. "Great coffee."

"I'll make the salad, at least."

"Already dressed the greens," Gib says. "Frittata's got two minutes." He glances at his watch, gives her a furtive wink before he disappears into the kitchen again.

She shakes her head, can't help but smile. He's messing with her. He knows her two-minute game.

Barry swipes a second tangerine, adding the peel to the pile. "There's surprisingly little out there about you." He pops another segment into his mouth, his eyes squinting from the tang.

Yes, and I like it that way. "I'm a private person," she says, lifting her chin.

"But you're passing up a windfall."

"I'm okay with that."

An uncomfortable silence balloons between them. Claudine can hear the cry of a seagull beyond the window.

Finally, with strained effort, Barry pushes himself up to standing, crossing the room to the sideboard. Her heart beats faster as she watches him pick up one of the photos.

"Wylie was such a great kid," he says. "When was this one taken?" He turns the frame so she can see the picture of Wylie hugging a stuffed turquoise Snowlet, the mascot of the 1998 Olympics.

His stalling tactic is so transparent she almost laughs. He knows the answer.

Still, the photo brings her back to that day, Wylie so inconsolable when she lost her beloved Snowlet in the crowd that Claudine skipped some of her usual warm-up to find the stupid thing, eventually replacing it with a new one that hadn't been trampled by the masses—although Wylie never knew this. Seeing her beaming face when it was back in her arms felt like as big of a victory as the gold medal she won later that day.

"Nagano," she says softly.

"That's it." He thumps the frame. "What's she up to these days?"

Hanging a Matisse? Claudine works hard to ward off any sign of grief on her face in front of Barry.

But she can't help feeling a deep ache in her chest, a hunger to freely touch her daughter's skin as she once had, a memory of how smooth it'd been. Claudine used to assure her daughter that a thin, invisible thread connected their two hearts, and this sentiment had eased Wylie's worried mind. They each have a little mole at the center of their breastbone, like the marking of a dull pencil. "See," Claudine had said, pointing to the two spots. "We're always attached."

Are they now? Still? By saying the wrong things and failing to show up in the right ways, Claudine has snipped that thread, allowing it to blow wild in the wind like a ruined spiderweb.

Claudine clears her throat. "Wylie's working at a museum in the Berkshires."

"She had such promise, didn't she?"

This guy. She stands up to retrieve the frame, sets it reverentially back on the sideboard. Then she turns to him, staring him down, wanting to cut the crap.

"I see what you're doing, reminding me that you know us, that you've always been a friend to our family. And that may be true, but it doesn't change anything. My answer is a firm no. Now I'm hoping we can enjoy a delicious breakfast together without talking about it anymore."

Barry stuffs both hands into his pockets, looking past Claudine to the choppy sea. His sigh is an anchor, weighted, as if all his grand plans have sunk under those white-churned waves. "I hoped it wouldn't get to this, and I hope this won't create bad blood between us, but you've left me no choice. I'm writing an unauthorized biography about you." He drags his gaze back to Claudine's.

Claudine gapes. "What?"

"I've got bills to pay. My ranch eats money."

"Then sell your ranch, Barry," she hisses. "Not my story."

"If we write this together, you can assure the book's accuracy. You can steer it. Without you, well . . . Who's to say I'll get it right? Or keep the right things buried." He removes a hand from his pocket and raps a knuckle on the sideboard at the word "buried," as if he's trying to indicate that he knows something—something *damning*. It sets off an internal alarm in Claudine.

"I won't be backed into a corner like this," she says through gritted teeth. "I'll disavow the book. I swear to—"

"All press is good press." He gives a cherubic shrug of his shoulders.

The vein in her neck pulses. "I'm going to find a way to stop you."

"The train's already left the station. I've got a publisher interested, and I'm headed to Switzerland on Friday. To interview your old pal Zosel Marie Schwarz. She invited me to Zermatt. She seems to have something she wants to get off her chest."

At Zosel's name, Claudine's face drains white.

Zosel Schwarz isn't just Claudine's old pal. She's the best friend Claudine's *ever* had, not to mention one of the strongest competitive ski racers she's gone up against. She was like a sister to Claudine, an aunt to Wylie—who even called her Auntie Zo.

And Zosel is the only other person besides Gib who knows Claudine's terrible secret. Not because Claudine confided in her in a best-friends-share-everything kind of way. No, Zosel figured it out on her own, confronting Claudine at the Salt Lake Games—just before Claudine wiped out and Zosel finally nabbed gold.

Claudine never called to congratulate her. They haven't spoken since.

"According to my timeline, you stayed with Zosel for a few months after her husband died rock climbing. When you and she were both around twenty-two. So young." Barry's staring at her, a tiny smirk forming on his lips—or is that in her imagination? "I'm guessing she'll have a lot to say about what a good friend you were during such a tragic time."

Claudine tightens her jaw, fighting to keep her composure, mustering the unfazed expression of the Stone-Cold Killer. On the inside, her mind races to piece this all together. Zosel's stayed silent all these years, but now she's suddenly ready to talk? Can this be true?

"Suit yourself, Barry," she says, like she's humoring him. "But I have a feeling it's not going to be worth the plane fare."

They stare at each other, a silent standoff that's interrupted by a humming Gib holding two plates brimming with thick slices of frittata and balsamic-dressed greens.

Gib stops short, slowly setting down the plates as he grapples with the scene in front of him. "Uh, everything okay? The mood in here seems to have soured."

Claudine doesn't tear her eyes away from Barry as she speaks. "Something came up for Big Bear. Unfortunately, he can't join us for breakfast after all. He's leaving just this very moment."

"Really, Claudine?" Barry asks, cocking his head.

"Really, Barry," she deadpans back.

Gib, still clueless, puts a supportive arm around Claudine's shoulders nonetheless and says, "I'm sorry to see you go."

I'm not, she thinks. Big Bear has become a big liability.

At the door, Barry pushes past Claudine, stops, and says, "Can I at least get a to-go container? I mean, have a heart."

"We're out," she says flatly. "There's a McDonald's down the road."

She closes and dead-bolts the door behind Barry with a definitive thud, not paying him the courtesy of seeing him off. A plan formulates in her mind, and she knows what she'll do next, narrowing her eyes, hearing the *click-click* noise of her boots locking into her skis, imagining sliding as close as possible to the start wand that marks the top of a race, gathering all her power. Kipper taught her to dogfight for every one-eighth-inch difference, one half second shaved from her time, and her nostrils flare with adrenaline as though she's about to launch herself downhill.

Barry Haberman is her next competitor. The ski run: Zermatt. The finish line: Zosel. She's got to get to her first.

Claudine doesn't care about the world knowing her dirty laundry, not really. But she has to protect Wylie from the truth. If she doesn't, and Wylie finds out what she was willing to do to win—well, there's no doubt about it.

She'll lose her daughter forever.

3

Wylie

STANDING IN THE CENTER OF THE WHITE-WALLED gallery space that's as large as an airport hangar, Wylie inhales, as if she just can't get enough of this place. There are currently two things she enjoys most in this world: her job here at the museum and chocolate-peanut-butter ice cream.

Both, she's been told, are not good for her. The ice cream because it's too sugary, too anti-keto. The job because it's *beneath* her.

She's sworn off the ice cream. The job? It's temporary—meant to be a stepping stone, a way to pay down her student loans while she makes a name for herself in the art world. But each day she has too much fun with her boss, Aileen, and each night, contritely, she vows to spend less time at the museum and more time painting.

Once again, though, painting her masterpiece will have to wait because it's install day. Wylie and Aileen get to finally hang up the art exhibit they've been carefully planning for months. As Wylie wields a crowbar to pry open three ship-ping crates marked "fragile," she's as giddy as a birthday girl, temporarily forgetting her CycleTron crash that morning. Seeing an exhibit in its full 3D glory, rather than on a com-puter screen, washes away all her angst.

Aileen, the museum's exhibition manager, puts her hands on the hips of her bright-blue coveralls, her headband hold-ing back a wave of messy curls. "A little to the left," she yells up to the small crew on ladders suspending overhead cables. Then she turns her attention to the crates. "Let's get a look at these babies, huh?"

They pull on their sterilized nitrile gloves and breathlessly extract the components of the exhibit, shuffling them to rest on carpet pads, careful not to damage any item.

"This should count as BodyFittest training," Aileen says, as they carry a papier-mâché ball that's as large as a car tire. "If you win next week, we deserve some credit."

Wylie laughs. *Ouch.* Her side aches from where she bashed it on the handlebars earlier. "You mean *when* we win." It has to happen. Everything in her life will fall into place once she and Dan come back from Berlin victorious.

"That's what I meant!" Aileen nods to the ball. "Doesn't this look like a glorified piñata?"

"Maybe there's candy inside."

Hey, they don't commission the artwork; they make it look good once it gets here, to this museum that's the gem of the Berkshires, housing an esteemed collection of contemporary art. Wylie was lucky to land the internship that led her to a full-time job as Aileen's assistant.

She loves spending time with Aileen. Wylie's basically friendless—nothing new, really. Just depressing, if she lets herself think about it too much. She's latched on to Aileen extra-hard, cling wrap on wet dough. But Aileen has a full life—a wife, a kid, her ceramics—and it's likely their work friendship means more to Wylie than it does to her. Aileen's got her son's violin recital to look forward to tonight, pizza for dinner, Netflix; Wylie's got burpees and lettuce wraps and a motivational fitness podcast.

Bending their knees, they lower the ball to rest on the pad, Wylie's thighs sore from her endless workouts. Another thing she's looking forward to after Berlin: no more training.

Dan's hoping to make a business out of being a BodyFittest winner. Not Wylie. You couldn't pay her to do another plank. One big win, that's all she needs.

Standing up, she spots Sonny, the new intern, holding a dented paper coffee cup, as lost as a kindergartner. *Poor guy.* She jogs across the space, wearing jeans that are more high-water hand-me-downs than trendy high-waisted mom jeans. Her long braid and bangs give her a wholesome vibe—a few snooty, snickering art students said Wylie's style channeled a pioneer woman. Confusing, considering she never wore dresses, let alone bonnets.

What she lacks in fashion sense she makes up for in kindness. At least, she tries to.

"Hey," she says, intercepting Sonny's walk to the garbage bin. "That belongs to *this* fellow." She nods to a twelve-foot-tall robot made of found trash nicknamed Mr. Crud.

Sonny frowns at it. "I thought it was trash."

"Well, yes, you're not wrong, but it's 'found' trash. The

entire robot is made of it. If you label garbage as found, it becomes art." She smiles. "Voilà."

"Oh no, sorry!" His eyes grow round. "I was trying to be helpful."

"All good. The artist will never know. I'll show you how to check the specs to find out where it goes. Follow me."

Involuntarily she imagines her mom seeing her now, reassembling trash art, and she winces.

"You quit skiing to hang up picture frames?" That's what Claudine had said the last time they spoke, the comment as stunning as a slap across the face.

It was the last straw.

They've been estranged ever since. Claudine left a flurry of defensive-sounding voicemails that only made Wylie feel worse. Her mom saw her as oversensitive. Thin-skinned. Said Wylie took a harmless comment too seriously—had always taken them too seriously.

Maybe Wylie's two-year silent treatment has been a little extreme, but she didn't know how else to defend herself against Claudine's inevitable next jab. And she can only imagine the jab that'd be coming her way now, as her career as an Important Artist has stalled out of the gates.

If Wylie's learned anything from her childhood, it's this: the purpose of life is to achieve on a grand scale. To "go big or go home," as Kipper used to say. To be a legend.

And there's never been a legendary exhibition manager, as far as she can tell.

So even though this job feeds her soul, and she's actually quite good at it—understanding how certain lighting might drop a viewer into the mood of a painting without washing out the colors, or how the spacing of installations invites a reflective, unhurried pace—there's always a little part of her thinking: *You're underperforming.* And that little part of her sounds a lot like Claudine.

Lately, though, Claudine hasn't sounded like Claudine. She's been texting her random little messages that pop up like daffodils. I hope you're having a good day. Or I'm thinking about you.

Say what?

They're so out of character that Wylie sometimes wonders if Gib is sending them.

She never responds. But she's started looking forward to them. Underneath her anger, she misses her mom. If only it felt easier to protect herself *and* invite her mom back into her life. That's why she's trying to wrap herself in success like it's padding; then Claudine won't be able to jab at anything—or if she does, it won't pierce through.

So no, she won't call Claudine back until she finally has a big win to show for herself, like BodyFittest Duo. Until she can deliver the news like it's a mic drop. *Booyah.*

Next week, she'll be a winner. Today, though, she's still a humble underperformer.

Around noon, Aileen says, "Let's break for lunch and hope Sonny doesn't put a boot through one of these balls while we're gone."

The museum's café is in a glass-walled greenhouse-like space, and Wylie notices that the early flurries have burned off. It's now so bright in the café—even with the weaker winter sun— that they've chosen a table not bathed in sunlight.

Wylie's lunch is an ice cream scoop's worth of tuna salad

over baby spinach that she brought from home to save money. She covers her mouth to block the fishy smell as she chews.

"When you get back from Berlin, we'll get up the collage exhibit by that Japanese artist," Aileen says. She's eating a made-to-order bruschetta that Wylie can't help but covet.

"I got my start in collages," Wylie says.

Aileen sips from her grapefruit Spindrift. "Somehow, I did not know that."

"And by 'my start,' I mean I started making them as a kid." For most of the year, until she was ten years old, her family followed the snow and the World Cup circuit—it's always ski season somewhere in the world—Claudine competing or training or testing equipment, Wylie homeschooled by Kipper. Forced to entertain herself, she made art with the things she could usually get her hands on: scissors, a glue stick, and cast-off magazines.

The hobby proved to be a lifesaver when she got older.

Wylie spears a cherry tomato with her fork. "When I was at the ski academy, sometimes I got nervous before my races." Nervous. Ha! That sounds downright jolly compared to the actual experience. "Making collages calmed me down." The sound of the scissors. The smear of glue. Creating a world where it hadn't existed. Tricking the eye with one image that, on second glance, was actually another. It was soothing.

Later, in art school, she abandoned collage, believing that painting held more gravitas, but she misses that medium, often wishing she'd trusted herself a little more, stayed in the lane that made her the happiest.

"You were under a lot of pressure," Aileen says. "In high

school, I was skipping class and taking bong hits. You were trying to get to the Olympics."

"The collages made me an oddball, though," Wylie says.

Aileen cocks her head, confused. "Why's that?"

"Have a hobby beyond skiing? Aileen, that's crazy talk!"

"Seems like it should be mandated. You want to be a serious athlete? Fine. But every day you have to do *something* creative so that you don't go off the deep end."

"You'd think," Wylie replies. Aileen has no idea how on the nose she is.

Truthfully, there was a lot that made Wylie an oddball. Awkward socially. Gifted physically, but with a mounting aversion to competition, as if she was covering her eyes and cringing through a horror film. At Burke, she had never heard so many *kids* talk knee tears—ACL, MCL, PCL—with crashes so inevitable that going under the knife was like earning your stripes. She had to psych herself up before every practice run, trying to rein in her breathing.

Then there were the obsessive-compulsive rituals she'd adopted that gave her a sense of security: checking and rechecking weather forecasts, cleaning and recleaning her ski goggles with a microfiber cloth, rebuckling her boots again and again.

To make matters worse, Claudine had followed her to Burke, joining the coaching staff to personally oversee Wylie's training. Having an Olympic-champ mom who pays you special attention puts a target on your back.

A memory pierces her. She's in St. Moritz, Switzerland, competing in the Junior Olympics, expected to win. Instead, she hid in the bathroom stall, too paralyzed with panic to compete.

A humiliating DNF stamped next to her name. Did Not Finish. Claudine would have amended it to "did not try." That's what she was yelling at Wylie as she pounded on the bathroom door, demanding that she get her ass up that mountain.

She snaps the lid on her Tupperware, balling up her napkin. No more talk about collages or skiing or going off the deep end. "What's new in your ceramics studio?" she asks.

"More on that later. What I really want to talk about is your job here."

"Oh?" Wylie's cheeks redden. Her first thought: *I'm getting fired.* Maybe Aileen just doesn't like her. Maybe she wants to work with someone else. Someone who doesn't bring tuna to lunch.

That is a fireable offense. A familiar pain zings in Wylie's stomach.

"You've become such a trusted member of the team," Aileen says.

But. Wylie's bracing for it.

"I honestly couldn't do this without you. I'm not sure how I ever did, actually."

But.

"You're clever and have creative ideas, and you're easy to work with. So . . ." Aileen drums her fingers on the table. "I'd like to offer you a promotion when you get back from Berlin. To exhibition comanager. No more assistant. I just got approval from the board. Whaddya say?"

Wylie's mouth falls open, a sound of surprise emanating from the back of her throat. She presses her hands to her reddened cheeks, shaking her head in disbelief. "Oh my gosh!"

Aileen reaches across the table to clasp Wylie's forearm. "It'll be more responsibility. Some longer hours. But you would be so great at this."

It's amazing to hear. Daily she battles a voice repeating that she doesn't belong, is an outsider in her own life, and she finds a reprieve here with Aileen among the canvases and the paint splatters and the found trash. The museum is possibly the only place where she is *not* an oddball—even if she wears high-water jeans.

Go for it. Stay in the lane that makes you the happiest.

But she hesitates.

Is taking this job going big—climbing the rungs, making an impact at the museum—or is it going home? Settling. Underperforming. Failing. Quitting, no more Important Artist.

You quit skiing to hang up picture frames? She can hear Claudine's voice in her head.

"What do you think?" Aileen asks, grinning. "We'll have so many laughs together."

"I'm flattered," Wylie says. "Truly. I . . ."

Before Wylie can land on a response, her phone rings. Dan. She hesitates to answer, but Aileen graciously nods at the interruption.

"Hey," she says. "You don't usually call me at work. Everything okay?" She starts to pack up her lunch bag, then halts as she comprehends what Dan's saying. "Wait, what? Slow down." Her hand flies to her collarbone as she listens. "I'll be right there."

But Wylie doesn't immediately spring into action. She's a statue of herself, an art installation, eyes wide, mouth open. Titled: *Woman in Fright.*

"What's wrong?" Aileen asks.

Wylie blinks. "Dan's on the way to the hospital."

4

Wylie

THE ER DOCTOR MOUNTING DAN'S X-RAY TO A LIGHT box is a man of towering height with hair the shade of Corn Chex. He has such an excessively jovial bedside manner—Wylie overheard him playing "got your nose" with an elderly patient—that it's extra-jarring to hear him deliver this solemn news: Dan tore his Achilles tendon running wind sprints.

"Rolled right up like a rug," Dr. DJ says, insisting they call him this. "Like a Swiss Roll. Like a Fruit Roll-Up."

"I'd say you were on a *roll*," the nurse interjects. They do a fist-bump explosion.

Noticing Wylie's horrified expression, he puts an oven-mitt-sized hand on hers, and his voice softens. "I'm sorry, just a little workplace humor. This must be really hard to hear." He turns to Dan, who's pale, propped up in a hospital bed. "And even harder to experience."

Wylie takes a tissue from the box the nurse extends, shredding it in her lap. She's been around enough injuries to know that this is a ghastly one. She shifts her gaze to Dan. The tiny *v*'s at the edges of his closed eyes glisten with wetness. "What happens next?"

Dr. DJ slaps the metal railing of Dan's bed, the reverberations causing Dan to grimace. "Well, Danny Boy's going to need surgery to reattach that tendon. He'll live in a boot for about three months; PT after that."

Dan, groggy on painkillers, opens his eyes and lolls his head in Wylie's direction. Through parched lips he whispers, "Ask him about the contest."

The answer is obvious, but she doesn't want to be the one to tell Dan they can't compete. The doctor can be the bad guy. "Doctor?" She can't bring herself to say "DJ."

He's scribbling on a prescription pad. "Hmm?"

"We're supposed to compete in BodyFittest Duo in seven days." She sees that he's written "Thai takeout?" on the pad rather than a prescription. Ugh, he sucks.

Dr. DJ gives a whoa-Nelly whistle as if a car dealer just quoted him an astronomical price for an obvious lemon. "It'll be a good six months before he starts to get back to his regular self. This is a *nasty* injury."

"*Nasty!*" the nurse repeats. She points at the prescription pad and gives Dr. DJ a thumbs-up.

The doctor stands. "Nurse Becky will be back in a bit with some paperwork and a brand-new pair of crutches. Well, not brand-new—they've seen their fair share of armpits—but new to Dan here." He squeezes the toes on Dan's good foot, but Dan doesn't respond. "I'm sorry about your competition,

Wylie. I'm sure you two will knock 'em dead next time. I'll be rooting for ya."

"Thank you." Her stomach twists as he whips the curtain aside, closing it again to give them privacy. Wylie scoots her chair closer to Dan, resting her cheek on his arm. He doesn't move, not to run his fingers through her hair to console her, not to reach out for consolation. He's somewhere else, floating in a sea of gloom.

Her heart aches for him.

And her heart aches for herself. She's worked so hard for this, pushing through the ten-mile runs wearing a weighted backpack and skipping so much as a nibble of sugar cookie at Christmas. The hours Dan's droned on about "mental toughness"—as if she didn't grow up being told there's no glory without sacrifice. Victory was within reach, so close that she was tasting the win, and, yes, she'd imagined—even rehearsed—that phone call to Claudine.

See, Mom, I am the best at something after all.

Beyond impressing Claudine, she's got a laundry list of other goals—get gallery representation, search for her long-lost dad, make a circle of good friends, for god's sake—and for some not fully rational reason, she's glommed on to the idea that winning BodyFittest will be the domino that starts it all. Who wants to be friends with a loser? Who wants a loser of a daughter?

All of that goes out the window now. No contest, no redemption, no reinvention.

She's hollow. But also, strangely, she feels a tinge of relief? She searches herself, looking for a fire in her belly, her beast mode railing against the travesty of Dan's injury. Instead, she notices the same sense of release she'd felt as a freshman at

Burke when a doctor proposed that her severe stomachaches could be stress-induced.

"Might I suggest she take time off from skiing?" the doctor had said to Claudine.

Time off from skiing.

How those four words had set Wylie's chest aflutter, as if she were standing in the middle of a giant board game, an alternative path unfurling.

"Yes," responded a deep pull inside her. "Yes."

And now, on the precipice of winning a different competition with the power to change her life, she feels an unexpected echo of that deep pull. Time off from competing. No more.

Dan licks his lips, nods to the paper cup of water on the side table. Wylie retrieves it, and he takes a long drink, hands it back to her.

"I'll email BodyFittest when we get home," she says. "Let them know we can't . . . You know . . ."

When Dan speaks, his voice trembles, maybe from the meds or the shock. "You have to compete."

"What?" Wylie leans closer, as though she's misheard him.

"You still have to go to Berlin."

She tilts her head, wondering if the painkillers are making him loopy. "But it's BodyFittest *Duo*. And now we're not a duo."

"We'll find you someone else. You're allowed an alternate."

"Who?" They've been training obsessively for two years. "It's so last-minute."

"We need the prize money, Wylie!" Dan's cheeks are as red and splotchy as a slice of salami.

"What are you talking about?"

Dan pulls his palm down his face, rubs his chin, and stares at the ceiling. "I'm in debt."

"In . . . debt?" The two worry lines between Wylie's eyebrows pinch in confusion. Her mind flashes to the green smoothies. His Apple Watch and tubs of Muscle Milk. The lavish birthday gift he gave her: a leather roll-up case for her graphite pencils and charcoal sticks.

"Things just got out of hand," he says.

"Your spending?" There's a chill in the room. She wraps her arms around herself.

"That, and"—Dan swallows—"then the sports betting."

"Excuse me?"

"I won a few times. And then I, well . . ."

She shoots up from the chair in one fast motion. "You what, Dan?"

"It got out of control," he says meekly.

"Are you fucking kidding me right now?" It's a rare swear word from Wylie. She puts a fist to her mouth, biting a knuckle, trying to stop herself from yelling. Never before has she raised her voice at Dan. She retracts or retreats, resents his controlling ways with a quiet, dignified air. But rage at him? No.

But now it's all she can do to contain her anger.

What an idiot she's been. A fool. Living this clean-as-a-whistle, straight-as-an-arrow life that Dan's laid out for them, working overtime at the museum while he occasionally takes substitute-teaching gigs and refs a few youth sports. And in secret, he's been gambling everything away?!

Then he was just going to . . . What? Use their winnings to pay his debt? Not tell her until after the competition? What about her chunk of the money?

This is a fireable offense, she thinks. Grounds to break up with him.

He pushes himself up to sitting. "It's just so easy. You can do it right from your phone." To prove his point, he reaches for his phone stashed on the table next to his water cup, opening the DraftKings sports-betting app. He flashes his phone screen at her. "See, I can bet on a game right here—" Dan starts to click a link, but Wylie swats at his hand.

"Don't *bet* on something now!" She closes her eyes, covering her eyelids with the heels of her hands. "How much do you owe?"

"Thirty-two thousand dollars," he mumbles.

Wylie keels over her belly as though she's been punched, her head hanging between her legs. Thirty-two thousand is well more than he makes in a year. "There'll be barely any prize money left. Did you ever stop to think about that?" she asks.

"I have a problem, Wy. I do." Then Dan hangs his head, starting to cry, his large shoulders shaking. "Please. Please, you've got to help me."

Wylie can feel her breath shorten; her chest constricts, so she stands up, pacing the room, drawing both her hands up and down in a Qigong movement to slow her heart rate. Goddammit, she wants to appear strong and pissed off and formidable. But her body has other plans. *Oh no. Not now. Please not now, not here.*

Where only moments ago she was cold, now sweat beads on her brow. The Qigong isn't working. Wylie grasps at the next grounding technique in her arsenal, the ones a counselor at Burke taught her and Claudine—although by then it was too late to salvage her skiing.

Um . . . Um . . . She closes her eyes, trying to invoke them. Find the exit door. That's one. She pictures the revolving hospital door, but that does nothing to calm her. The room grows hazy, her breathing more rapid and shallow. It's like a cinder block is pressing down on her chest, compressing her lungs. She flaps her hand in front of her face as she tries to figure out what else to do.

Dan's stopped crying. "Wy, are you okay?"

"I don't want this to be happening," she says, rapping her head with her palm to dislodge the panic.

"What's going on? Are you having a panic attack?" He knows about these panic attacks in an abstract way, but he's never seen one himself.

She rocks back and forth on her heels. "Mm-hmm" is all she can manage.

He sits up higher. "Okay, um . . . Everything's going to be okay . . . Shit, I'm sorry, Wy. Sorry I'm putting you through this. What should I do? Call a nurse?" His hand moves to the call button near his hospital bed.

She shakes her head violently. No nurse. She hates, hates, hates having witnesses.

"Water?" he asks, holding out his paper cup. "Take deep breaths?"

"Make a list." She puts her hands behind her head, winging out her arms, trying to encourage her lungs to gulp more air.

His forehead creases. "What?"

"A list. Anything. Name something." Listing items is a grounding technique meant to pull her mind out of distress.

"I don't . . . I'm going to call a nurse."

"BodyFittest exercises." She frantically twirls her hand in the air, a gesture of "get on with it."

"Dead lift?" He's utterly confused.

A moment later, between gasps of breath, she returns with "Kettlebell swing."

"B-Burpee?"

"Pull-up."

On and on they go, trading exercises until Wylie's heart rate slows, her breathing softens. Eventually she's able to open her eyes to see Dan's worried face watching her intently.

"Whoa," he says.

"Yeah."

He drops back against his pillows as if he's the one who's spent, an arm draped over his forehead. "That was intense."

"Oh, was that intense for you?" she snaps. He peeks up, hurt, looking so shell-shocked and small in the hospital bed that she regrets the sarcasm. "Sorry."

"No, it's okay. I deserve it. I'm the one who's sorry." He puts out his hand, but she doesn't take it, sinking down into a chair against the wall. Her body is damp. She just wants to curl up and sleep. "I shouldn't have asked you to do the competition. I'll find another way to pay it off."

But she's not really listening.

Gone is that sense of yawning freedom in her body. Her stomachache has returned, just as it swept back in when Claudine marched Wylie out the door of that doctor's office at Burke, muttering about the doctor being out of his lane.

What does she want to do? Find a way to compete? Quit?

How that word has trailed her. *Go ahead, be a quitter.*

"What are you thinking?" Dan asks. "You're making me nervous. Wy?"

No. She cannot live with herself if she bails. She'll do this thing, and she'll do it to win.

As for Dan's alternate, well, the sickening truth is that she knows only one person who has the physical prowess to step in on such short notice. One person who can compensate for inadequate training with pure grit, with a naked desire to be the victor.

Wylie closes her eyes, understanding what she must do. What she will do. Now she just has to muster the courage to do it.

5

Claudine

CLAUDINE, STILL ROILING AFTER BARRY'S VISIT, IS taking out her anger on her aching left knee. Sitting on the edge of the bed, she dips two fingers into a tub of Blue-Emu cream (she swears the stuff works better than any newfangled CBD ointment), and then she slathers the cold goop onto her knee with gruff impatience, like Kipper toweling her hair as a kid after a swim.

The CycleTron rides aggravate old racing injuries. It's her left knee—not the one rebuilt after her Salt Lake crash, but her other knee, with all her own parts—that gives her the worst time, perpetually inflamed.

On his side of the bed, Gib's propped against a husband pillow, reading Patti Smith's memoir. Or trying to—Claudine's jostling the bed so much with her seething movements that eventually he removes his glasses, closes his book, and rests his hand on top of it.

She glances at it, to see if it's trembling.

They're through the harried, horrible, terrifying first few weeks following his diagnosis when their world was turned upside down, but the reality is still a fresh wound. Claudine didn't find love like this until she was forty-two, six years ago, at a charity golf tournament in Newport Beach, California. That's when a dashing man sidled up to his tee and promptly shanked his ball into the trees, yelling "Fore!" in a theatrical voice, causing fellow golfers down the green to duck, and then to glare.

Only Claudine was standing close enough to hear him utter, under his breath, "Play."

She swiveled her head slowly and pinned her eyes on him.

"What?" he asked, mocking innocence, one hand jingling the tee in his pocket, the other rotating the handle of his golf club in wide circles.

"I heard that," she said, trying to decide if she was irritated. There was something charming about him in his white Ben Hogan cap and fitted blue golf pants, his eyes sparkling with mischief.

When she teed off next, selecting a nine iron for the long drive over a man-made pond, she said, "Four," only quieter, so she didn't throw everyone into a panic about a rogue ball, and then, under her breath, just for him, "Some." She raised an eyebrow—*touché*—and he chortled, slapping his golf-gloved hand on his thigh. It was on.

"Fore—shadow."

"Fore—arm."

"Fore—cast."

"Fore—runner."

Their silly game grew more nonsensical with every hole,

their laughter louder, their chemistry stronger. Claudine, shockingly, didn't even care who was winning.

"Fore—gone conclusion."

"Four—score and seven years ago."

"For—whom the bell tolls."

At the last hole, he said, "Seven!" and then, turning to her, "O'clock."

"What was that?" she asked, confused.

"The time I'd like to pick you up tomorrow night for dinner."

"What's wrong with tonight?" she asked, and so began the whirlwind love story of their lives, including an elopement and a move to the coastal town of Brookings, where they both enjoyed the obscurity, the fresh fish, and the joint promise to never play golf again.

Now she nurses a private devastation over what will be cut short, even as medical breakthroughs give them hope. They're settling into a new normal, like transitioning to an earlier bedtime routine on account of the disease disrupting Gib's sleep.

Still, 8:35 p.m. feels like old-people territory. So does the Blue-Emu.

"Remind me again why you can't just call Zosel instead of going all the way to the Alps," he says. "I'm asking not because I need you to stay, but it just seems like a lot on you."

She screws the lid back onto the cream, sets it on the side table, and repositions her legs under the covers, sitting up against the headboard. "Call her after going silent for sixteen years? You know how delicate this is. And important. I've got everything to lose." And with a phone call, Zosel could simply hang up. Block her number.

"So you're just going to ambush her at home?"

"Something like that, I guess." If she could've gotten to Switzerland in under two minutes, she would've.

"Not to offend, love, but that doesn't sound delicate." Gib looks at her kindly.

She throws up her hands. "What choice do I have, though? You know I'll never get Wylie back if Barry breaks the story. The *real* story."

He strokes his chin. "I see your point. I'm just curious about your plan."

She doesn't have one yet, not really. Knock on Zosel's door and beg? Intimidate her into silence? Will Zosel slam the door in her face? At least she'll have the element of surprise on her side. Her old friend will be absolutely shocked to see her.

"We should go into Medford early tomorrow before your flight, hit REI, get you some cold-weather gear for Switzerland. A new coat," Gibs says, as if he's outfitting her for a lighthearted excursion. She doesn't fault him his attempt at normalcy—she's been doing the same to him these past months about the Parkinson's.

"My old parka's perfectly fine."

"My love, you've duct-taped one of the elbows."

"It works. Still as warm as the day I bought it."

"A decade ago?"

Claudine shrugs. "You'll call Phoebe if you need anything while I'm gone?"

"I'm throwing a rager while you're away. Partying until dawn, like my old days. Inviting all the washed-up musicians I know."

She tilts her chin. "Just reassure me, please. I hate leaving you."

Gib chuckles softly. "Yes, she's on standby, should I need her. Which I won't." He reaches into the drawer of the side table, waggling his eyebrows like he's pulling out a sex toy. "Bow-chicka-wow-wow," he sings, shimmying his shoulders seductively, shaking a box at her. "How about a little bondage tonight?"

It's sleep tape. They're trying everything to improve his sleep, even bandaging their mouths shut to "enhance nasal breathing."

She gives a tired laugh just as her phone chimes. Every time she hears that noise, hope stampedes through her body that it's Wylie finally reaching out.

Every time, she's wrong.

And wrong again. CycleTron is responding to her request for sudden time off so she can go to Switzerland. She ignores it. No matter their answer, she's flying on a red-eye tomorrow night.

Still holding her phone, she pulls up the last message she sent to Wylie, frowning at the one-sided conversation. She shows him the screen. "Is she even reading these texts?"

He's already put on his sleep tape. "Mm-hmm," he says, handing her a strip. She takes it, darkens the screen.

"Are they making a difference? Soupy says I should keep showing up without any expectations. But it's hard not to hear anything back." Soupy—actually, Sue P.—is Claudine's therapist, but she and Gib have dubbed her with this moniker.

Gib mumbles from behind his sleep tape.

"Huh?" she asks, fiddling with her own strip, dreading smacking it across her mouth.

He lifts a corner of tape, speaking as if his jaw is wired shut. "I do. You're doing great."

Is she? To prepare for the day when Wylie's ready to speak with her again, Claudine's hitting therapy like it's a dedicated training plan, the same way she built muscle mass or tested new ski boots during summer skiing or learned to lead a spin class. She was hoping to change dramatically.

In, like, six weeks.

Of course, therapy—*talk* therapy—requires actually opening up to Soupy, and Claudine would rather ride her bike without padded bike shorts than do that. So her gains have been slow. And worst of all, for her: unmeasurable.

Claudine looks down, the ends of her bluntly cut hair sweeping forward. "I hope Dan's treating her right." She thinks back to the one and only time she'd met Wylie's boyfriend. She and Gib had taken them to dinner. She'd felt a flicker of concern when Dan sent back the bread basket.

"Wylie's an adult," Gib says, his words muffled.

Claudine nods. "I just miss her so much."

Gib gently pries his tape off. "I know, love."

"I'm scared," she says, her voice close to breaking.

"About seeing Zosel? Or something to do with Wylie?"

"Both, I think." Claudine should mention the sleep-tape method to Soupy. Threaten to slap some tape on her lips during a session and she'll morph into a chatterbox. "What if I can't get Zosel to back down? And what if Wylie . . . just never calls? What if I've already blown it? I've been the worst mom in the world."

Gib opens his arms, and she tilts into them. "I hate seeing you be so hard on yourself. All parents, from the beginning of time, have made mistakes. No one's perfect. And it's normal for children to push back, rebel, want boundaries—Wylie's just doing it a little later than some kids. She's stubborn. But she'll come around."

Claudine sniffs. He's right, but he wasn't there that day in St. Moritz. Wasn't on that phone call when Claudine mocked Wylie's new job. Hasn't witnessed Claudine at her worst. And if Wylie broke off contact over all that—imagine what she'll do if Claudine's secret gets out.

"Let's get some sleep," Gib says. "Or try, anyway. I'll get us new strips."

They lay facing each other, mouths bound, in the dark. It's not long before she can hear Gib nearing slumber, his out breath like the sound of a scuba diver, while she's forced to watch the usual parade of her failures—as a parent, as a friend. She's wondering if she'll sleep at all, when her phone rings.

She bolts upright, fumbling for it in the dark.

There on the screen is the name she's been waiting two years to see. Claudine whips her hand to her mouth, stripping off the tape so fast it stings her lips as she brings the phone to her ear.

"Mom?" Claudine hears when she answers, and she closes her eyes, allowing the voice, that word, to flow over her.

"Yes, it's me. I'm here. It's Mom," she replies.

6

Wylie

EVERYWHERE WYLIE LOOKS IS SNOW. A KNEE-HIGH sparkling-white blanket—*no, thicker,* a downy comforter—of snow. On the sloping chalet rooftops, steep as good sledding hills. On the mountains just beyond, and the ones even farther, their pinnacles edging up, looking, from her vantage point on the train whisking her out of Zurich, like sharpened pencils. On the truss bridges. On the compact village streets, burying pavement and, in some places, cobblestone.

She takes a sharp inhale of breath, nearly expecting the crisp, metallic *smell* of snow—she swears it has one. Instead she's hit with her mom's forever scent: Neutrogena soap. It's particularly pungent because Claudine's sitting right next to her. She's still shocked that Claudine agreed to be Dan's alternate. Though Wylie suspects she could have suggested anything—a culinary insect-eating tour, for example—and her mom would've jumped at the chance to reconnect.

It's mind-boggling to go from estranged to suddenly sharing such personal space. "Thank you for doing this with me," Wylie repeats bashfully.

"You don't have to keep thanking me," Claudine says. "I'm so glad that you called."

Me too, Wylie thinks—and not just because of BodyFittest. As they were figuring out travel logistics on the phone, Claudine had revealed that she was actually on her way to Zermatt that very next day to spread Kipper's ashes, so she'd just scoot to Berlin from there. Um, *hello?* Clearly it hadn't occurred to Claudine that his only granddaughter would want to be a part of that ritual. Or at least know about it?

She's trying not to hold it against Claudine—Wylie wasn't speaking to her, after all—but her brain cataloged the slight, even as she voiced her enthusiasm to tag along.

It sure felt like the right thing to do in the moment. Sixty miles—ahem, *kilometers*—into this train ride, however, and Wylie's not so sure. If there's ever been a geography that screams, "You didn't live up to your full potential," it's whizzing by as the train turns west toward Bern, ferrying them deeper into alpine ski country. She's jet-lagged and shot full of adrenaline. Her left foot is bobbing so violently she's liable to kick off her waterproof ankle boot and send it flying across the aisle.

Outside, the snow rate increases, the train twisting along as it climbs in elevation, the mountains jagged and cutting, wolf's teeth at an impossible angle. Remote chalets cling to outcroppings with no discernible roads to get there, tendrils of smoke looping out of chimneys. There are people out there, making a life in this inhospitable place.

This landscape is in her muscle memory, but it doesn't say: *Relax.*

Rather, it whispers: *Run.*

"You okay?" Claudine asks, leaning over.

Wylie shifts away, not ready for the kiss of their shoulders. "Uh, yeah. This is all just a bit"—she gestures around her—"sudden, you know."

"I know."

And that's it, that's all they seem able to say, already running out of words. Wylie just nods, staring at the pastry bag resting in her lap that holds the croissant that Claudine bought for her at the airport before Wylie had a chance to say "I don't do carbs."

She closes her eyes to avoid both the tempting pastry and the triggering scenery, trying to land on a conversation starter that will fill the next two hours. They opted for the faster train to Zermatt, rather than the Glacier Express, a glacially slow ride chock-full of tourists complaining about the photo glare on the windows.

Wylie and Claudine aren't tourists. They've come to do a deed. Get in, get out. Less than twenty-four hours, and they'll be back in Zurich to fly on to Berlin, where they'll win Body-Fittest Duo, and then go back to their separate coasts—East for Wylie, West for Claudine—and their separate lives. Wylie is keeping her guard up and her expectations low. She'll be cordial, kind, and grateful, but detached. Protective of herself.

It occurs to Wylie that they haven't talked about the reason they've come to Switzerland first. She turns back to Claudine.

"Where are the ashes?" she asks. It comes out sounding unintentionally accusatory.

"The what?"

"Kipper's ashes." Kipper, her grandfather, had also been a

skiing legend. The first Olympic gold medalist in the family. Claudine, the second. Wylie—*well*. Yeah.

"Oh, right." Claudine reaches down to unzip the side pocket of her backpack.

Wylie's expecting an urn or a container or even a crude plastic baggie puffed out with deep-gray human remains, as if Claudine's transporting playground sand. Instead, Claudine dangles a pendant necklace. Wylie squints at it.

"He's in here," Claudine says. "Well, some of him."

"That's all you brought?" It's got to be less than a thimble-ful of Kipper's ashes.

The pendant sways back and forth. Claudine stares at it, as if she's also confused by her choice. Even her yes sounds uncertain.

"Why here, Mom? Kipper didn't even like the Swiss."

A fair-skinned woman in an enormous mink-lined black Cossack hat glares at them from across the aisle.

"Sorry," Wylie mouths, holding up an apologetic hand.

Claudine leans closer to speak quietly. "Yeah, well . . . He liked the Matterhorn, didn't he?"

"Did he?" She's not trying to be contradictory, really. But she can't wipe the skepticism from her face.

"Of course." Claudine frowns at Wylie frowning and says, "Besides, it's symbolic. A great man scattered on one of the world's greatest mountains. He'd be honored."

Claudine calling Kipper a "great man" oversells it. Something's off.

Wylie studies her mom but decides to drop it for now. "Why aren't you wearing the necklace?"

"Oh, um."

"Here." Wylie takes the pendant, and Claudine automatically swivels in her seat, her back toward Wylie so she can fasten the necklace for her.

Claudine turns to face Wylie. "Plus it'll be nice to be back in some old stomping grounds together. I don't really ski anymore, but you could. I don't mind staying behind."

At this suggestion, Wylie can't calibrate her emotions. She smacks back against the seat, crossing her arms, plunging into petulance as if she's thirteen again. Her long braid, slung over her shoulder, suddenly appears childish, too. "I was wondering how long it'd take for you to start in on the skiing."

"I only meant for fun." Claudine looks appalled.

Okay, that's almost hilarious. Switzerland isn't exactly old stomping grounds in a frivolous, *fun* way. Wylie can't actually remember her mom ever even using that word. "Fraught" is a better descriptor for the times they've shared in this country. She can imagine the sound of Claudine's fist against the bathroom door in St. Moritz.

It'd be so easy to clam up right now, pout for the rest of the ride.

Then she forces herself to remember Claudine's texts: I hope you're having a good day! And I'm thinking about you. And her own resolve to be cordial, kind, grateful. She stares out the window, gathering herself.

The Swiss fly their flag almost as fervently as Americans do. In quick succession, Wylie counts six red flags with white crosses hanging from flagpoles mounted to the sides of buildings. Many of the homes have wide red shutters, as if the aesthetic is a neighborhood-association mandate. A cross-country skier cuts a track of fresh powder, a medieval cathedral rising in the background, snow falling all around him. It's brochure-worthy.

She clears her throat, returns to Claudine. "I could walk you through the BodyFittest Duo competition. What we'll be doing."

"Oh, that'd be great." Her mom gives her a relieved smile, seeming to appreciate the safe conversational ground.

"Do you know what a burpee is?"

Claudine pretends offense, her tilted chin and pressed duck lips an expression of "Who do you think I am?"

"Just checking. Barbell clean and jerk?"

"That one you have to remind me."

"I'll show you in the hotel gym. Plank, which I know you know."

"I'm the queen of the plank."

As the train begins its southward dip to Visp, they're buoyed by an old comfort topic: training. But it doesn't stretch far enough. Before long, the silence between them is voluminous once again.

Claudine nudges her. "You going to eat that? You used to love croissants."

Wylie stares at the pastry bag like it's a lap dog that will fire up a sneezing attack if she touches it.

"Well . . . I did already have breakfast." And by that she means her allotment of raw almonds and dried apricots, plus a coconut-flour muffin she packed from home. "But it smells so good, doesn't it?"

Claudine nods. "They just do pastry better here. And this coming from someone who usually doesn't give two hoots."

Wylie unsheathes the croissant, drawing it to her nose.

Just a whiff. *Buttery*. Her mouth waters. Then she puts the flat, caramelized bottom of her croissant against her mouth, reflecting a pastry smile in the window.

It doesn't fit her mood. She turns it upside down. A frown is better.

One tiny nibble sends her stomach grumbling.

If she records this pastry in her shared calorie-counter app with Dan, it'll balloon her daily tally. She used to get such a rush from keeping that number perfect—just enough nourishment for training. Wylie came from a sport she couldn't control—not the weather or the snow conditions, not the medal count, and certainly not her mind. Dan offered her something she could control: food and weight-lifting reps, a workout schedule alternating leg days and arm days and ab days. A manual for life.

But, damn, she's been missing carbs. And buying a *People* magazine in the airport felt like the first spontaneous, frivolous thing she'd done in years.

You know what? If she doesn't record the pastry in the app, it's like it didn't happen.

There's no graceful way to eat a croissant, so Wylie attacks it, angling a hooked corner into her mouth. Flakes of bread, like dried brown leaves after a lawn mower shreds them into bits, rain down on her sweatshirt, unnoticed. It's gone in a flash. She could eat three more.

Claudine smiles at her, and Wylie feels suddenly shy. It's one thing being weird with food, another having her mom witness the weirdness. She longs for the anonymity and voyeurism of the CycleTron touch screen. To see Claudine without being scrutinized herself.

At the next stop, in the town of Visp with its terraced vineyards, a man and a young boy enter the train, dust the snow from their shoulders, and scooch in across from them, their seats facing Wylie and Claudine as if they're a foursome out to dinner. The man—short, stiffly gelled black hair, a bright-blue Rossignol ski jacket—cracks a wide smile, his teeth like books crowded in a backpack, pushing over top of one another.

"Ciao. I'm Giovanni, and this is my son, Maximilian."

Wylie's not a rude person, and she's not normally grumpy with strangers, but she's too exhausted and taxed emotionally to chat with a pair of suave Italians—and, yes, the kid, at only four, is already suave in his designer jeans and equally shellacked hair. And she hates when people announce that they're skiers through the gear they wear *off* the slopes. "Wylie," she mutters.

"Claudine." Claudine crosses her arms, matching Wylie's stance, and Wylie feels a rush of affection for her mom.

"Are you on holiday?" Giovanni asks, ignoring the social cues the women are tossing at him like underhand softball pitches. "The forecast is predicting more snow. The skiing will be *perfecto*." He makes a kissing gesture with his hand to his mouth.

This situation calls for earbuds and doodling. In her backpack, resting at her feet, is the leather roll-up case from Dan. She's now slightly sickened by the memory of this gift, by her own naivete, knowing that even as Dan purchased it for her, he was also doubling down on bets that entrenched him in debt. But she won't transfer her frustration onto the leather case by refusing to use it. It's too perfect, with its twelve pockets and its sharpening tools, its leather strap that wraps twice like it's a belt fashioned around a rolled-up sleeping bag.

She reaches for it, then thinks better of it. Doodling in front of Claudine could invite an inquiry like: "Sold any paintings?" No. "Finished any paintings?" Also no.

Across from them, Giovanni wags a finger at Claudine, saying, "You look familiar."

Now there's no question; Wylie needs to get lost in a podcast.

Pulling her wireless earbuds from the front pocket of her sweatshirt, she notices the carpet of croissant on her pants. If she were alone, she'd wet a finger and dab at each golden flake, lifting it to her mouth to savor the flavor. But there's Maximilian staring at her, swinging his short little legs, likely thinking: *Americans really are slobs.*

Wylie makes a funny face, sticking out her tongue. Maximilian volleys back a funny face. Before she knows it, she's in a funny-face-off that she wishes she'd never started. *"Finito!"* she says to an insistent Max, who gives her a pouty lip. She's about to pop her earbuds in when she hears male voices from behind her start an a cappella rendition of "Don't Worry Be Happy."

She exchanges eye rolls with Claudine, an involuntary moment of solidarity. Buskers. *Ugh.*

Swiping through her phone, Wylie stops short at her podcast playlist: all athletic motivational speakers and fitness gurus. Dan's not here. Why keep listening to these?

Unsubscribe. Unsubscribe. Unsubscribe. Her heart beats fast with the treachery. Beyond her rebellion awaits an old fear. How will she fill her own feed, her own library, her own life, without anyone telling her what choices to make, even in the short term? Without Dan here, who will she be without structure and a clearly laid path to success? Unclear. Unclear. Unclear.

To calm her worried mind, she toggles to her meditation app, clicking on a link, sinking into the voice she's come to know and trust. She closes her eyes to the outside world, straightening her spine, releasing her jaw muscles. As instructed, she pictures a golden light spreading over her body, silently repeating the phrases. Such simple words. So out of reach on a daily basis.

You are enough.

You are loved.

You are safe.

She tunes out the Bobby McFerrin remix and little Maximilian whining to his father and Giovanni asking Claudine where she stores her gold medals and Dan's barrage of WhatsApp messages about sticking to the exercise schedule. She ignores her own brain asking: *Did I make a terrible mistake coming here with Mom?*

Before long, Wylie is asleep, and soon after, they arrive in the little village of Zermatt, population six thousand, swelling to three times that during ski season. As she and Claudine step off the train into the cold, thin air, she notices her mom reaching up to touch the pendant with Kipper's ashes. Wylie didn't know everything about her grandfather, but she knows this isn't the right resting place for him—even symbolically. So why are they really here?

7

Claudine

THE MOMENT THEY'RE OFF THE TRAIN, SETTING foot in an old-world village that Claudine knows well, the snow falling heavily, the wind snapping the Swiss flag, she scans the crowd for Zosel. The last thing she wants is to run into her. Not yet, with Wylie by her side. That'd be a disaster.

No, the name of the game right now is to skirt Zosel, hustle to their accommodation, duck inside, get settled in for the night, check on Gib. And then ditch her daughter so she can barrel back down these streets, bang her fist on Zosel's door. Gosh, just that image, that sound—*pound, pound, pound*—makes Claudine think of St. Moritz, Wylie panicking in the bathroom.

She glances at Wylie buckling the chest strap of her backpack. It's all she can do not to stare at her. Her daughter's so beautiful, with her strong shoulders and honey-hued hair, that electric smile she holds at bay around Claudine. There's a melancholy braided into Wylie's beauty now, and Claudine closes her eyes, knowing it's partly there because of her.

Whatever she says to Zosel, it has to work. There's already so much to make up for—*pound, pound, pound.*

Then Claudine will have to drum up some words to say about Kipper as they tip his ashes onto a snowdrift. On the phone with Wylie two nights ago, she'd made the idiotic mistake of telling her she'd already be in Switzerland and could easily meet her in Berlin. When Wylie asked why, she blurted out the first thing that popped into her mind: spreading Kipper's ashes—maybe because Barry Haberman had brought him up, reminding Claudine that she had yet to honor her father in any real way. Idiotic, though, because *of course* Wylie wanted to come along—and what was Claudine supposed to say? No?

Doubly idiotic because the cremation necklace—a gift from the funeral home that she called a "morbid party favor"—holds a laughably minuscule amount of ashes. She didn't have the heart to dump *all* of Kipper's ashes in Zermatt, no matter her conflicted feelings about him. Wylie's right—he had no special love for the Swiss, thought European skiers acted too superior, preferred the peaks of his own childhood.

Now she's got to wear the thing. She reaches up to touch it again.

"Nice duct tape," Wylie says, smirking.

"It's all the rage," Claudine says. Her bandaged-up parka sticks out like a trash-bag rain poncho in trendy Zermatt, where women dress for après-ski and find ways to wear form-fitting layers that are as warm as they are chic.

Passengers struggle to keep their suitcases from twisting directions, tugging them across the snow-packed streets, coats blown open by gusts, heavy snowflakes clotting eyelashes and accumulating fast on designer-brand hats. In step, Wylie and Claudine march past these newbies, backpacks on, as comfortable on snow as a pair of lynx. Claudine's head-held-high confidence hides the fear thrumming underneath, as well as the stiffness in her knee.

She gestures toward Bahnhofstrasse, wishing she'd told Wylie that where they're staying might not be *sehr schick*, as they say in this German-speaking town. That it might not be *schick* at all. Although the Swiss are reserved by nature, at least two hotel receptionists had guffawed at Claudine when she called yesterday asking to book two rooms. Even one was impossible.

They pass upscale boutiques and bakeries, luxury hotels and charming chalets, and the swanky Mont Cervin Palace hotel with its famed turreted windows capping a beige facade and dark wooden trim, historical meets elegance. The hotel's red horse-drawn carriage awaits a fresh batch of tourists. A horse paws the hard, cold ground, breath issuing out of its nostrils.

The noon sun casts a faint glow behind low-lying clouds, the wind strong enough to bend the tips of pines into a gesture of deference. Pellets of snow swing into her face.

She doesn't see Zosel, but she does see someone she recognizes.

Hi, old girl. It's been a long time.

Just above the red-shingled rooftop line of the ski chalets, she registers the crooked witch's nose of the Matterhorn piercing the sky. Claudine's nerves are calmed by the sight of the gray beauty. On the train, she'd stretched the truth a little about Kipper's enthusiasm for the Matterhorn, but it's always been one of her favorite mountains.

Wylie stops and stares. "Wow. I forgot how beautiful it is."

Claudine nods. "Do you remember we named her Mother Matterhorn?"

"Yeah, I think I do."

In her racing days, Claudine attributed personalities to ski runs, a habit that made some of the most notorious and technical runs on the World Cup circuit more approachable and less threatening—and, in a curious way, gave her and Wylie family members. The Olimpia delle Tofane in Cortina, Italy, was a beautiful and bold cousin who turned the heads of everyone she passed; the Stelvio slope in Bormio an unforgiving uncle pining for the old days; Lake Louise's East Summit a younger, energetic sister trying to keep up with the older kids; Garmisch-Partenkirchen's Kandahar a cheeky, risk-taking, sometimes arrogant friend who could back up his smack talk with action; the Lauberhorn in Wengen a great-aunt who was demanding to the bitter end.

As for the Matterhorn, although Claudine never skied it—few people have—she's always imagined the mountain as a matronly grandmother, firm but sympathetic, weathered and old but still regal, with a glint in her eye, the inhabitants of Zermatt all her grandchildren gathered in the folds of her dark-gray skirt.

Wylie's peering around as if she's beginning to recognize the place. "Hey, Mom. Does Zosel still live here? Wouldn't it be great to see her while we're here?"

There it is—exactly what Claudine was afraid of. They're here for less than ten minutes, and already her daughter is asking after Auntie Zo. And *of course* she is; Zosel had been seminal in Wylie's early life, age zero to ten. Until Claudine cut her off completely.

"You know, I heard she moved," Claudine manages to say after a beat. "Austria, maybe."

"Oh, really? Shoot."

"I know, right?"

"What happened with you two?" Wylie tosses out the question so casually—as if talking about the past, about major life moments, is something they've always done—that Claudine has to blink and reorient herself.

"Sometimes friends just grow apart." She ushers them forward, quick steps, just a few more blocks until they're standing outside the only place that had room for them.

"Is this . . . us?" Wylie's jaw actually drops as she squints through the curtains of snow. When she reads the sign, her voice is a question. "Hostel die Freude?" Underneath the hostel name is the motto: *Play first. Sleep later.*

The youth hostel looks worse than Claudine feared: an amped-up version of a traditional Swiss chalet, with a gabled roof and shutters in a garish red kissing the sides of each large window. Drawings of red vines, with little red leaves, are swirled atop the white paint, piped frosting, "Hansel and Gretel" style. Should anyone stumble home drunk or lose their way in a snowstorm, a multitude of colorful banner flags are strung from the window boxes, flapping in the wind as if other guests are leaning from the windows and waving handkerchiefs.

Claudine doesn't meet Wylie's questioning eyes. She's so sorry about the subpar accommodations, and so upset with herself for dragging them here, that her regret shape-shifts into anger and comes out in the wrong direction. "You were expecting a castle, your highness? It's just for one night." She instantly regrets the remark when Wylie lowers her eyes.

Really, Claudine? First you drag her to this hole, and then you act like she has no right to be pissed?

Inside, they stamp their boots on a faded mat that says, *Wilkommen!* Claudine takes in the interior, aghast. The lounge's bohemian decor collides with medical-waiting-room furniture, the chairs and love seats wipe-down-able. A tall bookshelf is crammed with used paperbacks. Three stacked wood pallets make up a coffee table. Holiday lights are strung up like loopy handwriting, next to T-shirts tacked to the wall, presumably for sale, catering to an English-speaking audience. One says: *You Matterhorn to me.* The other: *I'm Matterhorny for you.*

Ugh. If there's one thing Claudine hates, it's a location pun.

Deeper into the lounge, the wooden floor transitions to fake green grass, with three hammocks hanging from wooden beams, one sagging lower to the ground with the weight of a slumbering body. Next to the hammocks is a mural with a tropical motif: large hibiscus flowers, a toucan. Why would anyone come to Switzerland to pretend to be in Tulum?

I've made a huge mistake, Claudine wants to say to Wylie, who is turning in a slow circle to take it all in. But Claudine has never said anything remotely like that, so she squares her shoulders and steps up to the reception desk. If there was a bell, she'd smack it.

Behind the desk is a man, early twenties, his long, dark dreads spilling out the back of a maroon knit beanie, his T-shirt advertising a band called Fat Freddy's Drop.

Turning down the reggae music he's listening to on the computer, he says, "Hiya, how ya going? Welcome to Freude. My name's Koa."

He's a New Zealander; Claudine can identify his accent

from traveling to the country during its winter season to test skis. "I'm Claudine. And this is my daughter, Wylie." She extends her arm to Wylie, who is flipping through Michael Pollan's book on psychedelics.

"That's a good one, eh?" Koa calls out to Wylie. "Change your brain and shit." Then he looks at Claudine. "Sorry for swearing."

She raises her hand to show no harm's been done, then clears her throat, saying grandly, as if they *are* at the Mont Cervin Palace, "We're checking in."

"Sweet as," Koa says. *Oh yuck.* She'd forgotten that dreadful Kiwi slang that always made her want to respond, "Sweet as *what*?" He nods along to the music as he pulls up their reservation. "Last name?"

"Potts. Claudine Potts."

Koa's eyes snap up from the computer. He blinks once, twice. "*The* Claudine Potts?"

Her shoulders sag. Not again. But what did she expect in ski country? She fiddles with the stack of towels. "Uh, yeah, that's me." Next to her, she can feel Wylie bristling. Or is that her imagination?

"The Stone-Cold Killer!" he says, slamming a fist into his palm. "Your 1995 World Cup season was flipping awesome. I watch YouTube clips of you all the time. You didn't just ski down, you *bombed* down. You totally shred the gnar!"

"Oh! Well, thanks." Claudine's face prickles with pride. She doesn't normally like the attention—especially in front of Wylie—but her '95 season *was* flipping awesome. Even if he's calling her the nickname she hated.

Koa gestures from Wylie to Claudine, incredulous, hyped up. "This is your mum?"

"Yup," Wylie says, lifting her eyebrows and letting them fall. "Your mom is a *GOAT*. I'm in the presence of a GOAT." He performs three mini-bows in Claudine's direction.

"She *was* pretty amazing," Wylie says. Claudine is surprised to see her smile, as though caught up in Koa's enthusiasm. "A legend."

That word, from Wylie, doesn't cough out icily, as it could have, and now Claudine's entire being is warmed, as if she's sipping kirsch by a roaring fire. Which, by the way, is there a welcome glass of kirsch? A roaring fire? She mourns the absence of both even as she's mollified by the compliment.

Tucking her chin, in a soft voice meant only for Wylie, Claudine says, "Thanks, Wy."

"This is truly epic," Koa says, apparently so overcome that he has to pivot away from the computer, fist to his mouth, walk the few paces the reception area allows, and then return.

"I take it you're a skier," Claudine says.

"Yeah, for sure. In the summer, I'm a tramping guide—that's hiking, to you—and I ski year-round. This season's been stink, though. You heard they had to cancel the World Cup downhills here because there wasn't enough snow? That was crazy."

Koa says all of this as if he's presuming Claudine still closely follows the sport; she doesn't. She just can't.

Before she answers, he shakes his head, saying, "Climate change, bro. Glacier's melting. They called off summer skiing on the glacier for the first time ever. And get this. In November I was skiing on the Arctic Circle in Finland, and there were actual wildflowers poking up out of the snow, the pack was that thin. Trippy. Our sport's endangered."

"That's awful," Wylie interjects.

"True story," he says.

Claudine can hear Kipper in her head. *This generation can't stop whining.* Before he died, when this stuff was just starting to make headlines, Kipper's opinion had been that these climate change problems were overblown. This younger generation just couldn't deal with unpredictable weather. Varying conditions. That's part of the excitement of ski racing, he'd said. You get what you get, and you can't throw a fit.

She's worried about climate change, though, and taken on small measures to curb her footprint. When she and Gib eat out back home, she always brings her own Tupperware to avoid the foam take-out boxes if they have leftovers—and they always have leftovers, because she doesn't believe in throwing food away. But on a grander scale, she's assumed that someone—a genius inventor or, like, Sweden—would swoop in and save the planet.

Besides, what can she, as one former ski racer, actually do?

"Conditions change every year." For some reason, she's echoing Kipper's words instead of voicing her own concerns. Koa reminds her of someone, but she can't place it, and he makes her want to be a little contradictory. "That's part of the beauty of the sport. One minute you're skiing on ice, and the next race you're on powder. The best skiers adapt."

"Yeah, but this is extreme weather like we've never seen before," Koa says, cracking a knuckle. "And to be honest, the sport is partly to blame. All the emissions from flying racers all over the world and cranking out fake snow. And racers are crashing more too, because runs are faster. A reckoning is coming. A lot of the best racers are even calling for it themselves."

Claudine doesn't appreciate the implication.

Ah, she sees who it is now—Koa looks a little like Lark Pierce, one of her old ski technicians, a Sun Valley guy with shorter dreads and a rotation of Grateful Dead shirts who shot down her idea to try competing in men's skis, which are longer and stiffer than women's skis. She thought they might give her more stability *and* more speed. He laughed her off. Eight years after her retirement, Claudine watched in awe as Lindsey Vonn began competing—and winning—in men's skis.

"If you guys are in town next week, there's gonna be a rally in Davos to protect winter. And protect our sport. We're filling a van. You guys should come. Supposedly Mikaela Shiffrin and her mom are planning to make an appearance."

At these words—"Mikaela and her mom"—any last warmth toward Koa drains away, and Claudine wants to sarcastically repeat, *Mikaela and her mom, Mikaela and her mom.*

Claudine hasn't been following the sport, but she knows all about Mikaela and her mom, Eileen, and their special bond. Eileen serves as Mikaela's coach and manager and best friend—the same scenario Claudine had been hoping would happen with Wylie, when, in fact, the opposite is now true.

Making matters worse: Mikaela also graduated from Burke only a few years after Wylie. Just last week, in Pyeongchang, she won a gold medal in the giant slalom. She'd also openly described her battle with anxiety.

"Jealousy" can't even begin to describe how Claudine feels when she thinks about Team Shiffrin.

Mikaela's mom must have done it right. Whereas Claudine botched things big-time.

Scoreboard doesn't lie.

She gestures to a darkened window. "I'm glad to see there's a lot of snow now," she says, with a clipped emphasis on the last word so there's no question that she wants to quash this conversation. She can already hear Koa with his skiing buddies later, saying: *That Claudine Potts is a legend, all right. A legendary asshole.*

"Yeah, heaps, eh? Okay, let's get you guys checked in." Koa types a few more things, confirming their information and handing a waiver for Claudine to sign. He recites the hostel's rules: Quiet time starts at midnight (midnight?!), clean up after yourself in the shared bathrooms (shared bathrooms?!), no outside guests (that sounds civil, at least).

"But, um, Koa, where's the gym in this hostel?" Wylie asks, peering around.

"Yeah, nah, no gym."

"No gym? Like, at least a treadmill? Some free weights?" There's alarm in Wylie's voice.

"No, nothing like that. But"—and then Koa grins—"you could ski. That's a killer workout, as you know."

Wylie swings her head toward Claudine. "Don't say it."

Claudine lifts up her hands. "I wasn't going to."

Koa glances nervously back and forth between them. "No skiing, then?"

"No!" both women say in unison.

"Just our keys, please, Koa," Claudine adds. "It's been a long travel day."

"I get it." From little hooks hanging on the wall, Koa grabs a key for each of them, and as he turns back, he says, "You two are keeping it cozy as in room one-oh-four, straight down the hall."

Wylie grabs Claudine's arm, their first physical contact. "Mom, we're sharing a room?"

"All they had left." Claudine pastes a smile across her face. "Just like old times." As if nothing would thrill her more.

But truly, she's terrified. About the night ahead, and the reason she's really here.

Walking side by side down the hall, the women are two versions of the edelweiss, the alpine hotshot in the flower department, its blossom like Mother Matterhorn's woolly brooch. Wylie's wilting, drooping over herself in a petulant slump, and Claudine's blooming, thrusting her chest out in fake triumph.

8

Wylie

WYLIE OPENS THE DOOR TO THEIR ROOM AND faintly gasps. Bunk beds. In a space the size of a shipping container. Claudine and Wylie have to squeeze past each other like they're maneuvering down an airplane aisle.

"You go," Claudine says next to the bed, flattening her body against the wall.

"No, you go." Wylie steps back so her mom can pass.

They both stand still. They both step forward at the same time. They both lurch backward. Wylie would laugh, except she only wants to cry.

She couldn't care less about staying in fancy digs. She doesn't need gazillion-thread-count sheets or fourteen feather pillows stacked high on a king-size bed or little hotel soaps in the shape of the Matterhorn. Fancy, in her mind, means two TV remotes.

Quick scan here: Zero remotes. Zero TVs.

What Wylie does need, which she apparently should have specified, is a hotel fitness center and her own bedroom where she can regroup in private to keep her anxiety at bay. Now she has neither.

How to answer Dan's last message asking for a picture of the fitness center so he can supervise her training? She closes her eyes, longing for a safe place to land. This isn't it.

This is a strange land with troubled memories and a mom who can sometimes be mean. Such as Claudine's "your highness" comment. She'd used that one back in the Burke days too, to suggest that Wylie's anxiety was high-maintenance. It's disturbing how easily Claudine can shift back into this gear, delivering a little jab that seems insignificant but hits Wylie where it hurts.

So Wylie, in turn, picks up her old weapon: silence. Wylie can go all day without uttering a word. Without offering a response. Without so much as rolling her eyes.

Claudine, bent over her suitcase, appears oblivious to the icy nature of Wylie's current quietness. "Thanks again for what you said back there," she says. When Wylie doesn't reply, Claudine looks up, her face stricken, prompting Wylie to at least give her mom the courtesy of a nod.

According to Dan's schedule, they should be doing a quick cardio round. But there's no gym. She sends Dan a text relaying that she's safely in Zermatt, then she piles a change of clothes and a towel into her arms to ferry them to the communal bathroom down the hall. She smells, and maybe a shower will help her power through this jet lag. She closes the door without telling Claudine where she's going. It's obvious, but still.

The bathroom is painted a mossy green, with only one toilet in a stall, one sink, one shower, currently in use, and

71

a framed and faded picture of the massive Matterhorn. As she does with most art, even mass-reproduced photographs, Wylie studies it for a beat, admiring the way light and time and shower steam have streaked the image a shade of green lighter than the walls.

And although she'd never tell Claudine this, her brain begins to trace the fall line down the face of the mountain, curving around its features to find that perfect pocket, a marble run all the way to the bottom, and instinctually her hips sway left and right in a motion that's been embedded in her, a long, red-hot iron rod seared against her DNA.

In these moments, she misses skiing.

A voice from inside the shower—female, warbled, Broadway operatic—cuts through Wylie's reverie with "the sound of muuuuuusic."

What's with all the singing on this trip? Wylie rubs her temple, catching sight of herself in the mirror. The top section of her braid is loose and lazy, the end hanging sluggishly over her shoulder. Dark half-moons are stamped under her eyes. She lifts a hand up to trace the arch of her eyebrow. She has a thing with eyebrows, given that hers are so distinctive, perfect little rainbows, so different from Claudine's comma-shaped brows. In college, for a self-portrait assignment, she'd used a watercolor paintbrush size number four for her eyebrows, 2.4 millimeters. They came out thinner than she'd hoped.

Both in the mirror now and on the canvas then, she could find no lineage in her face, no link back to parents or family. Well, except Claudine's hazel eyes. If there were traces of her dad, Wylie couldn't pick them out. What would it feel like to know her own father? How will she ever find him?

She has one clue to go on: Her dad's last name is Fox, the

name monogrammed on a silver cigarette lighter that she discovered in one of her mom's old duffel bags. Her reasoning that it belonged to her dad: A ski bum would be a smoker. Right? It made sense to her nine-year-old brain. And judging by the way Claudine had snatched it out of her hand, Wylie was onto something.

The singer ends her song, turning off the water and, after a moment, whipping open the curtain to reveal a short, stocky older woman with a towel fashioned around her body and a towel wrapped tall around her hair.

"Oh!" the woman exclaims, her hand flying to her chest. "You are so quiet. I didn't realize anyone else was in here. This is usually a dead time for shower goers."

"It's okay. Sorry if I scared you. I just arrived." Wylie really wants to ask: *Why are you staying here?* She imagined she and Claudine would be the oldest guests at the youth hostel, but this woman looks a solid decade older than Claudine.

Her arms are covered in tattoos, botanical etchings of medicinal plants, their Latin names in cursive. She has the kind face of a chicken-noodle-soup maker, a fold-you-into-a-hug warmth, with mischief in her cornflower blue eyes, and a tiny ruby-studded nose ring twinkling from her left nostril. Her eyebrows, Wylie notices, are thin graying curves, like comets on the descent toward the bridge of her nose.

The woman nods knowingly. "Ah, washing off the airplane stench."

"Yes, exactly."

"I'm Bev." When she reaches out her hand, her towel falls open, flashing two plump acorn-squash-sized breasts at Wylie. "Oh geez. Titty time. Sorry 'bout that."

"No worries." Wylie averts her eyes to the Matterhorn

print on the wall, giving Bev privacy as she regathers the towel around herself.

"Anyway, I'm Bev—but everyone calls me Bibbidi."

"Bibbidi?"

"Like bibbidi-bobbidi-boo—you know, what the Fairy Godmother says in *Cinderella*. I'm a little witchy. Kinda like a fairy godmother." She winks.

Actually, the nickname is spot-on; Bibbidi looks *exactly* like a fairy godmother, minus a cloak and a star wand. "I'm Wylie."

"Oooh, I dig that name."

"Thanks."

"Old English, right? Meaning a willow. A meadow."

"How'd you know? Everyone just thinks Wile E. Coyote. That I'm going to hurl myself off a cliff." Which she sort of did for many years.

"I had a friend with the same name. She was a beautiful spirit."

"Oh wow. I've never met another Wylie."

"You have a beautiful spirit too, I can tell." Bibbidi cocks her head, considering Wylie, who, surprising herself, relishes the attention from a woman who seems so wise. Bibbidi clucks her tongue, nodding. "Yes, right, but just like a meadow, you can get trampled on. You can bend too much for others." She reaches out a consoling hand, gently grasping Wylie's forearm. "You'll take better care of yourself. I see that. You just have to be more careful, because giving to the point of breaking is a part of who you are."

At being recognized, Wylie's eyes prick with tears. She nods, peering at the floor to ward off a full-on crying attack.

"Thank you," Wylie whispers.

Why the tears? She lets herself sink briefly into the emotion. Her heart is wounded, and it's not the jet lag or being suddenly thrust into a tiny room with her mom or being surrounded by the landscape of her childhood. Dan sits in the center of it. He hasn't trampled on her, exactly, but he has spent three years microcontrolling her life while secretly losing control of his own. She's let him do it, invited and even relished the accountability and the rules, fearing that without it, without him, she'd tank. But then he lied to her, taking advantage of her bendable nature.

She's just not sure what to do about it. What she does know: it feels pretty good to have a break from him.

But maybe that's how it is with all long-term relationships. Maybe a little forced distance will help her more fully forgive Dan. Remind her what she loves most about him. Amp up her appreciation.

Or maybe it won't—and then what?

"Well, Wylie, my dear, I'm going to leave you to it." Bibbidi reaches for the door, but then she stops, staring at Wylie's feet. "You're not going to shower barefoot, are you?"

"Uh, yes." She knows this is the wrong answer, but what choice does she have? Claudine failed to give her a heads-up that they'd be sharing a bathroom with an entire floor of people.

"No, no, no, no, no." Bibbidi releases the door handle. "You can't ever go barefoot in a communal shower. You'll catch a foot fungus. Or something worse. Once, when I was traveling through Bali, I forgot my flip-flops and took a shower at a hostel anyway. Worst decision I ever made."

Wylie's eyes widen. "You caught a foot fungus?"

"No. I stepped on a turd."

75

"Gross!"

"Now I never shower without these little fellas." Bibbidi clicks the heels of her flip-flops together. "Go grab yours. I'll hold the shower for you in case someone else comes."

"I didn't bring any." Wylie is deeply dismayed.

"None?" Bibbidi looks even more dismayed.

Wylie shakes her head.

"You're gonna have to borrow mine."

"Oh, I can't do that."

"You can, and you must." Bibbidi removes her sandals, dangling them for Wylie to grab. But then she retracts them, peering at Wylie sideways. "But you don't have a foot fungus, do you?"

"No. I actually have pretty nice feet. Do you want to see?"

Bibbidi looks as if she might want to inspect Wylie's feet, but she says, "No, I trust you. Just drop them off at room one-oh-eight when you're done."

"Thank you. That's so kind of you."

"It's the way of the road. We've got to help each other out. Who knows? Maybe I'll need to borrow your toothbrush."

Wylie laughs; Bibbidi does not.

A few minutes later, Wylie's in the shower wearing flip-flops made for size-five feet. She's a size ten, and the back halves of her feet hang off like deli meat in a hoagie roll, her heels grazing the tile as she tries to avoid the drain, where there's likely to be the most foot fungus.

It's the first time she's taken a truly deep breath since touching down in Switzerland. She'd expected to be pummeled with memories of St. Moritz, but in the shower, as the steam slackens her clenched jaw, she finds herself thinking of Claudine's Salt Lake crash.

Claudine had been halfway down the course when she caught an edge trying to land a jump, tumbling in an almost cartoonish manner. Wylie, ten years old at the time, waiting at the bottom of the mountain with Kipper, stared at Claudine's unmoving form tangled in orange safety netting, willing her to move, funneling every ounce of her own energy to her mom via their invisible heart-to-heart strings.

"She's dead," Wylie said to Kipper, gripping his hand in sheer panic.

"She's not dead," Kipper replied, rubbing a gloved finger under his chin as he fixated on the medic team descending on Claudine. The crowd was unusually hushed.

"But she always waves at me after her falls. She's not waving."

"She will. It was a hard tumble, that's all. I bet she's just getting up real slow."

If Kipper thought she was fine, he would've pushed his way through the crowd, hounding someone for answers on her injuries, Wylie stumbling after him as he counted off all the things Claudine should have done better.

But Claudine was still, and Kipper was still, and that told Wylie that something was very, very wrong. He stayed locked, eagle-eyed, on the motionless form that was Claudine.

From the distance, an air ambulance approached, causing murmurs to erupt in the crowd.

Before long, Claudine was strapped to an orange medic stretcher that was lifted high, and then higher, into the air. Watching her mom dangle in the sky, Wylie heard Kipper say, "Come on, Claud, pull through," which scared her the most.

Claudine survived ski racing. Wylie survived ski racing. But the pair of them, as mother and daughter, had not. And she still has recurring nightmares about the accident.

In the shower, she thinks: *You're not that scared little girl anymore. You are brave and strong.* She closes her eyes, telling herself that from this moment forward, she will never again be a flimsy, willowy sapling underfoot.

No more getting stepped on. By Dan. By her mom. By anyone.

Wylie's come back to Europe to throw down. And she's not going to let a few snarky comments from Claudine blow her sideways.

9

Claudine

CLAUDINE'S STOMACH GROWLS. IT'S LATE AFTER-
noon, and she's only eaten that one croissant on the train.
She knows she should rally—get right over to Zosel's and push
herself onto European time—but her exhaustion is pressing,
her knee throbbing. A little lie-down, no eyes closed, before
she treks out? "I think that's fine," she says out loud, to herself.

Only, which bed is hers? Claudine doesn't want to assume
she gets the bottom bunk, although that's really what she
prefers. She stands there awkwardly, slightly swaying from
fatigue, texting with Gib, who's just waking up back home.

Wylie returns, freshly showered, obstinately quiet.

Claudine shakes her head wearily. The best thing to do
when a Wylie silent treatment descends: Wait it out like fog.
It'll burn off soon enough.

Although it did take two years last time.

"Want a Kind bar?" Claudine asks. She holds out two flavors.

Wylie picks Claudine's favorite, but no matter. Claudine rips open the packaging, biting into the seeds and cranberries. "Sorry there's no gym. But we're only here for one night."

Wylie nods again, her face void of emotions, and then, bless her, climbs up to the top bunk with her phone, leaving Claudine to roll herself onto the bottom.

Maybe this won't be too bad. The close proximity to Wylie could be a blessing, forcing them to interact. With two rooms, Wylie would have already disappeared inside, locking her out. Instead, she's just a few feet above, so near that Claudine can hear her daughter chewing.

She closes her eyes in gratitude for that sound.

It's her last thought before she's wrenched from sleep hours later by persistent house music thumping in the basement disco like it's the hostel's heartbeat.

Claudine blinks in the dark, trying to get her bearings, realizing that her little lie-down lapsed into an all-out slumber. *Oh no.* Wylie must have climbed down the ladder and turned out the lights at some point.

She checks her phone. Midnight. No way can she pound on Zosel's door at this hour. Although could she? It's a Kipper move. A sneak attack.

But no, that's just plain rude, and she won't sink to that. She'll slip out first thing in the morning, while Wylie's still asleep, before their train back to Zurich. Dammit, though. She wanted this to be already settled.

Bump, bump, bump. She shakes her head. Of course she booked a room at a place that morphs into a nightclub. There's no sleep impediment worse for Claudine than an electronic bass. Claudine would take traffic noise, people arguing in the next room, construction. Airplanes landing and taking off.

A garbage truck backing up. Someone opening a package of Twizzlers next to her head. Anything over the persistent sound of bass, as unignorable as someone poking her in the sternum. She gets up, fumbling through her backpack for earplugs. They turn out to be useless pieces of foam, as if she's trying to block a tsunami with a baseball bat. The bass slips over and under and through the earplugs, into the recesses of her brain, so that even during breaks between songs she can still here the phantom beat.

The music eats at her: Don't they know that people are trying to sleep? It's a hotel, for god's sake.

Oh, right. It's a hostel. As in, *hostile* to sleep.

Fully awake, she obsesses over Zosel. What if Zosel does slam the door on her? What if she's not home? What if she invites Claudine inside? That's the best-case scenario, yet it still causes a wave of pure dread. The two of them sitting across from each other in Zosel's living room like old times?

Pretty much any physical challenge on earth feels more doable to Claudine than a complicated conversation. She'd happily perform all the BodyFittest feats of strength—even with her bad knee—over figuring out what to say to keep Zosel quiet.

Zosel doesn't owe Claudine anything, especially after sixteen years of silence, after Claudine failed to congratulate her on her Olympic win.

She can picture Zosel's earnest, beautiful face in Salt Lake City like it was yesterday. "I think you should tell her the truth," Zosel had said, tipping her head ever so slightly toward Wylie, who was cutting up old magazines in a corner. That day marked the last race of Claudine's skiing career, the last time she saw her best friend.

As the bass drones on, Claudine screams into her pillow. It's now nearly 2:00 a.m. "Make. It. Stop," she mutters. In the bunk above her, Wylie doesn't stir. The girl can sleep through anything, Claudine remembers.

Eventually, she dozes again. A gust of wind wakes her, rattling the windows. She blinks. It's morning. The flimsy curtains on the windows, as translucent as wedding veils, do nothing to keep the room dark and cave-like.

Claudine stands up from the bed, peeking out the window, inhaling sharply at the sheer volume of snow that piled up overnight. The drifts are so tall—five feet or so—that she could open the window and gather a handful. She could climb right out, slide down the drift, and avoid the lounge and anyone passed out on that slippery sofa. She could plant her face directly in it, give herself a Santa beard.

On the top bunk, Wylie snores softly, just enough air to billow a tissue. Curled into a *c* shape, head to knees, her tawny braid unplaited, Wylie reminds Claudine of a fawn bedded down in a forest. It's what Kipper had called her, actually, when she exploded in height like she might burst through the ceiling and keep going. She'd needed to reacquaint herself with her skis and poles because she was inhabiting a new body.

Little Fawn.

Claudine had rather liked the nickname, until a few months ago in therapy, when Soupy mentioned that fawning is a trauma response that turns people into submissive people pleasers to avoid getting punished.

Soupy could be a real downer.

Sometimes, when Claudine thinks of Wylie's face before those races—well, she can't. She can't think about Wylie sitting in the bathroom stall before her final race, frozen, terrified, as though just putting on her skis might kill her. Unsure of what else to do, Claudine had parented like Kipper—pushing, prodding, refusing to make a big deal out of Wylie's anxiety.

After all, Claudine had gritted through her own nerves as a ski racer, gathered her mental toughness, not quit even on the days when quitting was so enticing. Those days she couldn't help but voice out loud to Kipper, "I don't think I can keep doing this, Kip."

His retort, always: "Go ahead, be a quitter."

Quitting was worse than losing. Quitting was the worst thing you could do, period. So Claudine had persevered.

It's been so hard to understand Wylie's block. Why someone who might have bested even Claudine's record couldn't force her body—and, mostly, her mind—to comply.

She studies her daughter, tenderness pirouetting in her chest, an unspooling of love like no other, and she almost, almost, sets her hand on Wylie's back, allowing herself just a momentary touch as Wylie's ribs arch with her breath. But then she pulls her hand back, dresses quietly, and slips out the door. It's time to do what she came to do.

10

Claudine

FOUR DAYS UNTIL BODYFITTEST DUO COMPETITION

"GUTEN MORGEN," CALLS A CHIPPER YOUNG WOMAN from behind the reception desk. "Are you going out? The snow is very much, even for here. It's quite windy. And now it has begun to rain."

All of this Claudine can plainly see herself through the window behind the desk.

The woman's name tag says Léa. She's got a top bun shrouded in an enormous black hoodie, nothing professional about it, and she's winged her eyes with heavy eyeliner like the feathers of a long-tailed widowbird. She might even be wearing fake eyelashes. Today's fashion is mystifying.

"I am going out, yes," Claudine says, stepping up to the desk. She doesn't want to send Wylie a text in case it wakes her. "If my daughter comes looking for me, can you tell her I'll be back in a few hours? I'm just . . . going for a walk."

"A walk? Are you very certain?"

"My daughter's name is Wylie." Claudine drums her fingers, deciding how to describe her daughter. "She's very tall, with a long braid."

Léa writes down this information into a notebook, although "tall" and "braid" don't seem too hard to remember.

"I will find your daughter," Léa says, with so much earnestness that Claudine wants to urge her to save some for later in life.

"You don't have to *find* her. She's still asleep in our room. Only if she comes looking for me."

Léa nods. "If she comes looking for you, I will tell her you are out." And then she reads from her own note. "And that you will be back in a few hours."

"Precisely, thank you."

"And you're sure, about going out? It is not advisable."

"Not looking for feedback," Claudine calls over her shoulder.

As soon as she steps outside, so many emotions collide at once from seeing this much snow again, from being in a ski town with its thin air, the smell of the powder and the burn in her nostrils, even the *sound* of the squish underfoot, and the jittery, intense full-body reaction from the prospect of going head-to-head with her former rival. Neurons fire in her brain as if today is race day, as if she'll soon be clunking in her ski boots, skis over her shoulder, to sit on a chairlift that will take her above the tree line so that she can do something beautiful and reckless, the snow her friend and her foe, her oldest playmate.

It's not, however, a ski day. A few hanging chimes swing wildly in the wind. Except for the town workers who are diligently shoveling the sidewalks clear, most people are either still sleeping or driven to stay indoors by the odd-for-Zermatt pairing of rain on top of snow.

From her parka pocket (calling a coat a parka really *does* make her feel warmer), she pulls out her phone as it navigates her. She knows this town, but with her nerves, she doesn't trust her memory to guide her to Zosel's. The screen is quickly pelted with fat raindrops. She increases the volume and drops it back into her pocket.

She passes the Mountaineers' Cemetery, commemorating so many of the people who've lost their lives in accidents in the surrounding mountains. *Too many,* Claudine thinks, averting her eyes, not wanting to study the headstones like so many tourists do.

Claudine hooks a right on Bahnhofstrasse, walking past the dome-topped Credit Suisse. Matterhorn Sport. Stefanie's Crêperie. The sprawling Mont Cervin Palace. Surely they don't have a basement disco.

The Matterhorn, its top half obscured by clouds, hovers over Claudine as she walks. The cloud cover allows Claudine to believe she's out of Mother Matterhorn's view, hating the idea of disappointing her on what's beginning to feel like a dishonorable errand if she were pushed to describe it.

Claudine and Zosel met when they were both nineteen-year-old baby skiers at Worlds. Zosel had the healthiest attitude toward competition that Claudine had ever encountered. Made possible because her parents weren't breathing down her neck. "They just want me to be happy," she'd once said. It had taken a long time for Claudine to believe, to see for herself, that this was actually true.

And then there was the envy Claudine felt when she watched Zosel ski, her style a mix of carefree and fierce, her curves around a gate like the swoop of a swallow, graceful and efficient, even playful. How her laugh would ring out in the start house. The *start house!* Where everyone else was solemn and poised and tense and edgy—Claudine earning her nickname with her stoniness—this young woman could be found chuckling over something. How did Zosel manage to give her all each race *and* be mostly unfazed by the results at the end of the day? A poor showing, just by a tenth of a second, would rattle Claudine for days. And piss off Kipper.

Married at age eighteen, Zosel seemed so self-actualized back then, independent. By twenty-two, Zosel was tragically widowed, and she turned to Claudine for comfort. Claudine did her best to be there for her, in spite of her surprise pregnancy.

When Claudine returned to the World Cup with a one-year-old Wylie in tow, people were shocked. Carting a baby on the World Cup circuit was like bringing a baby to a bar; it just wasn't done. But Claudine didn't have a lot of options. Who was she supposed to leave her with? Zosel was still freshly widowed, but she rallied to be by Claudine's side, a trusted second set of hands with Wylie.

The travel schedule with a kid was grueling. Long drives in an Audi minivan that Claudine rented separately from the team, thanks to sponsorship funds. Even longer transatlantic flights—and this was all before you could hand your kid an iPad. Each stop brought new food, new beds, new elevations, new time zones, new languages, new pharmacies for late-night runs to procure diapers, Tylenol, Band-Aids, a plush toy to play with in the van.

Claudine made it all up as she went along, with the help of some other girls on the U.S. team and Kipper, but mostly

Zosel, who poured all her love into Claudine's small family even though hers had just shattered. And it was like that for many years, until everything began to unravel.

Dear friends who grew apart. That's always been Claudine's line.

Siri in her pocket tells her to turn left.

A few paces later, there's the destination: a familiar two-story duplex apartment boasting the traditional white facade and dark wooden trim found in Zermatt, a balcony on the second level with the same dark, ornately carved railing.

Claudine takes a deep breath. "You have reached your destination" is still chirping. She silences the phone.

This is it. The person she's been avoiding for all these years. Can she do it?

She climbs the stairs to Zosel's front door. A wave of nausea roils through her stomach.

Zosel must hate me.

She steps back, glancing behind her at the looming Matterhorn, contemplating a mad dash back through the slushy, salted streets, past Léa and her top bun, and into her room, slipping into her now-cold sheets and shivering there until Wylie wakes. Wylie will never suspect that she had left.

Then she pictures Barry Haberman knocking on this same door.

Don't think, she coaches herself, hearing Kipper's voice. *Just do.*

And so, she knocks.

Nothing happens for a long moment. Maybe Zosel doesn't live here anymore. She hears shuffling on the other side, and the door creaks open, a draft of warm air rushing toward her. Zosel Marie Schwarz stands framed in the door, blinking in the light, sixteen years older than when the two were last together in Salt Lake.

"Claudine." Zosel's tone is straightforward, like she's been expecting her, and that alone catches Claudine off guard.

Zosel's wearing running tights and a lemon-yellow cable-knit winter hat with a pom-pom, as if the sudden rain has interrupted plans for a jog. Her blond bangs are swept to the side across her forehead like a curtain tucked behind her ear. Alpine skiers' skin ages faster, blasted by the sun and wind, although to Claudine Zosel looks timeless, even with the deep ruts bookending her mouth. Her blue eyes are as pale as ocean water on a globe.

"Zosel," Claudine says, matching the name with the person standing before her. She's aware of a distant thrumming, and for a moment she thinks: *That fucking base again.* But actually, it's her pulse pounding her temples.

"You've finally come."

With those three words, in the hurt that crests across Zosel's face, along with a flicker of guarded hope, as if she has never quite given up on her friend, and has, in fact, been waiting for this day, Claudine realizes with a sinking horror that Zosel thinks Claudine's arrived on her doorstep to make amends.

For as many times as she'd played out this conversation in her head, Claudine had never considered the possibility that Zosel might be willing to be part of her life again.

It's inconceivable. Zosel *knows* what Claudine was willing to do to win. What Claudine was willing to sacrifice for glory.

Her balance is off, and she reaches out to the doorjamb, so near Zosel that she could hug her.

Behind Zosel, from deep within the house, comes another

voice: *"Mama, wer ist das?"* A teenage girl, fifteen maybe, with Zosel's straight blonde hair and bright cheeks, bops around the corner, stopping when she sees Claudine. Zosel beckons her forward, gathering her under a wing.

"This is my daughter, Fränzi. Fränziska." Fränzi leans in to her mother.

Jealousy pangs through Claudine, watching their easy affection. *So this is what it's like to have a daughter who likes you.* Wylie can barely stomach a high five with Claudine, let alone this kind of warmth. A lean means everything. I surrender to you. I trust you.

No matter how much Claudine's achieved, Zosel's always had her beat when it comes to matters of the heart.

Stumbling to get her bearings, and perhaps even stalling, Claudine clears her throat. "Named for your old coach."

"Franz Blasi." Zosel nods. "Yes. Exactly."

Franz had been a good coach to Zosel. Masterful yet kind in a way that Kipper was not. Able to respect the human underneath the champion, especially after Zosel was widowed. She'd needed someone to prod her on *and* comfort her, and Franz Blasi did both.

Claudine often wondered: *What would've happened if Franz was my coach?*

"He's too easy on her," Kipper once remarked, explaining why Zosel remained squarely on the third podium for so many years. And maybe that was true. Maybe Claudine reigned supreme because Kipper was the opposite of easy.

"Fränzi, this is Claudine Potts. The best alpine skier in the world."

"No, that's not true." Claudine lowers her head.

"The fiercest, the fastest," Zosel continues. "And my one true friend for years."

Claudine's eyes burn a little. "And you were mine too."

"For a time, anyway," Zosel says, her face darkening.

"I know who you are," Fränzi says, reaching a protective arm around her mom. "You ghosted my mother."

"Fränzi, be polite," Zosel chides. "She's here now. We should give her the benefit of the doubt." Then she searches Claudine's face, looking for confirmation when she says, "Yes?"

There's no way Claudine can mention Barry Haberman now.

"Thank you," Claudine says, wishing for a rock to hide under. Mother Matterhorn, maybe.

"Okay, then." Zosel hinges the door wider. "Let's have coffee."

Claudine opens her mouth, then closes it. Opens it, closes it. If she tilts her head back, she could catch rain on her tongue. "I . . ." All her plans to charge inside slip away. Gone is her resolve to intimidate Zosel into silence. She's left with that same gnawing fear she'd had in Salt Lake that things are beyond her control.

What to do? She doesn't have the perfect words to make things right.

Fränzi's phone chimes. It must be bad news, because she flashes the screen at Zosel, her eyes big. *"Lawine,"* she says and groans.

Lawine. That word is familiar, given all Claudine's time in German-speaking countries, and she reaches back to the recesses of her brain. "Avalanche?" she asks, uncertain, slowly looking around. She didn't hear an avalanche. Didn't feel the ground beneath her shudder. "Zosel, what is it?"

Zosel takes the phone, reads the news. "It's an emergency alert. Yes, an avalanche."

Claudine's breath quickens. She knows that snow can propel, topple, sink, bury, and annihilate. An alpine skier can move as fast as a car on the highway; an avalanche, weighing over a million tons, can overtake a skier in seconds.

Kipper drilled into her how to look for the signs. Chunky snow was possible avalanche debris, an indication that one avalanche had already happened or that another was on its way. Shooting cracks beneath her skis—like cracks branching out of the epicenter of a rock hitting a windshield—could mean the snowpack was about to collapse. A *whumpf* sound—the technical term for air rushing out of the snowpack as if someone had placed a hand over a balloon, deflating it—could mean the world was about to crumble.

It's how she feels now—that the world is crumbling around her.

"I-I'm sorry, I have to go!" she says, scrambling back down the stairs as rapidly as she can, Zosel watching her retreat.

All she can think about is Wylie, slumbering in her bed, danger encroaching.

Her daughter, whom she dragged to this village.

Claudine registers no pain from her knee as she sprints away from Zosel's house, back down the street through the rain, slipping and sliding as she goes, imagining hurling herself over Wylie's body as the snow cascades upon them.

It may be futile, depending on the severity of the avalanche. But she's got to damn well try.

11

Wylie

LYING ON THE FLOOR OF THEIR ROOM, A WELL-rested Wylie—she didn't have the nightmare—curls into her one-hundredth sit-up. Her abs are on fire. But she doesn't let herself recover, instead flipping over to hold a plank for two minutes with arms so sculpted that she's the envy of everyone during tank top season.

Her morning routine's almost over. Where's Claudine? A solid night's sleep has thawed the cold shoulder Wylie gave Claudine yesterday for the "your highness" comment, and she's going to start off the morning of Kipper's ceremony day being warmer and kinder to her mom. Rain pounds against the window. Shame. It'll be a soggy, subdued affair for her grandfather. And a quick one too; their train leaves in four hours.

She presses back to child's pose, then keeps the position while she reads thirteen texts from Dan—all pep talks about training—and one from Aileen: Have you given any more thought to the promotion? Say yes! ☺

If she were to answer off her first instinct, it'd be: *Yes. I not only want this job, I'm going to slay at it.* She'd be silly to turn down a promotion. Who does that?

People focused on becoming Important Artists, that's who. She knows what Claudine would say: *Go for the gold. You want to work in art? Be the talent—grab the glory; don't just be the one adjusting the lighting.*

There are only so many hours in the week, not enough to excel at both; she can't take the job. It's settled, then. But it feels rude to break the news over text. She'll call Aileen later when it isn't two in the morning East Coast time. Dan too.

Maybe Claudine's at breakfast? Wylie could do some serious damage to a breakfast buffet right about now; dinner last night was a dinky Kind bar before she succumbed to sleep. As she dresses—black turtleneck tucked into jeans, unzipped maroon hoodie, rebraided braid—she reminds herself to stick to keto. High protein, low carbs. Four days to go. She may have faltered yesterday with that buttery croissant, but now she's back on course.

Just before she closes the door, Wylie notices Kipper left behind on the side table, the chain coiled around him. She snatches up the necklace, hoping Claudine won't mind, and fastens it around her neck. Then she strides down the hostel hallway, conscious of having Kipper so near before they scatter him in the wind, recalling the safety she'd felt when she'd slipped her small hand inside his callused one as he navigated them through the crowds at alpine races.

The dining room is jammed with guests sitting at round tables. Three Japanese women wearing itty-bitty backpacks hover around a laptop. An Australian couple are both tipped back in chairs, feet rudely on tables. Four young Portuguese men in various soccer jerseys with various iterations of Cristiano Ronaldo haircuts gesture animatedly, talking a mile a minute, as if they're still resolving an argument they were having in their room. Two British friends are politely inquiring if there's hot water for tea.

No Claudine. Where is she?

Wylie scans the breakfast offerings, or what's left of them, anyway. On the counter: an open loaf of sliced bread, just four slices left; a slab of hard butter; a messy jar of honey, as if the wooden dipper's been dragged around the outside rim; a jug of milk and two large plastic cereal containers, one with Switzerland's famed bircher muesli and the other empty; a half-full pitcher of orange juice and an urn of coffee; one lone apple.

Yuck.

She picks up the apple.

"Wylie!" she hears, and she turns to see an older couple sitting at a table near the massive stone fireplace, a fire warming the large room.

One woman is hunched, chewing glumly as if she's not allowed to get up until she's finished. The other's long silver hair, nearly reaching her elbows, has been dyed blue from its ends to her chin like an Easter egg half-dipped in dye. She's wearing a flowy blouse embroidered with butterflies. A sunray amulet is nestled between her breasts. Without her hair wrapped in a bath towel, it takes a moment for Wylie to register that it's Bibbidi beckoning her with a wide grin.

"Good morning," Wylie says, stepping closer, relieved to see someone she's already met. Someone who might have the

95

inside scoop on getting some decent food. Bibbidi seems to know the drill around here.

"Wylie, I want you to meet my wife, Erin." Bibbidi gestures *ta-da* with both hands at Erin, who has close-cropped hair, parted on the right, shaved on the sides with an electric razor's lowest setting, a pissed-off expression, and fantastic *s*-shaped eyebrows that dip with a pointed flourish on the outsides of her eyes. Her blue-and-white Columbia fleece is printed with pine trees laden with snow.

"Uh, hi," Wylie says.

Erin grunts a hello, and Bibbidi rolls her eyes. "Excuse her. She's grumpy this morning because they're out of cornflakes." Bibbidi nudges her shoulder against Erin's.

Erin stabs at her muesli. "This is reindeer feed. Do I look like a reindeer?"

"No," Wylie says, unsure if the question's directed at her.

"Exactly." Erin points her spoon at Wylie.

"It *is* quite chewy," Bibbidi acknowledges, flexing her jaw. "Your safest bet is probably coffee and toast. We found that apple on the floor when we got here."

Bibbidi's advice breaks the low-carb rule, but with few choices, Wylie follows it, returning to the table to join the couple. She'd like just a sprinkle of sugar (not getting tallied in the food app) for her coffee, but Erin parked the sugar bowl in front of her like she owns it.

"So, Wylie, isn't this place great?" Bibbidi asks, inhaling deeply.

Looking around, trying to see what Bibbidi sees, Wylie says, "Yeah. I guess."

"We love staying in hostels. It keeps us young. Doesn't it, honey bunny?" She places a hand over Erin's.

Wylie can't imagine Erin allowing a pet name like honey bunny, but surprisingly Erin winks back at Bibbidi. "Young and spry," she says. Wylie fights down the uninvited image of the two of them knocking boots in their bunks.

"Erin served in the first Gulf War as a mechanic," Bibbidi says, taking a sip of her coffee. It's a strange thing to announce unprompted.

"Hooah." Erin raps on her heart once with her fist.

"Thank you, um, for your service," Wylie says. She gives up trying to butter her bread, eating it dry. It forms a big lump inside her mouth.

Bibbidi continues. "You'd never guess it by looking at me, but I myself spent three unfortunate, stressed-to-the-max decades as a Wall Street trader. I worked for a guy who couldn't have made a buck without me, and knew it, so he paid me just enough to keep me. Golden handcuffs. The career bought me a beach house, but it did not buy me happiness. Then I met this one, left my husband, retired early, studied herbal medicine, and started traveling. And we don't intend to quit anytime—"

"Honey bun," Erin interrupts. "You're doing it again."

"Oh geesh." Bibbidi presses a hand to the side of her mouth in a mock whisper, as if she's letting Wylie in on a secret. "I talk too much."

Wylie shakes her head. She's been hanging on every word. "Not for me. I like hearing about your lives."

"I'll shut up so you can tell us about yourself. What brings you to Zermatt?"

Before she can answer, a young woman with a high bun zips into the room, circling their table, inspecting each of them.

"No braid," she says, behind Bibbidi.

Erin, too, gets an obvious "no braid."

Is this a Swiss version of duck, duck, goose?

She stops behind Wylie, clapping her hands. "Braid!"

Wylie grabs for her plaited hair, draping it over her shoulder a bit protectively.

"Can you stand up, please? Yes, you. Please stand up." The woman is already scooching back Wylie's chair. Wylie complies, exchanging perplexed looks with Erin and Bibbidi.

The woman claps again. "Tall!" Then she gestures to the older couple. "She is *sehr* tall, no?"

"Quite tall. And elegant, I might add," Bibbidi says.

Elegant? Wylie loves her.

"Uh, yeah, I'd say she's taller than average." Erin nods. "If you don't mind me saying so."

Wylie shrugs. "I don't mind."

"I found you!" the woman declares breathlessly.

"Oh?"

"You are Wylie?"

"Yes . . ."

"I am Léa," she says, placing a hand on her chest. "I work at die Freude. I've been waiting for you at the front desk. You didn't come to check where is your mom." She tsks at Wylie.

"No, I . . . figured she went out and would be back soon."

Léa deflates, robbed of the news she was going to deliver. "She went out . . . and will be back soon." Then she brightens, reading from a notebook, lifting a finger to clarify Wylie's error. "Actually, she's taking a walk. When I see her, I will tell her you are eating breakfast."

In this weather? Well, better be a quick walk. They need to honor Kipper, then hightail it for the train.

From beyond the door, there is a bleat of a pitch pipe, sounding like a single blow into a harmonica, followed by the snapping of fingers, and then a trio of young men—*oh no, not the buskers from the train*—strolls in, nearly sashaying, dragging each back foot slowly as they move as a unit. They're dressed in belted chinos and gingham dress shirts folded to the elbows, and they croon softly, notes that playfully glide up and down, like Fred Astaire tap-dancing up one stair and back down again, toying with the audience. Wylie vaguely recognizes the yacht-rock song.

Why do these guys assume everyone wants to hear them sing everywhere they go?

From the doorway, a fourth singer emerges—Wylie's not sure how she missed him—and glides to the center of the trio's half circle. He's tall, the only Black singer of the group, with a bald head and a slight pouch belly. Nothing about him would have grabbed Wylie's attention.

Until he starts singing. The first line: "Well, it's not far down to paradise."

Wylie's insides melt at the buttery sound of his voice, the ease of the notes on his lips, and in a matter of seconds, he morphs into the Sexiest Man Alive.

The Sexiest Man Alive is standing before her, also wearing chinos, but suddenly they're just the perfect amount of snug over his thighs, and she doesn't resent the other singers either, who are swaying, rhythmically snapping. Even the nerdy one with the glasses is sort of hot.

But really, she can't take her eyes off the soloist.

At the chorus of Christopher Cross's "Sailing," he moves his hand to his heart, the words floating, and she's impressed with his restraint, understands that he could belt this out like a show tune, and her mind drifts to how he might caress her gently, leaving her wanting more.

The song is little more than three minutes, and in that time, Wylie's imagined it all: a timid kiss that turns passionate, a night of bliss, *many* nights of bliss, getting married, having babies, him crooning to her and the babies. She wants to sail away with him.

Dan—who's Dan?

Abruptly, the song and the fantasy end. What in the heck just happened?

Bibbidi is on her feet, clapping, as are most of the guests in this room, save the Australians, who appear unmoved. Erin's frown looks like her version of a smile that says, "Not bad, not bad." Léa checks her notebook, as if confirming there's no rule against roving groups of singing men.

Wylie shifts in her seat, crossing her legs, confused by her instant attraction. She's unable to speak.

With the song over, the soloist and the three other singers turn back into mere mortals, all of them dorky, doughy, dressed like they just stepped off a ferry from Martha's Vineyard. Wylie blinks her eyes.

"Are you guys some kind of a group?" Bibbidi asks.

The soloist chuckles. "Yes. We're members of an a cappella group called Sings to Excess. There's usually nine of us, but there weren't enough rooms at the hotel, so some of us are staying here. I'm Calvin." He points to himself. "And this is Darren." Darren is a redhead with a flop of hair over his right eye and skin so pale it hurts to think about him on a beach. "That's Brandon." Brandon is as round as a glass-ball Christmas tree ornament, rosy-cheeked, with a scruffy beard and unruly curly hair. "And Jimmy." Jimmy, the scrawny guy with the glasses, could be David Byrne from Talking Heads.

"Well," Bibbidi says, flapping a hand over her face as if she's overheated. "Thank you for serenading us." She completes the round of introductions, and Wylie can barely make eye contact with Calvin when Bibbidi points to her.

Calvin retrieves a box just outside the door, jogging it back and flipping the lid open to reveal a stack of *Gipfelis*, the Swiss version of croissants. "We come bearing food," he says. "We noticed breakfast was *nicht sehr gut*."

At that, Léa whips her head to the food counter, appraising the offerings, pointing to items with her pen as if she's counting them.

"I'll take one," Erin says, holding up her hands, wanting a toss.

"It's really coming down out there." Brandon nods to the window.

"And it doesn't look like it's stopping anytime soon," Erin agrees happily.

Bibbidi picks up her plate. "What a generous gesture. I'd love one."

Léa, sniffing the milk, says, "The *Milch* is perhaps not at its best today. Nobody drink it." Erin clutches at her stomach.

"How about you?" Calvin offers the box to Wylie. The pastries *do* smell delicious, and she's actually really hungry. What's the harm in just one more nontallied croissant?

"Sure. Thank you." She notices that Calvin's eyes are golden brown, just like the underside of the pastry, caramelized to perfection. There's an invitation in his face, a playfulness, and without overthinking it, she puts the pastry up to her mouth just as she'd done on the train.

This time, a smile.

"Hi," she says, behind the pastry.

Calvin follows suit, masking his mouth behind his own croissant. "Hi," he says.

And there they are, *Gipfeli* smile to *Gipfeli* smile.

Before they have time to utter anything else, every guest's phone beeps with the clamorous sound of an emergency alert.

"What in the heck?" Erin asks.

They all extract their phones, reading the alert in unison. Avalanche. Worried chatter breaks out in the room in multiple languages.

"My word," Bibbidi mutters, her hand to her mouth.

"Mom's out there." Wylie jumps to her feet, face stricken.

And just as she does, the door bursts open, Claudine tumbling in, her coat drenched, her chest heaving, her eyes roving and, Wylie notices, a little deranged? Claudine takes a massive inhale of breath, leaning backward, as if she's trying to blow out trick birthday candles, and then she yells at the top of her lungs: "Take cover!"

The power flickers once, twice, and goes out.

12

Claudine

"YOU'RE SAFE," CLAUDINE PANTS, STILL GRIPPING Wylie's arm. They're huddled underneath one of the massive dining room tables along with five other guests. She pictures a ledge of snow poised somewhere above the town like the Grinch's sled, gunning to take them all out.

"What's going on?" Wylie asks, sliding her arm from Claudine's grip, rubbing it. All eyes stare at Claudine. "Is it bad out there?"

"I . . . No . . . But . . ." Claudine tries to remember what she saw as she was scrambling back to the hostel. It was a blur. Was anyone else even on the streets?

A young man—the spitting image of that singer from Talking Heads—says, "Has the avalanche *already* happened, or is it *about* to happen?"

"Yeah, that seems like an important distinction," says another young man.

"Is the village in danger, or is it higher up in the mountains?" Talking Heads asks. "We can't be all that shocked. The avalanche risk level was posted as high."

Wylie whips her head toward Claudine. "It was?" she asks.

Claudine is uncertain. Why, oh why, hadn't she checked something as simple as the avalanche risk level? Or discerned it herself with her years of knowledge, reading the danger signs? Big changes in weather—like what's happening in Zermatt with high winds, an unseasonably warm temperature, and massive amounts of snow, then rain—could cause the snowpack to slip away from the vertical face of a mountain like fondue on a tilted dinner plate, slow at first, and then all at once.

One of the Japanese women hiding under another table crawls on hands and knees to Claudine, imploring her for more information. "What's happening?" she asks.

Claudine's cheeks sizzle red with embarrassment. Zosel's and Fränzi's faces—did they look worried, or more put out, like the avalanche was a party pooper, about to ruin the day? Now she's not so sure. Her body had simply taken over; she'd fled without taking stock. If you're going to barge into a room and shout, "Take cover," you better have some solid evidence to back it up. "I don't know, to be honest," she's forced to say.

Rectangles of bright light glow under every table as guests check their phones for news.

"The hostel's Wi-Fi is out," the bald man says.

"Yeah, but the towers are still working," says Talking Heads. "Connect to 5G." After a beat, he says, "There's no news about the avalanche yet that I can find."

Léa is dialing numbers, trying to get through to someone,

while an older woman with dyed blue hair launches into a story about getting trapped in a New York subway for hours. "This reminds me of the time . . ." she says.

Beyond the table legs, Claudine catches a glimpse of actual legs, the woman with short hair who refused to dive under the table with them, instead pacing the floor, rapping on the walls, saying, "I think this structure could hold. Pretty solid build."

Wylie leans over. "Mom, you're breathing really heavily. Are you okay?"

"I just thought . . . Well. I panicked, I guess."

"Hmm," Wylie says, her eyes wide.

Claudine thinks she detects some satisfaction in her daughter's tone. "Panic" was a dirty word in the Potts household, a dangerous breakdown of mental toughness. If you talked about it, it was real, so you didn't talk about it.

Claudine's shocked that she just used the word herself.

Has Wylie inched farther from her and closer to Blue Hair? Also, *come on*. The woman's past the age of dyeing her hair such an outrageous color. She watches as the woman gingerly taps Wylie's hand, saying, "I think we should take a collective deep breath."

I'll give you a collective deep breath, Claudine thinks, miffed at this maternal takeover.

Koa strolls through the doorway with the gall to be whistling. "Oh sheesh, everybody, hiding under there isn't going to do any good. Come out. I have news about the avalanche."

All seven of them crawl out from under the table, unfolding their arms and legs, Claudine feeling creaky, her knee aching again—but not as achy, it seems, as Blue Hair. She reaches out a hand to help the older woman up, steadying her by the upper arm. Around the room, other guests follow suit, streaming out from their hideouts like they've been smoked out of a beehive.

"*O que está acontecendo?*" yells a Portuguese guest.

"Are we going to die, mate?" asks an Aussie.

"Should we make a mad dash?" suggests a Brit with a fringe.

On and on people lob out frantic questions, Koa lifting both his hands in a plea to quiet the crowd, until Claudine bridles her mouth with two pinkie fingers to give an ear-piercing whistle.

"Let the man speak!" she yells, and the entire room hushes. She tugs Wylie by the sleeve toward the fireplace and farther from the windows, just in case a sledgehammer of snow bursts in, hurling slices of glass and shrapnel from the building.

She *wants* everyone to survive whatever's coming their way, but she *needs* Wylie to survive.

Wylie shines her phone at Claudine. "Two hours until our train."

Claudine tries her best to appear calm. "Plenty of time."

"So," says Koa, swaying from side to side as if he's playing a virtual snowboard game. "There's been a mega-avalanche over the road and railway leading into Zermatt. And there might be another one coming. The risk level is at five—the highest it can be."

Murmurs in all languages shoot through the crowd, spreading like the red vines on the hostel's facade. It doesn't take a UN interpreter to understand the shared concern.

Léa steps forward, her notebook tucked into the crook of her right elbow, lifting up her other hand to calm the group.

"We are not, however, in any immediate danger." She tilts her head to Koa. "True?"

He nods. "Right. We're fine here in the village, but authorities are asking us to shelter in place while they assess the situation. Just as a precaution." Noticing the box of pastries, he says, "Oh, *Gips*. Sweet as. I could eat a horse."

His blasé attitude irks Claudine. "Is there a manager here? Someone trained to handle these circumstances?" she asks tersely.

Léa pipes up. "The owners of Hostel die Freude are on holiday in Thailand. So we're in charge." She beams, pointing to herself and Koa.

"Shelter in place for how long?" Wylie asks, worry lines creasing her forehead. "We're supposed to leave today." She's pacing the floor, checking and rechecking her phone for the time, reminding Claudine of the way she'd obsessively rebuckle her ski boots.

If this avalanche screws up Wylie's chance to compete in Berlin—which seems to matter to her a great deal—Claudine will never forgive herself.

"Unfortunately, I don't know that yet," Koa says between bites. "I will warn everyone that we might actually be stuck for a few days while they dig out the tracks. And they have to wait until the threat of another avalanche has passed to do that, so nobody gets buried as they work."

"Stuck?" asks the short-haired woman. Behind her, Blue Hair presses a palm against a glass pane as if she's energetically healing a wound.

"The road and the tracks are the only ways in and out," Talking Heads says with an eerie faraway voice, piecing it together, as if they've just solved a murder mystery but will be too late to save the next victim.

Next to her, Claudine thinks she hears a frightened whimper wind its way up Wylie's throat.

"How many days?" asks Wylie, wide-eyed and pale.

Koa rubs his neck, mulling it over. "Well, last year there was a level three, similar sitch, and we were stuck for two days. So I'd say five, since this sounds like a beast."

"Five days," Wylie whispers. "But that means . . ."

"Oh no," Claudine says, hanging her head in her hands. How could she let this happen?

Guests spring from their seats, reciting their travel itineraries as if they're lobbying an airline customer-service representative. But there are no planes, no trains, no roads out of this tiny, isolated village. It doesn't matter that the Brit with the fringe is supposed to be a bridesmaid in a Parisian wedding and the Aussies have nonrefundable tickets to Barcelona and the Japanese women are meeting with seed investors in Brussels, a meeting that took months to procure.

Or that Claudine and Wylie are competing in BodyFittest Duo in four days.

The competition that brought Wylie back to Claudine. The chance for Claudine to make things right between them. Now buried along with half a mile of railroad tracks.

I shouldn't have brought us here. Regret unfurls in Claudine's belly, and she slowly closes her eyes, sick at the thought of all the things she's done to get them to this exact moment.

She'll make it right. Somehow, she will.

She blinks her eyes open and turns to Wylie. To her surprise, she finds that she's now alone, standing before the fire. Wylie, always so damn quiet, soundless as snowfall, has snuck away. Claudine is left to watch the spectacle: angry guests demanding that someone fix this while a charred log in the fireplace caves in on itself, shifting so suddenly that for a moment Claudine thinks it's the thunderous sound of branches breaking under a tidal wave of white.

13

Wylie

WYLIE BASHES ITEMS INTO HER BACKPACK. HER sneakers. Her bunched-up pajamas. The toothbrush that Bibbidi might ask to use. There has to be a way out of here. Completely stuck? It's impossible. They have to leave.

Otherwise, it's two years of training down the tubes. No new life. No debt wiped clean. Another Did Not Finish next to her name.

All her plans are collapsing around her, taken out by stupid, stupid, stupid snow.

Her stomach pinches in pain, her chest squeezing. With each item she stuffs into her bag, her anger toward Claudine mounts. It's all her mom's fault they're here on some harebrained quest to spread Kipper's ashes. When, let's be real, he would have preferred Vail, where he grew up. Or Breckenridge. Taos. Whistler. Park City. Telluride. Killington. Mount Hood. A bunny slope at Sunapee!

It's not like Claudine's ever gone to the trouble to honor him before, despite Wylie practically begging for some sort of celebration-of-life ceremony after he died. Claudine always ducked the request until this random trip with this random timing, which has now left them trapped in a town where there's one road in and out. And she didn't even check the avalanche risk level. *Smart, Mom. Really smart.*

Wylie needs Dan to tell her what to do. If Dan were here, he would have already procured them exercise equipment. Had them up at dawn. Kept them eating right. Charged their cell phones, which, looking at hers, is nearly dead.

Hell, Dan would never get stuck in an avalanche. He would just *know* better.

But Wylie's too scared to use her remaining cell phone battery to call him. He'll flip out.

Another unwelcome thought pushes past Wylie's mental guards: *Do* they have a real shot at winning BodyFittest Duo? She'd brushed away any misgivings, riding the familiar notion that she and Claudine would dust the competition because they aren't like other people.

But now she sees the idea for what it is: Preposterous. Ridiculous. Dumb. Embarrassing. Just because Claudine's an insane skier and rides a spin bike like it's done something unforgivable to her doesn't mean she'll know what she's doing in a BodyFittest competition. She'll not only be jumping in cold . . . She seems injured. Wylie saw how hard it was for Claudine to get up from under that table, her leg stiff with discomfort.

There's nothing left to pack, so Wylie begins needlessly tearing at her sheets, pulling them off the mattress, unaware that she's sobbing, cleaving cries racking her body, snot streaking down her nose, Kipper swaying to and fro around her neck with every wild yank and tug.

A familiar constriction winds its way around her chest, tightening and tightening, the same sensation she felt in the hospital with Dan, and on so many race days before that.

She pounds on her chest, wishing she could dislodge whatever's trapped inside, blockading her breath. Every single time she's had a panic attack, she's certain it will stop her heart. How can her body bear such brutality?

She's vaguely aware of the door opening. Of Claudine rushing to her. Of her mom gently, and then with more force, removing the sheet from her fist. Guiding her to sit on the bottom bunk. Instructing her to breathe. A rhythmic circle motion on her back.

"Wy, we're going to make a list, okay?" Claudine says.

So Claudine remembers the listing technique, the one the counselor taught them after Wylie came home from St. Moritz with a DNF, disgraced. Claudine viewed the counselor's guidance as a last resort, a way to get Wylie back to racing. But by that point, nothing would do the trick.

Wylie's lungs constrict; she claws at her turtleneck.

"Lake Louise," Claudine says, her voice steady, yet tender.

It's the name of the Canadian World Cup ski-racing location, the words mustering their way through the curtain that Wylie's behind. "Lake Louise," Claudine repeats.

"I can't," Wylie sputters. She can barely heave out the words.

"You can. Just one at a time. Like stepping stones. Lake Louise."

Wylie's face is a stream of tears, her torso folded over her knees, hands on the sides of her head as if she can't bear the noise of something, fingers pulling the top of her braid loose. "M-Mammoth," she manages to say.

"Semmering."

Wylie's right hand has moved to squeeze her mouth, and she lifts it momentarily to say, "Maribor."

"Cortina."

"Park City."

"And where's the exit?" Claudine asks.

Wylie points behind her, toward the door.

A sodden fatigue seeps into Wylie as she gives up the fight, replaced by a swirl of emotions akin to the colored wax in a shaken-up lava lamp, floating to rest at the bottom. Stripped of her usual vigilance against touching her mom, she allows Claudine to draw her near, comforted by the crook of her arm.

Imagine if Claudine had taken this tack in St. Moritz, rather than blaming Wylie for not being able to muscle her way through. What a difference it would have made.

"How ya doing?" Claudine asks after some time has passed.

"I'm okay," Wylie responds wearily. She's far from okay, but at least she doesn't feel like she's going to die.

"I'm sorry we might miss the competition," Claudine says. "I should have checked the weather and the risk level before I brought us here."

Wylie wearily lifts her head to look at Claudine's face. It's the first time in her life that Claudine's delivered an apology without a qualifier.

I'm sorry I can't be there, but you know how much this race means to me.

Sorry I yelled. It's just that I know you can do better.

Sorry, but you're on your own if you quit.

The words are both comforting and disorienting. Wylie's

not sure how to take them. She sniffs, pressing away from Claudine, and she reaches to the side table for a travel pack of tissues. Her nose blowing is so loud and cartoonish that they both laugh, Wylie's chuckle slightly muffled behind the tissue. Then silence again, the pair motionless.

Wylie sighs deeply, then says, "I really need to be in Berlin. I have to win that contest, Mom."

"There will be other—"

"You and Kipper always taught me that the race right in front of me was the most important. Not to look for the next one. I need this, Mom. I just do."

Claudine takes this in. She nods with certainty. "Okay. So we'll find a way to get there."

"Really?"

"I'll give it everything I've got," Claudine promises.

Gratitude blooms in Wylie's chest. "Thanks, Mom." She draws the flimsy curtain away from the window. The rain has stopped, leaving behind drifts of snow that press against the bottom third of the glass, miniature hills and valleys. Wylie traces the undulations. "I've been riding with you," she tells Claudine, the admission tumbling out before she can catch it.

"What do you mean?"

"CycleTron. Three mornings a week." Why does this feel so cringey to share?

Claudine clears her throat, pauses, then clears it again. "I had no idea. I wish I'd known. It would've been a lot less lonely."

For the second time in this conversation, Wylie's surprised by Claudine's vulnerability. Come to think of it, she could see her mom as a little lonely. She's never had a lot of friends. *Just like me,* Wylie thinks. "You don't like being the fearless leader of the PottHeads?" she asks.

"I'm not fearless. And no, I don't."

Wylie glances at Claudine to see her face pinch, her lips puckered from biting the insides of her mouth. She doesn't expound.

"I don't usually lose it like this anymore, you know?" Wylie gestures to her tearstained face. She'd hoped to reveal a new-and-improved self, but she's already breaking down. "I'm stronger now."

A small part of her is hoping to hear her mom respond: *You were always strong.*

Instead, Claudine says, "This is all a lot to handle. An avalanche in a ski village, sticking you in close quarters with your old mom." She bumps her shoulder into Wylie's, trying to lighten the mood. "And I can only imagine how hard you've worked to make it this far in BodyFittest Duo."

Wylie's pulled another tissue from its packaging, and she spreads it out over the expanse of her thigh, smoothing it. "Yeah, it's been kinda grueling."

"How about for Dan? Does he find it grueling?" Claudine pauses. "Does he ever push you a little too hard?"

At the mention of his name—and a glimpse at what Claudine might think about her boyfriend—Wylie stiffens.

She turns to find Claudine's face flooded with concern. Maybe it'd be a relief to share that she's beginning to question life with Dan, but Wylie can't bring herself to trust Claudine. The past is still a treacherous ski route to navigate, like the Haute Route from Chamonix, France, to west Zermatt, unpatrolled, unmonitored, with deadly crevasses, storms rolling in without warning.

Just when you think you're safe, you're a goner.

"He's a really competitive guy," she says, brushing her bangs from her eyes. "He expects a lot of me, and I don't always deliver." Shame triggers a snide follow-up comment. "I think you can relate to that, right? You and Dan are actually a lot alike."

"Ah." Claudine forces a smile, but Wylie senses a shift in her mom. A cloud obscures the noon sun filtering into their window. With the sun swathed and the power still out, it's chilly in the unheated room.

Maybe Wylie shouldn't have said it—but it's true. Dan and Claudine are cut from the same compete-at-all-costs cloth. And Wylie doesn't feel like apologizing for pointing it out.

Snatching her sketchbook and leather roll-up case, she says, "I'm going to hang in the lounge for a bit. Just need to collect my thoughts." She strides to the door, pulling it shut, but not before she sees her mom slump to her pillow as if her shoulder's been pushed by an index finger, looking more defenseless than Wylie's ever seen her.

It makes her think of Dan, his beseeching eyes back at the hospital.

Wylie lifts her chin as she leaves the room. *I won't be made to feel bad for her.*

But as she's walking down the hall, Claudine pokes her head out of the room and calls out, "I'll get cracking on a plan to get us to Berlin!" And then Wylie does feel exactly that—bad.

14

Wylie

THE AFTERMATH OF THE PANIC ATTACK CHURNS through Wylie's body as she sets up shop in a window seat in the lounge, her bum on a cushion, her back against a wall, a sketchbook on her bent knees, affording her the best view of the Matterhorn die Freude has to offer.

Doodling, she hopes, will steady her nerves. Her mom is right; this is a lot.

From her leather roll-up case, she removes a graphite pencil. She tilts her head to study the Matterhorn, brings her attention to the blank sheet, and then makes quick tick marks on the paper as if she's fencing with the instrument. Between working and training and, okay, procrastinating, it's been a few months since she's sketched, and her hand is unpracticed. The Matterhorn's peak emerges, but it doesn't look the way she wants it to. It's too sloping, too narrow up top—*Here I go again.* The same thing happened in art school, seems to happen anytime she tries to draw or paint at home. She gets in her own head before she's captured anything on the page.

This is the opposite of stress-reducing.

Collaging, on the other hand, allowed a perfectionist to loosen the hell up. There's no way to perfectly tear a page, or to render, say, the Matterhorn, in its exact likeness when you're reproducing it through bits of paper. Make a mistake? Just cover it up, or fold that mistake into a new design. She'd found it so freeing.

She's suddenly aware of a presence next to her. Glancing up, she sees Léa staring out the window at the Matterhorn. "She stands alone," Léa says, launching into an unexpected monologue. "No siblings to the left or right. No one to lean against. That is why she is so strong. It is her sacrifice. She is the best mountain in the world." Then she peers down her nose at Wylie, giving her a pointed look. "We Swiss understand this. Put that into your drawing."

Wylie, dry-mouthed, gulps. "Thanks. I'll try."

With a curt nod, Léa disappears. Wylie stares at her sketch. She has no idea how to make it embody all of that—the mandate already piquing her stomachache again.

But what if . . . Well, what if she made a collage? Who's stopping her? She'd spotted a few magazines in the lending library when they checked in yesterday. She jumps up, grabs them, and heads to the front desk.

"Léa, would you mind if I cut these up?"

Léa frowns. "I meant to put into the recycling. It is not a problem."

Wylie grins. "And do you, by chance, have a glue stick and a pair of scissors I could use?"

"Glue stick and scissors," Léa says as she rummages through the desk drawer. "Ah!" Improbably, she holds up a glue stick. "A family checked out a few days ago. They left many things. Do you need this Elmo coloring book?"

Wylie laughs. "No. Just the glue and scissors, thank you!"

Back in her window perch, Wylie is a whir of excitement, feeling the way she did as a kid cutting up magazines in some alpine village. Just the sounds of the scissors, the tearing of paper—*Oh*, she loves it. Now, *this* is relaxing. An hour passes as she begins bringing the Matterhorn to life in a layer of shapes and patterns and shades of reds and oranges and blues and blacks, one side of the mountain bathed in bright light, the other side cooler as the sun sets.

Next she'll build in the Matter Vispa down below, tearing pages of blue rather than cutting them, wanting the rough-edged white to appear as currents of water.

Another shadow falls over her. She looks up expecting Léa, but instead it's Calvin, aka the Sexiest Man Alive, now just a normal dude clutching a paperback book. Wylie's lips, pegged in a concentrated straight line, tug up to a smile.

He gestures to the other end of the window seat. "Will I bother you if I sit?"

"Not at all. Let me just—" She scoops up her mess of magazine clippings, inches her feet back to make room, and Calvin plops down, one knee up, the other leg dangling over the side of the seat, facing her. A nervousness glides into Wylie's belly, a figure skater on ice, twirling, whirling. Her cheeks flush.

"It looks like a scone," he says.

"I'm sorry?"

He nods toward the Matterhorn outside the window.

"Doesn't it look like a powdered sugar scone? Makes me hungry just looking at it."

She squints at the mountain.

"Then again, I'm always thinking of pastries." He pats his rounded middle. "My tombstone will read: 'He lived for baked goods.'"

"Not: 'Here lies a man who can carry a tune'?"

"Pastries trump singing for me, any day. I had planned to eat my way through this town, trying every bakery. Now I might have to settle for that sliced bread in the dining room—which, I'm not a hater of sliced bread. Two pieces of white bread, ham, and a little mustard? That might be the perfect meal."

Wylie's mind momentarily flashes to Dan calculating calories of food he deems evil, marking a massive *x* over anything with a crumb structure, outlawing basic ingredients—flour, sugar, butter. If she were here with Dan, they'd eat only yogurt and fruit for breakfast.

Before she can stop herself, she blurts, "I want to do that too."

He laughs, lines forming on the outside of his mouth like extra-long dimples. "Which part?"

"The bakery part! I want to eat at all the bakeries in Zermatt."

His gaze sweeps to the quiet street outside, every resident and every tourist shuttered indoors. "It's a date," he says. "If we can ever leave this hostel."

The word "date" sends a shock wave through Wylie. "Oh, I . . . I'm so sorry. I didn't mean to give the wrong impression." She slips her fingers over the end of her braid. "I have a boyfriend. Back at home."

Now *Calvin's* eyebrows. Ooh, they're nice. Thick, soft angles, medium arch. Perfect, actually.

"I didn't mean . . . Not like a formal date or anything." Calvin fans the pages of his book, floundering a little. "Just an expression of speech, like, it's a date, on my calendar, and I will meet you there, but not, like, as a date or anything."

"Okay." She wants to bite on her braid to stop herself from grinning stupidly. "We'll just go eat a pastry. As friends. When we get out of here."

Eating pastries with the Sexiest Man Alive is definitely not allowed. She's breaking all sorts of rules.

"Cool," he says.

"Cool."

"I'm just going to read, then." He holds up the book. "I'll leave you to it." He signals to her collage.

"Cool," she repeats, wanting to smack herself on the forehead for playing it decidedly *un*cool. He opens his book, diverting his attention to the first page, and Wylie ducks her head down, staring at the magazine in her lap. How in the world can she concentrate—

"Do you by any chance want to play a board game?" he asks.

Oh, thank goodness. "Yes!"

Calvin tosses the book onto the table, jumps up, strides to the bookshelf, rifles through the options, and carries back a box split on all four corners. He holds it up. "Trouble?"

"I haven't played that game in years."

They choose their colors, and he gestures for her to go first, so she presses down on the Pop-O-Matic, which gives a hugely satisfying pop, tumbling the die in its dome like a popcorn kernel in a Jiffy Pop stovetop pan. Lucky six, the number that releases pegs from home to the playing track. She moves her yellow peg.

Pop. Calvin, blue, rolls a two. No can do.

Pop. Wylie, a three. Her peg inches forward.

Calvin: one.

Pop. Six for Wylie, setting free another peg.

"You're an artist?" Pop. Five for Calvin. He's stuck in purgatory.

"Oh, uh, sort of. I work for a museum."

"Doing what?"

She lowers her voice. "I'm an assistant exhibition manager. I help hang and create the art exhibitions."

"Wow. Do you like it?"

"I love it, actually." Pop. Five. Her first peg rounds a corner. She almost mentions the promotion.

In a hushed voice he asks, "Why are we whispering?"

Wylie laughs. "I don't know."

"What brought you to Zermatt?"

"My mom and I . . ." How to explain the entire situation in a single dose, an easily swallowable capsule, without going into Kipper's and her mom's skiing legacy and her almost skiing legacy and Dan, whom she really doesn't want to talk about? "We're competing in this fitness competition in Berlin, and we just stopped here on the way. For . . . fun."

"Whoa." Calvin protracts his neck, surprised. Pop. One. Poor guy. "That's an amazing thing to do with your mom."

Pop. Six. She's cruising. "Yeah, I guess it is."

Now that he mentions it, Claudine's really showing up, isn't she? Even beyond the competition. She hasn't made any condescending remarks about her art career, didn't pepper her with more questions about Dan when it was clear Wylie didn't want to talk about him, and helped her through that panic attack. And the way she'd been so protective over Wylie when she thought the avalanche was a danger. It's touching.

And how has Wylie mostly responded? With cold shoulders and silence, little jabs about Claudine's competitive nature. A competitive nature, by the way, that yielded five gold medals. So maybe her mom wasn't chill. How many champions are chill?

She'll do better, Wylie tells herself. Cut Claudine some slack. She can do that.

"Did your singing bring you to Zermatt?" she asks.

"I have a million more questions about this fitness thing," he says. "But, yeah. Sings to Excess is a professional a cappella group. We're on our European tour."

"Now *I* have a million questions. How long have you been with the group?"

"I graduated college three years ago, so since then. But this is my last year. This fall I'll be teaching music at a school on the North Shore of Massachusetts."

Wylie tosses up her hands in excitement. "I'm from Massachusetts too! The Berkshires."

"What are the odds?" His eyes shimmer.

She feels hot under his gaze, heat threading up her neck. "It's . . . uh . . . your turn."

Pop. Two. It's *really* not his day.

Nearby, the Aussie couple peer out another window, having an under-the-breath-but-heated argument. Wylie was having such a nice time she almost forgot about the avalanche, but now it hits her again. They're stuck.

"When do you think we'll get out of here?" she asks, popping with less vigor. All four of her pegs are in play.

"I have no idea. Maybe it'll be faster than Koa thinks."

"That's what I'm hoping. If we can't leave soon, we'll miss the competition." She mindlessly twists the end of her braid.

"Oh. That's awful. I'm sorry." His voice sounds genuinely remorseful.

"Thanks."

"The good news is that we're not in any danger here, and we're not stuck for life. Two days, five days, a week: at some point, we'll all go home."

Home. That word doesn't stir comfort in Wylie the way it should, doesn't conjure a safe harbor, a place to rest her weary head. She opens and then closes her mouth before she divulges more than she should to a man she's just met.

Outside, there's a grenade-like boom.

"What," Calvin asks, "was that?"

"Controlled avalanches, I'm guessing," Wylie says, remembering this familiar sound. "The snow patrol's setting off avalanches on purpose with explosives. It's sort of like opening up a dam to avoid a flood."

"Oh wow, yeah, I've heard of that," Calvin says.

From a hammock swinging breezily over the grass turf, Koa leans a head out and says, "She's right. It's a good thing. Means they're on it." The hammock envelops him again.

Wylie and Calvin exchange glances. "Didn't even know he was there," Calvin whispers. Pop. Four. He tosses his hands up. "I surrender. Want to go see what they have for snacks?"

She picks up a peg, studying it. "I should really work out. A few rounds of jumping jacks, at the very least."

"Is that how you like to spend your afternoons?"

"*Like* to? Not at all. *Have* to? Yeah, sorta." Wylie smiles, as if she's joking.

"I have an idea." He curls his lips in and bops them together, his eyes full of mischief. "Follow me."

Twenty minutes later, Calvin and his singing mates have pushed all the dining room chairs and tables against the windows, clearing a space the size of a racquetball court. Wylie's in the front, leading an impromptu exercise class, rolling her shoulders as a warm-up, with Bibbidi, the three Japanese women, the Brits, and Léa following along as Sings to Excess performs NSYNC songs. Erin stands in the back, inching her shoulders up and down to the beat, singing loudly, knowing every word by heart.

For the first time in two years, Wylie finds herself grinning during a workout, laughing as they sidestep through the Electric Slide, half the class going the wrong way, bonking into one another. She's enlivened by the joy in moving her body just for the sheer pleasure of it.

Watching the Sexiest Man Alive sing his heart out—his golden eyes occasionally meeting hers? That doesn't hurt her mood either.

15

Claudine

SO FAR, CLAUDINE'S FAILING TO HATCH A PLAN. HOW in the heck do they escape a remote, snow-covered town when there's only one road in? When they're not even allowed to leave the hostel? Her phone is tipping toward 50 percent battery life, and she'll have no way to charge it once it goes dead, so any minutes spent internet-searching or making phone calls have to be used wisely.

She's got Gib working on it after exchanging just a few texts. She even called Jasmine, her CycleTron handler, to see if they could help. But what can they do? They'd have to move heaven and earth, and also tons of snow, to get her to Berlin.

The only thing that's changed since Wylie left their room is that Claudine's knee has gone from painful to excruciatingly painful. Even if she pulls off a miracle getting them out of here, she can barely walk. Let alone box-jump.

Claudine checks her phone one last time before powering it down to save the battery. It's 5:30 p.m. *Holy cow.* Where's Wylie? She left to regroup in the lounge hours ago.

Sinking back to lie on her mattress, she thinks of Zosel's imploring face, of Fränzi saying, "I know who you are." And then Wylie, tearing at her hair, still in the grip of those merciless panic attacks, followed by Claudine saying something stupid about Dan that drove Wylie out of the room.

She's botching everything.

You're out over your skis again, Claud. Another Kipper-ism, his frequent critique of her ski stance, leaning too far forward, swinging wildly to regain her center. And he said it off the mountain too, whenever he found her to be inadequately prepared.

The thing with a posture is, you can make minute adjustments to stay in control. But in life, well, Claudine's never been able to find the center.

Hunger propels her out of bed. She tosses off the covers, blasted by the cold air in the room, feeling around for her shoes and her parka, her teeth chattering as she stuffs her arms in and zips it up.

The hallway is all murky shadows. Claudine makes her way toward the voices coming from the dining room, which must be the only warm spot in the entire hostel, thanks to the fireplace. She's eager to get there, to find Wylie and dinner, to get an update on the avalanche, but she makes her way slowly, her knee throbbing with each step. Finally, she pushes open the dining room doors.

At the scene before her, she stops short.

The room glows with light from the roaring fire and the half dozen miniature burners on each table, the flames licking the cast-iron bottoms of six red fondue pots. Around each table guests sit shoulder to shoulder, laughing and talking, their faces flickering in and out of view as they dip long fondue forks into the pots, drawing dripping cheese-coated bread to their plates.

It's beautiful. It's pure magic. And Claudine feels oddly left out.

There's Wylie laughing it up with the same folks that hid under the table with them earlier, but there are no seats left, and Wylie's not even noticing her absence. Claudine pivots awkwardly on her knee to slip out the door. Dinner will be another energy bar.

"Mom!" It's her name to no one but Wylie.

Wylie's raising her arm as if she's calling to Claudine among a crowd of people at a train station. It fills her with so much gratitude, this gesture from her daughter, that—oh heck no. Claudine Potts does not cry in public. She doesn't do it in private, for that matter. She takes a heavier-than-necessary step on her bad leg, wincing with pain. Hurts like hell, but better than letting her emotions brim over.

And then she approaches the table, stuffing her hands into her pockets and doing her best to walk normally.

One of the young men leaps up, saying, "I'll grab you a chair."

"Oh, that's not necessary," she replies. But it is. It so is.

She's desperate to join the group, dying to eat what's in that pot. Her mouth salivates at the smell of melted Gruyère. Closer to the table, she notices other items that had been gobbled up by the darkness: hunks of brown bread—*Ruchbrot*, she remembers—along with sliced pears and cherry tomatoes. Lightheaded, she now realizes that she could collapse with hunger. When did she last eat a proper meal?

"Did you get my text telling you about dinner?" Wylie asks. "I shut my phone off after I sent it."

"I didn't—probably because I had mine off. But that was nice of you." There's an awkward formality between them. Everyone must be noticing it.

"Mom, this is Calvin." Wylie gestures to the man unfolding a metal chair for her. The guests shuffle left or right, making room, and soon Claudine's shaking hands with Bibbidi (Blue Hair), Erin, and Jimmy (Talking Heads). Léa she already knows.

She sits down, discreetly straightening her left leg under the table.

"Were you limping?" Wylie whispers from behind her wineglass.

Claudine waves her off. "My leg's asleep, that's all." She notices that Wylie's wearing the Kipper pendant, and for the first time, she's glad she kept that thing, giving Wylie a way to feel close to him again. It seems like it's so easy for Wylie to remember all the good about her grandfather, and none of the bad—and that means Claudine's done one thing right, at least. Shielding Wylie was her intention.

"Wine, Claudine?" Calvin asks, holding up a carafe. She declines, never much of a drinker.

There aren't enough fondue forks, but Wylie passes hers to Claudine. Luckily she still recalls fondue rules, because boy is there a proper etiquette to eating food dipped in cheese. The Swiss won't hesitate to point out gaffes. She spears a square of bread, casts it into the pot, claims her cheese, and holds the long skewer aloft, allowing the excess to drip off. Then she reels in her catch, using her dinner fork to slide the bread onto her plate. Only then does she take a bite, eliciting a moan from the back of her throat.

"Oh dear god, this is good," she says.

"The key is grated nutmeg," Léa says. "Plus a bit of red wine. A little black pepper. The *Grossmutter* at the bottom is my favorite part."

"What's gross?" Erin asks, eyeing the pot skeptically.

"The *Grossmutter*," Léa explains. "It translates to 'grandmother.' It's the crusty cheese at the bottom." She smacks her lips.

Claudine swipes a bit of cheese from the corner of her mouth, licking her finger. The taste brings with it a swirl of memories: Bingeing on cheese and bread with Zosel and Kipper after World Cup races, Wylie, who never sat still at mealtimes, exploring their new accommodations for the night—sometimes a luxury chalet, usually a family-run inn.

Those were good times.

Now, squeezed together side by side, there's not a hairline between Claudine's shoulder and Wylie's, no shooting cracks. For this moment, they are fused.

Wylie signals for Calvin to pass her the carafe, and Claudine watches as she sloppily refills her own glass. *Hmm.* How many glasses has Wylie had?

Suggesting that she slow down would be the wrong move. Instead Claudine offers up a memory. "Do you remember eating fondue when you were little?"

Wylie's smile is so bright, it could be another candle. "I do. Didn't I once lose a Barbie shoe in the pot?" She takes another large swallow of wine, setting the glass down indelicately.

Claudine rollicks backward. "I forgot about that!" She closes her eyes, shakes her head, and covers her mouth with her hand. A muffled laugh elbows its way through her fingers.

Léa, overhearing, is horrified. "Your doll shoe in the *Caquelon*? No! That is against the rules. You never leave anything in the pot. The poor *Grossmutter*."

Wylie nods as the memory resurfaces. "I was trying to fill the shoe with cheese. I think I wanted to sip from it. But I didn't realize how hot the cheese was, so I dropped it."

"What's this?" Bibbidi asks, cocking an ear, leaning in.

"Her Barbie's shoe," Léa explains. "In the *Caquelon*." Her gesture toward the pot is exasperated, as if it's common knowledge that losing a toy in the fondue is an unforgivable faux pas.

Erin interjects, confused. "What's the *cock-o-loin*?"

"*Ca-que-lon*," Léa instructs, her horror growing at Erin's butchering of the word. "It's the fondue pot."

"*Cock-o-loin*." Erin gives the word a spin. Turning to Bibbidi, she repeats, "*Cock-o-loin*. Am I saying it right?" Bibbidi waves her off to hear the rest of the story.

"You didn't tell anyone until Kipper impaled the shoe with his fork!" Claudine exclaims. "There he was, talking away, dipping his bread, and out comes a tiny pink stiletto, dripping with cheese!"

Calvin, dredging a pear slice in the pot, says, "Then what happened?"

Claudine and Wylie look at each other, simultaneously recalling the scene moment by moment.

"He didn't even blanch," Claudine says.

"He pretended to eat it." Wylie's speech is slightly slowed.

"Just put it right into his mouth."

"We were all laughing and yelling for him to spit it out!"

"But he was making a big show of it."

Claudine mimics her father. *"Yum, what's in this? It's the best fondue I've ever had."*

"How old was I?"

"You must have been about six. You loved that ratty old Barbie. Not as much as your Snowlet, of course, but a close second."

"But I didn't like the name Barbie. I called her Fancy."

"That's right!"

Léa interjects. "Who's Kipper?"

"He was my grandfather," Wylie says, taking another large gulp.

"My dad," Claudine follows.

Erin, chewing her way through a tomato, says, "He sounds like a fun guy."

Claudine stiffens a little, suddenly bloated on bread and cheese and memories. "Yeah, he was a real barrel of laughs." From the corner of her eye, she catches Wylie shaking her head in annoyance.

"He could be, Mom."

Claudine's sigh is closemouthed, weary. "When he wanted to be, sure."

"For someone you didn't like all that much, you sure left me with him a lot."

Oof. A direct hit. Claudine touches the rim of her plate, and then her glass, buying time so she doesn't answer with her own angry retort. Everyone seems to be watching her, judging her mothering. "I didn't have much of a choice. And he was different with you."

Bibbidi reaches across the table, setting a hand on each of their forearms. "I'm sorry if this is a sore spot for you both." When neither Claudine nor Wylie break the silence, Bibbidi retracts her hands.

Calvin tries to lighten the mood. "What I want to know is: Why were you in the Alps eating fondue when you were six?"

"Yes, why?" Léa asks, her "why" sounding like "vhy?"

She can tell from Wylie's face—the way she seems to be powering down into silent mode—that this poor crew have really stepped in it. They were on safer ground discussing the melted-cheese recipe. Wylie's arms are folded across her chest, leaving Claudine to explain.

"I . . . um . . . was an alpine ski racer. So I— We"—she nods toward Wylie—"were on the World Cup circuit. I was competing, for many years. Until she was about ten years old."

"Wow," Calvin marvels. "What an upbringing. So you've been everywhere?" He's speaking to Wylie, who only nods. Then Wylie reaches for the carafe again, but Bibbidi intercepts it.

"How about a glass of water first, dear?" Bibbidi asks.

Claudine has the urge to duck for cover—and is shocked when Wylie agrees. *Agrees!* Claudine couldn't have gotten away with that.

"Wait a second," Erin says, pointing her fondue fork at Claudine like she's going to run her out of town with it. "You're not Claudine *Potts*, are you?"

Ugh, here it goes. She really doesn't want to do this whole oh-my-god-you-were-an-Olympian rigmarole. "I am, yes," she says.

Erin slaps a meaty palm on the table. "Holy frick, you

guys"—she gestures to Claudine as if she's a museum attraction—"she won a gazillion Olympic gold medals."

"Five, actually," Wylie says, seeming to forget her petulance. "And one silver. People always forget about that one."

That's sweet of Wylie to say. A stadium wave of appreciation and awe flows around the table. Léa, no longer irked about the Barbie shoe stepping on the *Grossmutter*, says, *"Ach du meine Güte!"*

Claudine shrugs off the accolades as if she's getting applauded for emptying the compost bin. To change the subject, she says, "Léa, is there fresh-grated nutmeg in this?"

"Claudine Potts," Erin repeats to herself. She leans over to Bibbidi. "Claudine *Potts*."

As Léa begins to mime pushing a nutmeg seed over a grater, Claudine thinks she's in the clear. No more questions, at least tonight, that could cause friction between them. Except Calvin is hell-bent on heralding his interest in Wylie.

"What about you?" he asks Wylie. "Do you ski?"

Claudine's face reddens, hidden in the shadows.

Wylie takes a deep breath before speaking. "I used to, yeah. Didn't have what it takes like my mom. Or grandfather." She brandishes the fondue fork like a conductor's baton, and Claudine has to lean back to avoid getting grazed. "Broke the line. No more legacy, thanks to *moi*." The weight of each word sinks Claudine in her chair.

"You had the most natural talent of any of us," Claudine says quickly. She means it to be supportive, to correct how Wylie seems to be putting herself down, but the way Wylie whips around makes her realize she's taken yet another wrong step.

"It takes more than talent to win," Wylie says, and Claudine hears the echoes of something she might have said to her daughter back in those Burke days. "It takes a winning mindset." Wylie taps drunkenly at her temple, then turns back to Calvin. "Which I did not have, much to my mom's dismay."

"You were trying your best," Claudine mumbles. *I now know.* It's true that Claudine didn't think so then, but she's come to a new understanding about performance anxiety, thanks to Soupy.

Wylie laughs wildly. "You thought I was a quitter. I couldn't get it together."

"Wylie," Claudine whispers, "I think this is a private conversation." A vast crevasse opens between them, a distance she has no clue how to cross. The guests fall quiet, the audience ill at ease. Seconds tick by. The flame in the burner simpers and reignites.

Claudine's too mortified to speak.

Bibbidi, bless her, claps her hands. "I think it's time to be serenaded. Calvin, would you lead your troupe in a few ditties?"

Sings to Excess doesn't have to be asked twice. In a matter of moments, they're huddling to the right of the fireplace, choosing their song before arranging themselves in an arched line. Then, with the soothing, low hum of a lullaby, as if they're rocking the entire room to sleep in the middle of a moonless night, they layer the first notes of another familiar song: "Silent Night," only the German version. *"Stille Nacht."*

It's past Christmas, but the dim lighting and the crackling fire, plus the unknowns of the outside world, the feeling of being hemmed in by snow, make it fitting. More than fitting. It waves a wand over the room, lessening the tension almost instantly.

And it gives Claudine a chance to collect herself. What just happened? Wylie's never spoken to her like that. As much as the words sting, as embarrassing as the public shaming feels, a part of Claudine is relieved that her daughter is letting her have it. Frankly, she prefers this to Wylie's silent treatments.

She'd never been able to give Kipper a piece of her mind.

Maybe there's progress in tonight, hard as it is. Maybe, underneath all Wylie's potent ire, there's an opening for Claudine to try and make it right.

Calvin steps forward, clearly the star. His voice is achingly beautiful. The others' voices swell behind him. If she were in her car listening to this alone, she'd press repeat. But this song is meant only for this room, this moment, and Claudine allows herself to be swept up in it, enraptured, temporarily forgetting her troubles.

Alles schläft. Einsam wacht.

The group switches to the English version, and soon the entire room is singing. It's mournful and joyous in turn, the song taking on a different meaning for everyone, some pining for loved ones, some perfectly content to be right here, right now.

All is calm. All is bright.

"Hallelujah" rings out, and Claudine hears Wylie join the chorus of other voices. Even though she can reach out and touch her, she misses her more than she ever has.

16

Wylie

WYLIE SHIVERS IN THE TOP BUNK, SOBERING UP. IT was a lovely evening, until it wasn't. At least she and Claudine hadn't gone to bed angry.

In fact, her mom was surprisingly affable toward her, in spite of the things that Wylie had lobbed at her. Wylie had meant them, yes—she's kept them simmering under the surface for too long—but it was indisputably crummy to let them break loose in front of an audience.

Calvin must think she's wretched. There's nothing more humbling than your crush watching you get tipsy and then *be mean to your mom*. Wait. Did she say *crush*? Oh, it's true. He's so easy to like. Wylie can't believe the spark in her chest, the gravitational pull of her body toward his, the way she's already seeking him out in every room, only to find that he's seeking her out too.

When he sings, *wow*. Wylie melts. Is it just her imagination, or was Calvin singing directly at her? "Silent Night" has never been so sexy. Shepherds quaking? More like Wylie quaking.

Quaking is definitely not allowed.

Has Dan ever stirred a longing in her? She has to admit that they've morphed into good friends—training buddies—rather than lovers who have wild sex. She was drawn to Dan by the life he was offering her, a sense of safety amid the chaos, not some burning magnetic passion. Even when they first met, they never really went at it like rabbits. And lately, they're more like . . . What's an animal that has sex every few months wearing a mouth guard out of exhaustion? They're that. Just like Dan's spending habits, Wylie's considered bringing it up, suggesting that she and Dan put some work into it. Add sex to the schedule, even.

But she hadn't. Because the alarming truth was that she didn't *want* more sex with Dan.

Up until meeting Calvin, she'd been fine to go on without this burning magnetic passion, didn't even know if it was a real thing.

Turns out, it is. It most definitely is.

Below her on the bottom bunk, Claudine's teeth chatter, tiny typewriter keys of white enamel pounding out a plea for help.

"Are you okay, Mom?" Wylie's shoulders are shrugged up to her ears, the blanket pulled tight. Her toes are frozen Vienna sausages. It's possible she could see her breath if it wasn't so dark.

"I'm . . . f-f-freezing . . . m-m-my ass off," Claudine answers.

How will they make it like this until morning? Wylie hasn't been this cold since . . . She thinks back. Oh yeah, that time

Kipper made her take another run when she was about twelve. They'd been in Minnesota, training for a season at Buck Hill. Claudine, retired at that point, was at a charity event for Buck Hill's ski team. The temperature plunged as the sun slipped down the back side of the mountain, ready for its own après-ski, casting the snow in a lonely gray pale. At the top of the run, Wylie's entire body seized up with chill, tears fogging her goggles.

"I don't want to," she told Kipper.

"Go ahead, be a quitter," he said, a dare he usually reserved for Claudine.

It was settled; the only way home was down. She willed her legs forward, stilled her worried mind, before pushing off from the start gate for two minutes of whooshing snow. As her skis carved left and right, a cry stuck in the back of her throat. Spindly tree-branch shadows reached out, spooking her.

No way home but down. She repeated it to herself until she *was* down, collapsing in a tangle of skis and poles, the cry bubbling up. Kipper, unfazed by her "dramatics," clapped her on the shoulder. "Now, that'll make a man out of you," he said.

Huh. She hasn't thought about that day in years. It had never happened again. Is that right? Yes, in her memory, that was the last time she skied with her grandfather, although she can't say why that was, exactly. Maybe her whimpering turned him away.

From the bottom bunk: "At l-l-least the d-d-disco music is offffff."

Disco music? She hasn't heard any music. Unspooling her arm from the blanket, Wylie pokes her head over the bed rail to catch a peek at Claudine. The darkness engulfs them both. "I'm worried about you, Mom."

Not just this brutal cold, but also Claudine's knee. She was *definitely* limping on their way back from the dining hall. Even tipsy, Wylie had noticed the way her mom struggled to get into bed.

"I'll b-b-be okay."

That's it. Claudine will be a popsicle before she admits needing help. Gathering her blanket, Wylie steps down the ladder, the chill in the floor instantly seeping into her socks. Feeling along the upper bunk so that she doesn't bang her head, she stoops toward Claudine.

"Move over," Wylie commands.

"What are you doing?"

"Just scooch over." Wylie pats Claudine's body. "We'll warm each other up."

It's a simple notion: huddle together to create warmth. But if Wylie's teeth are chattering too, it's partly from nerves.

Claudine obeys, flashing open her blanket. Wylie slips inside, layering her own blanket on top of them. Underneath, Claudine's body is quivering—she's in worse shape than Wylie realized.

"Turn over. I'll spoon you," Wylie says, the awkwardness of this type of closeness sobering her right up.

Hesitating for only a second, Claudine shifts onto her side to face the wall. Wylie wraps her arm around Claudine, tugging her tight.

"A-Aren't you c-c-cold too?" Claudine asks.

"Yes, but I'm fine. And we're going to be warm in no time."

The sound of Claudine's chattering teeth gradually slows, then stills, replaced by the sounds of breathing. What is Claudine thinking? Is she mad at her about her outburst? Does

Claudine feel as awkward as Wylie does? How long should she stay like this? Would it be rude to retract her arm?

Hoping that some conversation will take the intensity down a notch, and still thinking about her grandfather, Wylie says, "I'm sorry Kipper was so hard on you."

Quiet pools around their lumped forms. Claudine doesn't respond. *She's asleep,* Wylie thinks, her nose pressed against the downward slant of Claudine's bobbed hair. She can smell the Secret deodorant Claudine's worn for years, the Neutrogena soap she uses to wash her face. No frills. No gel-tip fingernails or painted toenails. No liquid foundation smoothed onto her face. Never lipstick. Wylie closes her eyes, trying to envision the contents of her mom's bag—not a typical mom purse, but usually a utilitarian backpack. White Tic Tacs. Boxes of raisins, little baggies of peanuts, for when her sugar was crashing. A black address book, before she carried an iPhone. ChapStick. Slim, cheap boxes of crayons for Wylie that they swiped from diners, only four colors, often broken.

Claudine's small voice is startling when she says, at long last, "He was doing his best, I guess. And it wasn't all bad."

It wasn't all bad. Wylie sees herself in this statement, defending Dan. *You don't understand him. Sometimes it's really good.* It sounds like settling, now that she hears Claudine say it. "Maybe his best wasn't good enough, then," she responds. "Maybe you deserved more kindness from him."

Claudine gives an almost imperceptible nod. "I'm glad you had a good relationship with him. I really am."

Wylie can hear the weighted sadness in Claudine, can almost feel her mom's body sag into the mattress. A protectiveness stirs in her. "I remember that time in Lake Louise.

You went wide around a gate, I think, didn't place. He really gave it to you after the race." She can picture it now, Kipper red-faced, fuming, humiliating Claudine in front of her teammates. Claudine's head bowed as if waiting out a storm.

"You remember that?" Claudine's talking at the wall.

"I'd forgotten it until just now." And then, emboldened, she says something she'd usually keep to herself. "It must've been hard growing up without your mom."

Claudine's mom, Clara, died in a car accident when Claudine was only two years old. They rarely speak of her.

Claudine shifts onto her back, draping her left wrist across her forehead, eyes open, staring at the wooden slats of the top bunk, just visible in the darkness. Wylie watches her profile, the strong nose and weathered face of a warrior. She can tell by the twist of Claudine's mouth that she's working up the nerve to tell her something.

A sudden hope blooms inside Wylie, despite being let down so many times before. Maybe this is it—the mention of Claudine's mom prompting a late-night confession about the identity of Wylie's father. *Fox*. Wylie stays still, as if a sudden movement will keep the words zipped inside her mom.

At long last, Claudine speaks again. "One of the reasons I coached you at Burke was to shield you from Kipper. The school had offered *him* the coaching post. I jumped in and suggested I take it instead."

It wasn't the reveal she'd been hoping for, but it's still a surprise. "What?"

"I know you thought I was just trying to be controlling. But there was more to it."

"Why didn't you just tell me that?"

Claudine's sigh is heavy. "I don't know . . . I guess I didn't want you to have a bad impression of him. You adored each other, for the most part, and I was glad. And—it's just complicated with parents, right?" She gives a little snort.

Wylie's mind flashes again to the cold night skiing.

"He taught you to ski, but that was different from *coaching* you," Claudine continues. "If he became your coach in an official capacity—well, I didn't think that'd be good for you."

"You weren't exactly easy on me either, Mom." Wylie has to say it, but she tries to say it with much more gentleness than she'd used in the dining room. She draws the blanket up to her chin.

"This is true." Claudine's quiet for a moment. "I've started seeing somebody."

"What?" Alarmed, Wylie props up on her elbow, half sitting. "Did something happen with Gib?"

"No! Sorry, I meant seeing a therapist."

"Really?" This revelation is even more shocking than the one about Kipper. She eases back onto the mattress.

"Trying to 'change old patterns.'" Claudine pulls her hands from under the blanket so she can use air quotes, giving a light scoff as if the term is silly, but then falls silent and sticks them back under the covers for warmth. "I know I haven't always been the mom you needed. I was hoping to get it right before we reconnected, you know? But I think it's going to take a long time."

Wylie's eyes well with tears. It's crazy to hear her mom say the words "therapist" and "patterns" with only a little sneer in her voice. This from a woman who thought Wylie could "tough it out"? It's hard to even picture the legendary hard-ass Claudine Potts sitting across from a therapist, baring her soul. Does she cry? Does she punch a pillow? What does she say about Wylie?

The thought of her mom making herself vulnerable in this way is a swaddle for Wylie's aching heart. All this time she's felt so alone in this world, wondering if Claudine had written her off. Turns out, she was trying to set things right.

"Careful, Mom." Wylie cracks a smile. "You're sounding like a millennial."

Claudine elbows her playfully. "Hush."

It's all a lot to process. Mostly, she just wishes Claudine had been honest with her from the get-go about why she came to Burke with her. The thing about secrets: it's the holding of them that's most hurtful, not necessarily the content. As if Wylie couldn't handle it. As if she didn't deserve to know.

But Claudine's chosen to tell her now, and that's something, isn't it? Yes, it's something.

If Claudine's being more forthcoming, maybe Wylie can match her.

She could fess up about Dan's debt. Declare how his betrayal has pushed her from feeling complacent about their relationship to seeing it for what it is: not good for her. How she'd actually like to break up with him, but doesn't know how—or if she'll be all right without him telling her what the heck to do each day. Admit out loud that, deep down, she doesn't want to compete in the contest. Share her confusing excitement about the work promotion, how it bumps up against what she's supposed to want in a career as a successful artist. And ask outright, again, about the engraved lighter. *Fox.* Her mom is evolving—therapy, who would've imagined? Maybe she can understand that Wylie wanting to know the identity of her dad is natural. It doesn't mean her mom wasn't enough.

"Mom," she whispers. "I want to ask you something else."

Claudine doesn't respond. Wylie lifts her head to look at her. Sleeping. *Damn.*

Meanwhile, Wylie's own body is tense, vigilant. Sleep feels farther away than Berlin. She's not exactly warm, but the coldness is bearable. Staring up at the top bunk, Wylie silently says, "Mom," her mouth opening like a puppet with no ventriloquist's voice to support it. She turns her head, just able to make out the rise and fall of Claudine's shoulders.

Understanding—an emotion that she hasn't experienced in a long time—circles once, twice, nestles into the side of her body like a sleeping dog.

THREE DAYS UNTIL THE BODYFITTEST DUO COMPETITION

Barry Haberman's Substack

Good evening, friends and skiers and ski-racing fans from all over the globe. I'm writing to you from my ranch in Big Sky, Montana, with a thrilling announcement. Your pal Barry Haberman has landed on his next writing project, and it's not just big, folks. It's *powder-day* epic.

Now, you all know I like to take my time deciding on my next project, wading through the ghostwriting pitches, deciding whose biography might be calling to me. This go-round, I didn't have to think hard; this is a person who's story I've wanted to tell for ages, and all signs are suggesting now's the moment.

A few clues: She was, and still is, elusive, known for dodging reporters and refusing media interviews, sometimes brusquely. She was nicknamed the Stone-Cold Killer for her eerie, almost trancelike demeanor in the start house before races. In recent years, she's traded her skis for a stationary bike, leading a pack of thousands of virtual riders, all while chirping her famous catchphrase: #dontthinkjustdo.

Points for those of you who guessed Olympian and World Cup winner Claudine Potts.

That's right, I'm penning the biography for the GOAT in women's alpine skiing long before Lindsey Vonn and Mikaela Shiffrin took the title. Aloof and private, there's still so much we don't know about the legend that is Claudine Potts, daughter of Olympian Kipper Potts.

And I'm going to finally spill all the beans. But first I've got to find those beans.

In the meantime, tell me in the comments what you'd like me to suss out about the Stone-Cold Killer. I, for one, have a lot of unanswered questions.

To support my newsletter, donate here. ◐

SKIDADDLE45: Why did Claudine switch her ski-equipment sponsor ahead of Salt Lake?

BARRY: The reason for the jump ($$) has already been widely reported on, but I do wonder if Claudine partly blames the skis for her injury. Will report back.

KENZIE10: Who was Claudine's biggest rival?

BARRY: Who wasn't her rival?? Jokes aside, I'd say Germany's Katja Seizinger. And possibly her old friend Zosel Marie Schwarz. Plus, she and Picabo Street were always vying for alpha status on the team.

PEGGYROGERS: Is it really true that former Swiss ski coach Franz Blasi fathered Claudine's child?

BARRY: Peggy, that's one of the most guarded secrets in ski racing.

GEOFFBETHOS: I'm curious about that too. Isn't it rumored that after Blasi was named FIS's interim race director of women's technical events in 1995, he gave her preferential treatment?

BARRY: That's a big accusation, GeoffBethos.

GEOFFBETHOS: I'm just repeating what I've heard. 1995 was Claudine's best World Cup. She won the overall title.

BARRY: All will be revealed in my book.

[LOAD more comments]

17

Claudine

AS CLAUDINE CARRIES A BANANA AND A MUG OF coffee back to the table to join Wylie for breakfast, the overhead lights of the dining hall flick on, electricity surging into the hostel. All the guests cheer and clap, someone yelling, "We're saved." She watches Wylie pull out a power cord from her bag, plugging her phone into a nearby outlet.

It chimes over and over again with notifications. Either Wylie's got a lot of friends back home or that's one worried Dan. Claudine pretends not to notice as Wylie glances at—and then ignores—the messages, returning to the table.

Claudine sits. "Well, this is a good sign, right? Maybe we'll get out of here sooner than they thought."

"You think? But they've still got to clear the tracks."

"True," she concedes.

Still, nothing's going to damper Claudine's mood. She just slept seven hours next to her sweet girl, arms touching—like the lean she envied between Fränzi and Zosel. If last night was nourishment, she could live on it all week.

They'd been so affectionate with each other when Wylie was a little girl. Back scratches and snuggles and comparing hand sizes, the easy, trusting way Wylie puddled over her in a chair, even as she grew taller than her. Claudine lived vigilant of the last moment her daughter would sit on her lap, hold her hand crossing a street, allow a stroke of her beautiful cheek, as if she could catch this fleeting moment like a firefly in a Ball jar and store it on a high shelf. But the last times came and went with little fanfare, no markers. That easy affection was simply gone, never to be reclaimed.

Now they're sitting together at breakfast, and maybe Claudine's getting ahead of herself, but she can't help imagining more breakfasts to come, more hanging out, taking trips, having adventures. It's so exciting. And so is the change she can see in herself. Yesterday she had offered Wylie an apology without an asterisk. She'd opened up a little too on the Kipper front. And she didn't lash out at Wylie in response to her criticisms. Soupy would be proud.

Now she just needs to fulfill her mission and then get them out of Zermatt. She's taken on harder challenges and triumphed, hasn't she?

There's a presence next to Claudine's left. She turns and jumps in her chair, a hand flying to her heart. It's Erin, her hair leprechaun-pant green. "Good lord, what is with the hair dye?" Claudine blurts. Bibbidi's too is freshly dyed a brighter blue.

"It doesn't look good?" Erin runs a hand over her cropped head, pouting at Bibbidi. "I told you it didn't look good."

"It looks good!" Bibbidi assures her. "*Doesn't* it look good?"

Her eyes widen as she stresses the question in Claudine's direction.

Claudine nods. "Uh. Yeah. It looks good."

"It doesn't!" Erin whimpers.

"No, no, it does," Claudine says.

"Really good," Wylie echoes.

"Thanks, guys," Erin says, toeing the floor in an aw-shucks-but-go-on manner.

Wylie gestures to the empty seats at their table. "Care to join us?"

Claudine bristles. It would've been nice to be just the two of them, but that's okay. She can deal. *See, Soupy? I'm going with the flow.*

A few minutes later, Erin and Bibbidi return with coffees and plates of strudel.

"Above and beyond that Léa managed to procure this strudel this morning," Bibbidi crows. "Can't beat the hospitality of a hostel!"

Is that true?

Bibbidi raises an eyebrow at Wylie and says, "You were into your cups last night. How are you feeling this morning? Hydrating?"

Step off is Claudine's first thought.

Although has Wylie had more than coffee this morning?

Erin plunks a forearm onto the table, leaning toward Claudine. "Okay, be honest. Did you ever bite your gold medals to see if they were real gold?"

A laugh flies out of Claudine. It's really hard to take Erin seriously with her Mountain-Dew-bottle-green hair. "Actually, they're mostly made of silver, with just a small amount of real gold."

"What? Whoa. Mind blown," Erin says, an exploding hand gesture next to her head.

"Mom, didn't I chew on the ribbon of your Olympic medal that one year? When I was teething?"

"Oh gosh, that was in Lillehammer. And no, it was the strap of my glove. I was up all night with you. I couldn't figure out why you were so fussy. Turns out you had a tooth coming in."

"And she still went on to win a gold medal in the super-G the next day," Wylie says. Claudine clocks the pride in her daughter's voice. Oh, sweet goodness, she loves that sound.

"Wait," Erin says, her jaw dropping. "You were up most of the night with a teething toddler, and then, like no big deal, went out and won Olympic gold the *next* day?"

Claudine opens and closes the hand around her coffee mug. "It was harder than it sounds."

"Find me a man who could've done that," Bibbidi says. "Or, for that matter, any other woman."

Okay, well, that's a generous thing to say. Claudine nods to Bibbidi.

"Did you like ski racing?" Erin asks.

Did she like ski racing? Such a simple question, with such a complex answer. Claudine eyes Wylie nervously as she says, "I craved the speed. It's incredible that humans can go that fast." Then, trying to read Wylie's face, she adds, "Terrifying too, don't get me wrong."

"I bet it was hard to retire. To give it all up. I've always wondered how professional athletes do that. One day you're an Olympian, the next day you're chopped liver." Erin seems to notice Claudine's frown, because she says, "Oh, excuse me, *you're* not chopped liver. But you get what I mean."

"I do," Claudine says. Not many people recognize this trade-off, this plight.

"I served in the army for ten years, deployed to the Gulf War, and when I got out, man, I had a heck of a time figuring out what to do next. Missed my friends. Missed the routine. Even missed the danger, if you can believe it."

"I can believe it. You know, my grandfather served. World War Two, in the Tenth Mountain Division. A soldier on skis."

"I didn't know there was such a thing," Bibbidi interjects.

"Oh yes," Claudine says. She can see her grandfather, Clifton Potts, showing her a picture of him and his unit, everyone outfitted in white camouflage suits that looked about as warm as children's slickers. "They climbed up mountains with their skis strapped to their backs more than they skied down them," she says.

"I'll be," Erin says.

"Mom, isn't it true that a lot of the Tenth Mountain guys came home from the war and started some of the ski resorts that are famous today?"

"Good memory, Wy. It is true. Your great-grandfather helped a guy named Pete Seibert start Vail."

"Whoa," Erin exclaims.

"And that's where Kipper"—Claudine puts a hand to her chest—"my father, learned to ski. Where he met my mother, who died in a car accident when I was young."

"Oh, I'm so sorry," Bibbidi says, just as Erin shakes her head and adds, "Geesh, that's tough luck."

"Thank you," Claudine says. It was so long ago, and she was so little that she rarely registers the loss anymore. Soupy had still nose-dived on that one, seeming to think growing up motherless, raised only by a relentlessly driving father who had the singular goal of making her a skiing legend, may have affected the way Claudine in turn raised her own daughter.

She might be onto something.

"Mom, why did Kipper leave Vail, move you to Mount Hood?"

At this, she does smile large. "By the midseventies, the hippies were invading Vail. And Kipper hated hippies."

They all laugh. Erin excuses herself to go fetch another slice of strudel. Bibbidi and Wylie fall into chatting about the other hostels Bibbidi's visited on her travels. Claudine savors the calm, normal, leisurely morning, finding she doesn't want to rush through breakfast in under two minutes. She doesn't want to rush it at all.

When Erin returns to the table, she's still brimming with questions, as if she'll never in her life have another chance to grill an Olympian.

"So where *did* you land, after you retired?" Erin asks as she pulls out her chair, plops down, and immediately begins scarfing her strudel.

At this, Claudine's chuckle is sad. She draws her finger around the lip of her mug. "Sixteen years later, I think I'm still figuring that out."

"She thought she'd be coaching me, right, Mom?" Wylie asks, in a surprisingly unsardonic tone. Claudine jerks her head up to study her daughter for signs of irritation, unsure if this is safe territory.

"Well . . ." Claudine says. Her instinct is to tread carefully. This might not end well.

"It's okay," Wylie says, as if it's all water under the bridge. "It's the truth."

"Plans change! It happens." She brightens her voice,

steering the conversation in a different direction. "Hey, fun fact: The first woman to summit the Matterhorn did it wearing a flannel skirt."

Bibbidi puts a palm to her face, tilting her head as she says, "That *is* interesting." It's unclear whether Bibbidi actually thinks this, or if she's just throwing Claudine a bone here. Either way, she appreciates it.

Erin, however, isn't digging the mountaineering trivia. She tucks a meaty fist under her chin. "What else don't we commoners know about the world of skiing? About the Olympics? Give us all the dirt."

"Oh . . . I don't know." Claudine glances at the door. She should go find out how soon the town will lift the shelter-in-place order so she can scurry to Zosel's. She needs to get that done, so they can leave as soon as they possibly can.

"Yeah, Mom, c'mon. Tell me something even *I* don't know!" Wylie's face is excited, hopeful, and, most of all, relaxed. It's nice to see that.

Maybe it's because Claudine's basking in Wylie's full attention. Or that she wants to show off a little in front of Bibbidi, a flex of her mama-bear muscle. Or that Erin seems genuinely interested, and Claudine hasn't held court like this in ages, talked about her past hardly at all. Or maybe she decides to play along because she's always pressed right up to the edge of reckless, still craves that speed, that danger, that sense of playing with fire.

She drums dramatically on her chin, and then says, "While everyone at home watching the Olympics thinks its sixteen straight days of family-friendly programming, guess what?"

Erin, riveted, pauses midbite of strudel and says, "What?"

They all lean forward, waiting for Claudine's big reveal.

Claudine leans forward too and whispers, "It's a sex fest." She shrugs, a mischievous twinkle in her eye.

"Mom!" Wylie gasps.

Claudine nods. "It's true. Think about it. Five thousand or so superfit athletes, bursting with adrenaline, nursing bruised egos or celebrating big victories, all housed in one place. Things get a little out of hand. So much so that the Olympic Village has something of a reputation."

"Mind blown"—Erin circles her head—*"again."*

Delighting in their shocked reactions, Claudine can't stop herself. "They even ship in condoms."

"The debauchery!" Bibbidi exclaims. "It sounds positively Roman."

They all cackle, and it feels so good to laugh with a group of people. Claudine honestly hasn't done that since—well, she's not even sure. Possibly years.

"And what about you, Mom?" Wylie waggles her eyebrows. "Did you ever have an Olympic hookup?"

"Ooooooh," Erin says, twinkling her fingers.

Claudine, sipping her coffee, nearly coughs it in Wylie's face.

Erin, in playful, teasing singsong, says, "She's getting all red. Must be true."

Claudine shakes her head no to deny it as she continues coughing, pounding on her chest with her fist.

"You okay?" Wylie asks, pushing a glass of water in front of her.

She nods yes as she tries to regain her composure.

Finally, she clears her throat, her voice still froggy, and says, "I was too focused to think about things like that."

This is a lie. When she left her first Olympics in 1992 as

a twenty-two-year-old star—having won not just one gold medal, but two—she also left pregnant with Wylie.

A pregnancy she didn't discover for three months. With all the hoopla that swept her up after the Olympics, Claudine was tracking her cycle as closely as she'd track the drama of a daytime soap. As in, she never watched it.

It's a pregnancy that she's always attributed to "just some ski bum."

She remembers sitting in the bathroom at the ski lodge of Mount Hood, her home mountain, holding the stick of a pregnancy test, staring out the window at the ski run that now bore her name. Then she shoved the pregnancy test stick deep into her glove, the glove deep into her bag, knowing that Kipper would never forgive her—and that she would never forgive herself—unless this baby became an asset. Not a distraction. Not a mistake. But a third-generation winner. Barely the size of a plum, and already Claudine had big plans for her.

How naive she was about parenthood back then. Not that she's any great expert now.

Wylie's phone chimes four times. She glances at it, still plugged into the wall, then sighs. "I should probably check in with Dan. He says he can't sleep until he hears from me."

With Wylie away from the table, Claudine gathers her wits. Playing with fire is one thing, but Claudine almost just burned everything to the ground. Why? She chides herself for getting caught up in the moment, for trying to show off. No more talk about the Olympics or ski racing or sexual trysts. Good grief.

"Mom." Wylie's voice slices the air.

Claudine looks up to see Wylie holding her phone, staring at her with an odd expression, confusion mixed with anger.

Every muscle in Claudine's body tenses. "What's up?" she asks, trying to keep her voice calm.

"Franz Blasi is my dad?"

Claudine goes as still as a hunted rabbit. "What?"

"Dan just sent me a link to a post. People are saying Franz Blasi is my *dad*." Her voice amplifies, turning heads in the dining hall. Bibbidi and Erin have the decency to look away, but they're not fooling anyone.

"That's ludicrous." Heat emanates from Claudine's body, creeps up her neck. "Wylie, I don't know why people are saying that, but it's simply not true."

Wylie speeds toward her, violently pulling the charger out of the wall as she walks. "It's all over Twitter, Mom! Trending." She's trembling with anger as she thrusts the phone at Claudine, who looks at the screen in her hands.

Claudine feels every single eye in the dining room. Is this happening? She's always shut down this conversation, the swift chop of her wrist like a barrier, dealing with it the same way Kipper would have. Eventually Wylie stopped asking, and Claudine thought matters were settled, that her daughter had accepted the story she'd given: Her dad was a ski bum who opted out of parenthood. And it was just the two of them against the world.

Claudine quickly scans the Substack, pieces falling into place. "Barry Haberman," she growls. "He's just trying to drum up an audience for his stupid book. I swear it's not true."

Wylie slams her fist down onto the table. "If it's not Franz Blasi, then who is it?"

Claudine is speechless. Just twenty-four hours in this hostel and Wylie's transformed into a confrontation machine. No more cold shoulder, no more loaded silent treatment.

Last night she'd taken some pleasure in the change, but now it's overwhelming. And just plain humiliating. Does Wylie really expect her to answer?

Erin leans over to Bibbidi, whispering, "Who's Franz Blasi?" Bibbidi shushes her.

All around them, guests murmur, hiding their phones in their laps to discreetly check Twitter. Not getting an answer, Erin pecks away at her own phone.

Claudine closes her eyes, tilting her chin up. She fights the urge to jam her fingers into her ears, like a kid who refuses to hear what's being said.

"Mom? Hello? Did you hear me?" Wylie's voice loses some of its angry edge, shifting into a resigned pleading, which is almost worse. "Can you just finally tell me? Who is my dad?"

"Wylie." Claudine lulls her head back and forth. "Let the past stay in the past. It's better that way, trust me."

This statement elicits whispered responses around the room. Apparently, some in her audience disagree. And Wylie is among them. "I'm an adult now," she says. "I have a right to know."

Why does motherhood have to be so impossible? She's tried her best, worked so hard to make a good life for Wylie while she was skiing, tried to fix herself with Soupy, jumped at the chance to make things right with this trip. Suddenly the weight of all her failures feels crushingly heavy, and she realizes: She'll never get it right. She'll never make it right. She'll never be a good enough mom in Wylie's eyes. Daughters deliver singular and specific blows, kissing you on one cheek only to slap the other, leaving your head spinning, a tangle of contradictions that's exhausting to parse out.

And in this moment, Claudine's exhaustion turns to

frustration turns to anger, a Sterno canister on high, ready to set the entire hostel aflame. Wylie seems to sense this change in her, and she takes a step back.

"Actually," Claudine says, her voice stern and unyielding. "I have a right to my privacy. And my right trumps your right. End of story!"

Erin tips her phone toward Bibbidi. "He was the old Swiss ski coach. Looks like he's in his eighties now."

Claudine snaps at Erin. "Could you just not right now?"

Erin bows her head, puts her phone on her lap, goes mute.

"*Your right trumps* . . . Do you hear yourself, Mom?" Wylie stamps her foot, paces away and returns. "What if I want to contact my dad? What if I want to have a relationship with him? Even if he is old." She lifts a finger and points it at Claudine. "You know what I think? I think you're keeping him from me all these years because you can't bear the thought of me having another parent. Becoming closer to him than I am to you. Finding out he's nicer to me than you've ever been."

"Wylie," Claudine growls through clenched teeth. "I am warning you to drop this now."

Bibbidi says, "Maybe you two should take a collective—"

"Stay out of this, Bibbidi," Claudine says, suddenly aware that, with the heat back on in the hostel and the fire roaring, she's absolutely roasting. "God, it's hot in here!" She stands up, unzipping her fleece.

She catches Wylie glance at Bibbidi, who gives her daughter a sympathetic smile—what is that, some sort of unspoken code? Because then Wylie pivots the argument into another realm altogether, saying, "I'm not going to let you walk all over me anymore."

Claudine is furiously stripping off layers of clothing,

slamming each item to the table, wrenching her wrists free from a clinging thermal top. "Oh, grow up. Somehow, you've concocted this story that I forced you to ski. Forced you to compete. You've conveniently forgotten that you *loved* skiing. Begged me to race for years!"

"I loved having an anxiety attack in the bathroom with you banging on the door and yelling for everyone to hear that I better get my ass on the chairlift?"

"You know, I'm sorry I didn't help you the way I should have, but I was trying. You didn't try at all to help yourself!"

Wylie balls her fists at her sides, taller than her mom, formidable in her stature. For the first time, Claudine realizes her daughter has the upper hand physically. "Or maybe I was anxious because I was scared of you."

Claudine charges past her, forcing Wylie to step back so they don't slam into each other, then she whirls around, the words flying out of her. "Yeah, well, you certainly weren't scared of me when you announced your retirement and we all had to change plans on a dime based on some whim!"

"My art is not a *whim*. It's what I like. What I've liked since I was a kid, if you'd bothered to notice. Not all of us care about being champions. Some of us think being a legend is stupid."

"You've made that perfectly clear. My accomplishments are stupid to you."

Every guest is staring at them, mouths open. You could hear a pin drop, a snowflake land.

Koa, as per usual, enters the dining room with his hands in his pockets, a mistimed jaunty whistle on his lips. "Hiya, everyone. I have an announcement." All heads swivel to Koa, but he frowns, seeming to feel the tension in the room—how could he not?—and he glances from Claudine to Wylie, the only two people standing, looking like two lionesses about to spring at each other. "Everything okay in here?"

"Oh, just spit it out, Koa," Claudine says, exasperated.

"Okaaaay," he says, clearly confused. He shifts uncomfortably. "So, uh, yeah. It's like I thought, I'm afraid. The avalanche socked in the train tunnel. They have to dig 'er out, but it's still not safe for anyone to work there yet. So we're here for five more days."

"*Shit*," Claudine spits, while Wylie puts a hand to the tabletop to steady herself. Moans and groans spring up from around the room.

"The good news," Koa says, speaking above the din, "is that we're now free to leave the hostel to go, like, shop and stuff."

"None of us want to 'shop and stuff,'" Claudine says. "All we want is to get out of this hellhole." She really means this hellish situation that she's created, but she can't stop herself.

Koa's shocked. "I wouldn't call this a hellhole. Zermatt is a luxury tourist destination."

"That Astroturf is luxury? The communal showers?"

"Sorry," he says quietly, lowering his head. Then he adds, his voice subdued, "There are a few helicopters flying tourists out of Zermatt."

Hope blasts in Claudine's chest like gallons of sprayed snow from a snowmaking machine. If she can get her and Wylie on one of those helicopters, she'll make good on her promise to get them to Berlin. And then maybe Wylie won't hate her so much.

"Koa," she says, before she turns to leave. "Next time, lead with that."

"It's based on priority, though," he calls after her.

Oh, please. He has no idea who he's dealing with. She,

Claudine Potts, Olympic champion, all-time legend, a GOAT, is priority *nummer eins*. She's never been one to seek special favors for skiing, but if it'll get her and Wylie a spot on a heli-copter—she'll take every last drop of it.

18

Claudine

WITH THE SHELTER-IN-PLACE ORDER LIFTED, THE mood outside is celebratory, and Claudine barrels down the middle of the street like a bowling ball, intent on breaking up the deliriously high-spirited party.

Twenty-four hours stuck indoors—plus missed flights and ruined ski trips and botched itineraries—have people clamoring for all the unnecessary and impractical things they wouldn't have bought otherwise: designer clutch bags; Gucci sunglasses; shiny, wrapped Lindt chocolates, purchased in bulk and with near hysteria, as if people believe the Zermatt store is the only retailer in the entire world.

Tourists stream out of the Migros *Supermarkt*, carrying paper bags of emergency provisions that will probably spoil when they opt to dine out. She cringes at the mindless spending.

The pain in her left knee ratchets up her agitation, and she almost craves an accidental bump from a passing stranger just so she can keep up her tirade, maybe spill a coffee on a stark-white puffer jacket purchased just that morning.

She scans for Zosel's lemon-yellow cable-knit hat with a pom-pom as she searches for the tourist office, following the lowercase blue *i* signs along the narrow Matter Vispa. The Swiss are notoriously good at labeling things. At a quaint bridge, tourists take turns stepping up to the railing to snap pictures of the Matterhorn. *"C'est magnifique,"* she hears a Frenchwoman say. And fine it is, though Claudine can't wait to be lifting off and saying au revoir to its magnificence.

The fight with Wylie eats at her, as does the thing she cannot say: *You do deserve to know your father. I actually agree with you. But you can never meet him.*

That's maybe the worst part of this entire situation.

Claudine slows her pace, noticing the line that's formed outside of the McDonald's on Bahnhofstrasse. Never has the fast-food chain appeared quainter, with its wood-trimmed windows and arched doorway reminiscent of a medieval tavern. What is everyone clamoring for? Happy Meals?

It's then she catches sight of the tourist office a good one hundred feet down the street.

She huffs out a puff of visible air in the cold morning chill, claiming her spot in line. Slowly, they inch along. Claudine checks the news headlines on her phone. "Twelve Thousand Tourists Could Be Stranded in Zermatt Until Sunday, Experts Predict." The competition in Berlin is over by Saturday.

Then she toggles to Twitter, sees the trending hashtag: #Blasibabydaddy.

Oh god. Does Barry have any idea of the shitstorm he's causing her? Or maybe that's the point. It's punishment for not collaborating with him.

Forty-five minutes later, her toes frozen, her left knee swollen, it's finally her turn to sign up for a lift out of here.

"Next," beckons a man wearing bright-red ski pants, a red parka with the distinctive white Swiss cross on the breast, and a name tag that says Jens. His protruding belly, straining the parka's zipper, suggests he'd get winded on a leisurely walk, but Claudine knows he probably skies Zermatt's slopes gracefully. Rather than a clipboard, he's holding a tablet, organizing the rides electronically. At his feet pants a giant Saint Bernard with a miniature barrel hanging from its neck stamped with the same Swiss cross. A glob of slobber clings to its jowls. Claudine retracts her hand instead of petting it.

"Hi, Jens. I'd like to sign up for a helicopter ride for this afternoon."

Without looking up from his tablet, Jens says, "And you vould like a snack mix on this flight?" The Swiss tend to pronounce their *w*'s with *v* sounds, but Jens's accent is particularly strong, almost as if he's putting it on: "*vould*."

She lolls her head from side to side, weighing the offer. "Sure."

"And a view of the Matterhorn."

"Well, I mean, if it's on the way."

"An in-flight massage, perhaps?"

Claudine folds her lips inward. "You're pulling my leg."

He peers at her over his glasses. "Yes."

She cringes, her voice going higher. "Can I still get on a helicopter?"

With his middle finger, he scrolls the tablet, angling it so that Claudine can't see the screen. "You vill be passenger number four thousand five hundred eighty-six."

"What does that mean, exactly?"

"Ve are able to evacuate roughly five hundred people per day."

Claudine pulls at her collar. "That's it?!"

"That's if the veather is good. If the veather is not good, zero people per day."

"So that means I can't fly out for . . ." She struggles to do the mental math.

"Ten days."

"The train tracks will be cleared by then!"

"Yes."

Claudine forces herself to inhale. Try again. "I have to get out of here sooner than that."

Jens gives a rueful chuckle. "You and everyone else."

"I'm desperate."

"Are you vith child?" He swoops his hand over his belly.

"Hardly."

"Are you unvell?"

She lifts up both hands. "Healthy."

"Okay. You do not qualify for priority status."

Claudine steps closer, talking in a hushed tone. Jens tilts his ear to hear her. "I'm Claudine Potts. The skier. The . . . Um . . . Well . . . I won a few gold medals?" And then, because Europeans revere the World Cup over the Olympics, she says, "And Crystal Globes." She smiles awkwardly, slightly sickened by the self-promotion.

"Ohhhhhh," Jens exclaims, his head launching backward, his mouth gaping open. The dog stirs, pressing to sit up, the slobber hovering like an icicle. "The champion ski racer! I thought I recognized you. These days, you're—" and then he mimics riding a bike with his arms.

"Oh, well, yes, that too."

Jens jerks his body, as if he's riding hills, jumping up and down from the bike saddle. "Like zhis?"

Claudine winces. "Sort of."

He stops abruptly. "I don't care for zhis. Vhy not skiing instead?" He begins to tally ski-related professions on his fingers. "Verk at a ski lodge. Verk as an instructor. Verk as a coach. Verk as a—"

She halts him with an outstretched palm, holding herself back from snapping that she's not looking for career advice. "I'll think about that. So where does this put me, on the list?"

"Okay, for the Stone-Cold Killer, I'll make an exception. Come back in one hour with your bag and passport."

"You're not pulling my leg again?"

"On this I do not joke." He yells this last part over the sound of an Air Zermatt helicopter coming in for a landing in a field nearby, momentarily pausing the rest of their conversation until the helicopter is on the ground, cutting its engine. She watches, squinting, as five people clamber out, retrieving luggage.

She points. "What's with those people? I thought everyone's trying to leave."

Jens glances over his shoulder. "Not everyone. Some tourists have reservations they want to keep. Or they have urgent business here. So we bring them—at their own risk."

Urgent business. Like Barry's urgent business? Claudine shields her eyes with a hand, trying to make out if Barry's in the bunch. He's not there, and she's being silly. He's not so desperate that he'd ask to be airlifted into an emergency zone. She shifts her attention back to Jens.

"Can I bring my daughter?"

Jens looks disappointed by the question. "That would not be possible."

"*One* extra seat—?"

"You understand I am allowing you to cut in front of four thousand five hundred eighty-five people." He frowns at the line behind her. "Now, you vill be back in one hour's time or no?"

It's not a real decision: Claudine would never leave Wylie. She's back at square one, no plan to get them out of Zermatt with a heroic rescue. How Claudine wishes *she* could just run away—away from the looming conversation with Zosel, from Wylie's questions, from the pain that comes from messing up motherhood again, and again, and again. Home to Gib and their safe little cocoon, the sound of him bustling around the kitchen.

"I'm sorry. I can't leave without her," she mutters to Jens.

"Suit yourself." He leans beyond her, beckoning the next person.

She shuffles to the side. Soupy would suggest she find the silver lining.

Shopping and stuff, she thinks sarcastically. Soupy would tilt her head, waiting for a real answer. Fine. Okay, silver lining. Well, at least the avalanche is blocking Barry from getting here, giving her more time to land on the perfect thing to say to Zosel.

19

Wylie

AS THE CROWD THINS OUT OF THE DINING ROOM, Bibbidi stays behind with Wylie, sitting next to her, patting her arm.

"How about a walk?" Bibbidi suggests. "A little fresh air might do you some good."

"I'm not sure I'm up for it."

Wylie used to have life as pinned down as a pressed flower, every moment of her days accounted for, every bite of food calculated, all the scaffolding holding her in place so she didn't . . . well, lose control. Ski off-piste. Now all her scaffolding has buckled, and she's had more panic attacks in the last few days than she's had in a long time. And more public outbursts than she's had, ever.

Because it's all just too much. Franz Blasi. The fight with her mom. Five more days here. No BodyFittest Duo. The prospect of telling Dan. Aileen waiting for an answer.

She puts her head in her hands.

"I'm sorry you're missing your contest in Berlin," Bibbidi says.

Koa, clearing away the breakfast bar, overhears. "It's not over for you yet, Wylie. Maybe your mum can get you two on one of those helicopter rides."

Wylie lifts her head up. "Do you think?" She wouldn't blame Claudine for hightailing it back to Oregon, if given the chance.

He pries a spoon from the honey jar. "Don't get your hopes up too high; the list is probably thousands of people deep by now. But your mum's achieved the impossible before."

"True." She gives a sad smile.

"I did hear they've cleared the snow from the town ice rink," he offers. "Conditions are perfect out there. Blue ski, little wind."

"That sounds like a delightful idea," Bibbidi says, clapping her hands. "And what an amazing concierge you are."

Koa blushes, holding a tub of dirty dishes. "Aw, thanks, Bib."

Bibbidi squeezes Wylie's arm. "What do you say?"

Wylie blows out a raspberry. "I don't know. I need to break the news to Dan. And I'm already so worn out from—" She gestures to the space, indicating the tiff. "I think I went a little overboard with the whole don't-let-anybody-trample-on-me thing."

"You were . . . Hmm, how to put this delicately . . ."

"Harsh?"

Bibbidi holds up two fingers to indicate "just a little."

Wylie winces. "Yeah. I'm either giving her the silent treatment or ambushing her in public. I can't seem to find a happy medium."

"Those happy mediums are hard to find, especially if you're unpracticed."

"She must be so mad at me. She's such a private person."

"She can't be too mad at you if she's waiting for what's probably hours in a helicopter line."

"That is nice, isn't it?" The morning, before their blowup, had been nice. Last night too. But their foundation as mom and daughter is so weak, so unstable, that the knocks shake them hard. And a big blow, like the Franz Blasi news—well, it feels like it could crumble their foundation to the ground.

"Very nice," Bibbidi concurs.

"I do deserve to know who my dad is, though, don't I?"

Bibbidi doesn't answer for a long moment, then says, "I can certainly understand why you'd want to know. And I can also see that your mom seems to have some pretty strong reasons for keeping that information to herself. Does she owe you it? I'm not really sure, to be honest. But judging from watching you both these past few days, I can say that I don't think your mom wants to hurt you on purpose."

Wylie bites her lip. "Yeah. But it still hurts."

"And you're entitled to that. Maybe telling you is something that will also hurt her?"

"I've never thought of it that way."

"It's impossible to be in anyone else's head."

"I just wish—oh, I don't know. I wish a lot of things, I guess. I wish it was different."

"Don't we all, my dear. Don't we all. Now—" She pats Wylie's knee. "How about you give this Dan a call, I'll see who I can rally for skating, and you can meet us at the rink?"

"Yeah, okay." Wylie stands up. "I'll see you soon."

But she doesn't immediately follow Bibbidi out. Alone,

Wylie stalls, staring out the window. After the fight with her mom and the Franz Blasi bombshell, she should be racing to seek solace in Dan. She's not. So she lingers, watching a shifting slant of sunlight over a square of snow as the sun rises higher.

It's only the prospect of fresh air at the ice rink that finally gets her moving.

Back in her room, Dan answers Wylie's FaceTime call on the first ring, the screen close to his face. He's scruffy and unshaven, his black hair messy, as if, in Wylie's absence, he's been worrying it with his fingers. It gives him a craven look. "What the F, Wy. I've called you nonstop. I've been up all night."

"Hi! Oh, really?" She frowns like she's inspecting her phone for a lose screw.

"What's going on there? You're not really stranded, are you?"

"Well . . . I mean." Twenty seconds into this phone call and Wylie's already on her heels. *No,* she tells herself. *You can do this. You just stood up to Mom. You're New Wylie.*

"The contest is in three days!"

"Yeah, I know. About that—"

Dan closes his eyes and shakes his head in a slow gesture of exasperation. "Don't do this to me, Wy. Don't tell me you're stuck. I have a lot riding on this. *We* have a lot riding on this. And I've been so depressed here without you, with my foot stuck in this boot, nothing to do but sit and think and not *move.* Having to stay with my parents while you're gone. Feeling weak and aimless." She's stirred by the vulnerability in his voice, that he's been depressed without her. But then his eyelids flash open, the anger in his voice mounting. "So do not tell me your little Swiss field trip jeopardized our entire future."

Internally, she staggers backward, all her intentions to be strong and unbending instantly collapsing. She can't even mount the obvious retort that *he's* to blame for jeopardizing their future. Instead, she finds herself grappling to get back on firm ground, to not be in trouble, slipping right into the shoes of Old Wylie. "No, I . . . I didn't. I was going to say that we *are* gonna make it." The lie shuttles past her lips.

"That's not what the headlines are reporting."

"Yeah, but there are helicopters."

"And you're going to get on one?"

She nods.

Dan presses the heels of his hands to his eyes and springs them away. Tears have formed, and now he shouts animatedly, pointing a finger. "That's my girl, Wylie! That's my girl! Of course you figured out a way. You're a warrior. You have made me the happiest man. I could just kiss you." He brings the phone close to his mouth. She winces. *"Muah."* He pulls back, grinning. "By the way, crazy about your dad. You seeing it on Twitter?" Now he's munching on something, licking salt off his fingers. Is he eating potato chips, a category of food decidedly not on their list? And at this hour? "Do you think it's the Swiss coach, babe?"

"I'm not sure." Could her dad really be Franz? Wylie knows Franz Blasi. Has met Franz Blasi. Is Claudine lying? "My mom says no." She doesn't want to talk about it with Dan, she realizes, and not just because he's still munching away. As if this tender topic is just casual gossip. His gorgeous face shows no sign of sympathy for what this new development might feel like for her. *I don't miss him,* she thinks. She's not even drawn to his ripped arms, his pecs bulging from his tight T-shirt. Dan may look like the cover of a romance novel, but he doesn't stir much yearning inside her. *I don't miss him at all.*

But he doesn't seem to notice. "By the way, FaceTime me when you work out later. I'll count your reps. I've got nothing else to do."

"I'm going to go"—she almost mentions ice-skating, but thinks better of it—"check in again on the helicopter."

"That's my girl. And, Wy . . ."

"Yeah."

"Don't *you* go falling in love with any ski bums while you're there."

Wylie's cheeks betray her; she blushes, but Dan doesn't notice.

Calvin. His kind eyes and buttery voice, his body—no sharp angles, all soft slopes, bunny hills—and his curiosity about her, about the world. Looking at Dan on the tiny screen of her phone, she feels a hard wave of guilt. "I won't," she says.

More than the helicopter, more than the gym, this strikes her as the biggest lie of all. She hears Claudine say, "You're out over your skis, Wy."

Maybe she is, tumbling forward, unable to right herself, cruising for a crash.

20

Wylie

WYLIE ZOOMS HER SKATES IN AND OUT IN AN HOUR-glass formation, pulling off an abrupt hockey stop, shifting her hips and spraying ice with her blades.

Calvin, too, isn't half bad, although he periodically steadies himself on Wylie's arm. In response, her skin crackles with electricity. She's grateful he wasn't at breakfast this morning to witness her *second* fight with Claudine.

Nearby, Bibbidi and Erin are both draped over the backs of chairs that they're pushing across the ice, appearing to demonstrate the self-Heimlich maneuver rather than learning to ice-skate.

"Look up," Wylie shouts, as they careen their chairs into each other, bumper car–style. The only other skaters using chairs are little children, and they certainly aren't Swiss. The Swiss, it seems, are born experts on the snow and ice.

And the Swiss—at least any local Zermatters—are steering

clear of the packed outdoor ice rink today. Except for Léa, who, it turns out, was a junior figure skater. She's holding court in the middle of the rink, performing waltz jumps, the headband of her earmuffs nestled in front of her top bun. Calvin and Wylie pause to admire her graceful lines.

"Wow. Léa's incredible," Calvin says, casting a hand over his eyes to block the sun.

"You know, I admire that she's still skating just for fun after competing for so many years when she was younger. I could never do that."

"No? Well, what do you do just for fun?"

Wylie cocks her head. "I've never done anything just for fun. I mean, art? At first, when I was a kid, it was just for fun." Wylie thinks about how good it felt to sit and work on her collage of the Matterhorn in front of the window. How long it's been since she's created art as a hobby.

"But not now?" Calvin asks.

"I mean, now there's just this pressure to be a successful artist. To do something with it, beyond just enjoying it. In my family, we achieve. As you might have noticed." Suddenly she loses her balance—the first time since she stepped onto the ice—and Calvin reaches out for her arm, steadying her.

"I got you," he says, and she has to admit that she loves hearing that.

Behind Léa, the Matterhorn is also showboating, reflecting thick golden sunrays into the sky as if it's a long-buried treasure chest pried open, fat gold coins piled inside.

"We see you too," Wylie calls to the mountain.

"The Matterhorn doesn't like to be upstaged," Calvin says.

"What do you think we look like from up there?"

"Ants," he replies.

An overly confident Erin tries to balance without the chair. She splats.

"Ants falling," he amends.

Wylie points toward Zermatt's ski runs. "Do you know that from up at Klein Matterhorn, you can see Switzerland, Italy, and France smashing against each other in a swell of glaciers and peaks?"

"Whoa, that's really cool."

"And," she says, holding up a finger, "you get a back side view of the Matterhorn. Looks like a different mountain. Sort of like when you meet someone without their typical Instagram filter, and you're left scratching your head, thinking, *Is that you?*"

"Like when you show up for a first date and the person's unrecognizable from their online-dating photos?" Just the mention of going on a date makes Wylie's stomach flip-flop.

Calvin's so easy to be with that she can almost forget about her terrible morning, about the lie she told Dan. Can almost forget Claudine's face as Wylie spewed out her pent-up rage and the shame cocktail that's followed, mixed with confusing pride for standing up for herself. And can almost forget the hurtful things her mom shot back. That art school was a whim.

He must sense Wylie's shifting mood, because he touches her arm, saying, "You must be so bummed about Berlin."

She does her best to smile. "Thanks. It's okay. What are you missing out on, by being here?"

"Two shows. One in Prague and one in Vienna. I'm not mad about it, to be honest. I was ready for this tour to be over, sleep in my own bed instead of hearing Darren snore."

Wylie laughs. Then, out of nowhere, she arches. An itch

attack, smack in the middle of her back. Reaching behind, she tries to scratch it through two layers of clothing and her coat, plus her gloved hands.

"You all right?" Calvin asks.

"Just . . ." Her body twists and jerks. "A bad itch." She flings off her gloves, trying again, the puffiness of her coat a barricade. She spins on her skates, a dog chasing its tail. "I can't reach it."

Erin pauses with her chair. "You're doing the Elaine dance. From *Seinfeld*." She punches the air with two thumbs-up fists, nearly falls, and claws for her chair's back.

"She's got an itch," Calvin explains as Wylie continues to lurch and spin.

"Ooooh, I hate that," Erin says.

Wylie's slung her arm up and over her shoulder, attempting to reach the itch that way, inching her fingers down her spine. Still, she finds no relief.

"Take off your coat," Calvin instructs.

"She should take her coat off!" Bibbidi yells.

"She's taking her coat off!" Erin calls back.

Wylie, in a panic, unzips her coat, flapping her arms to unsheathe them. The coat falls to the ice, and she hurries her hand up her back. Still, the itch is unreachable.

"Argh," Wylie shrieks.

"Let me help you." Calvin turns her body, flinging off his own gloves. "Is it here?"

"Up higher."

"Right here?" He scratches her skin through her sweatshirt, almost pinching it.

She inches her shoulders up and down. "That's not enough. Can you go under?"

"Under your . . . your clothes?"

"Yes! Just do it!"

Calvin slips his hand underneath the sweatshirt and her base layer, his chilly fingers sliding up her spine, finding the itchy culprit underneath her sports-bra band. "Here?"

"Oh my god, yes." Wylie closes her eyes at the sensation, stripped of all modesty. Scratching a hard-to-reach itch is the best feeling in the world. Pure heaven. Her shoulders begin to relax. Her heart rate steadies.

When she reopens her eyes, she realizes that she's leaning in to Calvin's chest, his hand still on her back, lightly scratching. What in the heck? Calvin's hand, her skin, his breath on her neck, the heat of their bodies fusing with the chill of the air.

It's incredible. Intoxicating. And well beyond the friend zone.

Wylie pushes off with her skates, gliding away, and then she turns around, unable to meet his eyes. "Well, that was embarrassing."

He chuckles. "Those itches are the worst. It always happens to me in the car, and I never have anyone to scratch it for me."

"Thanks for your help." He's probably not feeling the same charge, the skin on her back still pulsating from his touch.

Calvin opens his mouth to speak, but Wylie's afraid of what he might say. She cuts him off, pointing at Erin and Bibbidi, who are now both sitting next to each other on their chairs, people skating around them, Bibbidi's hair the ocean, Erin's the land. "Look at those two."

Bibbidi and Erin dip their heads toward each other, whispering, and then they both tip back, roaring in hysterics, slapping their knees.

"I hope I find that kind of love someday," Calvin says. "I want to laugh like that with my person."

Wylie can't help it now; she looks him full in the face to find his eyes shining at her, beams of sunrays, the Matterhorn's golden coins. Her face flushes. "Me too."

He picks up her coat from the ice, handing it to her. "Hey, I'm dying for a pastry. Want to hit up one of the bakeries on our list?"

Our list.

She should find a gym. She should declare that any outing involving pastry is strictly platonic. But she's so tired of living a life confined by *shoulds.*

He offers his arm, and Wylie takes it.

21

Claudine

CLAUDINE LIMPS BACK TO THE HOSTEL TO WRAP her aching knee. Call it procrastination, but she doesn't want to be in distracting physical pain while having a conversation with Zosel that will force her to summon all her inner strength. In ski racing, she took all variables off the table so she could perform at her best. She convinces herself that's what she's doing now.

She closes the door to her room, dejection slumping her shoulders.

From her bag, she retrieves a roll of Kinesio tape. She pulls down her pants to reveal the swollen bursa on her left knee. With her teeth, she rips off three short strips of tape, expertly applying them to the skin around the kneecap in a triangle, relieving the pressure on her patella. *Remember what it was like to have a dedicated physio team do things like this for me?* It's not just the care she misses, but the people—the steady cast of supporters, from ski techs to physios, who were her friends for so many years. When she retired, she lost touch with all of them. She'd had no clue how to extend the friendship, had felt too vulnerable to even try.

Besides, everyone wants to be friends with a champion. But when you're yesterday's news, you lose your appeal.

Claudine yanks up her pants and stands, bending her knee a few times. The pain has not magically disappeared. She trudges to the bathroom to splash some water on her face, opting to pee first, sitting on the toilet with her head bowed as if praying for something she desperately wants.

The one thing she desperately wants—to change the past— is impossible. Sometimes she imagines being able to turn back time, to rewind her actions in St. Moritz, placing a palm on the bathroom door instead of pounding on it, demanding that Wylie race.

Or rewind time even further, to that day in the Olympic Village when a man with an angular face and eyes the color of a gray winter sky plunked a tray down across from her as she swirled her spoon through a bowl of tomato soup, too nervous to eat. His nose was rounded at the very tip, and she imagined skiing down it, appraising everything like this: surfaces to ski off. Roofs, slopes, the flaps on milk cartons.

He raised his eyebrows. "Want to blow off some steam?"

Claudine needed to sink her agitation into something or she'd ski too wild to win. She sunk it into him.

Her pity party is interrupted by someone entering the communal bathroom. "Anybody in there?" the person asks, knocking on the door of her stall. Claudine's instinct is to draw her feet up—and then she's struck by how the pose, her pounding heart, her shame, the urge to hide while peering out through the cracks of a bathroom stall, mirrors Wylie back in St. Moritz.

Only the person on the other side is much calmer than Claudine had been back then. "Anybody in there?" says the voice again.

"Uh, yes, sorry," Claudine says. "Just one sec." She wipes, stands, flushes. When she emerges, she finds Erin doing an I've-got-to-wee-so-badly jig.

"Thanks," Erin says, squeezing past her.

Claudine's washing her hands when Erin emerges from the stall, sighing in relief.

"Ahhhh. We're all out ice-skating, but I drank so much coffee this morning that I had to run back to drain the lizard, as we said in the army."

"Got it."

"Wylie's a great skater. But Léa, boy. She's incredible." Erin angles around her to wash her hands.

"I'm glad Wylie's having a good time." Claudine can't meet Erin's eyes. "Listen, I'm sorry you had to witness all of that this morning. And yesterday. We're just going through a rough patch. That's lasted many years."

Erin nods, drying her hands. "Hey, no skin off my back. I don't have kids, so I won't pretend to know a darn thing. And I'm sorry I was googling that Franz guy at the table. Didn't mean to be insensitive."

"It's okay. I would've been curious too."

"Never pleasant to be internet-trolled. That must suck."

There's only one troll that Claudine's mad at: Barry. "I couldn't care less what most people think of me."

Erin runs a hand over her green buzz cut. "Hang in there, okay?" She makes a move toward the door.

To her own surprise, Claudine doesn't want to be alone just yet. "I wish I didn't trigger her so much," she says, oversharing, despair in her voice.

Erin removes her hand from the door handle. "You know, I went years not talking to my pops. We had a lot of troubles, he and I. One thing I realized later on in life—especially being married to Bibbidi, who likes to talk *everything* out—is that it's not going to be sunshine and rainbows every damn day, three hundred sixty-five days a year. That's not family. Family is real. So don't be scared about going a few rounds with your daughter. Doesn't have to mean you hate each other."

"That's true, I guess," Claudine says. She's never had it modeled that it's normal, even healthy, to argue, to contradict each other. If Claudine voiced an opposing opinion to Kipper, he'd say, "Suck it up, buttercup." Claudine never even tussled with Zosel on that day in Salt Lake. *I think you should tell her.* She'd simply walked away. And never came back.

What has Claudine modeled for Wylie? Silence.

"Arguing, in my opinion," Erin says, placing a palm on her chest, "shows that you care. You're not just fighting for the hell of it; you're fighting for the person to understand the real you because you care about the health of the relationship."

"Huh. Yeah. That's really helpful."

Erin gives her a hearty pat on the arm. "There's a lot of love between you. I can see it."

"You can?"

"From a mile away."

At these words, a cry could gurgle up out of Claudine. "Thank you for saying that."

"You bet. I'm gonna get back to the rink. Wanna come?" Erin aims a finger at her. "And it's not a pity invite. I swear."

This woman's got her number. She smiles, the warmth reaching her eyes. "Thanks. But I have a few things to do." She pulls open the door for Erin, following her out, heading to the dining room to get a banana. This day has had more ups and downs than a mogul race. Just when she thinks she can't sink any lower, along comes someone like Erin, bestowing a glimmer of hope in the communal bathroom of a youth hostel, of all places.

Claudine's got to laugh. But it also shows her just how isolated she's become in her life in Oregon. She complains about CycleTron, that most of her human interactions are virtual, but she chose that life. She retreated, preferring to pull away. Gib uses their house on a cliff as a launchpad, a better vantage point to see and interact with the world. But she's using it as a fortress, thinking that she's uninterested in getting to know people and uninterested in having people get to know her.

It dawns on her now that she's been missing out.

Passing the lounge, she hears, ever so faintly, the familiar voice and the cadence of CBS skiing commentator Tim Reynolds. But how?

She's drawn into the room. There, perched in the window seat, Koa's watching a ski race on his laptop. A race that must have taken place many years ago, given that Tim's retired.

Koa looks up, presses Pause on the computer. "Hiya, Potts. I'm watching your race in Nagano."

"Really?"

"Yeah, felt inspired after meeting you."

Claudine cringes. She hasn't exactly been kind to Koa.

"Want to check it out?" he asks.

"Oh, um." She hasn't watched old footage in years. "Sure."

Koa pats the seat, and she crosses the floor to sit down.

"I'm sorry for this morning." She's doling out *sorrys* left and right today. "When I was so rude."

Koa shrugs. "It's no big deal."

"No, it is. You and Léa are working really hard in a stressful situation. I didn't mean to be *that* guest who makes things worse."

"Thanks for saying that."

"And I don't think this place is a hellhole."

He chuckles. "We do have pretty nice mattresses, for a hostel."

"I will give you that."

"Here." Koa passes her the laptop. She holds it cautiously, not fully sure she wants to go down this road, be reminded of who she used to be.

"Don't be offended," he says, "but you skied this one ugly. In a good way."

That was her style, skiing vicious, ruthless, sometimes desperate, churning up so much heat underneath her as to scorch her own footing. Never forgetting what she had come there to do.

She took a lot of flak for that style.

Society, as she found out, is unnerved by a competitive woman. The world doesn't like watching a woman express her desire. And what is winning but the completion of desire? Deeply wanting something, and then going after it with every fiber in your being—it's unladylike, that much hunger meeting that much power. Undesirable. Inadvisable, in her experience.

Along with the media dubbing Claudine the Stone-Cold Killer, they also described her as: Bloodthirsty. Cutthroat. Aggressive. Ruthless. Merciless. Combative. Pretentious.

Bitchy. Kipper, who by any standard put her drive to shame, was never described in these terms. Kipper—or any competitive man, really—was considered hardy, resilient, motivated, dynamic, hungry, scrappy, brave.

But Claudine throw her goggles in defeat? Pump her fist too vigorously in victory? Acknowledge in an interview that she was "having the best season of her career, possibly the best season by any female skier ever," which by the way was simply true? Pour on the outrage. Pour on the shame and disappointment. Label her a bad sport.

She was misunderstood.

Claudine took no particular glee in defeating her competitors, watching their dreams deflate like airless wind socks while she walked away with a medal strung around her neck. She was always racing herself. Defeating her own weaknesses. Racing against the self that was unnerved by a mean comment or lost sleep from a teething toddler the night before. Winning meant triumphing over self, and that's what made it all the more compelling. The victories all the sweeter.

Perhaps the most confusing thing Claudine's discovered about being an elite athlete: When you retire, you're expected to turn off your competitiveness. As if it's as simple as turning a spigot. *Thank you for serving me, competitive streak, now you may take your leave.*

But she couldn't extinguish it, not fully.

Her hand is drawn to the space bar, pressing Play on the YouTube video, and there she is, tapping her poles together at the start gate, then hinging forward, the sound of the countdown start signal enough to flare her adrenaline even now.

Commentator Tim Reynolds says, "And now the twenty-eight-year-old American Claudine Potts is roaring back from that crash at Worlds last year, tore her left ACL, fractured two ribs. She's off to an aggressive start after being denied the gold in the downhill yesterday to German Katja Seizinger, having to settle for bronze, trying to clinch her fifth gold in the super-G today. Here's a series of tight, technical turns, and she's rewarded for her compactness, picking up a tenth of a second."

Claudine watches a younger version of herself shifting her weight from side to side, her inside hip only inches from the snow, her body armor smacking against the flags as she cut her own grooves, preferring icier conditions because she knew everyone else would struggle. Man, her performance was gutsy that day—almost violent in its swiftness, each turn around a flag a slice across a neck. Competitors dropped left and right from the leaderboard.

"She's skiing relaxed and clean, as compared to yesterday, when she looked unusually tense and rigid, taking too many wide turns," Reynolds says. "Today she's chosen a fall line hugging each flag—it's risky, but she's never shied away from risk. Along comes the Sun Terrace chicane that's been tripping up other skiers—"

Claudine's holding her breath, even though she knows the outcome.

"—but she masters it! Oh, she's bouncing around but manages to hold on, probably to the delight of her father, skiing legend Kipper Potts, cheering down below with Claudine's daughter, Wylie. She's flying into the downhill portion, tucking low, trying to pick up speed, and if she does it she'll be at the top of the podium. She's cruising. Can Claudine Potts do it again?"

Claudine's rigid still, remembering what this moment had

felt like, how close she'd been to letting it all slip away, but then—

"And she does! She does! By one-hundredth of a second, knocking Austria to silver and bronze, with Switzerland's Zosel Marie Schwarz denied a medal, winning the wooden spoon instead, and Seizinger falling to fourth. What an ordeal Claudine has been through. What a comeback! The most decorated female skier in the world adds another gold medal to her cache. Five gold medals. One silver. Fifty-one World Cup victories. Many call her the best female skier ever, and she's living up to the title. Tears of joy. Tears of relief for Claudine Potts as she hugs her dad and daughter. How incredible. The sun is shining high in Nagano today, not yet setting on this brilliant career."

Claudine leans back against the window seat, shutting the laptop. She swipes at a tear rolling down her cheek.

"Pretty epic, huh?" Koa asks. Claudine can only nod. "Whoa, you okay, Potts? Didn't mean to stir up anything for you."

She huffs out a laugh. "It's been an emotional day is all." It's not her performance that's moving her. It's seeing Kipper, alive and well, and then Wylie, so little, reaching for her. It's the way Claudine had lifted her from Kipper's arms, held her in a tight embrace.

She may never hug her daughter that way again.

"I also watched your Snowbasin race at Salt Lake," Koa says.

Claudine issues a sputtering sigh. "My swan song?"

"What happened there? I mean, that vertical drop on the course—"

"Two thousand feet." She nods, recalling it.

"Sheesh." He shakes his head. "But you didn't seem like yourself."

She looks down at her hands, examining the nail on her pointer finger. She's never really talked about what happened at that race with anyone except Gib. How the media had hounded her for answers, answers she really couldn't give. Answers she's not prepared to give Koa either.

But she can offer him a kernel of the truth.

"You know, at some point, a GOAT"—she gives Koa a bemused side smile—"has to face the fact that no one is the greatest of *all* time. Only *for* a time." She shrugs. "And my time was up. I knew it even before the race."

"How did you know?"

"My knees were pretty shot. I didn't want to listen to people saying that I was too banged up and injury-prone to compete. Maybe I should've."

"Mmm," Koa says, listening attentively.

"And then, well, fear settled in, like it never had before. Once you ski afraid—as you may know—if you're not able to fully commit, if you're holding back in any way, that's when you lose. And that's when you get hurt."

He gives one of his dreadlocks a habitual tug. "You fell hard. Pretty gruesome."

She doesn't have to watch a YouTube clip of the race to remember. "Yeah," she says. "Poor Wylie was watching. And she used to have the worst nightmares about it in the years after Salt Lake. I hated that I couldn't fix that for her."

"Left more than one mark, then, huh?"

"I'll say."

What she doesn't tell Koa: a different fear—separate from her crumbling knees—had, over the years, wheedled its way under her skin, been growing until it hatched on race day in Salt Lake.

What no one knew—not the media, not Kipper, not Wylie, not her coaches—is that a few hours before the race, Zosel confronted Claudine, and what she said, what she accused her of, shook Claudine to her very core.

Zosel's words—*I think you should tell her the truth*—proved to be her undoing.

The truth that has brought her back to Zermatt.

No more dilly-dallying. She stands, handing the laptop back to Koa, thanking him. As she strides out the door, she calls to mind her gutsiness, her win-at-all-costs mentality, heading back to Zosel's like she's taking the Sun Terrace chicane.

22

Wylie

IN ONE UNGLOVED HAND, WYLIE'S CARRYING A slice of *Bergführerbrot,* an only-in-Zermatt specialty from Bäckerei Fuchs, translating to "mountain-guide bread." Dense, jam-packed with fresh apples, figs, and a healthy dose of schnapps, the bread could either sustain her for a week or stop her up completely.

In her other hand, still gloved, she's carrying a new purchase: a pair of Adidas slides. Bibbidi's been nice to share, but she should have her own.

Calvin's making appreciative tones as he bites into a chocolate éclair. It looks good. She had to opt for the closest thing to a supercharged energy bar? Old habits die hard.

Old patterns too.

If a silent treatment is immature, so is a tantrum.

As soon as she sees her mom, Wylie's going to apologize. And when the time is right, when the moment is private, she'll bring up the topic of her dad again. Claudine has changed a lot, it seems—or at least she's trying to. She may not bend on this, but Wylie's going to try to at least have an adult conversation about it.

Calvin is the perfect distraction from her troubled conscience. On they stroll through the meticulously snow-cleared streets of Zermatt, occasionally stepping aside for an e-Bus, an electrically fueled vehicle—the only kind allowed in this car-free town.

It's been so long since Wylie's had a lazy afternoon with no immediate plans or goals that she's not entirely sure how to conduct herself. She has to keep from saying, "What's next on the docket?" If there's ever been a chemistry killer, it's the word "docket."

Not that there's any chemistry to kill. They're just two chummy-chum pals walking along, occasionally bumping arms, which thrills her heart.

After polishing off his pastry—he did offer her a bite; she declined—he wipes his mouth with a napkin, tosses it into the trash, and says, "I know you said you don't ski anymore. But do you miss it?"

"Oh, um, hmm. Good question." Would she offend the entire town of Zermatt by tossing the rest of this famed bread into the trash? She glances around for Swiss locals staring at her, realizes that no one's paying any mind, and sails the pastry into the can, where it lands with a thud. "I actually do miss it. There's nothing quite like skiing, you know? The wind in your face, the combination of speed and grace." Without realizing it, Wylie's shifting her shoulders from side to side as if she's demonstrating how to ski, her knees bent, her elbows pinned back. She closes her eyes. "But you know what I miss most? The sound of it. When I'm on a cruiser completely alone, and it's the *shush, shush, shush* of the snow under my skis. I can still hear it. It's a beautiful noise. A beautiful sport."

Wylie stills her shoulders, cracks one eye open to find him watching her with an amused look on his face. "What?" She laughs. "It *is* a beautiful sport. What are you staring at?"

"You're just adorable, that's all."

She stiffens, stands, balls up her face like it's a wad of paper. "You don't have to say that."

"I know." His eyebrows cinch together. "I'm saying it because you are. I like your enthusiasm for things. It's infectious."

Hearing a compliment—actually several compliments—is more than Wylie can handle, so she gestures for them to keep moving, stepping a little farther apart from Calvin to ward off their accidently-on-purpose arm bumping. She's vaguely aware that she must be confusing the hell out of him.

Behind them comes the jingling bells of the Grand Hotel Zermatterhof's horse-drawn carriage. They move aside to watch the two white horses trot past, pulling what looks to be a family of five. Around them, tourists shop and walk and dine at outdoor cafés, despite the cold, dressed in all manner of winter wear, from kids and adults in full-on snow suits and ski bibs to women in high-heeled boots with a hint of fur lining. It's odd not to see anyone clomping along in ski boots, carrying their skis on their shoulders like wooden planks at a construction site.

Flurries swirl around everyone, although Wylie has the sense that they're swirling only around the two of them.

"Do you regret quitting?" Calvin asks.

How much to divulge? Back on the skating rink, her instinct was to keep her cards close. Now she thinks: *What's the big deal?* After this captivity in Zermatt, she'll probably never see Calvin again—a prospect, she notes, that causes a pang in her chest.

"I didn't have a choice, really. I had to stop."

"The mindset thing you were mentioning at dinner last night?"

"Yeah, anxiety. It got really bad, at the end. I was having daily panic attacks."

Calvin frowns. "That must have been so tough."

Turning toward him, she says, "It was. My mom and I, we haven't ever really recovered from it."

"I'm so sorry."

"I'm working on it. *We're* working on it, I guess, in our own strange way." She throws her arms out wide in a show of nonchalance, accidently dropping one of the Adidas sandals.

He stoops to pick it up, handing the shoe back to her. "I appreciate you telling me that."

"Thanks." *I feel safe with you,* she wants to say, but doesn't. She gestures for them to start walking again. They come to an ice sculpture that has *Home to Winter* chiseled into its base, with a big circle up top framing the Matterhorn like a viewfinder. *An Olympic ring,* she thinks. *Mother Matterhorn takes the gold.* "My mom struggled to keep me skiing after she retired from the team. Financially, that is. I never fully recognized that."

"Really?" Calvin looks surprised. "I guess I assumed Olympic medalists are flush with cash."

"That's what everybody thinks. But the sponsors fade away pretty fast. She didn't have social media back then. I mean, look at Lindsey Vonn. She's retired, but she's got a huge plat-form. She can still make a lot of money from ads and spon-sorship deals. By the time I was fifteen, sixteen, Mom was pouring everything she had into sending me to a ski acad-emy, paying for my lift tickets, my fees for competing. She also coached me there, so that offset some of the costs and gave her an income. Even if I hadn't quit, if I'd made it to the World Cup circuit, we would've shelled out thousands. You only make money when you start winning. It's a really tough go. Some of those girls who never podium—I feel bad for them, all the sacrifices their families have made." Then she laughs. "Of course, a lot of the families are wealthy, so it's no big deal. But for us . . . Well, my mom was literally banking on me winning."

"Oh wow."

"Yeah."

When she explains it like this, Claudine's actions, the pres-sure she put on Wylie—a different side of the story surfaces. Claudine was trying to keep them afloat and keep Wylie doing the sport she'd previously claimed to love. On this clear, cold day in Zermatt, just hours after their fight, Wylie has a sudden understanding of how hard it must have been for her mom.

"And then . . ." She hesitates.

"What?"

"Am I talking too much?"

He laughs. "Not at all."

"Well, Mom—she thought coaching me would be her career." She recalls Erin asking Claudine where she landed after ski racing ended, her mom's sad expression. "And I guess I took that away from her when I quit. She's had to reinvent herself. *Has* reinvented herself, with the whole CycleTron thing. I should probably tell her how proud I am of her."

"I bet that would mean a lot coming from you."

Wylie pauses, considering it, picturing this conversation with Claudine. Maybe he's right. But she *is* talking too much. "Anyway, enough about me. Do you ski?"

"I love skiing. Was hoping to do some while we were here." With his hands stuffed into his coat pockets, he eyes the mountains, which are all but roped off. No trespassing.

"Did you grow up doing it, or did you learn as an adult?"

"I went to a junior boarding school in Massachusetts when I was in middle school. In the winters, every Friday, all the students went skiing, no matter what. I hated it at first; I was *terrible*. Like, bad. But it's one of those things I'm grateful for later. A skill I can take with me wherever I go."

They pass a happy brigade of families building snowpeople—big ones, fat ones, tall ones, squat ones, expertly dressed ones. Is that a Hermès scarf around that snowwoman's neck? Even the sticks poking out of the sides of the snowpeople are richly crafted, three perfect-pronged hands on every arm. Then Wylie notices the staff from the Mont Cervin Palace handing out the supplies—it's a hotel-sponsored activity for hotel guests only; those are definitely artisan-made arms.

Without meaning to, Wylie brushes her hand against his. He doesn't seem to notice, so she acts like it's no big deal, just two hands pinging off each other, as hands do. "It'd be nice to ski together sometime," she says.

She hasn't wanted to ski in years, besides cross-country, which she and Dan do for cardio.

Calvin again scans the mountains fencing in the town, his

eyes swooping down toward hers, bright and deep and kind. She'd like to crawl into the dip of his neck, burrow underneath his warmth. "It would be," he says, and Wylie goes liquid in her belly at the hint of suggestiveness in his voice.

They've crossed the river, standing outside the Hotel Antika with its long sloping roof, just across from the Mountaineers' Cemetery. Darren and Brandon holler for Calvin from across the street. He turns, lifts up his hand in greeting, and swings back to her. "We're giving an impromptu outdoor concert tonight at the Parish Church of St. Mauritius, right in the center of town. It looks like we're going to rehearse for a bit right now. Will I offend you if I go join them?"

"Not at all. I need to find a gym anyway."

"Didn't we just work out?"

She laughs. "What, the walk?"

"The ice-skating."

"Good one."

"I wasn't kidding! But will you come to the concert?"

Without meaning to, she licks her lips, and she sees him watching her mouth. "Calvin—" she says slowly, forcing herself to institute a boundary she's been blurring all day.

Cutting her off, he says, "As friends. Just as friends."

She smiles. "I'll be there."

23

Claudine

IT'S NEARLY THREE IN THE AFTERNOON, AND Claudine's gunning it for Zosel's as fast as her aching knee will take her, rehearsing what she'll say, aiming for a balance between pleading and threatening. Pretty wide goalposts. Angering Zosel could drive her straight to Barry. At the same time, Claudine's ego can't tolerate groveling.

Zosel, you have your reasons for wanting to hurt me. I understand. But if you go through with this, you'll hurt Wylie even more, and you'll ruin my future with her for good. So I'm coming to you mother to mother. You wouldn't want Fränzi to know if you had . . . if you were . . .

It's not coming out right. She stops on the sidewalk, presses her fingers to her forehead.

Jeez Louise, her knee hurts. She flexes it. In moments of uncertainty, Claudine's never been one to say, "Universe, give me a sign," but she's so miffed at her knee, and by the way she's bungling her practice monologue to Zosel, that she tips her chin up toward the sky as she wonders what to do about all of it, almost like she's asking for guidance. She's standing under an actual sign: *SportClinic Zermatt.*

Fine, she'll take the nudge.

A small voice inside her squeaks that she's making excuses, putting off the conversation she needs to have, but she pushes open the door of the clinic anyway. At the front desk, two stern receptionists turn her away, looking down their noses at her with haughty side glances at each other.

"We don't accept walk-in patients," says one, saying "walk-in" with a disdain usually reserved for "uninsured." So Claudine didn't know Dr. Elena Stoessel was fully booked for a solid six months. They don't have to be rude about it. Unlike Jens, they're unswayed when she offers her name, her status. She pivots to leave, curling her hand into the bowl of free mints just as the overworked doctor herself pops her head in the door.

"What did you say your name was?" Dr. Stoessel asks.

"Oh, um." She slowly releases the mints from her hand into the bowl. "Claudine Potts."

The doctor arches an eyebrow. "The skier?"

Claudine's hope lifts. "That's me."

Now Dr. Stoessel's full body appears in the doorframe. "I commend you on your career," she says. "I grew up watching you ski."

Claudine can't resist a quick peek at the two receptionists. "Thank you."

Dr. Stoessel frowns. "Your knee is giving you trouble?"

"Yes, painful with every step."

Much to the chagrin of the receptionists, who have grown even more hard-eyed and tense-lipped during this exchange, Dr. Stoessel says, "I can see you after my last patient. It'll be a while, so you can go and come back."

"Really? Wow. That'd be great." She imagines hobbling to Zosel's only to rush back here. *No.* She doesn't want to be under any time pressure. It all has to be just right. "I don't mind waiting."

Under the glare of the receptionists, Claudine fills out an intake form, sucking extra-loudly on a mint, the room emptying of patients. Then she briskly flips through magazines—one in English, two in German—as if it's a race to the back covers. One receptionist nudges the other, gestures with her pointy chin toward Claudine, and says something in German.

"Ich spreche Deustch," Claudine says loudly. Not true. They descend to whispering.

At 5:00 p.m., the final patient is called, and the receptionists gather their coats. She's mulling over some sort of clever and cutting last word when one of the receptionists pauses in front of her, pushes a piece of paper and a pen into her hand, and asks for an autograph.

"Will you sign?"

Claudine is momentarily speechless. "Oh. Sure, yes. Happy to."

"Vielen Dank," says the woman, nodding politely.

"Bitte sehr," Claudine says, still pretending she's fluent. *Huh.* Maybe she read that whole thing wrong.

And then she's all alone, waiting for Dr. Stoessel. She'll video call Gib.

"I'm sorry I didn't touch base earlier today," she says as hello. "How are you feeling? Are you taking your meds?"

"Slow down, Claud," Gib says. "Deep breath. I'm tip-top, never better."

"Come on."

"Just trying to get some good sleep is all. But otherwise, I'm doing okay. I promise. How are *you*?"

Claudine releases a haggard breath. "It's been a terrible day." She doesn't go into details about her blowup with Wylie, but her anguish is written all over her face. "This is basically a shit show. And I'm just . . . I'm just . . . Well, I'm not handling it well." Her eyes well with tears. *Again.*

"Oh, love," Gib says, his voice gentle. "It's understandable that you're emotional."

Ew. Some people hate the word "moist." Zosel detested the word "barnacle," disgusted by the idea of sea creatures sticking to the sides of things. For Claudine, her hate word is "emotional." But it's true, isn't it? She's probably more emotional than she's ever been.

"I know you're upset that you can't get to Berlin with Wylie. And I'm sorry I haven't come up with any Hail Mary to get you out of there. But I'm just so glad you're safe and sound," he says, talking through the screen. She knows he's propped his phone up against his coffee mug instead of using the cell phone mount she gave him to help with the tremors.

"Thanks. Hey, can you put your—"

He rights the phone. "How are things with Wylie?"

"Oh, you know, we're . . ." Her first instinct is to lie. To say, "Making the best of it." She doesn't like to show this floundering side. In her mind, Gib's already accepted or forgiven so many of the challenging aspects of her personality—things she would never stand for in a partner: moodiness, rashness, callousness.

I'm hard to love, she thinks, as Gib beams at her over FaceTime.

And yet there he always is, making it look like it's the easiest thing in the world.

And that's because, as Soupy reminds her, Claudine is also other things: strong, determined, loyal, sincere, interesting, with a deep well of tenderness and love to give. Sometimes Soupy and Gib convince her that this is true.

I'm deserving of love, Soupy told her to write down.

So she digs deeper, forcing herself to say, "She's not speaking to me. I don't think. Or maybe she is. Yelling at me is more accurate. And then I'm yelling back." Their fight flashes in her mind. *We all had to change plans on a dime based on some whim.* Why had she said that? "Like I said, total shit show."

"Wow. That's—"

"I know." When she glances back at the screen, she sees crown molding. "Your phone. I'm staring into the loving eyes of the ceiling fan."

"Whoops. There we are. Well, you know I think this competition was just a ruse for Wylie to spend time with you. She wanted to mend fences with her mum, and this gave her a reason to reconnect. Even if she's letting you have it. Better out than in."

Even if Gib is right—and Claudine's sure he's not—any mended fences are now broken. Maybe irreparably this time.

A text comes through. It's Wylie. Just seeing her name speeds Claudine's heart. "Hold on a sec, Gib. Wylie's messaging me." She clicks on the text:

We're going to a Sings to Excess concert tonight if you want to join.

"Oh," she says, surprised. Maybe Gib *is* right.

"What'd she say?" Gib asks.

"She just invited me to a concert." Claudine chews on her bottom lip, still studying Wylie's words. It's not an apology for earlier, but it's a gesture, an olive branch.

"See!"

A second text pops up. Any luck with the helicopter?

Oh. Okay. Claudine understands what this is. She shakes her head, feeling stupid. "She's just being polite. She really just wants to know if I got us a ride out of here."

"Love, that can't be true. You should go."

"I can't, anyway. I'm at a doctor having my knee looked at. I'm in agony. And then from here, I'm heading back to Zosel's."

"When it rains, it pours. Well, this avalanche buys you some time."

"Yep." She swallows hard.

"I miss you."

"And I miss that ceiling fan."

"Oh, sorry, there we are. Hello."

Claudine smiles, in spite of her agitation. "Hello."

"Right," he says. "Before I let you go, there's one thing. I have a confession."

A kernel of worry pops into her mind. Gib needing to admit something? That's not how this usually works. "Okaaaaay," she says, drawing out the word, tilting her head. "What is it?"

He inhales deeply, and then says in all seriousness, "I've ditched the sleep tape."

She bursts out a laugh. *"That's* your big admission?" She can't stop chuckling. How she wishes she could hold him now. Goose him on his bum. Rib him about the sleep tape for the next week. "Gib, I don't think that's going to make a huge difference, to be honest. People have been living without sleep tape for centuries."

"And look what that got them." He throws his arms up.

"Sleep!"

Pausing, he frowns. "True. Wearing it was downright dreadful."

"It was the worst."

"I hated it."

Claudine smiles at him. "You're free."

"I'm free. I'm free! You're right. See, this is why I need you back. I've been spinning my wheels without you."

"I've been spinning my wheels without *you*." They smile at each other. Somehow, just the sight of his face is a palate cleanser for this day, her awful morning, and as they blow each other a kiss goodbye, Claudine finds her outlook isn't so grim.

She hangs up. Dr. Stoessel appears, beckoning Claudine to walk ahead to the examination room so she can watch her gait. The doctor's "hmm" is troubling.

Claudine hefts herself up on the exam table, pulling up her pant leg to reveal her left leg, scarred from past surgeries.

"Could just be scar tissue aggravating you," Dr. Stoessel says as she manipulates her leg, tugging her knee forward, pressing against it.

Claudine watches the clock tick toward 6:00 p.m., hoping Zosel doesn't have evening plans. She turns her head to stare at an enlarged photo of the Matterhorn at sunset. Trippy because just two feet to the right, the mountain is still visible outside a window, golden in the few remaining minutes of daylight, art imitating life in real time. Rather than fade, the sunlight is having a last hurrah before nighttime wraps a fist around the sky, orange and pink party streamers bursting along the horizon. No wonder the Swiss can't get over this view. If you can't beat it, frame it.

She closes her eyes, exhausted from the jet lag and the lack of sleep and her body's melatonin kicking in with the setting sun. The fatigue is manifesting as a headache behind her eye sockets.

Dr. Stoessel applies pressure near Claudine's kneecap, causing her to wince.

"Tender?" Dr. Stoessel asks.

"Yes, very."

All of this—a physician examining one of her limbs; Claudine awaiting a prognosis, praying it isn't grim—is more familiar than it should be. How many doctors has she seen over the years? Too many to count. Occupational hazard.

Moving her gaze from the window, Claudine studies this doctor's concentrating face, her nose pinched at its tip, giving her the flared nostrils of a dragon, and her full mouth, imagining skiing over the prominent outline of her upper lip, two peaks and a valley.

Dr. Stoessel releases her leg. "Hard to say for sure without imaging, but the bursa near the knee joint is certainly inflamed. There aren't other red flags that are worrying me."

Plain old bursitis. Claudine closes her eyes and breathes a sigh of relief.

"I suggest a Prolozone injection. It is more regenerating than a cortisone shot. And it will help with the pain. Once you are back home, you should follow up with your orthopedist."

"I love Prolo," Claudine says. You name it, she's had it.

"And then try staying off of it for a few days. Rest it."

"I will," Claudine replies, the same way she always has, telling doctors what they want to hear, planning to do the opposite.

"Are you under a lot of stress? That might be contributing to the inflammation."

Claudine nearly laughs. "An avalanche's worth," she says.

Dr. Stoessel nods solemnly. "Oh yes, I'm sorry about that. One of the downsides to living here. We are at the mercy of the weather. But do not stress at what cannot be avoided." She tosses up her hands. "It is what it is. Best to now enjoy your time here even without skiing. And your knee will thank you." She prepares the injection, and then sterilizes Claudine's knee with a cold antiseptic wipe. "Little burn. Ready? Breathe." She pricks Claudine's skin, driving the needle deeper. "You'll feel some pressure now."

Claudine grits her teeth as a pocket of fluid plumes under her skin. "I feel it."

"Good." Dr. Stoessel disposes of the needle in the sharps container and then rubs her fingers over the injection site, spreading the Prolozone. "This will help."

Maybe it's her call with Gib, his kindness, his support, being loved despite her shortcomings, and maybe it's the good doctor's steadying hand on her leg, the experience of being cared for, the tender response to Claudine admitting that she's hurt—a wellspring of tears catches her off guard yet again.

Get it together, Claudine, she admonishes herself, using her sleeve to wipe her cheeks with extra force.

"Are you okay?" Dr. Stoessel peers at her in concern. "I know it can sting."

Claudine just shakes her head, embarrassed. "Perfectly fine, I promise." She sits up, unrolling the pant leg down from her thigh, bending her knee back and forth, the Prolozone acting like a squirt of oil to the Tin Man's joints. Good as . . . Well, not new. But better than before. She nods toward the now-darkened sky. "Thank you so much for staying late for me. I'm really grateful."

Dr. Stoessel's gloves snap as she peels them off. "It's really no problem. And it turns out you are not my last patient of the evening." She wheels her stool to the waste-basket with a practiced kick of her foot. "Actually, I believe you know her."

"Oh?" Claudine raises an eyebrow. There are only two people she knows who live in Zermatt, and only one of them is a "her." *Oh.*

Oh *no.*

"I am Zosel's sister-in-law."

"You're Zosel's . . ."

"Sister-in-law, yes. She married my brother."

"Her second husband." Why does Claudine say this?

"Yes, well." Dr. Stoessel's amused look falls away for a moment. "Yes. Our girls are cousins and best friends."

Claudine's mind is ticking fast. "How sweet."

"Like you, she still has pain from old ski injuries from time to time. She's popping over for a treatment."

"That's . . . so convenient for her."

Claudine should also find this convenient, the opportunity falling right in her lap. What a lucky, lucky day.

But the last thing she wants to do is see Zosel while she's so . . . Fine, she'll say it, *emotional.* The thought of breaking down in front of her doesn't fit the reunion she'd envisioned.

In her mind, she'd be stalwart. Steady. The person storming the ridge, ambushing her competitor. She needs all her wits to do this right, her one and only chance.

She'll talk to Zosel, she will, but now's not the right time. She needs to be more . . . in control.

On autopilot, Claudine stuffs her feet into her boots, cinching her laces, tying them too quickly. She has to start over, her fingers trembling.

Gone is the Stone-Cold Killer fighting to keep her family intact. In her place is a woman who's just scared to look Zosel in the eyes again, flooded with the instinct to flee—only this time she can't blame a natural disaster.

It's just her own cowardice.

She finds it hard to breathe, the room shrinking in size. Was it always this small? She pulls at the neck of her sweater.

"It's possible she is here now," Dr. Stoessel says, her voice sounding tinny, far away. "I'll bet she'll want to say hello."

Claudine jams her hand through her coat sleeve. "That's okay!" She attempts a singsongy voice meant to mask her mounting angst. "I'm sure you're eager to get home. I can catch up with her another time."

Dr. Stoessel tsks. "She speaks of you often. I am sure she has many things to say to you. I'll go fetch her."

"No . . . That's—" Dr. Stoessel is already out the door, leaving Claudine to say "not necessary" to herself.

Damn. Many things to say to me? She spins in a circle, unsure of what to do, hating the feeling of being cornered.

Down the hall comes the sound of two voices, Zosel's laugh ringing out just as it used to in the start house.

I can't do this.

She scribbles "Bill me" on a notepad, knowing the office

now has her paperwork on file. Then she slides the window open and hefts herself through it, kicking a pile of snow onto the floor of the exam room. Slides it shut. Stands, hurrying as much as her left knee will allow.

Feeling more like a quitter with each shameful step.

24

Wylie

THE TOWN OF ZERMATT SURE KNOWS HOW TO make the best of things. In the village center, a large bonfire warms a ring of tourists, and local volunteers hand out mugs of kirsch and hot cocoa, bowls of steaming *Bündner Gerstensuppe*, a barley soup with vegetables and cured meat. The mood is festive and jubilant as everyone mills around the Parish Church of St. Mauritius to hear the young men of Sings to Excess serenade the stranded.

As promised, Wylie's there too, arriving with Bibbidi, Erin, and Léa. They huddle, sipping kirsch, Erin audibly slurping her soup. Wylie extended an olive branch to her mom by inviting her, but she's nowhere to be found.

Talking to Calvin about her mom's sacrifices—looking at their history in a more objective way—has shifted something in Wylie. They've spent very little time together since they've arrived here, and in spite of their harsh words this morning, now she's craving more time with her mom, just as she had as a girl. The apology she hopes to deliver still knocks around inside her.

Plus, she doesn't love the idea of Claudine plodding around this village by herself. Seems lonely.

The singers gather in formation, another half circle, this one larger, with every group member present. Calvin catches Wylie's eye and nods. She nods back.

Erin nudges her shoulder. "What's up with you two, anyway?"

"Nothing." Wylie hopes the darkness hides her reddening cheeks.

In her coat pocket, her phone buzzes. Dan again. She doesn't answer.

The crowd hushes as all nine members of the group crisply snap their fingers in unison, hinging one hand up and then the other with every cadenced sway of their hips. A vocal percussionist acts as a mouth drummer, setting the rhythm for Stevie Wonder's "Signed, Sealed, Delivered." The voices blend as a symphony: bass, baritone, tenor. A man steps out of the semicircle, singing the lead.

Wylie frowns that it's not Calvin.

Next to her, Erin hums the song, slipping out a few off-key words between bites of soup. Bibbidi wears an expression of rapture. Léa nods along. Wylie looks from face to face to face in the crowd, moved by a love for humanity—all these people, from all over the world, inexplicably stuck together, sharing music and food. It's beautiful, and she feels remarkably more at peace than she has in a long time—even in the midst of the Twitter mayhem about her dad.

Oddly, Wylie finds herself hoping that Claudine came up

empty with the helicopter. Out in the real world, Wylie has none of this.

No pack of goofy friends.

No sugary-sweet drinks.

No magical nights filled with music.

No burgeoning crushes—which she knows is wrong. She *does*. But being trapped in a European village has transported her, inviting her to swap the food calculators and the fitness regimens and the overtaxing boyfriend for a more forgiving approach to life. A gentleness she's never imagined could be hers.

Sings to Excess seamlessly transitions to its second cover. Only the vocal percussionist and the lead singer begin the song—again, someone who is not Calvin.

At the first few notes of a 2013 song that topped the pop charts, and is still a favorite, recognition dawns on people's faces. It's Lorde's "Royals."

The vocal percussionist sounds so much like a drum—or someone beating their hands on a table—that Wylie searches for a hidden instrument. Is he actually doing that with his mouth? All the singers' voices swell to carry the chorus, and a second percussionist layers a "dom dom," almost like a wool-felted drumstick struck against a large bass drum, hollow, but not empty.

Erin's digging this tune, as if it really gets her. She sings every word, lifting her arm up high and pointing her finger at the makeshift stage, timing it to the beat.

Wylie smiles to herself, appreciating that this side trip to Zermatt, while wildly inconvenient—and competition ending—has introduced her to a motley crew that's sworn off extravagance in the heart of a luxurious town.

The crowd moves and sways and sings the lyrics, everyone's breath visible in the cold night sky, lit up by the orangish-red backdrop of a bonfire. In this moment, not a soul would opt for a helicopter ride out of here.

Wylie even feels a warmth for the Italians from the train, Giovanni and his son, Maximilian, whom she spots across the church courtyard, devouring a Toblerone in the shape of the Matterhorn.

Standing next to Giovanni is a jowly, large-framed man who seems to be staring directly at her. Something about him makes Wylie nervous. She gives a curt half smile and a lift of her eyebrows to show the staring is not appreciated, then looks away. When she peeks back, he's gone.

Weird.

For the third and final song, Calvin does step forward to sing the lead. Sings to Excess saved the best for last. He brings his hands chest high, cupping them as if he's drawing water to his mouth, and then he opens his lips, casting out the first line with such measured force that it takes her breath away.

"I was born"—this word he holds, toying with it, before leaping to—"by the river"—again, a suspended breath—"in a little tent."

Murmurs ripple through the crowd. Bibbidi appears to collapse into Erin, who puts her arms around her, propping her up.

Goose bumps prickle across Wylie's arms, and it's not because she's cold.

The other eight singers usher in, supporting Calvin's voice, almost as if they've gathered him by the legs to hoist him into the air.

Several of the singers are performing so theatrically it's

nearly comical, scrunching up their faces like producing the notes physically aggrieves them. Redheaded Darren gestures emphatically with his fist as if he's begging a lover not to leave him. Jimmy, a tenor, appears to press his palm down in order to get a leg up on a high note, elongating his vocal cords. Curly-haired Brandon pushes his hand into his abdomen, bending slightly in the stance of a bellyache, before standing upright to outline the shape of a curvy woman. Some snap. Some clap, two fingers into palms like the clang of symbols.

Taken separately, each performer is sort of ridiculous.

But together, they're brilliant, practiced professionals.

Standing serenely in the middle of it all is Calvin, and Wylie feels her heart give a little.

Then she senses a presence next to her. She glances left. Does a double take. It's the jowly man with the staring problem.

Weird, again. She shuffles toward Erin, a little annoyed that this man is pulling her attention away just as Calvin is singing the last lines, his arms outstretched to the heavens. The crowd goes wild—or as wild as a crowd goes on a cold night in Switzerland, most people having to clap against the cups and bowls they're holding.

"Excuse me," says the mystery man, craning his neck to make eye contact with Wylie. He's American, she notes.

"Yes?" Wylie's voice hints at perturbed. She just wants to congratulate Calvin and the rest of Sings to Excess.

"This is a strange question, but are you . . . Are you Claudine Potts's daughter, by chance?"

Her eyes widen. Being recognized by a certain ski crowd hasn't happened since Wylie was young. She folds her arms across her chest. "Uh, yeah, I am."

He laughs, shaking his head in amazement. "I thought it was you."

"Can I help you with something?"

"I'm just a big fan of your mother's." He sticks out his hand, and she reluctantly shakes it. "What, might I ask, are you doing in Zermatt?"

"Um." She's not giving some strange fan any personal information. "We're just here for nostalgia's sake." Distracted, she peeks a glance at her friends chatting with Calvin. She wants to get over there.

He lifts a furry eyebrow. "We?"

"Me and my mom, yeah." She steps to the left, peering around him to get a better view. Bibbidi is turning in a circle. Calvin scans the crowd. It's clear they're looking for her. She cups her hands to her mouth and shouts, "I'll be right there!"

The man shakes his head, as if he's mystified in a pleasing way. "Claudine Potts and Zosel Schwarz back together in the same town. I'll be damned. Let the drama unfold."

This attracts Wylie's attention. She stares at him, rereading the situation. "What'd you just say?"

"Claudine and Zosel, both in Zermatt. Have you all been catching up?"

"I have no idea what you're talking about." The man is now officially creeping her out. "Besides, Zosel moved to Austria."

He chuckles. "Is that so?"

"Yeah . . . I think so."

"And who told you that?"

"My mom . . ." She trails off. "What'd you say your name was again?" She takes a step forward, wanting to pin down why he seems to know so much about them.

"The intrigue deepens." He rubs his hands together in an evil-villain sort of way.

"Your *name*?" she presses him.

"Oh, I didn't say." A bizarrely smug smile spreads across his face. "But your mom's wrong. Zosel Schwarz most certainly does still live in Zermatt."

Then he lumbers away, leaving Wylie standing alone and confused.

25

Claudine

BACK TO THE HOSTEL CLAUDINE GOES, HER HEAD hung. If she had a tail, it'd be between her legs. She can't look at Mother Matterhorn, whom, she imagines, must be deeply disappointed in Claudine's lack of valor.

Why is it that every time she sees Zosel she loses her nerve?

It's preposterous, really. Claudine has faced fear head-on in every ski race. Would have even conquered the world's hardest run—the Kitzbühel Streif—if women had been allowed to do it. But put Claudine within arm's distance of Zosel and she's running for the hills, her brain and body revolting.

Through a tavern window she sees a merry-looking group of people laughing and eating. If only she could turn back the clock to just last night, when she was dining on fondue with a similarly merry group, all her prospects seeming rosier.

She can make excuses all she wants about not being the one in charge or not being in the right headspace, but the truth is that Claudine just about had a *panic* attack back there. Not only did she have to find an exit, she climbed out of it. Luckily the window had been close to the ground.

Maybe this is how Wylie felt before a race.

What in the hell is going on?

And to make matters worse, she's crying for the *umpteenth* time today. Kipper would be absolutely appalled. *You're not actually* crying, *are you?* she hears him say.

Across the Wilkommen mat she drags her sorry ass, relieved to see that the hostel lobby is empty and already darkened, save for a square of light shining from the reception area. Claudine's aim is to tiptoe past, avoiding an evening conversation with whoever's working and hiding her tearstained face.

She's near the hammocks when Koa calls after her.

"Hiya again, Potts."

She halts, turns slowly around. "Oh, hi, I didn't see you there."

"You don't have to whisper. No one's here, as far as I know." He's staring, once again, at a computer screen, and he doesn't break his gaze away to look at her.

Claudine knows from Wylie's text that everyone's at a concert. She still hasn't answered her question about the helicopter, hating to disappoint her.

"You're working a lot today," she says.

"Yeah, I wanted to give Léa some real time off. She's been putting in some long hours." For such an upbeat guy, his voice sounds glum.

"Ah." Claudine steps forward, toward the light, tugged by a sense that Koa could use a friend. He finally looks at her, his face a sag of worries, his eyes rimmed red.

Hers must be too, because at the same time, they both say, "You okay?"

They laugh.

"I've been better," she says. "If I'm being honest."

"Same."

She can't imagine he wants to confide in her, or that he wants to hear about her problems. She looks around the lounge, trying to figure out what to say.

Mercifully, he saves her by asking, "You hungry?"

"So hungry."

He nods toward the dining room. "Follow me."

Penne bathed in butter, salt, pepper, Parm. Has there ever been anything better?

Koa whipped up the dish from his personal stash of food, and she's eating with Gib-level gusto and appreciation. The pasta is working like the sleep tape at home. Claudine hasn't opened up like this with anyone besides Gib—not even Soupy—in years.

"So you've had a chance to talk to your friend a few times now, but you keep running away?" Koa's been listening intently, not prying for left-out details, such as who the friend is or why Claudine has come this far to see her.

She wipes her mouth with a napkin. "It has the strangest effect on me. My whole body shuts down. Just now, before I came back to the hostel, I literally *ran* away from her. As fast as my banged-up knee would take me. But I just knew I wasn't ready to have that conversation, you know? Something about it wasn't right." She chuckles a little at the absurdity.

"If I had to put this in skiing terms, it sounds like you bailed." Koa spears three penne on his fork, fits them all in his mouth.

"You're right. I *did* bail." She shakes her head. "I'm so embarrassed."

"Okay, this is going to sound cheesy, but sometimes the cheesiest things are the truest." He spears another three penne. "When you bail skiing, it's often because you're about to take a hard crash, so you purposefully fall so that you can control the damage. It's a form of self-protection. The safest thing to do is bail, you know? Maybe, with your friend, the safest thing to do was get the heck out of there before you crashed, emotionally."

She sets down her fork, watching him chew, bowled over by his insight. "Koa, you might be onto something."

"You'll get there with your friend. Just give yourself some grace. Listen to your gut and dodge her until you're ready."

Dodge her until I'm ready. Maybe there's no shame in that. In listening to what her body is telling her.

"Thank you. I can't tell you how helpful this is to hear."

"And if you're not ready to talk to her, write her a letter. It's a lost art."

"A letter?"

"Even if you don't end up sending it. Maybe it'll help you get your thoughts straight so you don't feel as panicky the next time you see her. It's what I did with my ex about a year ago. Never ended up sending it, but it was still cathartic."

"I wouldn't even know where to start."

"How about, 'Dear'?" His mouth quirks up into a smile.

She laughs. "You're almost better than Soupy."

"Who?"

"My therapist." She waves away his questioning look about the name Soupy. "So why was your night a bummer?" Koa's face goes ashen. Misreading it, she says, "You don't have to tell me, if you don't want to."

"Ah, there was another World Cup crash today. At Kvitfjell. Young Italian skier. He's a buddy of mine. It's not looking good for him. Poor guy's *munted*."

"Munted?"

"Broken. Paralyzed. At least, that's the chatter."

Claudine clasps her hand over her mouth, closing her eyes. "That's . . . horrible. I'm so sorry we've been going on and on about my silly problems."

"It's the pits." His shoulders drop as he shakes his head, still trying to come to terms with it.

"How did it—"

"Same old story. Not enough real snow, too much ice underneath the fake snow. These skiers are going too fast. I know the name of the game is speed, but this is crazy, bro."

"Not enough snow in Kvitfjell? That's so unusual."

"That's what I was saying the other day. Things are changing. It's not good."

Koa ticks off the grim statistics—number of races cancelled from lack of snow or extreme weather, the increase in grisly crashes, the outlandish lengths ski towns are undertaking to keep the snow they have, and the environmental groups calling for an immediate halt to ski racing in order to protect what's left of all the glaciers. This time, she doesn't contradict him. She just listens.

When Koa's done speaking, they fall silent, both of them churning with anxious thoughts about this new reality. Finally, he turns his face to Claudine's, his dark eyes wide and entreating. "What should we do to protect the sport we love, and towns like this one? Our friends? Protect winter itself?"

The thing that crushes Claudine the most is that Koa thinks she might have the answer.

26

Wylie

TWO DAYS UNTIL BODYFITTEST DUO COMPETITION

WYLIE'S IN THE TIGHT GRIP OF HER RECURRING nightmare.

She's ten years old at the Salt Lake Olympics, clutching her grandfather's hand as a helicopter lifts Claudine, strapped to an orange medic stretcher, high into the air. The suspended stretcher spins in the wind.

Wylie and Kipper watch helplessly, the crowd at the finish line pushing in on them, people yelling up to the helicopter as the stretcher spins faster, in a way that Wylie knows can't be right or safe. A woman nearby is loudly praying, all her words gibberish. Kipper's too still, too rigid. Wylie tugs on his sleeve, but he doesn't take his eyes from the sky.

All at once, a body slips from the stretcher straps—it's not Claudine, but Wylie—and Wylie on the ground is watching another Wylie tumble back toward the jagged rocks below. She startles awake on the top bunk, her eyes flashing open.

Soft morning light filters in through the curtains. Her heart is racing as she gathers her bearings, hears her mom stirring in the bed below her. She'd tiptoed in late last night, and the two of them haven't seen each other since yesterday's blowup.

With her thumb and forefinger, she pinches the space between her eyes, settles her head back on the pillow. *It's over.* She means the nightmare. And also ski racing. *It's over,* she repeats.

Without meaning to, she issues a sigh from deep within her belly.

Claudine yawns loudly.

"Sleep well?" Wylie ventures. When she closes her eyes, she can still see the spinning stretcher.

"Disco music," mutters Claudine.

"I didn't hear anything."

"You slept through it."

Not peacefully. She sticks her head over the side of the bunk. "What are you doing today?" Her mom never bothered to text her back yesterday. She must still be angry.

Claudine cuts off the tail end of another yawn as she says, "I couldn't get us on a helicopter yesterday. I'm going to try again. See if we can get a lift out of here." She pushes her blankets off, moves herself to sitting up.

"Mom, you don't have to do that. I think it's hopeless."

"You never know. Maybe a bunch of people took their names off the list."

"Really, it's okay," Wylie says emphatically.

"Nothing about this entire situation is okay."

Oh. Wylie's not sure if that means Claudine wants to get away from her. It stings. Measuring every word and tone and inflection for the amount of love it carries can become an exhausting chore.

She sinks back onto her pillow and pulls her blankets to her chin, wondering if either of them is going to address the elephant in the room: Franz Blasi. Yesterday's fight. She acted like a jerk, yelling at her mom that way, and yet now that she has the chance, Wylie's finding it so hard to simply apologize.

She can't let it go. Her mom, more than anyone, should understand the desire to have two parents. Why does she want to deprive her of someone else to love—especially when their family is already so small?

Imagine if, on that day in Salt Lake, she'd had a dad who was more emotionally available than Kipper? Or had taken her somewhere else while Claudine raced—to do something kids like to do, maybe. Wylie wouldn't have had to see that accident. The nightmares wouldn't plague her still.

Claudine stands from her bunk and lifts the curtain away from the window, the sky a monotone whitish-gray wall, lit up from behind by a straining sun. Dan would know how to blast away the despondency that settles in after her nightmares. "Let's get those endorphins going," he'd say, such a common phrase in their relationship that they turned it into "dorsal fins going," sometimes relying only on the gesture: a shark fin hand to the top of the head.

He's not all bad. She *should* get her dorsal fins going.

"And what are you doing today?" Claudine asks, in what sounds like an afterthought.

"Um. I'm not sure." Wylie's yearning for her mom to interpret the "I'm not sure" for what it is: an opening to do something together. For Claudine to suggest an activity, or to

226

take the lead on talking about yesterday. Apologize first, for the awful things she'd said to Wylie too. She can't bear the vulnerability.

Claudine nods, then lets the curtain drop. "This town is just too small," she mumbles to herself.

Wylie's fragile heart fills in the rest of the sentence: *For the both of us.* She feels young and exposed in her bed. Close to tears. Scared. She watches as Claudine stretches her arms up over head, bending her left knee back and forth as if she's checking to see if the appendage still operates.

"Mom?"

"Hmm?"

"Never mind."

Claudine looks at her, concern crossing her face as she reaches out to press a cool palm against Wylie's forehead. "You're kind of pale. Do you feel sick?" Wylie closes her eyes under her mom's touch. "You don't feel hot."

"I think I'm just tired."

"It's probably the elevation." Claudine's hand lingers on Wylie's forehead and then swoops down her cheek once before lifting away. Wylie misses it immediately.

She closes her eyes and sees the strange, jowly dude from the bonfire, remembering his certainty that Zosel still lives in Zermatt. Then why did Claudine tell her differently?

Something about all of this feels off—just as off as her mom choosing Zermatt for Kipper's ashes. Claudine hasn't even mentioned the ashes since they've arrived! She's never even missed the pendant necklace that Wylie's now wearing.

Surely Claudine didn't *lie* to her about Zosel moving, right? She just got it wrong. Like, maybe last Claudine heard, Zosel moved to Austria, but now she's back? That's plausible.

People move all the time, and if they'd lost track of each other, then this makes sense.

But why *did* they lose track of each other to begin with?

Claudine's explanation—"sometimes friends just grow apart"—is as maddeningly scant as her line about Fox. "He was a ski bum who didn't want to be a dad."

There's got to be more to it. Claudine and Zosel were so close. Practically family, all of them. Wylie called her *Auntie Zo*, for goodness' sake. It's been a long time since she's thought of Zosel, but now that she applies her adult brain to Claudine and Zosel's friendship breakup, she can't stop wondering if there was a rift. And if so, about what?

If that guy last night was right—if Zosel does still live here—maybe Wylie can find her, ask her all the questions her mom refuses to answer.

"Wy, did you make this?"

Wylie presses herself up to sitting to see Claudine holding her collage. Her mouth falls open. "Where did you get that?"

"Sorry—it was sticking out of your backpack. I hope it's all right that I looked at it."

Heat flushes up Wylie's neck. She wants to snatch the collage away, press it to her chest. "Um . . . I guess so."

Claudine's studying the Matterhorn. "It's really"—she taps on the paper, the silence stretching as she seems to search for an adjective—"good."

"Thank you," Wylie says, past a lump in her throat. It's shocking—but really, really nice—to hear Claudine say something positive about her art. Coming from Claudine, "good" is glowing praise. She'd once asked out loud if a fellow student's modern-art painting had been drawn by a child, to Wylie's great embarrassment.

228

Claudine sets the collage down right where she found it. "You know, you could sell that collage. People would pay money for something like this. Maybe your museum would even display it."

There it is, the reminder, the commandment that's always steered the Potts family: It's not enough to do something for sheer pleasure. You have to capitalize on it. Make it count. Prove yourself. Only then do you have value.

Ski racing is over, but this mentality is not. Wylie sinks back onto her pillow.

27

Claudine

GOOD? WYLIE'S COLLAGE IS "GOOD"? CLAUDINE could kick herself. This is why she's always afraid to talk about art. She knows nothing! Now she's gone and used the world's stupidest, blandest word.

But the collage *is* really good. Wylie made the Matterhorn look so alive, pulsing with emotion, using only torn-off bits of magazine pages. How did she do that? Claudine could almost make out the facial features of the grandmother she pretends is embodied in the stone, as if Wylie had reached in and pulled out the vision from her own mind.

All of that seemed ridiculous to tell Wylie, or it would've come out muddled, so she'd pinned a mediocre accolade to the work of art that her daughter somehow managed to whip up amid the chaos of the past few days.

She's not blowing smoke when she says Wylie could sell her artwork, that it deserves to hang in a museum, but she gets the impression that this offended Wylie somehow. It's all so confusing. Measuring every word and tone and inflection as a reflection of whether you're failing as a parent can become an exhausting chore. Mikaela's mom would've come up with a better—

No. Stop it. She's not going to do this to herself anymore.

Here's what she is going to do: march back to the helicopter line.

Getting to Berlin is increasingly far-fetched, but Claudine hasn't lost all hope—something she learned from her ski-racing days. You never count yourself out. Five days before Nagano in 1998, she'd had a brutal case of shin bang, an excruciating injury to the tibia not uncommon for skiers. Every time Claudine put her boots on and leaned forward, pressing her shin against the boot liner, she cried out in pain, reduced to tears. If her condition didn't improve, competing was unlikely. Still, she didn't count herself out, committing to a steady rotation of ice, rest, stretching, ibuprofen, and lidocaine cream, while her ski tech fiddled with her boots, making minor adjustments to the ski-boot liners that had been custom-made for her legs and feet. The weather delivered her another gift: warm temperatures and soft snow, which mercifully pushed the competition back by one day, giving her more time to recover. Come race day, Claudine was ready. It wasn't perfect—but nothing in ski racing ever really is.

This doggedness was always what separated Claudine from the pack. And it's what's going to get her and Wylie out of Zermatt.

As she's gathering up her coat, her phone rings; it's Jasmine from CycleTron.

"Claudine! How are you and your daughter faring in Sweden?"

"Hi, Jasmine. We're in Switzerland. And thanks again for trying to help us bust out of here." Claudine has to wonder how actively Jasmine was pursuing rescue plans, if she had the country wrong.

"No problem. I'm sorry we couldn't do more. Do you mind if we switch to FaceTime?"

Ugh. "Sure." She drops her coat, plunks down to sit on the ground so she can outstretch her left leg, her back propped up against the side of the bed.

Their video screens connect. Jasmine's obviously working from her Los Angles home, white AirPods in her ears, a view of her living room wall behind her: white bookshelves devoid of books but with three bowls in consecutive sizes and varying metals—gold, silver, bronze—that remind Claudine of Olympic medals, a ceramic matchstick holder with matches as tall as the nearby unlit candle, and a wooden sign that says *You are the Rachel to my Monica.*

Jasmine squints. "Where are you, like, staying?" Her vocal fry is grating.

Claudine glances behind her at the bunks. "Oh, um. A youth hostel."

Jasmine laughs. When Claudine doesn't join her, Jasmine's eyes widen. "Wait. Are you serious?"

"Yes."

"Do they let . . . non–young people stay at youth hostels?"

"I told them I'm twenty."   •

"Ohmygosh."

"So don't say anything."

"I won't," Jasmine says with sincerity. "I would never."

Is this mean? Yeah, a little, but Jasmine's also letting her little dog lick her face during a work call.

"Anyway, Claudine, before we get into the BodyFittest Duo stuff, and congratulations, by the way, on competing with your daughter, that's the cutest—"

"Thank you."

"—thing ever. You're welcome. We caught wind that Barry Haberman, the sportswriter, is writing a book about you, and we are absolutely thrilled."

"Wait, what?" Claudine tilts her head. Uncomfortable on the floor, she tips to her right hip to try sitting at an angle.

"Your book? About your life? It's perfect timing. As you're outlining chapters with him, we just have a few ideas to discuss. We don't want to be controlling at all. Like, *at all*." She slices her long, lavender-painted nails through the air. "But wouldn't it be neat if your book ended on CycleTron sort of, you know, pulling you out of retirement? And now you have this extended CycleTron family, and all of your PottHeads, who love you, and you love them, and you're so happy now, where before you were kind of treading water—and even if you weren't, you could play that up a little—because our market research shows that a lot of our members come to us feeling dejected and unhopeful. You and this book, and then, of course, CycleTron, would give people hope that they can turn their lives around too. So." She purses her lips proudly.

There's so much to take issue with in that diatribe that all Claudine can say is "Whoa."

"I know!"

"No, I mean, there's been a huge misunderstanding. I have no plans to write a memoir, assisted by Barry or otherwise."

"That Barry guy—"

"It's unauthorized. I want nothing to do with that book."

Jasmine's dog is angling to lick her nostrils, so she pushes its muzzle away, saying, "No more, Ross." Then she gives a nervous laugh. "Don't you think your PottHeads deserve to get to know the real you?"

"No."

"But why?"

Claudine dimples her cheek with her pointer finger, her right elbow resting on the bottom bunk's mattress. "I don't owe anyone anything." As she says it, she wonders if this is what she sounded like to Wylie when she asked about her father.

"You don't have to write a tell-all. Just write a tell-*some-things*." She collides her palms together, her nails ten church spires. "You win, we win."

Ross may or may not be humping the pillow next to Jasmine. He's mostly off camera, but his tail is intermittently visible in a way that suggests thrusting.

Telling Claudine Potts that she should think about how her book might benefit CycleTron has the opposite effect of motivating her. Every word of her next sentence comes out through gritted teeth, articulated with potency. "I am not writing a memoir."

Jasmine leans closer to the screen. "You could see this as an opportunity. Bolster your CycleTron following, maybe double it. Once the book comes out, we can set up a media tour, get you on the *Today* show. Even announce that you're signing *another three-year contract with us*."

No glee over the contract renewal comes her way. "Media tour?" Claudine's overheating, and she unbuttons her cardigan. "I'm not that interesting, I promise."

"You're a legend, and you know it."

"This is so absurd."

Jasmine is now so close to the screen that Claudine can see the etching of her lip pencil. "If you want to continue to be the face of CycleTron, then you need to actually be the face. Up your game. There are dozens of other retired athletes gunning for this."

"I never asked to be the face!"

"What's good for you is also good for us. CycleTron could certainly outline some incentives. Sweeten the pot, so to speak. Because as I said, when your brand goes up"—Jasmine points heavenward—"so does ours."

Claudine balls her hand into a fist and presses it to her mouth, staring at the carpet, thinking. Finally, she says, "I'm speechless."

"Right? It's going to be amazing!" Jasmine's smile is a bright-white snowdrift hiding a sinkhole. Now Claudine is chilled to the bone, and she wraps her arms around herself, wishing for time to think, time to talk this over with Gib.

But why? What's there to think about?

She closes her eyes for a moment, shaking her head, searching for the right words. "It's not happening. I want no part in a book or a media tour or building my brand."

Jasmine's lips twist in shock. Her eyes blaze with anger. "I'm sorry?"

"I ride with CycleTron to get people moving and keep people moving, and I am genuinely touched that my riders feel a connection to me. But when my rides end each day, so does my responsibility to them."

"What are you saying, Claudine? I strongly urge you to write—"

Before she has time to change her mind, Claudine blurts

out two words she's never said in her entire life: "I quit." She lifts her hands up as if she's backing away from a poker game.

I quit. What a rush. It feels awesome.

Jasmine, dropping the best-friend facade, issues a mean-girl laugh. "You can't *quit.*"

"I can, and I just did."

"You have a contract."

Claudine mimes ripping up a contract. "Don't care. I'll figure out a way."

"Ohmygosh. You're going to regret this. Like, a lot."

"Doubt it! Also, Ross is a sex fiend, get him some help."

Claudine hears only half of Jasmine's outraged scoff before she hangs up.

28

Wylie

WYLIE'S TRYING TO FIND ZOSEL'S HOUSE FROM memory; she's been there before, but not since childhood. So many of these chalets look the same—dark wood, red shutters; dark wood, red shutters—that she gets turned around.

She lets out a huff of air, her breath visible in the cold of the morning, frustrated that everything looks foreign and vaguely familiar at the same time. But it's not only that. The morning's still weighing heavy on her too: the ski-crash nightmare, the thing Claudine said about her collage—"You could sell it"—the fact that she's got to tell Dan the truth about the competition. Not to mention that she still hasn't gotten back to Aileen about the promotion.

What to do to get her dorsal fins going? Dan would talk his way into using another hotel's fitness center for a power hour of weight lifting.

Yes, but what would *Wylie* do?

She's rooted in place, unsure. Somewhere up in the mountains comes the boom of another avalanche detonation, and it snaps her out of it, awakening her to what's right across the street: the cutest little café and creperie with a red-trimmed door the color of an old British phone booth. *Maybe this.*

Inside, she's nuzzled by warm air and chatter and the sound of the espresso machine, the café's interior welcoming with its vaulted, exposed-beam ceiling, its wood-paneled counter.

Wylie just loves the old-world charm of this town, how it collides with the modern day: a woven basket holding oranges and grapefruits rests atop the counter, while nearby patrons Instagram photos of cappuccinos so large they could serve as bathtubs for Wylie's old Barbie doll.

Every seat is taken, so while she waits for one, she unzips her coat and steps up to the counter to watch a stoop-backed, gray-haired gentleman, who looks to be pushing seventy, command the crepe station. He's got two crepes going at once, using a wooden, T-shaped tool to spin the batter, spreading it into thin, nearly translucent circles over the sizzling crepe pans. Then he swoops up a long, slender spatula, slicing just underneath the crepes to flip them over in fluid, flawless motions.

"You're an artist," she says, mesmerized.

He chuckles. "I've been doing this since I was fourteen."

She eyes the menu. "What's your favorite flavor?"

"Nutella and banana. Simple. *Lecker.*"

A young Italian woman with sleeve tattoos is also working behind the counter, and she whacks the portafilter of the espresso machine onto the wooden counter as if she's trying to squash an insect. Then she nods toward the window.

Wylie glances behind her to realize she's indicating a recently vacated table. She smiles in gratitude, moves to hang her coat on the chair, and returns to the counter to order a full-fat latte and the crepe master's favorite.

Oops. There goes her diet again—although Wylie feels less and less guilty about it with every mouthful she puts between herself and her old life in Massachusetts, making her "oops" more mischievous than contrite.

Back at her table, while she waits for her food, she closes her eyes, a memory of Zosel flitting in with a humming-bird's swiftness. Wylie's eighth birthday at Copper Mountain. Zosel's gift—an art-history book called *The Art of Art: A Primer*—was wrapped in shimmery purple paper that beamed back a watery reflection of Wylie's wide eyes shaded underneath the umbrellas of her eyebrows.

The best part of this gift was that it demonstrated Zosel's respect for her. An adult book, given to a child. Wylie felt her spine grow six inches with pride. Zosel had seen her. Had noticed her burgeoning interest in art. Had encouraged it, in her gentle way.

How does someone give such a loving gift and then disappear two years later? It doesn't add up.

Claudine is still withholding her dad's identity, cutting off her inquiries with a swift hand chop—but she can't stop Wylie from finding Zosel. Wylie's an adult now. She should have done this years ago.

The Italian server delivers brunch, the crepe folded like a letter in an envelope, dusted with powdered sugar. She savors the first sip of latte, cuts into her crepe with the side of her fork, relishing the combination of hazelnut and chocolate and banana. Nutella had been a World Cup staple, Wylie dipping pretzel sticks straight into the jar as she jostled in the back seat of their rental van, driving from one alpine village to the next.

It's freeing to eat like she used to as a kid, with total abandon for calories.

She looks up to see the crepe master watching her, and she gives him two thumbs up. He nods in appreciation, bends his head back to his work.

Franz Blasi would be around his age, she realizes. He could still be spry and full of life and have a lot of good years left. A handful, at least, to get to know each other. Does she believe Claudine?

She alternates bites with sips, pulling out her phone to look up Franz Blasi. In a few clicks, there he is—a younger version of him, anyway, old photos of him coaching. She zooms in, trying to detect a likeness in his face, not sure if she's dismayed to find none, though it could be hard to tell, she reckons. She sets down her phone.

If it's not Franz, who else could it be? Why would Claudine guard her dad's identity so tightly? She thinks of what Bibbidi said in the dining room the other day, that her mom's not necessarily trying to hurt her by keeping this secret. That maybe she's trying to protect herself. But from what? She remembers that accusation on the Substack that Claudine might've been the beneficiary of some preferential treatment during her 1995 season. That can't be it. Her mom would never cheat, partly out of ethics and partly out of ego; cheating is admitting you're not really the best. Plus, Claudine can barely accept someone holding a door for her, let alone favoritism.

Outside, beyond the window, she recognizes a few

members of Sings to Excess displaying the frustrated gestures of a group trying to collectively decide where to eat. With them is Calvin, who looks toward the window, sees Wylie, grins, and jogs to the door.

How can she feel this thrilled to see someone she barely knows? She tries to temper her enthusiasm, bite back her smile.

"Hey," he says.

"Hi."

He nods toward her crepe. "That looks incredible."

"It is." She wants to offer him a taste, but that feels too intimate.

"Want to hang out with us today? We're going to check out the famed wooden houses of Zermatt."

"The Hinterdorf."

"You pronounce that so much better than I do. I'll just stick to 'wooden houses.'"

She laughs. "It's so cool, you'll love it."

"So you'll come?" It makes her heart pitter-patter, seeing how much he's hoping she'll join him.

"I wish I could, but I can't. I actually have a few things to do."

"You have the cutest little smudge of chocolate on your face," he says. "I can't be that guy who doesn't say anything, and then you see it in the mirror later and think, *WTF, Calvin!*"

"Here?" She points to her forehead. She's not really even that embarrassed. Not with him.

He snorts. "No, just near your mouth." He picks up her napkin. "I'll get it."

"Oh, okay." She juts out her chin as Calvin gingerly swipes

a corner of the napkin on the outside edge of her lips, and her stomach squeezes—in a good way, for once—as she imagines pulling his hand to her mouth, kissing it.

His hand lingers for a beat, as if he's also lost to his own imagination, and she wonders if he's about to cup her cheek. But he pulls his hand back. "There," he says. "All cleaned up."

She thinks of retorting with a flirty *But I like it dirty*, but that's pole-vaulting way over the line. "Thanks," she says instead.

"Can we have dinner tonight, just you and me?" His eyes sparkle at hers.

"Um . . ." She shouldn't. She really, really shouldn't.

"As friends." He holds up his hands to show his innocence, although that touch on her mouth felt anything but innocent. "It just feels like our time here is fleeting."

Wylie's voice is reflective, almost mournful. "I know."

"I like hanging out with you."

"Me too." She twists the napkin in her lap, what she says next going against her own moral compass. "Okay."

"Okay?" His eyes light up.

"Yes, okay." She holds up a clarifying finger. "As friends."

"Totally."

"Your *other* friends are waiting." She swats his arm.

He turns to leave, then turns back. "See you tonight."

Wylie nods, and he bounds out the door. She squints through the midmorning sunlight filtering in, watching his a cappella buddies throw their arms around his shoulders, their laughter filling the air. Calvin has been a welcome surprise. If she has to be stuck in Zermatt for a few more days, at least it means more time with him.

And time to find Zosel. Maybe even Franz?

But she's got to tell Dan the truth.

She owes him a phone call, but she opts for a text instead, worried he'll back her into a corner somehow and, just like last time, she'll end up making promises that she can't keep. And if Claudine couldn't get them on a helicopter yesterday, chances are even slimmer today.

Hi, bad news. We can't get on a helicopter after all. Too many people on the list in front of us. I'm so sorry we'll miss BodyFittest Duo. But we can try again next year.

Then she deletes the last line. She doesn't want to be with Dan next year. Or even next month. And if that's the case, why be with him for even one more day?

That's a conversation she does owe him over the phone.

For now, she'll start with this message. She takes a deep breath and hits Send, relieved that now Dan knows. And the competition is off. About his sports-betting debt, well, he'll have to find a different way to pay it off.

Before she can take another sip of her coffee, Dan responds.

Another DNF for Wylie Potts. Why am I not surprised?

Did Not Finish.

Wylie's jaw drops. Tears prick her eyes. She knew he'd be disappointed. Frustrated with her, even. But she never imagined he'd lash out like this, hitting the center of her most bruised wound.

He's ultracompetitive, and he can be controlling, but Wylie's never pegged him as cruel. You learn a lot about someone by how they respond and treat others in times of crisis, and she's realizing that up until Dan's injury and his sports-betting admission—and all that's set into motion—it's been mostly smooth sailing. She's never seen him under real duress.

This, she understands with a jolt, is what it looks like. What's in store for her down the road, if she stays with him. She can't. She won't.

Not only does she not miss him, but she doesn't love him anymore.

Even as Wylie arrives at this conclusion about Dan, "another DNF" circles in her mind. Maybe his words hurt so much because they're true. She always has been, and always will be, a quitter.

She glances around, the once-friendly noises of the café becoming louder, menacing, even, the whir of the milk steamer not unlike the sound of wind rushing in her ears as she skied downward, and she wants to cover her ears with her palms, quiet it all, push it away.

But it's her thoughts that are the loudest, a schoolyard bully on repeat: *quitter, quitter, quitter.* Everything big in her life she quits.

Only losers don't finish. Disappointing, second-rate losers.

An anxiety attack gathers like a storm cloud. With horror, she senses it grow, her breathing becoming rapid and shallow. She grips the sides of the table, her head bowed, willing it to stay away. Pain spikes in her stomach like she's a butterfly pinned to a mounting board, still alive, trapped and frightened.

She reaches for her bag, groping for her earbuds to listen to her meditation app—but her vision blurs with more tears and she comes up short. *No!*

Maybe she actually yells this, because in an instant the Italian server is beside her, setting down a cup of water. "Everything is okay?" she asks.

But Wylie can't speak, can only shake her head no, and the server runs a hand over her back in a soothing circular motion, bringing the cup of water to her mouth. "Drink."

Complying, Wylie takes an ungraceful gulp, water dribbling down the sides of her mouth that she wipes at with her sleeve. Slowly, the attack abates, never picking up full steam, Wylie coming back to herself. She's painfully embarrassed, hoping she didn't cause a scene. She can't bring her eyes to the counter to see if the crepe maker is watching her too.

The server crouches down, hands on the edge of the table, chin on her hands, her dark eyes on Wylie's. "You are sad?" she asks in her Italian accent.

Is Wylie sad? She thinks for a moment, *really* thinks, taking stock of herself, like someone patting their own body for a lost wallet or a pair of missing spectacles.

"No," she realizes, her voice garbled. "I'm mad." She juts out her bottom jaw. Not just mad, but livid. Livid at Dan for making her feel small.

"Good, eh? Sad—" The server makes a *pfft* sound. "Sad, you are stuck. But mad—" She zooms one palm across the other, like a moped taking off. "Mad is like, uh . . ." She searches for the correct English word. "Petrol, yes? Petrol."

"Yes," Wylie says, a new resolve building. No more getting walked on, remember? She's not a sapling. She's petrol itself, liquid and flammable, capable of burning up everything in her path with one spark.

The server pats Wylie's shoulder, satisfied. "Good girl. Another *caffè*?"

Wylie stands. "No, I'm on my way out."

She's not quitting the competition. But she's not competing

for Dan. Or to prove a thing to Claudine. She's going to win for herself—it's an all-encompassing pull that drowns out the desire to locate Zosel or Franz.

Striding through the streets, clear mountain air chilling the insides of her nose, Wylie decides: she and Claudine have to find an escape route to Berlin. It's not over yet. And she knows just the mountaineering guide to help them.

29

Claudine

EN ROUTE TO THE HELICOPTER LINE, CLAUDINE spies a lemon-yellow cable-knit hat with a pom-pom, and the woman underneath it. How can they be crossing paths this much? Claudine shoots a look at Mother Matterhorn, as though she has her hand in it.

Dodge her until you're ready.

Claudine ducks into the Matterhorn Museum. Worried that Zosel might be able to see her through the exterior glass walls, she pays the entrance fee, stepping farther into the museum and farther back into the history of Zermatt.

Before she can even hang up her coat, she's swept along with the crowd, down the stairs into the museum's main exhibit: Zermatlantis. In front of her, a know-it-all father explains to his kids that Zermatlantis—a clever mix between the words "Zermatt" and "Atlantis"—is an underground rendering of the village in the nineteenth century.

Claudine didn't know this little tidbit, but she regrets learning it from this guy, who's actually reading from a pamphlet and passing it off as his own knowledge.

At the mouth of the stairs, she spills out with the group, transported to a past world, the air cool and musty, the room lit up with ceiling-hung theater lights. She walks in the opposite direction of the know-it-all, who's now talking loudly (reading) about old architectural styles.

She trips once over the cobblestone square as she takes in the surroundings: the whitewashed facade of a chalet with red shutters nearly as tall as her; dark, wood-paneled stables with fake farm animals; the mountain guide's house with its narrow bed; the local pastor's home with its long-lost prayers and cries and sins and omissions; a tiny teahouse.

Claudine's never been a fan of history museums—stopping to read the plaques even less so—but here, she's spellbound. It's as if she's woken up in an alpine village two centuries ago, and the effect slows her thundering heart rate. Zermatt is a truly magnificent place, and in the scrum of the last few days, she's failed to appreciate it. Down in this shrine to the past, she even forgets about Zosel for a moment.

She wishes she could bring Wylie here. Enjoy it with her. But if she can't answer Wylie's fundamental question about her father, will they ever have that kind of relationship?

Claudine takes a deep breath, smelling mouse poop.

A group of tourists circle a glass-enclosed piece of rope draped over a red velvet cushion. Claudine's versed in Zermatt history enough to know what this is: the broken rope from the first ascent up the Matterhorn in 1865. Four of the seven climbers died. The rope didn't hold.

She shudders. This village might be quaint, but the Alps eat people up and spit them back out. She spots a long wooden bench underneath the eaves of a fake tree in the middle of the square. The cortisol spike from quitting CycleTron has worn off, leaving her shaky and wiped. It was a rash decision. What will she do now? How will she fill her days?

Claudine drops to the bench like an acorn, emitting a sigh. She longs to get home to Gib, have him as a sounding board. She doesn't want to stay in this country for another millisecond, reminders of her former life swirling around her, glories and failures.

This visit to Zermatt, she's had only failures, no glory.

Sitting farther down the bench is an old man in a navy-blue fleece, his legs out straight, his arms crossed at the wrists, and his eyes closed as if he's warming in the sun. Claudine glances his way, looks back to study the red shutters, and then pauses, tilting her head.

No way.

She beams her gaze at him again, studying his profile, his shock of thin white hair like a cresting wave, the unmistakable ruddy skin of a lifetime skier, branded by the sun and wind. Then she looks around her, as if there's been some sort of setup.

I mean, what are the chances? she thinks.

Unsure if the man is sleeping or merely resting, she pivots her body toward him and whispers, "Franz?"

He doesn't respond. Okay, so it's not him. Claudine's going to drop it.

She pivots back.

He is *from* here, but what would he be doing in this museum? She leans to the right, her voice louder. "Franz?"

To her delight and shock, the man—Franz—opens one eye

like a slow-moving iguana, peering at Claudine. His other eye snaps open, and a smile unfolds on his face.

"Claudine Potts," he says, his Swiss accent familiar, as thick as porridge.

"Franz Blasi." She smiles back.

"It's been a long time." He's neither delighted nor shocked to see her, acting as if he's always known they'd run into each other again. "What are you doing back in Zermatt? Not skiing, I hope. This avalanche." He tsks.

"It has been a long time." She's still processing that Franz Blasi, in the flesh, is sitting next to her. Gib will never believe it. "No, I'm not skiing. I'm just here . . . for a walk down memory lane." She gestures to the room. Then her curiosity gets the best of her. "Why are you down here? I thought this place was only for tourists."

He closes his eyes, nodding, a small chuckle tangling in his chest, turning into a cough that takes time to tame. It's strange to see the once-powerful Franz Blasi, such a dominant figure on the mountains, reduced to this hunched and hacking man.

When Franz finally clears his throat, he says, "I'm here for a walk down memory lane too. Zermatt has changed so much. I like pretending I'm in the old days."

"Are you still skiing?"

"My knees are *nutzlos*." He slaps his knees with his hands. She laughs. "Mine too."

"Besides, the skiing is . . . How should I say? It's *Scheisse*." He spits the word to the floor. "The glaciers are receding. They're melting faster than ever. One day, they will be gone. Not before my lifetime." He points a finger at her. "But possibly in yours." Thumping his chest with his fist, he says, "It hurts my heart. It will be a great loss for Switzerland. For everyone. But especially this village. Down here, I can pretend that everything is as it was."

Listening to his projections, Claudine's own heart hurts. If Franz is worried about climate change, it's real. He might be the least alarmist person she's ever met. It's a dizzying prospect, the disappearance of this terrain, the glaciers retreating as if pushed back by a marching army, revealing dark, ugly rock below, and then soon, with sunlight and rain, meadows will emerge, trees and flowers and wildlife, beautiful in its own way, but not the same. Not skiable.

For the second time, Claudine shudders in this dank underworld.

"That makes me sad too," Claudine says. It's an insufficient response, as was her "I don't know" to Koa last night when he asked what they should do.

A silence settles between them like a third person wedging their bum on the bench. Claudine studies her hands. Finally, she leans over past the silence and says, "Oh, get this: people are speculating that you're the father of my daughter."

Franz slowly raises an eyebrow, searching Claudine's face. She shrugs and cracks a sly smile, and at that, he tips his head back, issuing a cannonball of a laugh shooting straight out of his mouth, loud and hard. He slaps his thigh, utterly tickled.

Claudine laughs too at the sheer absurdity of it all. She can't stop laughing, in fact, tears wetting her cheeks. It's a rare belly laugh, and she welcomes the release.

Franz holds his elbows with crossed arms. After a long moment, he leans toward her and says, "I do know the real father. Of your daughter."

Claudine's body goes still. "You do?" she asks quietly.

He gestures for her to come closer, so she does, inching along the bench. He brings a withered hand up to cup her ear, whispering, and her eyes grow wide. He sits back, staring straight ahead.

"But how did you know?"

Tapping his temple, he says, "I saw you leave together. I did the math."

30

Wylie

WYLIE FINALLY FINDS KOA RESTING IN A HAMMOCK. She nudges him with her thigh, accidently sending the hammock swaying.

"Hey, can I ask you a quick question?"

He removes his AirPods. "Sure, shoot. Just steady me. You really sent me rocking."

She gives an embarrassed laugh, stilling Koa. "Sorry! I'm just amped up."

"You're stronger than you—well, no, you look strong too. What's up?"

"There's a hiking path from Zermatt to Täsch." She thrusts her phone at him, the screen pulled up to a web page for the Zermatt-Täsch Railway Trail. This is their escape route.

Täsch is a town three miles away that's not been impacted by the avalanche. From there, Wylie knows, is the train to

Zurich. From Zurich, the plane to Berlin. Once in Berlin, world domination. On a small scale.

He takes the phone, nodding. "Yeah, natch. You can for sure hike from here to Täsch. But only in the summer. It's closed for the winter. Snow-covered."

It's just as Wylie thought. "Can you get us skis?" she asks, nearly breathless with excitement.

"Wait a tick. What are you planning?"

She grins. "We're going to ski out."

"Bro, you can't do that. It's an avalanche zone."

"I knew you'd say that. But look—" She grabs her phone back from him, pulls up another website. "They've dropped the avalanche risk to level three. See?"

Realizing she's dead serious, he sits up from the hammock, gripping the sides like it's a canoe, his face full of worry. "Level three is not nothing."

"But it's not level *five* anymore. And they've been setting off controlled avalanches like crazy. We'll be fine."

"Wylie, you're not hearing me. It's dangerous. You'd be off your rocker. It's going to be slow going and really hard to cut a fresh track. And you of all people should know that you can never totally predict avalanches. I think you're gonna have to let that go."

"I can't." Her smile falls away. "It's worth the risk to me. I just can't go back to my old life a loser. A quitter. Someone who hides in a bathroom. I need this, Koa." They stare at each other, Koa still not budging, so Wylie applies a little more pressure, trying for a lighter tone. "If anyone can make it through that pass on skis, it's me and my mom. You said so yourself. She's achieved the impossible. And if they change the risk level any higher before tomorrow, we won't go."

Koa shakes his head. "The snow's deep as."

"The trail's marked, though. I'll bring my compass."

"Sure, but—"

"I grew up on snow."

"I know, but—"

"Please. *Please.*"

He hesitates, drawing a palm down his face, and even as he says "You'd need backcountry skis," he's still shaking his head, like he can't believe his own complicity.

"I'm comfortable on those. And we'd need ski boots too."

"Your mom probably won't agree to do it. She was pretty spooked the other day. I mean, she did yell for everyone to duck under the tables."

"Koa, that's where you're wrong." A strange calm settles over Wylie. "Claudine doesn't believe in quitting."

Koa sighs. "I'll get what you need. But I don't like this. I really don't."

Wylie reaches out to grip his hand. "Thank you. We'll go tomorrow."

"Leave before seven a.m. so snow patrol doesn't catch you and turn you back. And if they do catch you, don't tell them you got the skis from me." He gives her a pointed look.

"I won't. I promise. Besides, we'll be so fast that we'll be uncatchable."

"I think you're overestimating yourself, Wylie."

"Never!" she sings as she sails to her room.

She shoots Claudine a text, linking to the trail: I found a way out of here. We'll cross-country ski on this tomorrow. Let's leave at 7:00 a.m. We'll spread Kipper's ashes along the way.

Every win, she reassures herself, has an element of risk. It's like Claudine and Kipper taught her—if you ski afraid, you're dead. So they won't ski afraid. They'll be fast and fierce and flawless. Banishing any nagging worries, she gathers up her towel.

Her next step: glam up.

If she'll be gone tomorrow, she's going to party first—just like the Hostel die Freude promises.

31

Wylie

IN THE HOSTEL'S SHOWER, WYLIE USES A TINY PAIR of traveling sewing scissors to trim her unruly nether regions. How long has it been since she's groomed? She can get a good two inches if she pulls her curlies straight. Also, has anyone ever gotten injured by doing this? Like, accidently cut skin? Ended up in the hospital? She thinks of Dr. DJ and the fist-bumping nurse, how they'd joke about an injury like that.

A few more snips, and she sighs, giving up. It's not like she's planning to bed Calvin, anyway.

She pulls on jeans and another tight-fitting turtleneck that she hopes is sexy in an athletic way, raking a brush through her hair, deciding on no braid.

In the mirror's reflection, she catches a glimpse of the Matterhorn print. Her mind flits to the danger involved in her escape plan tomorrow, and a nervous energy charges through her that she shuts down immediately.

The door swings open, Bibbidi huffing, her arms wrapped around two towels and an overstuffed dopp kit.

"My dear!" She bellows a greeting.

"Let me help you." Wylie removes the dopp kit from her clutch.

"Thank you. My back is still aching from ice-skating." She hangs up her towels and clothes on two little hooks, and then presses a hand into her lower back. "Why are you getting all gussied up?"

Wylie's face reddens as if she's just been caught with those sewing scissors. "Having dinner with Calvin."

"Ohhh," Bibbidi says, a knowing smile on her lips.

"As friends!"

"He's a pretty handsome friend."

"Haven't noticed." Wylie shrugs one shoulder.

Bibbidi reaches out her palm. "Here."

"What?"

"I'll brush the back."

"Oh, uh, okay." Wylie hands over the brush. Bibbidi begins, tenderly pressing against the back of her head with one hand as she pulls the brush through to her tips, and she's struck by how intimate a gesture it is. How nurturing. She could fall asleep like this.

It's been ages since someone really took care of her. She watches herself in the mirror, Bibbidi's body mostly hidden behind Wylie's tall frame, the botanical tattoos on her arms rising and falling with every brushstroke.

After a silent moment, Bibbidi says, "How are things going with you and your mom?"

Wylie's shoulders inch up toward her ears just a smidge, a protective stance. "That's a complicated question."

"You mean a complicated answer?" The brush catches on a snag, but Bibbidi gently pries it free.

She closes her eyes. "Extremely."

"I don't mean to meddle."

Wylie sighs. "We'll be okay. We just have some things to work out." Bibbidi is quiet, rhythmically brushing. Does Wylie actually believe that she and Claudine will be okay? Will they work things out? What are those *things*, really, if she had to boil them down? Does she even want to stay in touch with her mom after Berlin?

Again she studies the Matterhorn print on the wall, how the gray pyramid's four distinct ridges point perfectly toward the four cardinal directions, as if the mountain is a compass. *Tell me what to do,* she thinks of asking Mother Matterhorn, only Wylie doesn't have the same relationship to mountains that Claudine has. Claudine, who sometimes preferred mountains over people because she said people could let her down. Who could easily cut off a human side of herself when she was clicking into competitor mode. Having a mom nicknamed the Stone-Cold Killer meant some of that coldness was aimed at Wylie—especially when Wylie displayed weakness. Claudine got so confused, angry, even, that Wylie didn't share the same ability to shut down fear. Go stony. Be cold.

Is the Stone-Cold Killer still in her mom, or has she been exorcised? Here in Zermatt, Wylie hasn't really seen that old side rear its head in Claudine, but they've been together for only, what? Three and a half days? Feels like a lifetime, when in fact it's been no time at all.

Another thought emerges: *Is it safe to be my true self around Mom?*

Huh. Maybe that's the crux of it.

Her head bobs with the motion of Bibbidi's brushing, and ever so quietly Wylie says, "I'm a disappointment to my mom." That's the crux of it too.

Bibbidi tilts her head, taking this in. "And she's a disappointment to you."

Wylie frowns. St Moritz. *Pound, pound, pound.* And, "You quit skiing to hang up picture frames?" How those words had stung. "Yeah, in some ways she is."

"Mmm."

"I bet you are a really good mom, Bibbidi."

Leaning out from behind Wylie to make eye contact in the mirror, Bibbidi asks, "What makes you think I have kids?"

"Oh, I assumed, I guess. You just have such a maternal vibe."

Bibbidi takes hold of both of Wylie's shoulders. "Turn." Wylie shifts, now able to see herself in the mirror only from the corner of her eye as Bibbidi comes more fully into view, brushing the right side of her hair. "I do have two children. They're grown now. But I found parenting exceedingly challenging. It tested me constantly. The number of times I lost my patience. Yelled. Messed up. And I was so hard on myself about it. So hard." Bibbidi squeezes her eyes shut as if pained by the memory. "I think you should ask yourself: What makes a 'good' mom"—she air quotes the word in the mirror—"and what makes a 'good' daughter?"

Wylie thinks about it. Well, a good mom doesn't shame her daughter about a new job. She understands why her daughter would want to know—would deserve to know—who her father is.

But then again, maybe she shows up on a bum knee to do

her best in an admittedly crazy contest, just to help her kid. Maybe she dusts herself off after a parenting wipeout and tries another run.

As for good daughters, well, aren't they supposed to make their parents proud? Fulfill expectations? Or maybe none of this is true at all, and her perspective on moms and daughters is totally warped.

"I don't know, exactly," she answers.

Bibbidi guides Wylie to turn again, facing her toward the other side of the bathroom. "The only advice I can offer on the topic: Right now, she's not allowed to mess up because 'good' moms don't mess up. And you're not allowed to go your own path because 'good' daughters do as they're told. The sooner you both see each other as fully formed people, not just a mom and a daughter, the freer you'll both be from expectations. And then you can have a real relationship. An authentic relationship. You can have shortcomings and flaws and still love each other. Does that make sense, or am I babbling? Sometimes I babble. They could have nicknamed me Babbidi."

Wylie can't laugh at the joke. Any sound that comes out of her next will be a cry, so she keeps her mouth shut, warding off the tears. Instead, she nods.

She's never seen Claudine as anything but her mom. What would it be like if they both acted like they were meeting for the first time? What would she love about Claudine?

Bibbidi, finished brushing, squeezes Wylie by both shoulders. "Promise me, whatever happens next between the two of you, you'll be careful. I can't say why, but I just have this ominous feeling. It's there, and then it's gone." Her hand makes a poofing gesture in the air.

Wylie manages to keep her face neutral, but she can't repress a small shiver. "I promise," she says, knowing full well their trek tomorrow morning will be the opposite of careful.

To distract Bibbidi from prying any further, she lifts up a lock of her very straight and squeaky-clean hair, eyeing the dopp kit. "You don't happen to have anything in there to zhuzh this up?" She's never said "zhuzh" in her life.

"Oh, do I ever."

And that's how Wylie exits the bathroom with hot-pink highlights.

32

Wylie

WYLIE AND CALVIN ARE SEATED AT A TABLE ACROSS from the bar at Restaurant Stadel, so near the server stand that Calvin reaches for another clean knife and fork after he clumsily knocks his silverware to the floor.

"By the way," he says, "I like the pink."

She fingers the ends of her hair. "It's silly."

"If I had hair, I'd dye it pink."

"That would look really good on you."

They beam at each other.

Calvin picks up his menu. "Let's feast."

So they do: a basket of brown bread; cognac-marinated grilled prawns; a plate of air-dried beef because, in Calvin's words, "Why not?"; a Swiss staple: shredded-potato pancakes called *Rösti*, served in a piping-hot cast-iron skillet, this version dubbed the Matterhorn for the bacon, cheese, and fried egg piled on top of one another like alternating thermal base layers of warmth; and a white wine mushroom risotto that makes Wylie moan with pleasure. Plus, two glasses of red wine each.

It's decadent and delicious and even a little dangerous, Wylie leaning into her desires in a way that's been off-limits for so damn long.

They talk mostly about the food, not because they have nothing else to say, but because they're giddy for it all—the give of the rice, cooked perfectly al dente; the thin slices of beef that filter the candlelight when they hold them aloft, a heavenly stained-glass window of meat; the crunch of the bottom layer of *Rösti*; the bread, downy soft, that sops it all up.

Talking about food brings them back around to Wylie's fondue story.

"Barbie shoe aside," says Calvin, "it's incredible that you were exposed to foods like fondue from such a young age. Me—I was probably eating a Lunchable while you were fighting over the *Grossmutter*."

"You know, I've never had a Lunchable."

"It's not too late." He smiles. "Seriously, it sounds like you had an extraordinary upbringing."

"Mmm," she agrees, sipping her wine. "But extraordinary gets exhausting because you have to keep it up. Speaking of extraordinary, you could go on *The Voice*. Be the lead in a band. Make an album—" She stops short, hearing her mom's voice in the suggestion.

He chuckles, seemingly unbothered. "Sings to Excess has a few albums."

"Calvin, I just realized I sound like my mom right now."

She clasps a hand over her mouth, shaking her head. "I'm sorry! She's always pushing me to do something more with my art, and here I am doing it to you!"

"My parents do the same thing. It's not totally their fault. Our culture conditions us to think we should be doing more. I'll *always* sing. But I don't need acclaim. Or an audience. I sort of want to try some things I'm not good at—just for kicks, you know?"

No, Wylie does not know. "Like what?" she asks, nearly scandalized.

Calvin wobbles his head. "Oh, I don't know. Maybe cake decorating?"

"Do you know anything about cake decorating?"

"Not a thing. But I want to learn how to make my kids—if I have kids—really cool birthday cakes. A soccer ball or water-slides with swimmers in inner tubes—whatever they're into. It's just something I've always thought about."

It's so fitting that one of his expressions of love would involve cake. She smiles, imagining him piping the frosting of an edible soccer ball.

"What cake design would you make for me?"

"Hmm . . ." He studies Wylie in a way that makes her melt on the inside. "Ah! I've got it. I'd make you a cake decorated as the Trouble board game."

She bursts out laughing. "I am the master at that game."

"And you're also trouble, at least for me. So it has a double meaning." The restaurant lights dim at just this moment, as if Calvin and Wylie have surreptitiously ducked into a closet together, shut the door, shut everyone else out, their bodies pressed together. His eyes seem to darken too with his first overt blurring of the line, his admission of the effect she's having on him.

"Calvin," she says. "I don't mean to be trouble for you."

"I know. You can't help it." He shrugs as if it's no big deal, but he's still staring at her intently. He's set one hand on the table, and she could easily reach out and entwine her fingers with his. She swallows. How much to tell him about Dan? She opens her mouth to speak, but their server is upon them, lighting the votive candle at the center of the table, her accent sounding like a reprimand. Did they leave room for dessert?

It breaks the spell. They veer back into the friend zone, laughing and joking.

Calvin shakes his head. "Not for me. If I look at the dessert menu, I'll have to get something. You?"

"I'm glad you're saying no because I would have forced that dessert down my gullet. I think you've created a monster."

"Well, at least I didn't create a Muenster, because that's a cheese."

Wylie snorts. "That's a really dumb joke." Even as she cracks up, she knows there's a new, undeniable charge between them.

"Thank you."

The server is not amused.

And the server is even less amused when they're the last to leave the restaurant.

In what's becoming their favorite pastime together besides eating, they stroll. She's turned off her phone, not wanting another rude text from Dan to plummet her mood.

She looks around, marveling. Zermatt is magnificent at night in the winter. The quaint lampposts along the street curve up and over like Little Bo Peep's staff, each light illuminating the snow. Here and there, string lights cascade over the window railings of chalets and boutique hotels. After the warmth of the restaurant, the air outside offers an invigorating chill, reminding Wylie of the relief of pressing cold packs to aching muscles. Above them, the night sky is a crisp sheet of unfolded origami, stars twinkling like fireflies, the full moon a clock ticking down. Hidden in the darkness, where they can't see, Wylie imagines the Matterhorn snoring softly, bedded down beneath a quilt of clouds.

The streets are also party central.

Groups of newfound friends stagger and sing and sway. Wylie and Calvin hear songs in German and Spanish and Japanese, duck past a couple with Scottish accents having a surprisingly cutthroat snowball fight, admire a mermaid ice sculpture made by two Polish friends who are crosshatching her tail, and stop to warm up at another city-sanctioned bonfire, holding up their hands as if they're pressing them against a wall of heat.

Along the way, they play lightning round, Wylie feverishly learning everything she can about Calvin. Only she knows that this is their last night together in Zermatt. She doesn't share her escape plan, not wanting him to worry—or to try to talk her out of it.

"Horror movies or comedies?" he asks.

"Comedies," she answers. "Always lose your keys or never?"

"Never. You?"

"Always."

"Okay . . ." He tilts his head, thinking. "Sleep on planes or awake the entire time?"

"I'm out. I can sleep anywhere."

"Same!" They bump each other, a shoulder high five.

"Operation or that game that slaps you in the face with whipped cream?"

"Neither. Both would give me a heart attack."

They've stopped outside of a nightclub, the music thumping so loudly they can feel the vibrations through the soles of their feet.

"Dancing or no dancing?" Wylie asks.

Calvin grins. "Dancing. Always."

"Should we?" It's a gutsy question. She bites her lip, watching Calvin's face.

"You mean, like, now?"

"Sure! Unless you're tired." In the suspended seconds before Calvin answers, a shooting star of worry whizzes through Wylie's mind. What if he's not having as much fun as she is? What if he's just plain tuckered out, and the idea of being in his comfy bed is much more enticing than a crowded club?

She's the one who should be prioritizing sleep, the morning trek just around the corner now, but being responsible feels like drudgery. Wylie Potts wants to live it up.

Calvin's smile is so big and beautiful Wylie has to close her eyes to savor it. "Let's do this, Wylie. But you might be sorry. Once I start, I don't stop."

33

Claudine

IT'S NOT GRATIFYING TO PACE A ROOM THAT'S JUST a smidge longer than bunk beds, but Claudine's been rambling wild-eyed and breathless back and forth between the bedposts for the last hour, trying to flush out her angst.

This afternoon, following Franz Blasi's shocking admission, she'd wallowed on that museum bench until closing time, long after the Swiss coach patted her knee, groaned himself up to standing, and left the old world for the modern one. After that, she'd slipped into a restaurant that doubled as a piano bar. The mournful sound of the piano keys matched her mood as she sat low at the bar, picking at a dinner of salmon on toast until the bartender cleared her plate and set down her bill with a you-can't-loiter-here-unless-you're-drinking kind of briskness.

Back in her room, she's coming to terms with a few chilling realizations.

The first: Keeping the truth from Wylie may not be as simple as controlling Zosel. If Franz saw Claudine slink out of the dining hall at the Olympic Village, who else might have put two and two together, "done the math"? With Barry's digging, it's really only a matter of time before he hits on what he's looking for, isn't it?

If she had to pick a ski term to describe her situation, it's "yard sale." Meaning a crash so hard you lose all your gear, everything. Wylie, gone; job, gone; secret, inevitably coming to light.

So if she can't stop it, what can she do instead? Her heart thuds so rapidly in her chest she can almost hear it.

Then she hears another noise, and *you've got to be kidding me right now.*

Boom, boom, boom. The floor below her hums with the vibrations of disco music.

Claudine halts, reaches a hand out to one of the bedposts, and bows her head to her outstretched arm, grinding her teeth. How has this infernal noise already started? She could murder someone, she really could. She really might.

Shake it off. She cracks her neck from side to side, yawns her mouth open to loosen her jaw. She can't afford to be distracted right now because on top of the whole your-secret-is-emerging-like-those-wildflowers-in-the-Arctic-Circle thing, Wylie's sent her a text message, outright declaring that they're skiing through an avalanche zone in the morning to escape Zermatt.

That sounds about as safe as trying to fly off a roof with cardboard wings.

And now, Wylie hasn't responded to Claudine's last four texts, including: Wy, let's figure this out together.

She bristles at the transactional nature of her daughter's message, how she almost seems to be saying, "Risk your life if you want to finally be a 'good' mom."

And she does, desperately.

Just as Claudine couldn't really deny her daughter the opportunity to come to Zermatt to spread Kipper's ashes, she now feels equally backed into a corner. How does she say no—especially given what's waiting around the corner for them? The truth that's going to hurl them apart and—*boom, boom, boom*.

"Oh my f-ing god!" She tosses up her hands. The glass pane in the window rattles from the music. She walks to the door and throws it open, sticking her head out. The music is even louder in the hallway. She looks the other way, sees no other guest who's equally aggrieved. How is she the only one bothered by this? She slams the door shut again, searches for her stupid earplugs.

Both have ear gunk. Gross. She tosses them in the wastebasket.

Get a grip, Claudine.

She checks her phone. Still no reply. Where *is* Wylie? She studies the hiking route again. Then she pulls up the avalanche risk level—the one she should've checked before they came here—finding that it's at level three. Could be worse.

Still, it's . . . It's negligent. Yes, that's what it is.

But maybe so is *not* helping Wylie? She cannot win. She—*boom, boom, boom*.

And *pound, pound, pound*. The bass taunts her, could easily be her fist on that bathroom door, a memory she can't ever seem to scramble away from, as if the music is designed to remind her of her failings, is drilling it home. *Pound, boom, pound, boom.* The sounds entwine, angry and relentless. *Get your ass up that mountain!*

Claudine picks up her pillow and screams into it.

With the pillow mashed against her face, she folds both sides against her ears, muffling the noise only slightly. And it's not like she can stay like this all night.

She drops the pillow, attempts a steadying breath. *I am a woman who once raced through fog so thick you could slice it like a piece of pie. I will not be bested by this bass.*

Again, she tries to apply her mind to solving her problems. Zosel, Barry, Franz Blasi, the secret, Wylie's faulty escape plan. It all loops in her mind as the band plays on—or, in this case, some deejay's laptop hooked up to really, really loud speakers. It's all she can focus on, zeroing in on the *boom, boom, boom* as if it's a car alarm going on in her own head.

Enough.

She strides again to the door, yanking it open, this time not looking or caring if there's any coconspirators against the racket, hurling herself down the hallway. If no one else is going to put a stop to the mini-Ibiza happening in the basement, she will.

Soupy would tell her to—*Can it, Soupy.*

She plunges down the stairwell to the basement, annoyed that each stair is responsibly lit by a square LED light stuck against the wall—and yet this hostel can't follow its own noise ordinances. Allow its guests to get some fucking sleep!

At the door to the *Disko,* she curls her lips in, clenching her fists, almost welcoming the release that's about to happen when she goes a little apeshit on everyone's ass. She can't control much right now, but that bass is going to stop. She won't hesitate to rip a cord out of a wall, power down what she imagines are speakers as tall as the snowdrifts outside. Maybe Wylie's even here too, whooping it up, ignoring her texts.

Then she thrusts open the door, sucks in air as if she's the wolf about to blow the house to the ground and—*Oh*.

The die Freude dance floor is the opposite of crowded. There are no throngs of ravers. No tourists jumping up and down to the beat. No drunkard yelling, "Shots, shots, shots." No Wylie.

The *Disko* is dead save for three people: Bibbidi and Erin, plus a deejay.

The deejay's wearing headphones, eyes on his laptop, head nodding to the beat with the solemnity of someone playing for thousands instead of a lone couple with hair the color of gumballs gyrating wildly to the techno music. Everything about the room is makeshift. The deejay booth, up on a riser, is nothing more than cheap wood painted a royal purple, the music thumping out of what looks to be two home-karaoke-machine speakers. The walls are haunted-house black, with a laminate checkered floor in alternating purple and black squares. Above Bibbidi and Erin spins a sad little silver disco ball that tosses dots of bright-white light onto the ceiling, the floor, the walls.

Her mouth falls open. She's been driven half crazy by these two, in this sorry excuse for a nightclub?

Before Claudine can recover from her shock, she's spotted. Erin casts a pretend fishing line in her direction, trying to reel her to the center of the dance floor.

Oh hell no. She waves her off, yelling, "I don't dance!" But the music is too loud.

Erin recasts her line. Claudine doesn't take a step closer. *"I don't dance!"*

Bibbidi, wearing a long dress that looks like ten silk scarves layered on top of one another, Dansko clogs, and her sunray amulet, has abandoned her techno moves, if she ever had them, and is now doing the swimmer, arms in the freestyle motion before she plugs her nose, pretending to submerge herself.

Erin, who's been reeling her line in for way too long, *again* casts it into the deep purple-and-white abyss of the dance floor. What's it going to take to stop her? Surely she can read Claudine's lips. Well, Claudine's not yelling again.

Instead, she mimes grabbing ahold of the fishing line with two hands and giving it a good yank, tugging the entire rod out of Erin's hands. Then she snaps the pretend rod over her bent knee. There. Done. Ha! That'll kill the party.

Across the dance floor, Erin draws her shoulders up to her ears like a bruiser who could bench-press three Claudines. But Erin isn't angry. She's . . . crestfallen? As if Claudine destroyed her actual fishing rod. Bibbidi stops swimming. They both stare at Claudine until Erin lowers her head.

Regret and humiliation stir inside her. She likes these two women. Why'd she have to go and do that?

She doesn't really know how to do friendships, and the weight of that hits her. She'd skipped over the typical rites of girlhood because she was always skiing. The truth is, she's never been out dancing with friends. She'd never, not once, gone to the movies with friends. Never shopped at a mall with friends. Never swapped recipes, sweaters, taken a girl's trip. In early adulthood, she had Zosel, but their friendship had the framework of the World Cup, of traveling in unison to follow the snow like a band of nomads. Nothing about that life was normal. Then she'd ruined it.

Maybe that's also why the music's irked her so much. Not

just the *pound, pound, pound* mimicry. Each beat announces what's missing in her life. Fun. Friendship. Frivolity. It all seems so easy for everyone else.

The deejay presses his lips to a microphone and says, "DJ Deli in the house coming straaaaight atcha all the way from Newchester, Vermont." Then he points at Claudine. "This one's for you."

With a click on his laptop, the music shifts. The techno disappears, and the song "Groove Is in the Heart" by Deee-Lite fills the room. Erin and Bibbidi cheer.

Claudine is frozen. She doesn't dance. She. Does. Not. Dance.

Does she? Maybe she could. As if of its own volition, her foot begins to tap. Her shoulder bops up and down. Still, she stays rooted. It's odd, but joining Bibbidi and Erin in the middle of the dance floor is more frightening than taking on the gnarliest downhill course. She's got no muscle memory for this, no road map.

Her hips wiggle, her body bypassing her brain. *Don't think, just do.*

She can feel Kipper in the room with her now, saying these words, urging her forward. Nodding. Sometimes he was soft with her. Loving, in his own way.

Don't think, just do.

One foot in front of the other, and now she's on a purple square.

Another step forward, black square, as if she's a chess piece. Purple. Black. Purple. Black.

She must look insane crossing the floor like this, but Bibbidi and Erin are dancing fools who also look insane.

She gathers her courage and rushes forward, skipping

squares, Bibbidi and Erin opening their arms to include her. No need for apologies, judging from their grins. Here on the dance floor, she has a fresh start.

Song after song, they bop and move and flounce and thread and duck and curl. No one is good. Everyone is amazing. Claudine has masterful control of her body—has never lost control—but now she just lets go, the music flowing through her. It's terrifying. And . . . great.

Next to her, Erin, materializing another nonbroken fishing rod, pretends to cast a line toward Claudine, and Claudine, laughing giddily, crooks a finger into her cheek, allowing herself to be hooked.

When Black Box's "Everybody Everybody," comes on, Claudine is surprised to find that she knows the words. They all shout-sing the "ooh ooh ooh"s.

The lyric "sad and free" pulls a string in Claudine's chest, setting her awhirl. Oh yes, she wants to be free. Is freedom a possibility for her? A release from guilt? Shame? Can she have freedom without the sadness? As she twirls, her arms outstretched, her head thrown back, Bibbidi and Erin orbiting around her, both in their own worlds, she suddenly realizes that the answer isn't in shushing Zosel and continuing to lie to Wylie.

Freedom is coming clean. Freedom is making amends. Maybe that's why she's really here. Somewhere in her subconscious was a little knowing, growing spark. She'll never be able to move forward with her life—funny that she'd been riding a stationary bike for two years—if she doesn't first patch up the past.

She hasn't had the guts to talk to Zosel face-to-face on this trip, and now she's run out of time. Because she will meet

Wylie at the trailhead in the morning. Her daughter has never really asked for much, and now she's asking. Claudine can do this one thing, danger be damned.

But before she goes, Claudine is going to take Koa's suggestion. When she eventually climbs the stairs from the *Disko*, she feels forever changed in some way. At the front desk, she pilfers a sheet of paper and an envelope. She'll write Zosel a letter.

And give her the apology that's twenty-six years overdue.

34

Wylie

INSIDE THE CLUB, WYLIE AND CALVIN FALL INTO a rotation of dancing, laughing, hydrating, collapsing into sticky booths, and dancing again, each song an invitation to inch their bodies ever closer, brush fingertips, kiss thighs.

When Dua Lipa's "New Rules" comes on, Calvin, along with the crowd, goes wild. He takes her hand and draws her to him, then he spins away, losing himself in the song, dancing with abandon.

Wylie watches as Calvin belts out all the lyrics while he dips and spins, bumping into another woman, apologizing and instantly befriending her, the two of them counting Dua's rules with extended fingers. He's so confident. So joyful.

He's a really cool person, she thinks.

The playful vibe changes with Khalid's "Better," dancers coupling off, and from across the dance floor she sees his eyes on her, taking her in, nodding as if he's appreciating the view, desire written all over his face, in the flexing muscles of his jaw. Wylie, in turn, finds that she likes being appreciated in this way, with him. She's never considered herself a striptease kind of girlfriend—never danced sexily for Dan—but here, in the darkness of the club, she rolls her hips suggestively as Khalid sings, "You say we're just friends." Then she turns in a slow circle, giving him a view of her ass, rolling her body like it's a wave, her arms above her head, hands circling languidly. When she turns back, he's upon her. A hot current shoots through her, every nerve ending alive with the anticipation of what they've been denying themselves since they met.

"You're killing me," he growls into her ear, and his breath on her neck instantly makes her warm between her legs.

She bites her lip, putting a palm to his chest, and he spreads his hand on the small of her back, pulling her into him. They grind together to the beat, unhurried and indulgent, her hands slipping down his back, his hands running the length of her sides, under her arms. In response, she pushes her chest into him, and he groans again.

Calvin lifts his hungry gaze to stare into her eyes, their faces inches apart. He kisses her neck, and then moves to her jawline, and finally, finally, their mouths meet.

It is the most erotic thing that's ever happened to Wylie. But in the back recesses of her brain—because she's only mentally broken up with Dan—she also knows that this is wrong, that she's crossed a line.

Mustering every ounce of inner strength, she breaks from the kiss, shaking her head. "Let's go talk outside."

They weave their way through the crowded dance floor, Wylie nearly turning around to kiss him again. But no. She wants to be honorable toward Dan and do right by Calvin, so they grab their coats, pass the bouncer, and head out into the frigid air.

She faces him, her body still aching to be close. "Hi," she says.

"Hi."

"Sorry I stopped us."

"You don't have to be sorry."

"Can you stop looking at my mouth like that?" She swats at him. "You're making this harder."

"'Kay, I won't." He gives her a lazy half smile.

"I like you a lot." She blushes with the admission.

He reaches out to tug on the zipper of her coat, pulling her a little nearer. "I like you a lot." It'd be so easy to stumble back into his arms.

Wylie forces herself to be brave, to ask the question that scares her. A question she would've never had the guts to ask before she came on this trip. "Outside of Zermatt a lot or just, like, because you're stranded here and maybe you're bored?"

He tilts his head. "Wylie."

"What?"

"I'd leave here as your boyfriend if you'd let me."

"Really?"

"Yes. I haven't met anyone like you in, well, ever."

"Well, it's just that . . ." She reaches out to touch his fingers. They clasp both of their hands, holding them up between them at chest height.

"You have a boyfriend already. I know." He sighs, looking off into the distance. "Feels too good to be true, because maybe it is."

"Calvin, I'm breaking up with him. Not because of you, but because I'm realizing he's not the right person for me. But I need to deal with things at home before we . . . I can't just . . . It isn't fair to—" She releases his hands.

He nods. "I understand."

"You're not mad?"

"No." He runs a palm over his bald head, tugs a dark-green beanie from his coat pocket. "I respect that. And I can hang out in the friend zone. For real this time." Calvin pretends to outline an imaginary box, steps inside it. "Oooh, it's actually warm in here."

Wylie laughs. "Can I come in?"

"No! See, that's a mixed signal. You can't join me in this tiny box where we'd obviously have to make out."

"Okay, right. I'll do better."

"Do better. And I'll do better."

"Look at us doing better."

Maybe it's a good thing she's leaving in the morning. As soon as she's home from Berlin, she'll let Dan know it's over. And then maybe she and Calvin can find each other outside of the friend zone.

"This is going to sound kind of crazy, given how much we ate at dinner, but I'm sorta hungry," Wylie says.

Calvin gasps. "Me too!" He addresses the bouncer. "Do you know where we could get something to eat this late at night?" Lighting up his phone, he checks the time. "Oh wow, I mean, this early in the morning. We just danced until almost four."

She grabs his arm, angling the phone screen in her direction to see for herself. "Are you serious?" It's very possible she won't sleep at all before she and Claudine set off.

The bouncer is prepared for this question. He jots a street intersection on a piece of scrap paper. "Knock on the black door," he says.

Wylie and Calvin are elated with what seems like a secret speakeasy for early-morning snacks. They trill on down the street, invincible, defying their exhaustion and better judgment and responsibilities.

Ten minutes later, Calvin's rapping on the black door of an unassuming building.

Wylie stamps her feet to warm them. "It doesn't look right."

There's no answer. Shrugging, he says, "Maybe we should just call it a morn—"

The door flies open like it's been kicked in a cop raid. Briefly they see a hefty, scowling woman in a white chef's hat and uniform before they're engulfed in a fog of bread flour, as if they'd hovered their faces over a mixing bowl just as the flour sack was poured in. They wave the cloud away, Wylie coughing, and as the flour thins, a scene emerges beyond the woman in the doorframe: a bustling, industrial-sized kitchen with dozens of bakers kneading dough, ducking underneath the hot trays of bread and pastries sliding out of the oven, reaching across one another for rolling pins, sprinkling ever more flour from their high-held fingertips. Wylie's amazed they couldn't hear the noise from the street, a swirl of voices and accents like spices in a cardamom bun, the clanking of steel mixing bowls, the whir of the industrial mixers, the groan of the oven doors peeling open.

It's bread heaven, Wylie thinks. The smell alone is enough to entice her through the door, as if she's a Looney Tunes character following a visible waft of baking croissants.

But they're not meant to enter, made apparent by the woman's thick arm stretched to block the door. *"Das Brot?"* she barks.

Huh? Calvin and Wylie exchange perplexed looks, and the woman rolls her eyes. Keeping the door propped open with her foot, she leans back, and when she tilts forward again, she's holding two loaves of brown bread and a quarter of a stick of butter. "Here," she says in English, and Calvin, wide-eyed, steps forward to claim the items.

To Wylie, she holds out an empty palm. *"Sieben Franc."*

"Oh, right." Wylie digs in her purse. The woman snatches the money, allowing the door to slam shut, the noise and the bakers and the pastries vanishing from sight.

But not the smell. Bread heaven emanates from the loaves in Calvin's arms.

"Wylie, it's still hot," he whispers reverentially. He hands her a loaf. She draws it to her nose, inhaling deeply.

She closes her eyes. "Oh. My. God."

"I know. This might be the best thing that's ever happened to me."

"Me too."

"Let's find a bench."

They turn a corner, each loaf a miniature heater, warming their chests. And there, under a Little Bo Peep streetlight, is a bench, as if it's been positioned just for them, a stagehand scurrying off the set before the curtain lifts.

"Is this real life?" Wylie asks. "I feel like I'm in a play."

"It's like we're the only ones alive."

The street is silent, the bench a cold, snow-packed seat, but they don't care. Dawn won't break for at least two more hours.

"Cheers," Calvin says, tipping his loaf toward Wylie. She clinks back, and then they tear into the bread, taking turns smearing the butter on the chunks they've clawed off.

They eat and moan and chew, smiling at each other through full mouths.

Calvin hears the sound of running feet before Wylie does, turning his head to look in the other direction, down a street that's no longer empty. There's a jogger in the distance, coming their way, moving at a fast clip, especially given the snow.

"Wow, now, that's dedication," Calvin says.

"Even I wouldn't get up this early to train," Wylie says.

The jogger nears—it's a woman—her yellow knit hat bobbing up and down with every stride. Barely noticing Calvin and Wylie, she steps into the pool of light around the bench, giving a distracted wave, not breaking pace. The light illuminates her face, sparking a hundred memories in Wylie of a person, a friend, an auntie, that she hasn't seen in a very long time.

"Zosel?" she asks, on instinct.

The woman in the yellow hat stops in her tracks and wheels around.

35

Wylie

ZOSEL EMBRACES WYLIE AS IF WRINGING OUT THE time they've lost, each moment the hug lasts equaling a year they can reclaim, and Wylie clings on against a gust that could redivide her from a person she held so dear from such a young age.

Then they step back to take each other in.

"You look the same!" Wylie says. And Zosel does, only more comfortable somehow, like a favorite yellow sundress that's tumbled through the dryer, the color slightly muted, the fabric softer, but still with the same shape.

"You've grown up!" Zosel exclaims, one hand to her own cheek in shock, the other still holding Wylie's arm.

Emotion swells in Wylie's chest: It wasn't just her childhood imagination inflating their closeness. Their bond had been real.

Behind Wylie, Calvin shuffles his feet.

"Oh, Calvin! Oh my gosh." Wylie reaches back for his arm, creating a chain linking the three of them. "This is Zosel! A dear friend of our family. I haven't seen her in years." Wylie's cheeks are burgundy-wine red, her words tumbling out. She turns back to Zosel, not believing her good fortune in running into her like this. "I was just trying to find your house today. I mean, it's been, what? Fifteen years?"

"Sixteen."

Zosel's surety in this number stretches Wylie's heart wider.

Calvin extends his hand. "It's really great to meet you."

"Likewise." Zosel inches her coat zipper up toward her neck. Addressing Wylie, she says, "I did not know you were in town too."

Wylie's face drains of color as she tries to parse out the meaning of that sentence. "What do you mean 'too'?"

"Your mother . . . She came to see me a few days ago. The morning of the avalanche." Comprehension dawns on Zosel's face as she nods slowly. "She didn't tell you."

"No." The bread in Wylie's stomach is suddenly brick-like. "Mom told me . . . She told me you moved."

"I've always lived here."

Wylie realizes she has no idea what's true and what's not. Why are they really in Zermatt? "Why would she lie about you living here?"

"Oof." Zosel rubs her forehead with gloved fingers. "You should really ask your mother. This is not my place."

Wylie shakes her head in frustration. "If there's something she doesn't want me to know, trust me, I won't get it out of her."

"That sounds like Claudine." Zosel sighs.

"Can we talk?" Wylie knows she should be catching a few hours of rest, but now talking to Zosel—and getting to the bottom of why Claudine snuck out to see her while claiming she'd moved—seems urgent.

"Yes, okay. You two come back to my house for coffee."

"Thank you," Wylie says, breathing a sigh of relief. Maybe now she'll finally get some answers.

"My bed is calling my name. But you go ahead." Calvin yawns. Wylie can tell he's faking it, but she's grateful. She wants to talk to Zosel alone.

Now it's Calvin and Wylie hugging, their bodies a natural fit, long and lanky melting into cushiony and strong. He briefly brushes his lips to her cheek and then locks eyes with her, holding on to her hands with his.

"See you on the next stop of our pastry tour," he says.

"See you." *And goodbye,* she thinks, sending up a little prayer that this hug happens again back at home, after Berlin.

Their fingertips linger; they pull apart. And then, like a dream, he's gone.

Zosel and Wylie link arms, walking toward Zosel's house. It turns out to be a spot Wylie has unknowingly passed several times since arriving in Zermatt. What else has been right underneath her nose?

36

Wylie

WYLIE SITS ON ZOSEL'S LIVING ROOM COUCH, accepting a hot mug of coffee. They whisper; Zosel's daughter, Fränzi, is sleeping. Her husband, a banker, is away on business.

"She'll sleep until eleven," Zosel says. "She went to bed last night with a headache."

"Can you imagine being allowed to sleep that late when you were a teenager? Not getting up early to train every day?" Wylie asks.

Zosel shakes her head. "That would not suit her. Fränzi has her own gifts, but not skiing. Or, at least, not competitive skiing."

The coffee and the excitement of seeing Zosel make Wylie feel surprisingly alert, given the hour, and she takes in the room: family pictures on the bookshelves, Zosel's Olympic gold medal hung in a frame on the wall next to a mounted pair of old wooden snowshoes. Wylie sets her mug down on a coaster, amused it has a charcoal sketch of the Matterhorn that apparently not just tourists appreciate.

She prefers her collage to this sketch. This one is hard lines, no shadows, strict in its boundaries, harsh in its rendering. Yes, the mountain is fixed in place, but to Wylie it's also living, breathing, flexing—at least, that's what she's trying to capture in her collage.

She wonders if that makes any sense. Pictures it written on an artist statement. But that prospect, her name on the placard, doesn't make her as happy as it should.

Not the same type of happy as sitting on the window seat, cutting up strips of magazines.

From a wooden basket, Zosel extracts a white faux-fur throw blanket and hands it to Wylie before stoking the cast-iron wood-burning stove, its long stovepipe carting the smoke up and out of the house. She nestles down on the couch, removing the yellow knit hat she's been wearing, tousling her blond hair, tucking a strand behind her ear.

"We supposedly came to spread Kipper's ashes." Wylie lifts the pendant out from under her shirt. "He's in here."

Zosel gingerly cradles the pendant in her hand. "Hello, Kipper." Her voice is soft. She settles the pendant against Wylie's chest. "I have fond memories of him."

"I do too." *For the most part.*

"He was very kind to me." But then she frowns. "But why his ashes in Zermatt? He rather hated the Europeans."

Wylie pounds the couch with a first. "That's what I said! Zosel, I have so many things to ask you." The pendant necklace seems to sway on her neck, an Ouija-board planchette pointing toward the truth.

"I'll answer what I can. What's mine to answer. Why Zermatt for Kipper, I cannot help."

Wylie licks her lips. She doesn't want to fire-hose Zosel with questions, so she asks the most important one first. "Is Franz Blasi my father? People are saying it might be him, and if it is, well, I could get to know him."

The skin around Zosel's eyes crinkles as she chuckles softly. "Franz? My old coach. This is a question I can and will answer. Oh no. Certainly not. No."

"Are you sure?"

"Franz is gay. He lives with his longtime partner. He never showed any interest in women, as far as I know."

"Oh." Wylie's both relieved and disappointed. On this, at least, Claudine told the truth. Her tired eyes are dry, and when she closes them, she sees pinprick spots, and then zigzags of light, like white calcite veins in a slab of limestone. Fault lines in a foundation. She's reaching a level of exhaustion that could push their escape trek from risky to heedless.

From down the hall, Fränzi calls out. *"Mama, wo sind die Kopfschmerztabletten?"*

"Sorry, Wylie, one moment. I need to find some headache pills for my daughter." She pats Wylie's knee, stands up, and heads down the hallway.

Wylie glances at the clock on the wall. It's five-thirty in the morning. An hour and a half before she's due to meet Claudine.

Charged up with anxious, exhausted energy, she also stands, crossing the floor, pausing to look at some photos that Zosel has framed on her bookshelves. Beneath the frames are several thick photo albums with dates, and Wylie selects the one that says *1990–1995*. Maybe there are some early pics of Claudine in here.

Back on the couch, she turns the plastic-covered pages, each one heavy with pictures.

"Oh my gosh!" she says out loud, to herself. There's Claudine and Zosel, both fresh-faced, innocent-looking, full of vigor, walking with their skis slung over their shoulders. Zosel appears to be midsentence, and Claudine's head is bent, as though listening intently. Underneath, Zosel's written: "Austria."

Another image: Claudine in this very house—Wylie recognizes the living room window, although the furniture is different—pregnant with Wylie, her belly and cheeks round, her hair past her shoulders. She's looking up in surprise, a melancholy to the downturn of her mouth, everything in the image a shade of brown or taupe or khaki: the wooden walls, Claudine's hair, her sweater. The only bright item in the picture is the tangerine she's peeling. Zosel's scrawl says: "Zermatt."

A third picture: Kipper scratching his head with one hand, irritation in the tips of his fingers, pointing to somewhere off camera with the other, while Claudine, fist on her hip, gives a sour-mood sulk. "Kipper and Claudine, Cortina."

It's the grandfather she sees in her mind when she imagines him. His head of dark hair, speckled with gray, his broad shoulders, his eyes—the eyes of someone who had backroom wisdom.

Seeing these pictures is like stumbling through another door, an alternate universe. Wylie studies the tangerine photo again. *She was so young,* Wylie realizes, bringing the picture closer. *Just a child herself.*

She peeks at the clock. Six-fifteen. *C'mon, Zosel!*

On the next spread, there's no Claudine. Instead, an image of Zosel and a tall young man with his arm around her shoulders, pulling her to him. She's in a white turtleneck sweater and high-waisted jeans, and he's wearing a striped red-and-black shirt with a fur-lined jean jacket. They look sharp and hip for the times and achingly attractive, an air of invincibility about them, the world their oyster. "Zosel and Reynard."

The room is quiet but for a hiss and pop in the fireplace. Outside, a distant, pale-pink light is edging out the darkness, as if Wylie's swiped an oil-pastel pencil to the bottom of a canvas shaded in with her charcoals.

The man looks oddly familiar, and Wylie is struck with the sensation of having known him, rather than just known *of* him. She vaguely recalls the story: Zosel a widow at a young age, her husband, Reynard, killed in the nearby mountains while rock climbing.

She shifts her eyes to the next image, this one of Reynard standing next to a snowdrift, laughing, measuring his height against it. *So* tall. She turns another page, greedy for another picture of him.

This next one makes her breath catch in her throat. It's a makeshift memorial high in the mountains, a white flag flapping in the wind, several teetering cairns, a bouquet of yellow flowers, a wooden cross.

On the ground, overtop the scree, are three letters spelled out with rocks: F O X.

F O X . . .

Fox? Fox. *Fox.*

From her cursory understanding of French, she suddenly remembers the translation of *Reynard* is *fox*. It must have been his nickname. All these years she'd had the clue, but never made the connection.

She jerks her head up, eyes toward the window. The sunrise is blooming now, pinks and golds and oranges hefting the night off its shoulders.

She looks back down at the image of Reynard. His eyebrows: rolling hills, perfectly arched, crooked pointer fingers. Just like hers. His height.

The monogrammed lighter. The makeshift grave. Wylie's hand rests over her mouth.

It startles her when Zosel sticks her head into the living room. "Wylie, I'm so sorry, but Fränzi has a fever. I hate to cut our visit short, but I need to tend to her. Will you come back later?"

Wylie lowers her hand, swiftly shifts a pillow over the photo album. "Oh, um, yeah. No problem."

"Thank you. Get some rest and come back this afternoon. Good?"

"Yes."

"Kiss kiss."

Once more Wylie turns her face to the window, the sky aflame, a first-birthday candle atop a world that's just shifted underneath her feet. She's immobile with the shock of it all, the anger submerged in the depths of her, not surfacing yet. Grief and sorrow keep her pinned to this couch, the clock ticking on the wall, eating away at her lead time to beat snow patrol's detection.

Her mom did this. Did this. Did this. It's worse than *pound, pound, pound.* Worse than anything Wylie could've possibly conjured up.

And Zosel had known, hadn't she? Yes, she'd known, Wylie's suddenly certain of it.

The deception injects Wylie's anger with air bubbles, rising it to her stomach, her chest, her throat. She has to tamp down a scream. All she wants to do is flee. Get far, far away. It's exactly what her instincts had told her on the train ride here: she can never relax in an inhospitable landscape like this or let her guard down with her mom.

She glances at the clock one last time. Nearly 6:30 a.m. She doesn't have time to get back to the hostel, and she will not, under any circumstances, share one more minute with her mom in that tiny room.

She powers up her phone. Numerous messages ping across her screen—a few from Dan and several from her mom. She doesn't read any of them. Her fingers fly over the keyboard as she instructs Claudine to bring her pack and ski boots to the trailhead. Wylie will meet her there.

And if Claudine won't come with her? Fine.

Robotically, she stands up, crosses the floor, and replaces the photo album on the shelf. She lets herself out. Emerging from the house a different person, she walks with the fast, loping gait of Reynard, a low wind rustling her hair like a father's hand on her head.

37

Claudine

CLAUDINE CLOCKS JUST A FEW HOURS OF SLEEP, rising before the sun to write the letter to Zosel with a semi-fresh mind. She owes her that, at the very least. There's not really enough time in the world, enough words, to do her justice. But an honest effort is better than nothing. And she wants to get her thoughts down on paper before Wylie whips through the door from what appears to be an all-nighter.

She closes her eyes to summon her courage, then writes "Dear"—that's the easy part—and she chuckles a little, shaking her head, the tiny moment of levity helping to loosen the knot in her chest. But how to get beyond this first word? What do you say to someone you've wronged so badly? In this case, *don't think, just do* doesn't apply. She can't just shut down her mind and shut down her heart, relying on her body. She's got to open herself up.

This might be the scariest thing she's ever done. She takes another deep breath, and then she dives in.

Dear Zosel,

I came to Zermatt to talk you out of telling the world about me and Reynard. I was going to rail and yell and fight and even plead if I had to. My main goal was to keep you quiet. To stop Wylie from finding out. To keep what I did hidden from her forever because I was so ashamed. I am so ashamed. I still can't believe I did what I did to you.

Claudine pauses, giving herself a moment to think. How much to share about that day in Albertville?

She was twenty-two years old, about to compete in the first Olympic downhill race of her career. Reynard was the furthest thing from her mind as she stared at her tomato soup in the dining hall, a freight train of adrenaline coursing through her body. She craved a pressure-release valve for some of that energy.

In walked Reynard, strutting with the barrel-chested ego of a bullmastiff. Accustomed to making decisions in fractions of a second, she knew instantly that she would use him. He'd slept with half the Olympic Village, rumor had it, rumors that sometimes got back to Zosel, hurting her deeply—although she didn't leave him over it. He always managed to woo her back, a cycle that was hard to watch. Until Claudine realized she could use it to her advantage, reckoning that a little tussle with Reynard would be like nothing more than a cortisone shot to the hip, or an adjustment to her ski boots, all of it preparing her to perform at her peak—collateral damage be damned.

Technically, Reynard propositioned her, believing their tryst was all his idea, but Claudine knew better. She predicted what would happen if she coquettishly batted her eyelashes at him.

She winces at the memory, at all she was willing to sacrifice in order to win.

When she discovered she was pregnant, Claudine had planned to tell Zosel the truth. But only a week later, before she'd drummed up the nerve, Reynard was killed in his climbing accident, crushed by a serac dislodged near the summit of the Grand Combin in Switzerland. Zosel needed Claudine in her hour of grief, and Claudine rose to the occasion, flying to Zermatt to shepherd her friend through the first awful weeks of shock and sorrow. Bathing her. Cooking for her. Urging her into the fresh air.

Feeling sick about what she'd done the entire time.

Claudine couldn't break the news then, of course she couldn't. But the baby continued to grow inside her, until one day Zosel said, "When are you planning on telling me?"

She remembers how her mouth fell open, shocked, believing that somehow Zosel had intuited her secret. "I . . ."

But then Zosel said, "I can see that cute baby bump. It's okay to share happy news with me even if I'm sad. *If* you're happy about it, that is."

"Oh." Claudine's hand moved to her belly. "Mixed, actually. It'll complicate skiing."

Zosel arched an eyebrow. "And the father?"

Here was Claudine's chance. But she didn't take it. "Just some ski bum back home."

The lie was born. And as Wylie continued to grow, so did the lie.

Claudine bends over the page, the hardest part in front of her.

I've given up on keeping what I did a secret.

In therapy—yes, even me!—I've been practicing the art of the apology. Literally sitting across from my therapist and saying, "I'm sorry," and seeing that the bottom doesn't fall out. That saying sorry isn't so scary. All those practice apologies have been preparing me to deliver the one I've owed you for far too long. I'm ashamed it's taken me this long, and that it took a trip here to finally understand why I felt so compelled to come.

So here it is: I'm so sorry. I'm sorry I made such a horrible choice that day. I'm sorry I deceived you. And I'm sorry that I threw away a friendship that mattered so deeply to me.

I'm sorry I never told you the truth, year after year.

As time passed, Claudine's self-hatred had mounted, the guilt expanding like an invisible monster in the room that only she could see, taunting her from the corner, following her to bed, rousing her in the middle of the night, whispering to her as she soared down a mountain.

Sometimes Claudine watched Zosel and Wylie—reading a book together, walking down the street, Zosel's hand falling naturally on Wylie's head—and she thought: *Zosel should be Wylie's mom. She's better at this.*

Because Claudine knew that underneath it all, she was a bad person. And she had proof: her daughter, whom she loved. Whom she couldn't fully enjoy because of the betrayal she represented.

From the time Wylie was a baby, she looked just like Reynard. Even Zosel's former in-laws commented on it when they came out to support Zosel at a race in Méribel. "This is so crazy, but she looks like Reynard, doesn't she, Zosel?" said Reynard's mother wistfully, grabbing on to Zosel's wrist. "Oh, how I wish you'd had a child together."

Claudine was stricken, her face ghostly pale. Zosel, misinterpreting, reached out to her moments later, out of earshot from her mother-in-law, to try to assuage Claudine of any guilt. "I'm glad one of us is a mother," Zosel said earnestly. "And Wylie is such a joy in my life. Please don't feel bad."

Oh, but she did. She so did.

There were other clues too: How Claudine always conveniently excused herself from the room whenever Zosel talked about Reynard with other people. Just before Salt Lake, Wylie had a growth spurt, shooting up like an asparagus spear, tall and lean, and Claudine was desperately afraid that Zosel would recognize Wylie's strut, a certain way of swinging her arms so like her father. Her face was filling in too, revealing even more of Reynard in her rainbow-arched eyebrows and strong nose.

Her fear was justified. Zosel did see it, and Claudine witnessed the moment it all seemed to click for her friend, the understanding dawning in Zosel's eyes as she stared at Wylie, her mouth falling open in disbelief for the briefest of moments, replaced with an eerie knowing look that chilled Claudine, as if her suspicions were confirmed.

I'm sorry that you had to confront me about it to learn the truth. I'm sorry that when you did, I got angry and stormed out.

Claudine's pulse is racing. A thousand apologies doesn't feel like enough.

I'm sorry I never called. I'm sorry it's taken me this long. I'm sorry I thought I could come here and bully you into submission. I'm sorry that this is a letter and not a conversation. I have fallen short of what you deserve in so many ways.

I hope you can forgive me. I understand if you cannot.

I want you to know that I'm planning to tell Wylie. She deserves to know, and I don't want her to find out any other way. You can tell Barry anything you want. I won't try to stop you. I'm done hiding. Whatever comes next, I want to face it head-on.

She momentarily closes her eyes, still unsure if she can absolve herself, more interested in this self-forgiveness as it relates to Wylie. How it will shift the matrix in their relationship.

I hope you can meet Wylie as an adult sometime. She's incredible. A beautiful soul.

With deepest affection,

Claudine

She sits back and sighs, experiencing a peace of mind she hadn't expected, and she wraps her arms around her shoulders to give herself a hug. It's been a long, self-punishing twenty-six years. Then she folds the paper, stuffing it into the envelope, eyeing the door to their room.

Where the heck is Wylie? Claudine goes to the window, pushing aside the curtain. Outside, the darkness has retreated, giving way to what looks to be a stunner of a winter day. A fresh layer of snow has fallen overnight, and it sparkles, diamond-like, under the first slices of golden morning sunlight.

There's always something magical about being the first one to walk on new, clean, bright snow. It seems fitting to Claudine in this moment, when she also feels renewed.

But there's a disquiet gnawing at her—about this escape route, about Wylie's whereabouts. She picks up her phone to try calling her again, only to see that Wylie messaged her fifteen minutes ago—she kicks herself for silencing her notifications. She scans the message quickly, hungry for her daughter's words. Wylie's amending the plan. And a lot of it falls on Claudine. She surveys the room, the items she'll have to pack for Wylie—and swiftly, in a rush. Isn't this how it always is: moms have to pick up the mess.

She sets her timer. She packs everything in two minutes flat.

At the desk, she scrawls a note for Koa, asking him to deliver the letter to Zosel later that day, when Claudine and Wylie will already be long gone.

38

Claudine

CLAUDINE LUMBERS DOWN THE SNOW-CLEARED street, one thirty-five-pound backpack slung over each shoulder, four heavy ski boots cradled in her arms. She's already sweating. And her knee—*Don't think about it.*

Near the trailhead, she spies Wylie standing with her arms crossed, looking huffy. Irritation wafts off her. Oh, goody. She's in a *mood.*

And Claudine's the one doing all the heavy lifting. "Can you come take one of these?" she manages to yell. It's only then that Wylie jogs toward her, arriving red-cheeked and puffy-eyed, as if she's just finished a good, long cry.

"Are you okay?" Claudine asks, forgetting her own chagrin. She drops the boots and swings both packs to the ground, grateful to be rid of the cumbersome load.

Wylie glares. "It's after seven, we should go." She offers no thank-you for carting her bag, no explanation for her absence last night or this sudden change in plans.

"It took a while to get here with all this stuff alone."

Wylie only nods, hefting up her pack and leading the way the last one hundred feet to the trailhead. Claudine, still recovering from the exertion, is slow to catch up, and when she does, Wylie's already uncinching the drawstring to the top of her pack, rifling through it, sticking a long arm in to pull out her snow pants and gloves. She watches Wylie step out of one shoe to thread a leg into the pants, and then the other. She snaps the waist button.

"You're not going to change into thermals? You're wearing jeans."

"No time." Wylie doesn't so much as look at her. She's stuffing her feet into her ski boots, clasping the buckles.

Claudine assesses the trail, her entire body sagging with the realization that her hunch was right; trying to ski out is a very, very bad idea.

The snow is everywhere—*well, of course it is*—and there's just so much of it, layers upon layers, as if they could sink down and never resurface. The branches of the surrounding pine trees are heavy with it, bowing toward the ground, loaded catapults. Only the very top of the hiking sign is visible, like a hand poking up, waving for help.

Along with the back-country skis, Koa's left them two avalanche beacons to wear—a precaution, should the worst happen, but the devices only worry Claudine. They're attempting to thread a needle, sneak past an awning of snow before it descends. Maybe that snow will stay put, settle in. Or maybe it won't. They could have hours. Minutes. Only seconds.

Kipper would chew them both out for even considering it.

Claudine reaches out to touch Wylie's arm, but she pulls away. "This isn't safe. I mean, just look at this trail. It's not one." She gestures to an open field of white, deep snow. "We'll be cutting slow tracks, especially with these heavy packs." She considers cracking a joke about how long it'd taken her just to cart the packs to the trailhead but thinks better of it. "We'll be in the risk zone for too long. And you're not even wearing the proper gear. I'm sorry. But no."

"You wanted me to keep hurling myself down a mountain at ninety miles per hour, but *this* is dangerous?" Wylie pulls on her gloves.

Claudine ignores the barb. "I know how badly you want to get to Berlin. But I'm not sure we'll make it."

Wylie clicks into her skis. Her stubbornness is frightening. "I can't allow you to do this."

"You can't *allow* me to do this?" Wylie scoffs haughtily. "I'm an adult."

"Then make an adult decision." Claudine crosses her arms. "You're acting like a child. You know better than this."

"And why should I listen to you?" Wylie's eyes are stormy, her tone withering. "Have your decisions been so responsible?"

At that, Claudine feels a flicker of fear. What is she alluding to? Where *has* she been all night? "Look, if you want to hash some more things out about us, our relationship, I'm up for it. But back at the hostel. Let's go."

"You go. I'm getting to Berlin. I know it doesn't matter to you, but it does to me." Wylie pushes off, silent, stoic, her skis trying to push open a path like the bow of an icebreaker. But the snow is so deep that Wylie's forced to immediately change tack, having to take high steps, more like she's wearing snowshoes than skis.

"Wylie!" Claudine yells, her voice frantic, but it's no use. Her daughter won't come back.

What to do? She rifles through her options. Waking up Koa for help. Summoning ski patrol. Both of those will take time, time she doesn't have if she wants to keep Wylie in her sights before she disappears through a grove of trees.

Hastily, Claudine steps into her ski boots, clicks into her skis, grabs her poles, strings the avalanche detector around her neck. She can't let Wylie go alone.

Before she shoves off, she looks up at the Matterhorn. She's never been superstitious, and she's not religious, but she does believe in the power of communing with mountains. Do they look like fools, two prideful humans who think they are above the whims of nature?

"Look out for us down here," she says, and then, with groaning effort, her skis find Wylie's grooves in two narrow lanes leading away from Zermatt, the canyon walls of the snow as high as her knees. She inches forward in stilted bursts. It's been years since she's been on cross-country skis. She's always hated the laborious shuffle, the diagonal stride. Why would you ski flat when you could fly down? Her hands shake as she grips her poles.

Last night's dancing seems to have negated the effect of the Prolozone injection, and her ballooned left knee makes her movements uncoordinated and strained.

Wylie glances back, a look of surprise on her face—maybe to see her mom following at all, or at how slow she's going. But she does not stop, pulling Claudine into what feels like the belly of the beast.

Her knees are rigid, partly out of fear and partly because her left knee is throbbing. From somewhere deep inside, she recalls how to do this, activating her core as she pushes off, then glides. It's not pretty; her skis are coated with snow. As the person breaking the track up ahead, Wylie must not even be able to see the tips of her skis at all.

Push off, glide, Claudine repeats as a mantra. Kipper used to roll his eyes at the cross-country skiing Olympians. "That's not a sport, it's a pastime," he'd say. *You're wrong, Kip,* she thinks now. *This is hard.*

Her ski poles punch the snow, a soft, muffled crunch like a pencil jabbing into Styrofoam. The wind picks up from behind them, a gentle cooing in the ear, a sweet-nothing whisper. The rising sun refracts off the snow. Claudine squints behind sunglasses. They both drive their elbows back with their poles, their heels lifting off from the skis with every glide forward.

She's winded, breathing hard. The elevation is getting to her, the pack weighing her down.

Digging an escape tunnel through the snow with plastic spoons could be faster. Sweat dampens her base layers as her heart rate soars.

Push off, glide.

It looks like they have so far to go.

Something must be tearing a tiny bit inside Claudine's knee with every push off, glide. How can it be only bursitis?

I don't think I can keep doing this, Kip, she thinks.

Good, quit. Be a quitter. What's stopping you? she hears.

From the Matterhorn's vantage point, Claudine knows they are mere specks. Pieces of lint. Small as sunflower-seed shells, inconsequential.

A memory blasts in. Claudine's ten years old, on the ski

slopes in Mount Hood, desperately needing to pee, sunflower seeds the only snack she's had that morning. No cute snack container. No plastic baggie. Just ski-jacket pockets packed with seeds. It was snowing, or rather spitting, tiny meteorites smashing into the planets of her cheeks.

She needed to use the bathroom. She needed more than squirrel food. She needed to unthaw. Then she'd be ready again.

But those basic needs were a weakness, and Kipper was in her face. All those CycleTron riders nostalgic for their barking high school coaches had never encountered someone as intense as him. There was the fleeting pleasure of the warm urine before it froze, stiffening her snow pants, chapping her bare skin. The shame she'd felt when she'd peeled off her pants in the lodge, smelling like a latrine.

Claudine would've done anything to stave off her father's fury. Even pee her pants.

She's never told Wylie: *Those stomachaches, I had them too.*

Instead of commiserating, instead of connecting on common ground, Claudine had showed her no mercy. Kipper had pressed upon Claudine that only accomplishment—the medals, the records, the triumphs—made life meaningful.

On this, he had been wrong. They were not enough. Now she found that they hardly mattered at all.

What would she give up for the chance to do things differently with Wylie? To not pass Kipper's wrongness on to her own child? All the medals, the records, the triumphs, the accomplishments that mean nothing at the end of the day, not really, not measured against a life of deeper purpose, of unconditional love.

Here now, the falling snow crashes into her face just as it

had back then. She fights for every inch, the pain in her knee intensifying, screaming at her. Eventually, it's too much.

"Wylie!" she calls.

Wylie, fifteen feet in front of her, glances over her shoulder.

"I need a break," Claudine yells.

Surprisingly, Wylie does a full 180, skiing back to her. The girl is a machine. There's no way Claudine would retrace her steps if she didn't have to.

They face each other, skis to skis. Winded, Claudine says, "Give me a second." She looks behind her, can still see the top of the trailhead sign. They've probably made it only less than a quarter of a mile. Not even halfway.

She turns back to find Wylie's removed her sunglasses, and she's shooting daggers at her.

Maybe Claudine's slow, imperfect, insensitive—but does she deserve that look? She's here, isn't she, fighting through the pain? "Are you going to make me guess what's wrong all the way to Berlin?" she asks, trying for a smile, hoping to keep things light.

"Was Reynard my father? Zosel's Reynard?" Wylie's jaw is set, her nostrils flaring.

The smile slips from Claudine's face. Every muscle in her body tenses. Tentacles of wind push underneath her sunglasses, causing her eyes to tear up and crust at the corners. "How did you—?"

"It doesn't matter. How could you?"

Claudine makes a strangulated noise. Her chest constricts, as if the weight of snow is upon her. She chokes out, "Let's do this when we're safe and sound."

"Right, that's so fucking typical. Your terms." Wylie's anger slashes her face. "Answer me." When Claudine fails to produce words, Wylie's voice breaks. "Answer me, *please*."

Tell her, Claudine urges herself. But all these years keeping one thing unsaid makes it excruciatingly difficult to finally say it. Claudine just swallows.

Above them, the sky darkens, and, in spite of her thundering heart, Claudine takes notice of the shifting weather. Gone is the sun, pasted behind clouds like Wylie's early collages made of Elmer's glue and construction paper. Yellow for sun, white for clouds, black for storm. She scans the horizon. They're sitting ducks, vulnerable to whatever brews out here, and this kicks Claudine into action. If she can just force herself to tell Wylie a little, give her something, then maybe she can convince her to turn back, where they can talk properly, in safety.

Her eyes land on Wylie's, and finally she speaks four small words with the largest significance: "Reynard is your father. He's . . . I . . . We . . ." Tears flow down Claudine's wind-burned cheeks, rivulets running straight to her chapped lips. She tastes the saltiness mixing with her own shame.

Wylie hinges forward as if she might be sick, her hands still clutching her poles. She immediately straightens up again. "Why didn't you just tell me? All these years?"

"I was going to tell you in Berlin. I just—"

"I don't believe you." Wylie's eyes blaze. "All this time I thought he was out there somewhere, that he was alive, that someday you'd give me a chance to know who he was and meet him, or that I'd find him myself, somehow. And you never told me otherwise. Never told me he was dead. It's such a double whammy, Mom, don't you get it?"

Claudine lowers her head. Never, not even when Kipper was reaming her out, has she felt lower.

"I can't believe you'd be this selfish. To do what you did to Zosel. And then to keep it from me. Why?"

As a child, poised at the top of a run that scared her to her core, Claudine had experienced this feeling—like resignation—that the only way home was down. The only way through was to plunge right into the fear and come out the other side, somehow. "Because I'm deeply ashamed, Wy. Deeply ashamed. And I didn't want to lose you. It was such a stupid, stupid, rash mistake that's been following me for years." A gust of wind dives at them like sparrows chasing away a predatory hawk, lifting a swirl of powder from the ground. "But I can't say that I regret it. Because then I wouldn't have you. And you are the best thing, the absolute best thing, in my life."

Wylie opens her mouth and roars with fury into the wind.

Claudine holds up an entreating hand. "You have every right to be angry. Maybe you'll never forgive me. But I'll never forgive myself if something happens to us out here. *Please.* Let's go back." Claudine nods toward their cut tracks. She lifts one ski out of the snow and then the other, turning her body gradually like the shadow on a sundial. "This isn't safe. Zermatt is closer."

Wylie pivots her skis in the opposite direction.

Claudine faces Zermatt. Wylie faces Täsch. The Matterhorn hovers above them both, its peak out of reach of the storm that's just getting started.

Wylie won't be dissuaded. "Just leave me alone, Mom. I don't want you with me."

Claudine is powerless to stop her daughter from looping her hands back into her ski-pole straps, charging forward into the face of danger.

39

Wylie

WYLIE CAN'T GET AWAY FROM HER MOM FAST enough. She can't bear to look at her, doesn't even recognize who she is, and she uses her anger to power up beast mode, putting everything she has into pushing forward.

Each memory, even the good ones—the Barbie shoe and the back scratches and the Nutella on long drives—now takes on a different hue. Of all her criticisms of Claudine as a mom, she's never known her to do something so dishonest, to betray her friend in such a heartless way, to not disavow Wylie of the notion that her dad was alive, and to do it all as her fingers trailed up and down the sides of her spine, as she laughed with all of them over fondue.

He wasn't a ski bum. He'd been a ski racer, a mountaineer. He's dead. And Claudine would have gone her entire life hiding this fact, had Wylie not discovered it herself.

Telling me in Berlin my ass. She shoves her poles into the snow, but for all her blazing ire, she's making slow, painful progress, which only incenses her more.

Wylie's not an idiot; she can see the weather conditions are changing rapidly, knows she's being hotheaded.

But she will not quit. Not this. *Go ahead, be a quitter.* Never. Especially now, with Claudine telling her to quit. Urging her to give up, for the first time in Wylie's life.

She peeks behind her, annoyed to see her mom still following, albeit slowly. Wylie knows she can outrun her. Leave her behind in this stupid country. Go to Berlin without her.

And, yeah, okay, without Claudine she won't have a duo, but she doesn't care. She'll pull a stranger off the street to be her partner. They won't win, but whatever. She is duty-bound by one thing: undoing her quitting streak.

The wind suddenly rushes at her, deafening. Wylie looks up, her hand shielding her eyes to see an Air Zermatt helicopter coming toward them, flying at an angle, brawling with the wind. A man in a red parka stands in the frame of the chopper's doorway, motioning with his arm at Claudine and Wylie to go back to Zermatt.

Go. Go. Go.

Maybe the sensors have already alerted them. An avalanche is in motion. Precious seconds to spare.

Go. Go. Go.

He motions one last time before the helicopter lifts up and away, flying low to the ground back to Zermatt. Back to safety.

From behind her, Wylie hears Claudine yell, "Come back!"

"No!" Wylie yells over her shoulder. They're mostly inaudible to each other, the wind plucking their words from their mouths, pocketing them.

Minutes pass as she wrestles her way forward. When, at

last, she glances back again, she doesn't see her mom. Claudine's vanished. It's snowing tiny, bite-size crystals, and Wylie has to squint as if she's peering through television fuzz. *Where is she?*

"Mom?" she calls. Did Claudine actually turn around? *Good,* she wants to think, but Claudine's disappearance rattles Wylie, and she pivots around much more arduously this time—she's growing cold and tired from the physical output; wearing jeans had been a stupid idea, an overhasty choice, maybe even a way to punish her mom, but it's catching up to her now.

She squints her eyes again, yelling, "Mom!"

About thirty feet away, she spots a figure on the ground, a hand waving at her. Claudine has fallen.

Without giving it another thought, Wylie shoots toward her like a rocket, her adrenaline flaring. She can't leave her mom like that, no matter how angry she is. But the wind, in this direction, is a wall, a flat palm, restraining Wylie. She knows that the lactic acid in Claudine's thighs is beginning to pool and tighten, potentially causing her muscles to stiffen and cramp, her body losing too much heat as she stalls there. If that happens, it'll be impossible for Claudine to ski back to Zermatt before hypothermia descends.

And then . . . *Oh god.*

What has Wylie done? *Mom!* She digs deep within herself, mustering up all her power and energy, finding fuel in her empty tank—one of Dan's favorite motivational fitness lines. That life, her old life back in Massachusetts, is so far away now. She thought riding that bike felt hard, forgetting a sweat towel was torturous? It was nothing, not even in the ballpark of this agony.

When, at last, she reaches Claudine, her mom's parka has sprouted a polar fur, snow on her eyebrows, snow on her hat.

"Are you hurt?" Wylie yells.

"It's my knee! I can't get up! I'm stuck!"

"Here!" Wylie slides her skis parallel to Claudine, reaches out.

Claudine clasps Wylie's hands, and Wylie heaves until she's righted Claudine, brought her up to standing.

Wylie's panting. She's so exhausted, everything—the all-nighter, the run-in with Zosel, the revelation about her dad—hits her all at once. How will she ever make it to Täsch?

Claudine, her teeth chattering, says, "Listen to me, please." She draws her gloved hands together in a prayer pose. "We could die out here. You can see that, can't you? The weather's just getting worse."

Wylie nods. "I can't give up, Mom, I can't just quit."

"Sometimes it's okay to quit, Wy. Sometimes it's the right call."

"Why didn't you ever say that, then? In St. Moritz!" Wylie's cheeks are red emergency flares against the snow, her bottom lip twitching. "You made me feel like such a disappointment."

"I didn't know what I was doing—I'm still learning—and I was scared. I felt like it was my job to keep you on a certain path. I was wrong, Wy. You've never been a disappointment."

"I need to be great. To prove that I'm great."

"Oh, honey. You already *are* great. You always were."

At this, Wylie's arms go limp, and she hangs over her poles. Imagine all that could have been saved if Claudine would have said this to her, if she had gathered her up in her arms in St. Moritz and whispered, "It's okay. Your worth isn't measured by whether you race today. You are enough. You are loved. You are safe."

Instead, Wylie's had to hear that from a mediation app, drill it into her own brain, teach it to herself.

"I'm sorry, Wylie. Truly."

The weather rages, the wind and snow compassionless.

"We have to leave now," Claudine pleads.

Wylie looks at the trail ahead, snow upon snow, no clear path. She's straddling two worlds: Zermatt and Berlin.

Which way to go? What does she want? To be at the top of the podium, at last? Or something else, something . . . softer? She thinks of board-game birthday cakes and slow afternoons making collages and the particular satisfaction of holding a spirit level in her hand, watching the bubble gradually center, determining whether a framed painting is exactly horizontal.

Maybe the anxiety attacks were not her body's failing, but rather, her body's wisdom. Alerting her, loud and clear, that she was embarking on the wrong path.

Where's the exit?

Back the way she came.

And what's her body telling her now?

To turn around and claim the life she really wants to live.

Not giving up, but going forward, with some clarity about what actually makes her happy.

She inches her skis toward Zermatt, and then another, stutter-stepping, slower than she should be moving. Every moment on the trail is a moment of risk, and she understands that more strongly than ever now. A mild snowstorm can turn ferocious on a dime, which is what happens now.

It's a squall, winter's impulsive and unrestrained cousin, causing havoc. Claudine and Wylie are gulped up in a cloud of snow, the world around them vanishing as if it's been smothered in Wite-Out.

"Mom!" Wylie howls. "I can't see." Her heartbeat is on a stampede, her adrenaline screeching at her to run. Is this the first huff of an avalanche barreling down at them? Are they in an avalanche now? Wylie can't make heads or tails of anything, up or down, ground or sky. Her eyes are useless.

"I'm here," Claudine yells back, and Wylie can hear the terror in her mom's voice.

"What do we do?" Wylie flails her arms around wildly to find something to hold on to. She catches Claudine's sleeve, grasps her arm tightly. There's another deafening roar of wind, blasting them from all sides, and Wylie whimpers, "Mom."

40

Claudine

CLAUDINE'S HEART IS A TATTERED FLAG HEARING her daughter stripped of all defenses. Crying out for her.

This is another start gate, she thinks. *The race of my life. Two minutes or less—go.*

She recalls the cemetery back in Zermatt. The broken rope on display in the museum. Reynard's tragedy. Koa's paralyzed ski buddy. These mountains will not claim them too. They will not be another sacrifice laid at the feet of the Alps.

Another sacrifice in the pursuit of greatness.

She squeezes Wylie's arm in reassurance, then turns her own skis back to Zermatt, bounces her knees, feels for the tracks they've already put down. Tracks that are quickly filling in with snow. But this is the way, and she knows it.

"Follow my voice," she yells to Wylie. "Yes? Say yes, so I know you're with me."

"Yes!"

Claudine shoves off, her body stiff and cold and frightened, feeling one hundred years old, creaking into motion like a rusty train climbing its way through the altitude. Beneath her skis, she can sense the groove of the tracks. She pushes the tips of her poles into the ground, feeling the give of the snow underneath as she reblazes the path for Wylie. How long the squall will last, she has no idea. How much time they have before an avalanche, she can't dwell on.

Glancing quickly over her shoulder, her eyes search for flashes of color, Wylie's hot-pink hair. There is only white, the two of them skiing through a cotton ball.

What should she do?

The list. Claudine begins their game of Marco Polo, this time not a grounding technique but a way to tether them, to keep their minds from being crippled with fear.

"Lake Louise!" She waits for Wylie's answer, desperate to hear that she's still behind her. There's no response. "Lake Louise!" she screams with all the might she can muster.

What if Wylie's not there? What if she's lost her? Claudine begins to yell again. "Lake—"

But then she hears a voice, muffled by the wind but still there, not as far away as she had feared—Wylie's on her heels. She bends her ear, trying to make out what, exactly, Wylie's yelling. Bizarrely, it sounds a lot like, "Raspberry . . . scone."

Wylie yells it again. "Raspberry scone!"

Claudine, pushing through the pain in her left knee, is momentarily confused before she understands. No more ski towns. They have to find a new language. And so she lobs back, "Cinnamon bun!"

A few seconds later, as if their words are traveling a great distance, or through the string of a tin-can phone, Wylie yells, "Lemon tart."

Claudine tosses back: "Blueberry! Muffin!"

"Cream puff!"

"É ... clair!" Every word is strained and difficult, but if they don't keep this up, they'll break the chain. Lose each other completely. And so they press on, Claudine's knee past the point of burning so that she doesn't feel it anymore, their incoming route now buried so that Claudine's moving on instinct, trusting herself that this is the way back. She is the tugboat; their lives depend on her pulling them to safety.

Above them, she knows, although she can't see her, is Mother Matterhorn. This calms Claudine somewhat as she soldiers on, as does knowing Wylie's wearing Kipper around her neck. *Don't think, just do.*

From behind her: "Croissant."

Out of clever types of pastry, Claudine shouts, "Donut."

At some point soon, or maybe now, they'll ski through that grove of trees. All Claudine can do is hope that she doesn't barrel into one—that Wylie can stay locked in the tracks she's laying down—and periodically she pauses to thrust her ski pole in front of her, tapping around to connect with something.

Always, it's only air, so she pushes forward.

The path seems interminable. The storm is ceaseless. Over and over, Claudine restarts the clock in her mind when she senses two minutes are up, that unit of time she knows by heart, one hundred and twenty seconds that have shaped her life. Out here, their progress is the opposite of fast. Nor is it unhurried. It is both urgent and protracted. And so damn hard, possibly the most grueling thing Claudine's ever done.

There's still no end in sight, but maybe that's because they can't actually see it. They plow forward, each pastry they yell a beam from a lighthouse, the thin, invisible thread connecting their two hearts more vital than it's ever been.

But then, unexpectedly, from the edge of the storm, as if the storm really is a cotton ball with a defined shape, the tips of Claudine's skis emerge. A few measures behind her comes Wylie.

They are out. They are safe. They survived.

At the trailhead, near the CLOSED FOR WINTER sign, the women pop off their skis, their limbs trembling. "We made it," Claudine exhales, tears stinging her eyes. She rests her hands on her knees, breathing hard. Things out there could have taken a wildly different turn, a tragic turn, and Claudine knows that they're lucky and dumb and tough, all bundled together.

Wylie drops to the snow-packed ground as if she's a shipwrecked sailor who's just found land. She stays lying on her side, gasping.

From behind them, the squall lifts just as assuredly as it descended, the world coming back into focus. There's the grove of trees they skied through. There's the village, awaiting their return. There's the unfazed Matterhorn.

The shift is stupefying. Wylie rises from the ground, and they peer around in shock and wonder as the snow stops falling altogether, revealing a bluebird day—bright-blue sky, sunny, cloudless, calm. Trees brushed free of snow. Optimism hanging in the air.

It's as if the storm never happened at all. Could never happen again.

They turn to face each other. Claudine lifts one arm toward Wylie, more exhausted than she's ever been in her entire life—and Wylie lunges into her arms. Their hug is tight and firm; no last gasp of wind can squeeze between their two bodies. They hold each other, Claudine repeating, "My girl, my girl, my girl." In response, Wylie gives way to a sob.

41

Wylie

THE DAY OF THE BODYFITTEST DUO CONTEST

"I'M STILL MAD AT YOU," WYLIE SAYS TO CLAUDINE the morning after their calamitous attempted escape. She's a mosaic of emotions—a collage, really. Sleek magazine strips embodying acceptance. Roughly torn bits of anger. Circles of sadness. Swirls of confusion, curiosity, caution.

Mostly, though, she's trying to make sense of it all, bring into focus a new image of her life and her mom and dad, and while she does that, she's vowed not to shut Claudine out—as long as Claudine promises no more lies. And she has.

"I know," Claudine replies, sitting on the floor of their dorm room with a bag of ice on her knee.

Fresh from the shower, Wylie's expertly plaiting her wet hair into double French braids. "I might decide I need space from you again."

"I understand."

"I don't know if I can trust you."

"I get it."

Wylie nods. There's no question that her mom is showing real signs of change—especially the way she's acknowledging Wylie's pain, making no excuses. It won't change the past, but maybe it will shift their future. Maybe the tough, fierce parts that made up the Stone-Cold Killer were the parts that showed up in her mom on the trail in order to guide them home. And maybe the other parts—the coldness, the stoniness—Claudine's shed for good.

"Okay," Wylie says. "Just so we're clear."

"I respect whatever you decide to do," Claudine says, standing up with a groan, wincing as she gathers her towel and clothes to head to the shower. At the door, one hand on the door handle, she says, "You saved my life out there yesterday. If it hadn't been for you—well, thank you for coming back for me."

"You wouldn't have been out there if it weren't for me, so. Yeah." They both chuckle nervously.

"Can I say one more thing?" Claudine asks. Wylie shrugs. "You're really remarkable. I haven't told you that enough."

Wylie reddens, embarrassed yet moved, casting her eyes down, those words a balm to her heart. "Thanks," she says.

"I mean it."

Wylie's not sure what else to say—they're new to this intimacy, and Wylie's still guarded. Maybe some of this is too little, too late; maybe some of it's right on time. Without complete clarity, she gives Claudine a closemouthed, fragile smile.

As Claudine swings the door shut, Wylie calls out, "Oh, and by the way—be careful in the bathroom. Bibbidi's in there, and she's got hair dye."

When she has the room to herself, Wylie does what she should have done days ago. Calls Dan. No FaceTime. No text. Just a good old-fashioned phone call.

Today she should be in Berlin competing with Dan. Instead, she's breaking up with him.

There are a lot of ways this could go down, dozens of accusations she could make, but she wants to keep it short and courteous and kind. Less risk of being backed into a corner or saying something she doesn't mean or receiving a cruel blow.

There had been love between them, and she's grateful for that.

But there hasn't *always* been love between them, and she cannot abide by that any longer.

Quickly, steadily, she says her piece as Dan listens quietly. "We want different lives," she says. "We have different goals. Neither of them is wrong, but it means that our life together . . . Well, it's over now."

She hears him inhale a staggered breath. Knows he's likely running a hand through his hair. Would be pacing the floor if his leg wasn't in a boot. Finally, he says, "We could still be on the same team, without, you know, being together. You're an amazing athlete."

The fact that this is his first reaction—keeping their team intact—cements her resolve.

"Thank you. But I want to decide how to use my gifts—and how to spend my life—and not have it decided for me."

He begins to cry a little, and she's crying too—you don't spend three years with someone and get through a breakup tearless. Dan sniffs loudly, as if he's wiping his nose with his hand, and she gently ends the call, having said what she needed to.

Afterward, she stares at her phone, her relief like a break

in the storm. She dries her eyes. Those are the last tears she'll shed about Dan. You don't spend three years with someone like Dan and not feel a little elation when you're free of him.

Fighting fatigue, desperately hungry, she sends one more message, this one to Aileen. *If you'll still have me, I'm in.*

⌐

Forty-five minutes later, in the dining hall, Erin and Bibbidi are sitting where they first sat, and the breakfast options are as skimpy as ever. Erin's even eating another bowl of bircher muesli, but this time, as Wylie approaches their table with a cup of coffee and another questionable apple, she hears her say, "You know, this colon blow is growing on me. Might even bring some home."

Seeing Wylie, Bibbidi claps her hands in delight. "Wylie, my dear. I just gave your mom a bit of a makeover in the bathroom."

"Uh-oh."

"You're gonna love it. Brings out her eyes. And how are things between the two of you?"

Wylie opens and then closes her mouth. It's impossible to explain all that's transpired in the last twenty-four hours, so Wylie simply says, "We're finally making some inroads." Which is true. She pulls out a chair and sits down.

Erin slaps the table. "Your mom cut a rug at the disco night before last."

Wylie pauses just as she's about to bite into the apple. "Excuse me?"

"Busted a move. Boogied down. Tripped the light fantastic. Rocked the casbah."

"We couldn't keep up with her," Bibbidi adds.

"My mom? Claudine Potts? *Danced?*"

Erin leans back in her chair, arching her arms overhead, presumably to make room for more muesli. "In the basement nightclub. She's got some real moves."

Bibbidi elbows Erin playfully. "This one's got a bit of a crush."

"I'm impressed is all." Erin's face shines red. She catches Bibbidi's eye and lifts her hands in embarrassed agreement. "Okay, fine, maybe a tiny one."

A smile arcs upward on Wylie's face. Then she points a finger at Erin. "She'll *crush* you if word gets out that she 'boogied down,' as you say."

"What happens in Zermatt stays in Zermatt." Erin winks.

Wylie, for one, hopes not.

The dining room is filling up. The Japanese trio are hunched around a laptop, reviewing their pitch deck for a rescheduled meeting. Koa and Léa enter, both holding the hand of a different Brit. As for the Australian couple, all this forced togetherness has them eating at tables in opposite corners.

Sings to Excess appears in the doorway, no serenade this time. No box of *Gipfelis*. And no Calvin. Wylie's heart droops at his absence.

Jumping straight into another relationship would not be smart, she tells herself. She's itching to get on Zillow and search for one-bedrooms where she can sprawl out with her collage supplies.

As Erin turns her attention to Brandon from Sings to Excess, diving headfirst into a conversation about granola versus muesli versus porridge—"And what is gruel, exactly?" she asks, tapping her spoon to her lips—Bibbidi reaches her hand to gently squeeze Wylie's forearm. Their eyes meet.

"I'm glad you're safe," Bibbidi says knowingly.

What, exactly, Bibbidi thinks she knows, Wylie's not sure. She nods back, saying, "Me too."

Wylie picks up the apple. Instead of eating it, she twists its stem, each rotation a letter in the alphabet. Each letter standing for the first name of the person she's meant to marry. A children's pastime, but still so fun.

A...

B...

C...

Bibbidi pats her arm, gesturing with her chin that someone's standing behind her. The apple stem spins backward from *c* as Wylie swivels to find Calvin, bald head gleaming, a little puffy under the eyes from lack of sleep but with a mischievous smile as he plunks a box of chocolate éclairs onto the table.

He picks one up and puts it to his mouth. "Hi," he says from behind the frosted pastry.

"Hi," she replies, her breath caught in her chest. She'll always, for the rest of her life, spring for this pastry. Wylie Potts has eaten her last gluten-free, carb-free, sugar-free, yummy-free food.

Erin's about to take a massive bite of an éclair when she pauses and asks, "Do you guys sing 'Can You Feel the Love Tonight'?" With her free hand, she clasps Bibbidi's. "It's our song."

Boy, do they ever.

With Calvin leading, Sings to Excess brings the house down. Even the Aussies gravitate toward each other. Bibbidi is watching wide-eyed, her mouth slightly open. Erin leans past her and whispers, "This one's got a bit of a crush."

Bibbidi, join the club.

42

Claudine

CLAUDINE'S TAKING KIPPER FOR ONE LAST JAUNT in Zermatt. Rather than wearing him around her neck—that's just too much for her—she coils the pendant in her parka pocket.

On her way out the door, she pauses at the front desk, Koa reading a book instead of doomscrolling on his computer.

She taps the counter. "Hey."

He looks up, folds a corner down to mark his page, and says, "Hiya."

"Thank you. For the skis."

"Gotta say, I'm glad you turned back." Koa blows out a relieved breath. "Wylie filled me in. That's one heck of a tale."

Claudine's not sure what Wylie told him, exactly—if she mentioned their fight on the trail, anything about Reynard—but Koa isn't treating her any differently. How she'd feared people finding out, Wylie finding out. Now she has, and the world spins on. She wasted so much time, not sharing the truth.

"It was wild out there," she says. "The weather changed so fast."

"That's why we love it, though, eh?"

It's true; she loves winter. Capricious, gorgeous, powerful, waning winter. It suddenly hits her: she's going to do whatever's in her power to hold on to winter, to preserve the ski seasons and the snow-capped mountains. Mother Matterhorn, in particular, who would not be the same without her white-laced shawl.

"Look out for us down here," Claudine had said.

Look out for us up here. Claudine can almost hear Mother Matterhorn's reply now, spurring her to take some action.

Maybe some of her PottHeads will even take up this cause with her. She's got clout; she should finally use it to remind people what they love about winter. Skating and snowboarding and skiing and snowshoeing, in hero snow and on powder days, through the gusting temperatures that make you earn it, and on those singular, precious bluebird days that sweep in only a handful of times, so memorable you can name them. For the traditions wrapped around winter like a scarf, the hot cocoa and the warm saunas and the snowball fights and the clunky gear and the particular delight that is an untouched snowfall before a boot breaks the glittering surface.

It's almost as if letting go of her darkest secret—facing her shame—has opened up space, allowing her to consider what else her life could hold. Soupy had once asked her: "Wouldn't it be nice to be free?"

Yes, it would be. It is.

She taps the counter, almost nervous, as if Koa might rebuff her. "About that rally in Davos," she says. "Do you have room for one more?"

Koa is baffled before he breaks into a grin, pulling on a dreadlock, nodding. "Sweet as. Sweet *as*."

Outside, the light is dimming, a book being shut on the day. Claudine's wearing a thin knee sleeve underneath her pants, ibuprofen coursing through her veins. Her gait is still purposeful—to her, an amble sounds like a unit of measurement, not a leisurely way of moving through the world—but on this outing, all the fire and fear are gone, discarded like wet wool mittens back on the trail she will forever remember as a "real son of a B," another Kipper-ism. She and Wylie could have lost their lives out there. She's grateful to be alive. She's grateful for a lot of things.

She sticks her gloved hand into her pocket, clasping the pendant. "I'm going to release you to the wilds," she says to Kipper. "You never liked to be cooped up."

And neither does she.

With her secret out in the open after more than two decades, Claudine feels lighter than she's felt in years. She's no longer the woman in the corner, her nose to the wall in a time-out, administering her own lifelong punishment.

Not to say she's off scot-free. Claudine has atoning to do. And she meant what she said to Wylie about giving her time and space. It's a fair request, one she understands. She'll do her best to hold their relationship with a loose hand, not clamp down on it with all her might.

She's so caught up in her own thoughts that she very nearly walks right past Barry Haberman sitting on the patio of a café.

A very glum, very bundled-up Barry Haberman, staring into a pint of beer.

She sidles up to him, and he peers up at her, does a double take.

"I almost didn't recognize you," he says. "With the hair."

"Oh, right," she says, running a hand over her bob, as red as a maraschino cherry, thanks to Bibbidi. "It's a little brighter than I intended, but what are you going to do?" She laughs. *Okay, so it is* sort of *a riot.*

"Matches the Swiss flag."

Geez, maybe not. "You must really want to write that book," she says. "Not even an avalanche could stop you."

"Yeah, well, my heroics were for naught." He tilts his glass, slanting the amber liquid.

"What do you mean?"

"Zosel gave me the cold shoulder." Barry sounds like a rejected teenager.

"Did she change her mind?"

He gives a sheepish shrug. "I may have stretched the truth a little to you. She'd already turned me down. I was hoping to show up on her doorstep and sweet-talk her."

"Stretched the truth?!" Claudine is aghast.

Barry opens and closes his palms to show he's empty-handed.

"Do you have any idea..." She trails off, looking at the horizon, conjuring her outrage. But what's the use? If it hadn't been for Barry, well. She'll leave it at that. She can't stand giving him too much credit. "Does this mean Big Bear is calling it quits on a book about my life?"

He sighs, bottom lip folding down. "It's looking that way. I think I'm going to see what Picabo's up to these days."

"She already wrote a book. You know who you should try? Mikaela and her mom."

Barry's eyes widen. He wags a finger at her. "Now, there's an idea. Can I ask you one thing?" Barry asks.

"No."

"Just something I've always been curious about?"

Oh dear. Here it is. "I'd rather you didn't."

Barry's never met a boundary he's respected. "Is it really true that you ripped down a stuffed moose head from a lodge after you lost a first-place finish in Killington?"

Claudine has to laugh. "*That's* what you want to know?"

"It's just one of those rumors that's swirled around. I always thought I'd be the one to put it to rest."

"I'll say this: moose heads are heavier than you might think." Then she gives him a devilish wink before leaving him to drink a second beer.

At a bridge over the Matter Vispa, she weaves through a smattering of tourists leaning over the railing to watch the narrow river churn. Beyond is the Matterhorn, beautiful and large and fragile all the same. She pulls Kipper from her pocket, the pendant a silverfish in her palm glinting in the winter sun. Her fingers curl around it. Incredible how such a man, feared and loved, could be ground to dust.

It will be the same for Claudine one day. What will Wylie think as she releases her to the wind? She lets out a relieved sigh, free from being able to control it. What Wylie thinks, and what she does, will be up to her.

The metal pendant grows cold in her palm as she stands waiting.

"Mom," she hears. It's her name to no one but Wylie. She turns to see her child, with the loping gait of her father, join her on the bridge. Side by side, they stare at the river before taking stock of the village, snow-covered roofs, string lights turning on as the day peels away. It really is a magnificent place, but Wylie's right; Kipper wouldn't want to be scattered on a mountain here.

She unscrews the lid of the pendant. She didn't cry when Kipper died, and she's not crying now, but her heart squeezes. Without allowing herself to fall prey to sentimentality, she says, "Safe travels, you old son of a B," before tipping the opening of the pendant toward the water below.

This river will flush him out from the mountains. Beyond to the sea.

"No way home but down," Wylie says.

And while Kipper travels south, and Wylie rejoins her friends, Claudine turns back to the snowy village, pulling the letter out of her parka pocket, searching for a lemon-yellow cable-knit hat with a pom-pom. There's work to be done yet.

ACKNOWLEDGMENTS

Thank you, Zibby Owens and Anne Messitte, for believing in my second novel and allowing me to do my favorite thing. Thank you also for creating an author-centered experience for me and all the Zibby Books authors. My editor, Bridie Loverro, tirelessly went round after round with me on this manuscript until we got it exactly right (even when we were both simultaneously texting each other from our respective pediatricians' offices). Thank you for your guidance, wisdom, and friendship. Many thanks also to Kathleen Harris for your keen editorial notes and for shepherding this manuscript across the finish line. A huge bouquet of gratitude to the entire Zibby Books team for launching this book into the world with such love and care.

Thank you to my agent, Hannah Brattesani, who helped me brainstorm the bones of this novel, and offered sound, reassuring advice and support along the way. I feel lucky to work with you.

I'm also lucky to have a small band of early readers who gave me invaluable feedback during various stages of this book. Carly Wahl, thank you for reading this manuscript several times, and for hashing out plot holes at a moment's notice—and just keeping me generally sane and laughing. Alexandra Russell, thank you for reading an early version, offering insight, and rooting for me throughout. Sandra Miller, thank you for stepping in toward the end to read those all-important first few chapters. Thank you to Rob Stewart for brainstorming a cappella group names and coming up with the brilliant Sings to Excess. A hug of gratitude to Meghan Riordan Jarvis for that late-night chat on the Cape to therapize Claudine and Wylie. A hiya and thank-you to my New Zealander friend Hanna Butler for reviewing Koa's Kiwi dialogue. Thank you, Sarena Neyman, for reading my cross-country ski chapters.

I'm so grateful to the librarians, booksellers, and Bookstagrammers for supporting this book and using your platforms to share it with other readers. Thank you!

I loved conducting research and interviews for this novel. I'm so grateful to the Olympic skiers who answered my naive questions. Thank you, Sarah Schleper, Toby Dawson, and Josh Sundquist. Additional gratitude to Sarah Schleper for reading my entire manuscript and correcting any ski-lingo errors. Thank you, Phoebe Hallahan, for talking with me about your ski-racing journey. I'm in awe of all of you. Heaps of thanks to sports psychologist Dr. Jim Taylor, for helping me understand the very specific mindset of ski racers, and how performance anxiety might affect an athlete at the top of her game.

Several books were instrumental in my research, including Picabo Street and Dana White's *Picabo: Nothing to Hide*, John Fry's *The Story of Modern Skiing*, and Nathaniel Vinton's *The Fall Line*. FIS Alpine's YouTube series *Down the Line* was both helpful and riveting.

I got the idea for an avalanche socking in my main characters from a 2018 headline, when an actual avalanche stranded thirteen thousand tourists in Zermatt. I'm so grateful for the Zermatt-based locals who chatted with me about that experience, including director of Zermatt tourism Daniel Luggen and Air Zermatt's manager of ground operations Sandro

Imboden. Swiss glaciologist Matthias Huss lent his time to talk to me about climate change's impact on glaciers. Thank you to Russell Bollag-Miller for chatting with me about what it's like to live in Zermatt, and to Sydney Suttor for sharing what it was like to be among the stranded tourists.

A massive thank-you to the country of Switzerland. You sure are gorgeous. Thinking I was a better skier than I actually was, I once tried to ski down a glacier in Interlaken—only to get stuck at the top, paralyzed with fear (I see you, Wylie). Thank you to the retired Swiss ski instructor who helped me ski down. It took us only two hours. I never got your name, but in my mind, you're Franz Blasi.

A big shout-out to my extended family for your love and encouragement. To my late mom: Thank you for that one special summer when we embarked on weekly outdoor adventures together. I'll never forget getting stuck in that canoe, paddling against the wind in vain. Your spirit is in these pages.

I've reserved my biggest thank-you for my husband, Alex Bartlett, who is the best sounding board, supporting my writing life with incredible generosity and keeping me laughing on the days when I'm filled with doubts. Also, he always catches the things in my manuscript that no one else does, like Barry plus Gib equaling Barry Gibb, the lead singer of the Bee Gees. Thank you, love. To my kids, Lisle and Satchel, thank you for thinking that every book on our shelves was possibly written by me. Shows how much you believe in me. I adore you both.

Finally, to the winter season itself: Thank you for the gift of cold and snow. I won't take you for granted. I'll do my best to protect you.

ABOUT THE AUTHOR

MEGAN TADY, a journalist and editor, is the author of *Super Bloom*. She founded Word-Lift, a communication consulting and copywriting firm. Originally from Nebraska, she now lives in New England with her husband and two children.

@megtady
www.megantady.com

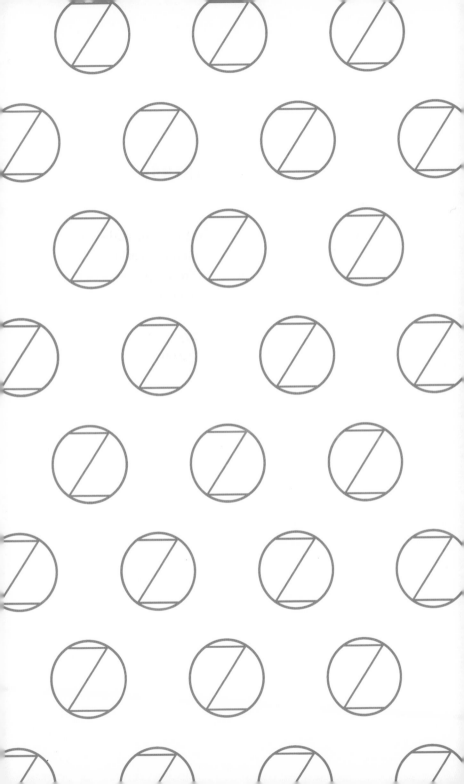

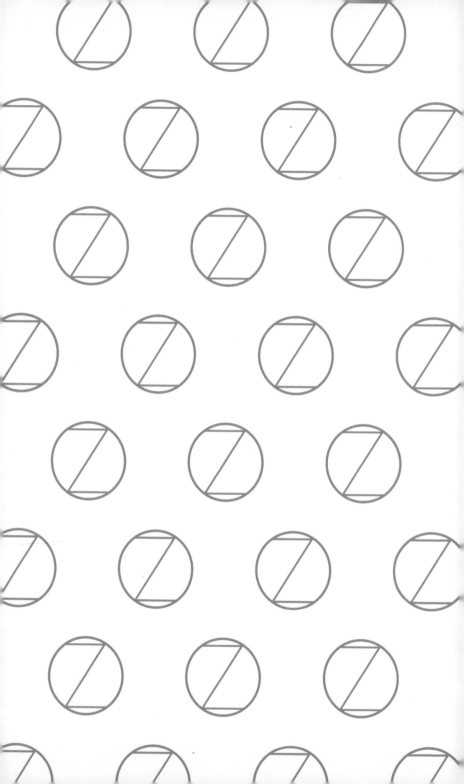